GALIMAR

Episode 2

JASON AND THE CIRCLE OF SEVEN

by

DAN ADRIAN

Galimar – Jason and the Circle of Seven
First Edition

First Print Edition: August 2020

ISBN:

(Paperback): 978-1-945925-13-9
(e-book): 978-1-945925-14-6
(Audio): 978-1-945925-15-3

Cover: Paul Kimber

Interior Design and
E-book Programming: Slaven Kovacevic

Editing: James Zumwalt
Brynn Shepard
Brooke Zumwalt

Content Consultation: Brooke Zumwalt

For Kierstin.

TABLE OF CONTENTS

PROLOGUE

"WOULD YOU LIKE SOME MORE coffee, sir?"

Doctor Nixon McConnell, or "Nix" as most called him, sat looking deep into the fire. So deep in fact that he didn't even register that his assistant had even asked him a question. No ... his thoughts strayed to a place far away from his present location. It was a place where a man goes when he is alone with his quiet thoughts. A place where the hidden person of the heart will come out for adolescent dreaming, and the occasional play.

"Sir?", asked Frank.

"Huh? What was that?" said Nix as he was roused away from his reverie. With an exaggerated wide-eyed look on his face, he realized that while his pre-frontal cortex hadn't *listened* to the original question, his brain had still *heard* it. Recognizing the question now, he responded "Oh, sorry. Yeah. Here you go."

Extending his cup toward his assistant, Nix felt the weight of the warm brew as it poured. "Thanks," said Nix as his lips once again tasted the bitter but somehow satisfying liquid.

For his part, Frank had noticed that his boss was uncharacteristically quiet this morning. It was actually a wonder that you could detect anything that was quiet in this cacophony of the rainforest. They had come here to the island of New Caledonia about seven weeks ago, and it must have taken a full week before either of them could get any sleep. Neither of the men were unfamiliar with sleeping in tents and waking up to a breakfast served around a campfire, but somehow the other times they had respectively camped out under the stars, it just seemed ... quieter ... at least for Frank. Nix seemed unfazed by it though.

To call Nix his "boss" was, while technically accurate, more of a misnomer ... that is if you were to judge from the way Nix treated his associate. True, when he was hired to go on this research trip to study a specific species of intelligent crow only found on this island, his stated duties would be to maintain the camp, provide cooked meals, and assist in any other way that Nix deemed appropriate to accomplish his goals. Those goals, by the way, were to study this species of crow and to see if there were any environmental influences that caused an enhanced intelligence. Or ... maybe it was the isolation in this part of the world? The population of crows was evidently large enough to support appropriate genetic diversity in the species which was one of the first observations that Nix had made. As a rather well-known biologist and genetic researcher from MIT, this, of course, was one of the first questions he had to answer upon getting to the island.

Once again Frank took note of the demeanor of his boss and wondered to himself. Where was he this morning? It certainly wasn't anywhere on this island right now. "What's up, boss?", asked Frank.

Looking over to his assistant, Nix once again smiled at the notion that not much had missed Frank's notice. "Oh ..." a smile broke out on his face as he responded, "I was just thinking about Emma."

Emma Elise Wesson was Nix's fiancée, and she was still living back in Cambridge. He was hopelessly in love with her, and she was completely smitten with him. Lately, he had to work hard not to waste the day away daydreaming about her.

Frank smiled. He knew how in love Nix was with Emma. It had been a regular subject of their evening discussions around the fire. "Well," said Frank as he smiled a wide toothy grin, "Unless the purveyors of your grant money are just as enamored with your lady love, I suggest you and I get to it this morning!"

"Yes Sir!", said Nix with a magnanimous salute and a fake buck-tooth grin. They had truly become good friends. Gathering up their things to be packed away and hanging up the foodstuffs from a rope dangling from a tree, the two made short order of their morning chores in preparation for going back to the lagoon.

That lagoon was, in fact, something that neither of the men had to be coerced to visit. Shortly after arriving on the island, and after making the trek to this part of the island where some of the indigenous people said a lot of the crows that they were studying lived, they happened upon the lagoon where the birds seemed to congregate. After talking to some of the locals for a while, some of the older men said they were aware of the lagoon, and they even believed it was where some of the spirits of their dead ancestors lived. They said that the spirits came out at night and danced in the water and, in fact, some considered the crows to be the embodiment of their ancestors. As a result, their visit was met with quite a lot of resistance from the locals. It was only after the researchers had assured all involved that their interest was only in observation and that they would cause no harm to the birds, that the islanders agreed to allow the visitors to stay.

Secretly, Nix had intended to take genetic samples back with him to Cambridge, and he especially had hoped to take a living male and female bird back with him. At this point though, he didn't know quite how he was going to pull that off. While the village elders had agreed to let him stay and do his observations, still

... Nix and Frank observed that there was always a villager or two popping up out of the blue as if to check on what the good doctor was up to. He had the feeling that he wasn't completely trusted.

Meanwhile, Nix and Frank made their way from the campsite and began their trek across the small oval-shaped valley. They were camped on one end of the valley, however much of their attention focused on an area way over on the other end where a waterfall emptied into a lagoon whose beauty regularly took their breath away. One time, Frank observed that its color wasn't unlike another lagoon he had visited in the Philippines named Kawasan Falls. The pooling of water underneath the falls took on a pale blue-green color and looked as if it had been colorized by a cartoon artist. The surreal beauty was breathtaking to behold, but in fact was only half of the mystery. Almost five weeks ago, Nix and Frank came to the lagoon at night to see if the activity level of the animals was any different than what they had observed during the day. That was when they were astonished to discover that the rocks in and around the entire area actually glowed with the same color as was seen during the day. Initially, he theorized that there must be some sort of phosphorescent algae adhering to the rocks, but he later discovered that even the rocks with no algae glowed with this same blue-green hue. Frank had voiced concern that maybe the rocks were naturally radioactive, but that was quickly disproved. Nix was truly perplexed, and since he wasn't a trained geologist (he was, after all, a biologist and genetic researcher), he sent samples of the water, algae, mud, and rocks back to his alma mater and asked that they try to identify this mineral that he had discovered. He didn't know it at the time, but his use of the word "discover" would work quite well in his favor.

It only took about forty minutes to arrive at the observation site today, only to discover that their main observation point was now occupied by an uninvited guest. Arriving with their normal stealth so as to not startle the population of crows that lived here, they soon realized that this "guest" who appeared rather pudgy and not well suited for field work like this was already there and had sufficiently and loudly disrupted the peace of the flock.

Rather annoyed at the flagrant disregard for their work, Nix approached the intruder who at the time was crouched down near the edge of the water and who was facing away from Nix. "Can I help you?"

With a decent modicum of effort, the man stood up and turned around, and it was only now that Nix recognized the man to be Doctor John Siegel, who was the head of the materials sciences lab where Nix had sent the samples.

"Doctor McConnell," said the out of shape, yet well-appointed man, "mighty fine-looking piece of water you have here. How has your research been going doctor?"

Doctor Siegel often went by the name Doctor Livingston, since his full name was actually Johnathan Livingston Siegel, named by his parents after a favorite book of theirs. "Doctor Livingston, I presume" said Nix. He then added "Well it would probably be a little better had you not scared away the subjects of my study here doctor" said Nix with a mild edge to his voice. "It will probably mean this day will be a wash as far as observing the crows I came here to study."

"Well, I apologize for that doctor," said the contrite man, "but I had hoped to catch you, and I didn't know where you were camping. I would have gone there instead."

"We chose to camp far away from this area because we didn't want our presence to influence the behavior of our test subjects." Then gesturing to a divot in the canyon walls on the other side of the valley where they stood, he then explained: "We are camping about 30 minutes that-away at the bottom of that granite cut-out."

"Well, once again I am sorry to disrupt your work here, but I had to come and see the lagoon myself."

Up until now, Nix hadn't really thought about how odd it was that his visitor was here in the field. Aside from the fact that biology wasn't his field of study, it was rather obvious that the good Doctor Siegel wasn't well suited for the humid and decidedly dirty environment that this part of the world offered. As Doctor Siegel had obviously traveled a long way, Nix decided to be conciliatory. Nodding his head, he said "Apology accepted." Then cocking his head to the side, he added: "What brings you to my favorite getaway spot?"

"Well, I'd like to explain that to you," responded a smiling Doctor Siegel "but I was wondering if you might have a place to talk that had a little more refreshment and a little less dirt?"

"I think we can mostly work that out, although dirt is a rather normal commodity in this part of the world" responded Nix. Turning to Frank, Nix then said: "Frank, would you hot foot it back to camp and rustle up some refreshments?" Knowing that the trek back would be slowed by his rotund visitor, he added: "We'll follow behind you and see you there."

"You got it boss!" was Frank's quick and smart response. Turning on his heels, the ever-responsive assistant took off toward camp, followed shortly by the two doctors.

As expected, it took about twice the normal amount of time to get back to camp. The visiting doctor wasn't really in the mood to talk about the nature of his visit while huffing and puffing through the trek. The walk back to camp involved a slight grade since the lagoon was about three or four hundred feet in elevation less than the location where the camp was. Eventually, though, the two men made their way back, and the offering of liquid refreshment was immediately and gratefully accepted.

Allowing Doctor Siegel to get his wits about him, Nix took the time to get his things in order. Since he was going to have a rather lackadaisical day due to his visitor, on the walk back to the camp, he had decided that he would perhaps get some sleep today and return to the lagoon tonight for some nocturnal observations. At least the day wouldn't be a total washout.

After a short amount of time, Doctor Siegel spoke up to Nix as he was passing by. "So, doctor, I know that your complete first name is Nixon. I don't think I've ever heard of that name being used before, at least as a first name." Then seeing that this may have been received as a jibe, he added "I like it, mind you. I think it sounds sophisticated."

Nix had had this particular conversation with people over the years countless times and didn't really relish having it once more, although this may have been the first time that someone thought it sounded "sophisticated."

"Well, I was born in 1974 during the whole 'Watergate' debacle" replied Nix, "and my parents being staunch Republicans decided that they would name me after the president to show their support."

"Oh really?" said Doctor Siegel with a raised eyebrow. "And how do you feel about that?"

Taking a seat near his visitor and looking into the unlit fire pit, Nix looked like he was choosing his words carefully which, by the way, he wasn't. He just knew that he needed to show that his words were well thought out. They were in fact; he had just arrived at these particular conclusions about 30 years prior.

"Well you see" replied Nix, "while the things President Nixon did in his earlier career were really great such as the forming of alliances with China, and the effect that had on the creation of détente between the United States and the Soviet Union," Nix paused, "still, the involvement he had with the Watergate scandal really marred my opinion of the man. I've always subscribed to the motto 'You know the right thing to do. So just DO IT.' For that reason, I rarely go by my full first name."

"I can understand that" conceded Doctor Siegel. "I'm a democrat myself, but I remember feeling like there was a real black eye put on the overall credibility of the engine of politics. It was bigger than just a partisan thing."

The two men stared at the coals that were remnants from the morning fire. Being the middle of the day, the fire wouldn't be needed until later tonight when the meal was to be cooked.

After a short amount of time, Nix spoke. Knowing the answer already, but wanting to be courteous he asked, "You make it out into the field to do research much?"

The ensuing snort from his visitor revealed that his veiled courtesy was not very well disguised. Thinking how badly he had fared in the simple walk back to the camp, Doctor Siegel replied: "I think the answer to that question is rather obvious." Then with an open-handed slap to his belly and with enlarged eyes, he added "wouldn't you say?"

Seeing that he had been caught, and seeing the self-deprecating humor of his guest, Nix immediately broke out in laughter, which of course was accompanied by Doctor Siegel as well as by Frank who was bringing a paper plate with various crackers and cheese for the men to snack on. The laughter had broken the last vestiges of ill regard on Nix's part, and the three men now enjoyed a short bout of relaxed conversation until Doctor Siegel brought the conversation back to a more serious-minded subject.

"Honestly though, I came here to talk to you more about the samples you sent back to my lab."

Scrunching his eyebrows together, Nix thought for a moment. He had actually forgotten about the samples he had sent five or six weeks ago, and had the doctor not mentioned it now, he probably wouldn't have given it much more thought.

"The samples? Oh, that's right. Those probably ended up as paperweights on your desk, didn't they?"

"Not exactly" replied the doctor enigmatically.

"Oh?"

“No. Oh the water and algae samples were sent to the bio departments for analysis, and the last I heard they didn’t find much more than …” Doctor Siegel paused for a moment while he pulled a slip of paper from his shirt pocket containing the names of the species that he knew Nix would be interested in “… Charophyta and Spirogyra species.”

Nix nodded, instantly recognizing the species, and registering that they were exactly what he had thought it would be.

“Sill though,” continued Doctor Siegel “the rock samples came to my desk, and I have to tell you they are really causing a stir.”

“A stir?”

“Indeed. Doctor McConnell are you familiar at all with the periodic table of elements?”

“Not really. My work doesn’t have much call for the regular use of it.”

“Well, my boy,” said the older gentleman, “Trust me … you are going to be getting VERY used to it now.”

“Oh? And why is that?” asked an intrigued Nix.

“Ok, so a little background here” said Doctor Siegel. Gesticulating his hands in the air, he proceeded to draw on an imaginary blackboard. “You see, back in the late 1860’s a Russian chemist named Dmitri Mendeleev first published the table based on a bunch of observations that he had made. It was a tabular arrangement of the all chemical elements known at the time, and they were ordered by their atomic number, electron configurations, and recurring chemical properties. The ordering showed periodic trends, such as elements with similar behavior in the same column. Overall, the elements on the left are metals, whereas non-metals such as the noble gasses Argon, Neon and the like are on the right.

“The groupings in the table show the relationships the elements have with each other, and due to the arrangement of the elements, chemists such as myself are able to predict the behavior of elements based on the proton-neutron-electron configuration, even though we may have not run across those particular elements yet. Follow me so far?"

"Yep" replied Nix. Some of this was coming back to him from his chemistry courses when he was in college.

"OK. So up to this point, we haven't been able to observe elements much past atomic number 118 named Oganesson. Even then it has to be synthesized in the lab, and the non-isotope version of it only lives for around point seven milliseconds before it decays into simpler elements. Still, though we are able to calculate and predict that sitting out there at atomic number 126 would be an element that is what we have always referred to as an island of stability. We didn't know exactly what the properties of that element would be, but we could predict that the trend of increasing instability of elements farther up the table would halt once we made it to 126. The kicker though is that we have never been able to prove if an element of that atomic number was actually stable since it has never been discovered or even synthesized."

"Oh, I see," said Nix.

"That is ... until now" said Doctor Siegel with a rather large smile on his face.

"What do you mean?"

"Well my good man, that sample you sent me turned out to be the prodigal child of the Periodic Table of Elements. That sample turned out to be the elusive element 126!"

Now it was Nix's turn to have the wide eyes. "Really!"

"Yes. And that's not even the half of it" responded Siegel. "We started doing some testing on the element, and it has properties that are completely re-writing the textbooks. Once we reported the results of our tests to the senior leadership at the institute, the President, Chancellor, and Vice President for Research essentially demanded I get myself down here to find the man responsible for the discovery of the newest entry to the periodic table of elements," then with a pause to enunciate the seriousness of his words he added "which we have named 'Connellium' in your honor. Not only that ... due to this, it is generally accepted among my contemporaries that your discovery will assure you a Nobel Peace Prize."

At this point, the muscles in Nix's face lost all control, and his mouth gaped. In a bit of comic relief, Frank unintentionally dropped the plate he was holding, and his cheese and crackers went flying across the ground near the feet of the men. For his part, Nix was having a difficult time finding his voice, but eventually said the first thing that came to his mind which he instantly regretted since it sounded so lame.

"You're kidding!"

"No. Not kidding. But I think you'll find what the element can do even more amazing."

Looking at the cold coals in the fire pit, Nix said: "How could that possibly be more amazing?"

"Well the element by itself doesn't really do much. But when you mix it with a few other elements and add some electricity ..."

Doctor Siegel paused.

"... it repels gravity and floats in mid-air."

CHAPTER 1

We ought to esteem it of the greatest of importance that the fictions which children first hear should be adapted in the most perfect manner to the promotion of virtue.
– Plato

DID YOU EVER GET THE feeling that you were riding a wave of greatness? A feeling where even though the events of your life up to this point had led themselves to amazing and incredible things, you somehow knew in the deepest parts of your soul that more was just around the corner? Young couples often feel this shortly after their wedding as they are settling down into their new normal. Politicians regularly feel this shortly after winning elections, and each and every new employee at a new job looks forward to the future with eager anticipation, knowing down deep that they will remain excited and pleased with whatever the future has to offer.

But then, as is often the case with the human animal, the newness of the experience wears off and once again we are left gazing toward the horizon. This dichotomy of the human spirit is often blamed for men sailing away on ships to new worlds, but the male species certainly has no monopoly on wanderlust. Psychologists call this pattern of thinking "Hedonic Adaptation", which is defined as the tendency of us mere humans to quickly return to a relatively stable level of happiness, regardless of whether the events or life changes experienced are either positive or negative.

With Jason and Dennis singlehandedly having saved the entire human and Galimarian races by utilizing the XYZT Transportation Device, or simply the "Portal" as they like to call it, our heroes quickly found themselves having to get used to new "normals" as well. Actually, all in their close circle of friends and acquaintances had a lot to get used to now.

Once all of the Galimarian people had been awakened from their slumber in the underwater habitat by Jason, Dennis and the rest of the team, each individual eventually returned to their respective lives, albeit with a considerable amount of interest in what their lives would now be like.

Jason and Mikki, on the other hand, returned to their home in Sonora, California along with their son Jace Junior. Being that Mikki was now privy to all that Jason did professionally, it wasn't unusual for Jason to discuss with her various events of the office. This new "normal" between the two of them, though, took a little getting used to since his work was so secret. Even 99.9% of all personnel at the Pentagon had no idea that the facility where Jason and Dennis worked even existed, let alone that the portal existed or that it had the site-to-site transportation and time travel capabilities that it had. Even so, while it was now allowed for Jason to talk about the technology that he worked on with his wife (by presidential decree, by the way) they had to be ever diligent in keeping things incredibly secret.

This whole secrecy thing was actually a bit strange for Mikki, and it took a little while for her to get used to it. Since she now had a security clearance that many in the top intelligence agencies of the United States didn't even know existed, one requirement that the president put upon Mikki was that she had to take a crash course on exactly how to treat top secret and sensitive information. The classroom course she took was held at the pentagon and her classmates were some of the more elite in the various bastions of military intelligence. As Mikki sat in the classroom, there was more than one occasion when she spied sideways glances from the other majors, lieutenants and captains in the class who were wondering why someone who appeared to be your garden variety young stay-at-home mom was even there. One and all had participated in side discussions amongst themselves as to how she could possibly need to be in such a position to handle top secret intelligence. One and all felt that there must have been some sort of clerical mix-up to land her in such a class ...

... and one and all were thoroughly and completely wrong. Her knowledge of the Island of New Galimar, and her conversant knowledge of the Galimarian language meant that along with her husband, she was an indispensable asset to the office of the President.

After relations had been established with the Galimarian people, Dennis decided to take some time to connect with his new romantic interest, that of Patricia Lynne Marlowe, or Lynne as she liked to be called. Dennis' hand was still a little stiff after having suffered the bullet wound from Admiral Brinstock's sidearm during the showdown in the portal room between Jason and the admiral. The injury was healing nicely though, and Dennis wanted to introduce Lynne to some of his family back in his hometown of Tomball, Texas. He was more than gratified to see her fit into his family dynamic like a glove, and it took all of about thirty minutes for his dad and mom to take him aside and inform

Dennis that he had better hang on to this one and not let her get away.

Lynne had to go through the same security classes as Mikki, in fact Lynne was a student in the same class. She didn't raise the same number of eyebrows as Mikki though since Lynne had a military background, though she was in the reserves, and so that did happen to strike some of the others in the class as slightly odd.

Jose settled into his new occupation, that of being the sole owner of a huge vineyard in Spain. This occupation was bittersweet for him since the land he now owned was the same land where he had been born some seven hundred years before. It was the same land where the preponderance of his memories had been forged, however it was those memories that left him somewhat melancholy in the evenings. He remembered playing with his boyhood friends along the river that cut through the valley in the middle of the real estate he owned. He remembered evenings by the fire as he listened to his mother hum while she prepared the evening meal. He also remembered having to lay his mother to rest in a spot that hadn't been touched in the last seven hundred years. It took him a little bit to locate the gravesite, or what was left of it, but when he did, he cleared away the brush and rendered it as a shrine to a woman for whom he had great respect.

From the moment they laid eyes on each other, Terri and Khreelon were very much in love and truly enjoyed the time that they could now spend with each other. President Michaelson requested that Terri take on the job of being an Ambassador and field representative of the President of the United States to the island of New Galimar, and the presidential liaison to the ruling body of New Galimar known as the Grand Council. Terri was humbled and reverently took on the job given to her by the office of the president, much to the chagrin of her supervisor at the New York Museum of Natural History. Up to that point, that supervisor had hoped Terri would be on board long enough to complete the job of cataloging the inventory in the massive downstairs museum archives, and so now he had to find someone else to do the job.

As a side note, it was slightly comical when the museum administrator then turned to Lynne asking her to take on the archive project, only to discover Lynne's own resignation on his desk. Lynne had decided to work closely with Dennis, and with her military background she became a secondary liaison between the Grand Council, the President of the United States, as well as the Pentagon.

Terri and Khreelon decided to split their time between living in her apartment in Brooklyn Heights, New York and living in Khreelon's apartment on New Galimar. Any time they wanted to move back and forth between the two, all they had to do was ask Jason or Dennis to fire up the portal and, Voilà!, they were in their other apartment.

After the events centering around Yellowstone and the demise of Admiral Brinstock, President Michaelson, had a lot to consider. He was now the only sitting president that had ever made contact with beings of another planet, and that in and of itself naturally led to the need for new foreign policies that were decidedly different in nature than any other policies that had been drafted before. The political engine behind him had already been making plans for his reelection and so it came as quite a shock to his political party constituents when he declared that he would not seek reelection even though the campaign trail was almost done and over. The party had to scramble to offer up a replacement candidate, but there were many that were more than a little angry that he had backed out. This move all but guaranteed that his campaign rival would win the presidency, which in fact he did. Before leaving office though, President Michaelson created an office for himself that would be in charge of relations with people of other planets. The existence of this office would be known by only an elite few. Even the incoming president wouldn't learn of its existence until a few weeks after he had taken the oath.

Now that Admiral Brinstock was no longer alive, his former office had to be filled, and that was done rather quickly. The president had told the secretary of defense that the Admiral had been part of an undercover operation, and that during this mission he had lost his life. President Michaelson felt that any more information needn't be shared with the secretary, and so a military funeral ensued in honor of the fallen soldier. In a short discussion between President Michaelson and Admiral Brinstock's assistant Lieutenant Flume (who had continued as the assistant to the new Deputy Chief of Naval Operations), it was discussed how even though Admiral Brinstock had the psychological break that he did causing him to be guilty of some definite crimes against the state, there was still an entire naval career where he had served his nation admirably. This was reason enough to see to it that there would be an honorable memorial held in his honor, and even though there was nothing to bury, a casket holding his uniform, and various other medals and diplomas was lowered into the ground at Arlington National Cemetery.

And so, such was the life of those who had been part of the greatest adventure ever experienced by any human up to that point. While millions of people interested in such things fantasized on what it would be like to meet and interact with beings of another planet, Jason, Dennis and the rest of the team actually had the pleasure of living that dream. Even to them, it was surreal to wake up in the morning and know that you had been instrumental in the survival of not only your own species, but even that of another planet. It was nothing short of amazing to all of them.

The Galimarians understood what it was like though. Their race had stretched out into the cosmos many years before and had met other races themselves. Their interactions with these races led to some of the most enriching and fulfilling relationships and interactions ever.

All interactions except for one.

This one particular contact with a species of another planet was actually the first planet where Galimar had discovered intelligent life. It was events on this same planet that caused some of the most sweeping changes to the main body of laws followed by all Galimarians. These laws, known as the Testimony of Galactic, Land and Maritime law, dictated that Galimar would only share its advanced technology with races that had socially developed to the same level as Galimar. It ensured that such technology wouldn't end up being in the hands of people that might use it for purposes that were less than virtuous.

What could possibly have happened on that planet to cause such heartache on the part of all Galimar? What heartache caused the Grand Council of Galimar to change their foundational laws?

The answer to these questions come from events that happened many years ago in the distant past of Galimar, in a solar system far far away ...

CHAPTER 2

ABOUT THREE PARSECS, OR A little over 900 trillion kilometers from the planet Galimar, in an unremarkable solar system locally referred to as the Pantheon consisting of only seven planets (and a lot of moons that have never been colonized), there lives a planet that is fairly commonplace in terms of its appearance. About fifty percent of its surface is water, which obviously means the other half is land. The land masses have the typical graduations between hotter climates of the deserts, to those that are more tropical and green. The oceans are uniformly green in hue.

This planet is commonplace and really wouldn't merit much of a second glance, except for the fact that it happens to be in that narrow band of distances from its sun where the water is neither boiling off into space, nor is it solid ice never to melt. It also happens to be the right size thus generating enough gravity for its atmosphere to remain against the surface, and at its core is a rotating mass of molten iron resulting in a magnetosphere responsible for protecting the planet from cosmic rays and solar winds coming from its yellow dwarf sun. For these reasons alone, it might merit more inspection by a passing race just to see if perhaps it has even a trace of life. Most planets like this have no life, but some do.

This planet, though, not only has life, but it has an enormous supply of it. Its most remarkable feature happens to be that one of those life forms is not only a bipedal race, but that race is what can be classified as "intelligent". This newly industrial civilization has progressed to the point where its more learned individuals are only now embarking on a wonderfully varied journey of discovery into many different disciplines of science including the biological, geophysical and chemical world around them. Some of the centers of civilization have begun to use new inventions (to them at least) that allow for locomotion as opposed to using animals to carry them from one place to another.

This race calls their planet ... Traxis.

The history of Traxis up to this point is one that is rather similar to that of many other planets that have intelligent life. Throughout time there have been many occasions on Traxis where the repeated ebb and flow of political history played its well-known song, a ballad where certain groups of Traxians would segregate themselves from other groups, and then claim their socio-economic philosophies are better than that of other groups on the same planet. These groups generally would find themselves clustered according to natural geographic features on the planet and, as is typical with such young civilizations, such attitudes are the basis of many bloody conflicts that have occurred over many millennia.

Not all of those on Traxis act the same way though. While most Traxian people have a more combative and warlike mentality, there are some who seem to naturally rise above the murmur of racial grandstanding. For one reason or another, these ones seem to find themselves among the more cultural and philosophical populous, and so they are doing their best to shape the minds of young ones in the universities to see that science and discovery is the one and only way that a person can find true fulfillment in life, and not with the competitive nature of nationalism and the inherent rise and fall of different arrogances and ideals. They have no idea that by living their lives in this way, they have taken on the same force actuating their minds as more enlightened races in their same galaxy.

Resistance to such change has been formidable, and revolution towards enlightenment has been slow in coming, but it has been steady. About 70 years prior to the events of this story, there was a landmark treaty that had been signed between the countries of Traxis that essentially stopped most of the conflicts on the planet. It was agreed that the conflicts were causing an unbelievable amount of suffering on the part of those who had no way to fend for themselves, and that something had to be done about it. It was at this same time that some of the major political alliances had the ability to completely destroy each other, thus creating a framework for what many referred to as "Mutually Assured Destruction". What made it particularly unnerving was that these countries had the ability to launch a devastating attack on their enemies, but none of these ideological groups possessed the ability to perfectly defend themselves from an equally destructive attack coming their way. A peace treaty was obviously needed.

Such a treaty eventually did come into existence though. The treaty was called the "Treaty of Vordoon", named after the island where it was signed. This island was a designated land that was owned by none, and so it was a place of common ground for all nations. Locations on the island for meetings and negotiations were created allowing for the peaceful coexistence of the people of Traxis. The tenets of the Treaty of Vordoon all center around six basic rules:

- All military actions occurring at the time of the treaty would immediately cease.

- All arsenals for each nation would be decreased to, at most, only ten percent of the current stockpiles, while at the same time, the stockpiles had to be equal among all nations.
- All existing non-contested borders would be honored by all nations.
- Any borders that were contested at the time of the treaty would be divided vertically, north to south, without consideration to natural resources or topography.
- A central organization called the "United League of Vordoon" (or "ULV" for short) would be established where all nations would consistently meet and air out any differences.
- Where there was a disagreement between nations that could not be resolved, the different sides of the disagreement would be presented to the uninvolved members of the ULV body, and the body would pass a binding ruling on how the difference would be settled. The ruling would be decided by simple majority vote.

Animal and plant life are remarkably diverse on Traxis. There are animals that range from very intelligent small animals that are no larger than one's finger, to simple minded animals that are larger than some of the trees of the planet. Life can be found on not only the land masses, but under the surface of the oceans as well. Aside from an amazing biodiversity in the oceans, there also happens to be an intelligent race of beings that live exclusively under the sea, however the Traxians that live on land have yet to discover this peaceful race. This oceanic race does of course have a name, but that name can't really be pronounced unless you have water flowing past your vocal cords. It basically sounds like the "Colwyns", but ... not really.

One thing that makes the land based Traxian people different from a lot of planets is that there are not just two specific genders to its people, but there are actually three. When procreating, one gender (that some might call "male") contributes the equivalent of sperm, while a second gender (that could be called "female") contributes the egg. These two genders deposit their contributions into the third gender which is known as "remale", where the fertilized egg will incubate and be carried until the child is born. For this reason, all three genders can rightfully be considered parents to the child. Marriage unions generally start out as a union between any two of the three genders that find themselves in love, but eventually those two will add a member of the third remaining gender to their union once someone is found that they both have fallen in love with. There are times when a couple decide that having a child isn't really important to them, and in those cases, the remaining gender is never sought.

Names on Traxis also take get a little getting used to. The family name always comes first, then the personal name. If you see the name "Tenovis VinBlinaee", the names of all members in their immediate family start with Tenovis, but the personal name of that person is VinBlinaee. Also, each personal name will start with a prefix which indicates their personal gender. "Bar" is the prefix for males, "Vin" is the prefix for females, and "Ren" is the prefix you will always find in the names of remales. So, in the previous example, you automatically know that Tenovis VinBlinaee is female.

Our story begins on a day that is mostly like any other, except for one very important difference. Today, Scientists in this barely industrial civilization of Traxis will try to determine the origin of a very strange device.

A device that doesn't seem to have originated from anywhere on the Traxian planet.

CHAPTER 3

Professor Nestoph BarStenson was getting ready to leave home for work. It used to take at least an hour to get to work in the carriage pulled by his favorite two steeds in his barn, but ever since he was able to obtain one of the new self-propelled ambulators, the ride to his laboratory at the University of Smorona now only took about fifteen minutes. Having worked there in the astrophysics department for most of his professional life, BarStenson is rather familiar with long quiet days and nights observing the heavens through massive telescopes and trying to unlock the secrets of the universe by what he sees. Discoveries seemed to be coming regularly these days among him and his contemporaries, and in fact it was only recently that a colleague of his successfully detected a seventh planet in the local solar system. This feat was quite amazing considering that it was so far from Traxis.

Today though wasn't going to be quiet. Not by a longshot.

"Honeys, have you seen my glasses?" said BarStenson while gliding around the family room. Looking up with a look of mild exasperation, he spied not only his female mate VinSanna, but also his remale mate RenTshoy nursing their newborn baby.

Looking up at him from the morning newspaper she was reading, VinSanna smiled and strode over to stand in front of him. With an even wider grin she kissed him, reached up, and dislodged the pair of spectacles that were sitting on top of BarStenson's head, placing them on his nose. "You know Mr. Nestoph," said RenTshoy from across the room, "there's an old saying about how if it was a serpent ..."

The two then started laughing much to the chagrin of their male mate. "Sometimes" he said, "I get the feeling like I'm getting ganged up on!"

"Oh, you love it and you know it", replied VinSanna.

"Mmmm Hmmmm ..." was the only reply he was able to manage in the face of such collusion on the part of his mates. They were right of course, but he wasn't about to relinquish that little victory to them. Not right now at least.

Once the overall level of laughter died down, VinSanna then asked, "So what are you going to be doing today our husband?"

BarStenson thought about his answer for a moment while taking a bite of his toast. He knew that the task of the day was classified top secret by the government lackeys that had basically invaded his department the day before, and so he wasn't allowed to say what was really going to happen. No, but he needed to come up with something that was reasonably plausible to his ever-inquisitive mates. He decided he would have to make a pit stop in the office of his colleague, Professor Linson, and talk to him briefly about his planetary discovery. He meticulously avoided anything that came close to lying to his mates, and so he would go there for five minutes today to satisfy his sense of truthfulness and propriety.

"Remember how I told you that Linson BarJamoor discovered a seventh planet, and that he published his findings last week? I'm going to stop by his office and talk about the effect of red-shifted light on his detection equipment. I'd like to see if he learned anything that I can put to use in my research" replied BarStenson.

Ok, maybe ten minutes.

As BarStenson predicted, VinSanna and RenTshoy looked at each other and simultaneously made like the very thought of such a conversation was putting them to sleep. BarStenson was pleased that his reply was received exactly the way he had hoped and would result in no more questions about the day. No, today was not only a hush hush day, but it was one that he was extremely looking forward to personally.

The next ten minutes consisted of him listening to his mates discussing what they were planning on doing that day, and him mildly paying attention to the subject matter. He seemed distracted this morning, but that wasn't necessarily unusual and so it didn't raise any further interest on the part of his mates.

All too soon, it was time to make his way to the lab, and so donning his hat and coat, he bid farewell to his mates and left for work. It only took about ten minutes to get to the lab today, and it was one of those trips where, after you get there, you can't remember the trip itself. Thinking about it, he decided that he needed to be more careful traveling at such high speeds. No need to risk life and limb in these ambulators!

Once he entered the building and made it to his office, he dropped his hat and coat on his chair and went straight to the observation room where the object of interest had been laying since the day before. A couple of his grad students were already there talking amongst themselves while looking it over. They weren't touching it of course since Professor Nestoph wasn't there and he was the head of the team that was asked to determine what this thing was, but still, that couldn't quell their excitement over what it could possibly be.

"Gentlemen" said BarStenson as he approached the two hovering over the object.

"Professor" said each as they stood back away from it as if they were possibly doing something they shouldn't have been, which they weren't.

There before them was the object of interest and slowly, almost reverently, BarStenson approached it as it lay on a soft mat on top of an observation table. It appeared to be a smoothly rounded object that was roughly cylindrical in shape, and it had a metallic silver outer shell. On the side of the object were two appendages that appeared to be fully articulatable, however it was obvious that they could be folded back into the body of the object as if it needed to allow for an aerodynamic shape. That this was a robotic probe was clear, but its goals were not. There were markings on the outside of the object, and there also appeared to be what one would call a "head" unit on one end that seemed like it was built to spin around in any direction. On the other end were tracks and wheels that allowed for it to move. Small shiny glass windows were in various places, and there seemed to be access panels peppered all over.

As he was setting down his briefcase, he looked over to the object and said, "So what do we know so far?"

"Well ..." said the student on the left, "we know that it was discovered by two hikers in the upper altitudes of the Emriis national forest. They said that they had decided to go off trail for a while to ... uh ... explore" the grad student glanced to the other, and the other let off a small smile, "and they said that as they came to a clearing, they heard a noise that sounded mechanical, and not something that would be normally heard in the forest. After walking toward the noise, they eventually came to a meadow where they saw movement amongst the brush. They quietly came up toward it and saw it moving around unaware they were there."

Pointing at what appeared to be an appendage coming out from the side of the object, the other grad student then said "Yeah, and they said that these arms were moving back and forth taking things from around it."

"Taking things?" asked Professor Nestoph.

"Yes" replied the first student. "For the lack of a better description, it appears it appears it was gathering samples from the plant life around it and then ... digesting ... or at least doing something with it behind this door here." The student pointed at what appeared to be a door on the belly of the beast.

"Hmmmm ..." said Professor Nestoph as he walked forward to the item while putting on his glasses. As he approached, he observed some of the markings, and how some of those markings were on the door itself.

"Has anybody been able to decipher these markings?" asked the professor.

"As you requested, we sent drawings of them up to the chairman of the language arts department, Professor Sulvan, but we haven't heard back from her yet."

The professor didn't respond as he continued to look it over. Reaching into a drawer underneath the table where the item laid, he pulled out a magnifying glass and looked into one of the glass windows. "Interesting" he said more to himself.

"What's interesting?" asked one of the students.

Handing the magnifying glass to his student, he responded "If you look closely at this window, you can see that behind it there appears to be what looks like a lens of some kind." While letting the student look at it for himself, he got a faraway look on his face and said "You know how they have been doing that new thing that where you can make images of things through lenses and then put the image on paper where it will stay permanently? I'm wondering if this can do the same thing."

"You're talking about a camera, right? I've seen those things and they are pretty big. You think this has one completely inside of it?" asked one of them.

"Now, my young apprentices, is the time for nothing but questions. We mustn't get into the habit of looking for too many answers before we know what the questions are in the first place. If you do that, it can be all too easy to pursue a line of assumptive logic that doesn't take into account all the observable facts."

"Yes sir" replied the two students.

Just then the phone rang and one of the students walked over to answer it.

"Hello?"

"Yes, I'll get him for you"

Looking over at Professor Nestoph, he said "Professor Nestoph, there is a man from the governmental center that wishes to speak with you."

The professor handed the magnifying glass to the other student and walked over to the wall where the phone was hanging.

"This is Professor Nestoph."

"Yes, Professor Nestoph, this is Braydeen BarKaze from the office of scientific intelligence. We spoke last night when we brought the object to your office."

"Yes Mr. Braydeen. What can I do for you?"

"Professor, I'll get right to the point. As I said to you last night, the object in your current possession has been classified as top secret by the Prime Officer himself, and to that end I have to insist that dissemination of information about it be cleared by my office first. Do you understand?"

"Yes, of course" replied a now quizzical Professor.

"Well Professor, I was made aware that your grad students have shared images of the writings on the outside of the item with a Professor Sulvan. Is that correct?"

Now recognizing the reason for the current line of questioning, BarStenson replied "Professor Sulvan? In the language arts department?" On hearing that name, the two grad students looked up and instantly thought to themselves that they might be in trouble for having sent those pictures over, although it was the professor who had suggested they send them,

"Mr. Braydeen, while I can understand that you need to keep a lid on this project, you must first realize that Professor Sulvan is a very trustworthy individual. I have worked with her for the better part of two decades and wouldn't have any problem trusting her with anything on this project."

"Oh, I'm quite aware of her track record and I have just cleared her for working on this project, but I must stress to you that ANY leaks of information MUST and WILL be cleared by this office first. Do I make myself clear professor?" curtly replied Mr. Braydeen.

Unaccustomed to being strong-armed by anybody, the professor paused and then said "Completely."

"Thank you, professor. You are authorized to use the services of Professor Sulvan, but I trust you will impress upon her the secrecy of this project. Thank you, professor." The caller then hung up the phone without waiting for a response.

Professor Nestoph slowly hung up the phone and as he turned back to the observation table said the first thing on this mind.

"Rude."

"What was that all about?" asked the tentative grad student, fully expecting to be chewed out for having shared that information with the language arts director.

"It was one of those suits that dropped this thing off last night. Apparently, they want full control over who hears anything about it. We have to clear any dissemination of information about it with their office first."

"Sorry for getting you in trouble professor." Said one of the students.

"Eh ... don't worry about it" replied the professor with a conciliatory tone. He knew that he wouldn't get the best the students had to offer if they were worried about every step they took.

The now relieved students went back to their observations. One of them walked around to the other side of the object and took another picture of some similar markings.

"Would it be all right if I sent this picture to Professor Sulvan too?"

"Yes" replied BarStenson. "She's been cleared for ..."

Just then the phone rang again. The phone ringing so much was something that didn't happen very often at all in this department.

Picking up the phone himself since he was still close to it, BarStenson answered "Astrophysics. Professor Nestoph here."

"Yes, professor Nestoph. You're just the person I wanted to talk to. This is Professor Sulvan from the language arts department."

"Yes professor, I'm glad you called too. I was just on the phone with the department of Scientific Intelligence, and they ..."

"... and they asked you to make sure I know that this is classified information. I know. I was made quite aware of that myself by one of them this morning" interrupted Professor Sulvan.

"They got to you too, huh?"

Laughing, she replied "Yes. They seem to be very good at keeping the lid on things, even if they don't know what they are keeping the lid on."

"Yeah," agreed BarStenson, "Seems like the name 'Office of Scientific Intelligence' is somewhat of an oxymoron isn't it?" The two of them shared a small amount of laughter.

"I suppose it is, but in fact that is why I was calling, or rather the pictures your students sent is why I'm calling. I've been looking over these markings all morning and I can't place it as any known writing, either modern or ancient. It's something that is completely unknown to me. Are you sure it wasn't placed there as a prank?"

"I'm sure" answered BarStenson. He then added "This thing appears to be legitimate, and the more I observe, the more questions are raised."

"Interesting. Would you mind if I came by to get a closer look at it?" asked the language arts professor.

"Not at all." answered BarStenson. "It would be my pleasure. The monkeys at the governmental center have cleared you for this project, but I'm afraid you'll have to come alone since nobody else can know about this."

"Not a problem" came the reply. "I'll be right over."

They shared a parting greeting and after hanging up the phone BarStenson came back over to the table.

"So, after the hikers found it, what happened next?" asked the professor.

Looking up from taking a close look at the object, the taller of the students replied "According to their statements, they said that after watching it for a while one of them moved to get a closer look and in doing so made a sound. They thought they may have stepped on a twig that snapped. Anyway, when that happened apparently this headpiece swung around and pointed this part

…" the student pointed at a protrusion on the head piece, "… at the hikers. The two of them froze, not knowing what was going to happen next. Apparently, both the hikers and this object sat there for a few minutes without moving. They said that after a few seconds, all the lights on the object seemed to shut off, and that is how it has remained until now."

"Lights? Where did it have lights?"

The student pointed at four of the small glass panels and said, "They said that glass panels here, here, here and here were really bright when they came upon it, but then went dark like they are now."

"So, these are lights" said the Professor.

"Apparently so" replied the same student.

The room remained quiet for several minutes while all three made their observations. One of the students was exceptional in his ability to draw, and so a big part of his method of observation involved detailed drawings of the item. He felt that drawing something forced him to observe details that others might have all-to-easily skipped.

After a few minutes, there was a knock on the locked door, and after checking to see who it was, the door was opened and in came Professor Sulvan.

"Hello Gentlemen" greeted the cheery instructor. Her blue eyes didn't seek out those of her companions though, she was much more interested in the object itself. Approaching the observation table, she shed the items she had been carrying onto the floor and whistled under her breath. With eyes darting back and forth she asked, "Have you done any metallurgical analysis?"

"Not yet. We actually just got it last night and are only now figuring out what we want to do" replied the older grad student.

The younger of the two reached over to a list of tasks that the two had been making before Professor Nestoph arrived. "Here's a list of what we thought would be a good place to start" said the younger one.

Professor Nestoph took the list and reviewed each step. "These are good. You might want to include an acid etch analysis of the metal cabinet."

"That's right" added Professor Sulvan. "You might also want to..."

Just then, a definite click happened in the object and what sounded like a motor began to make a sound. All in the room froze and watched the object to see if there was anything that was going to change. After about fifteen seconds, the bravest of the group who happened to be the visiting professor started to take a step towards the object when all of the sudden one by one each of the glass panels on the front of the unit lit up. The object that had been laying on its side then extended its articulated arms and up-righted itself such as it was now sitting on its wheels and tracks on the one end, and what was now being thought of as the head was now sitting on the top.

The head unit swung itself in a circular direction until the part of the head that was more pointed stopped while pointing at the group of professors and students who had, by this time, gravitated toward each other into a tightly knit grouping.

Just then, they heard something strange come from it.

"Beyezhzhoo - Gahnn Eeooeh Beyeahl Roieye"

"Did you hear that?" asked a very excited grad student. The two professors didn't pay attention to which one said it.

"It sounded like a man speaking" said Professor Sulvan. "Didn't it?"

Just then it happened again.

"Gahnn Eeooeh Roiahkheye Ooehth Habahth Haeye Ahleye Staheeohnnm"

"It did! It sounds like a man talking, but it's a language I've never heard before" added the very excited linguistics professor. Professor Nestoph mentally noted that if this professor hadn't ever heard it before, it must be something that wasn't from anywhere around here.

BarStenson approached the object and spoke. "My name is professor Nestoph BarStenson. Who are you?"

After a few seconds another set of sounds came from the unit.

"Oh Ahroi Zheyegeyezh Oonneye Eyennmohnneyeeyel Nnvahlthb. Haeye Khnnooha Eeooeh Ahleye Thleeohnnm Thoo Gooroiroiehnnohgahtheye , Nehth Haeye Gahnnth Ehnnveyelstthahnnv Eeooeh . Fzheyeahsteye Kheyeeyef Thahzhkhohnnm"

Professor Nestoph looked around himself to the others in the room to see if anybody knew what was being said, but the bewildered looks on the faces that he found told him they were just as lost as he was.

Looking back at the object, he said "I'm sorry, I don't know what you are saying."

Meanwhile ... far away from Traxis at GASEA headquarters – Planet of Galimar

N'Darth sat back from his terminal and let out a big breath of hot air. He hadn't actually realized that he was barely breathing but his lungs HAD to have a reprieve and they made their needs known in no uncertain terms.

He had arrived at work that evening with the greatly laudable and prestigious, yet equally boring job of monitoring the data feeds from a few of the deep space probes that had been sent out to some planets that had been spied as candidate planets where vegetative life might be found. It was his job to quantify the data that came in, and to contribute to an overall list of planets where Galimar might one day visit to explore and discover more about the universe around them. Upon getting to his post one began to review, one by one the feeds that were coming in to his workstation, but eventually he came upon one probe, the one designated as NX-62, as not responding. In fact, it hadn't been sending any data for the last 22 hours.

"Great. Looks like we might have a dead bird" he said under his breath.

Reaching to his keyboard, he called up the logs outlining the last transmissions from this probe.

- Acquiring candidate for new sample.
- Analyzing candidate with spectral analysis.
- Found organic compounds, carbon, H2O, proteins, natural sugars.
- Transmitting image of sample to Mission Control.
- Proceeding with level two sample analysis.
- INTERRUPT: Unexpected input. Secondary systems shutting down.
- Awaiting command.

This immediately intrigued N'Darth because it was very rare that a planet actually had complex life on it. From that initial spectral analysis, it seemed that this probe might have found it and it might even be something qualifying as vegetation!

Noting that the probe apparently sent back an image file, N'Darth called up the images folder dedicated to this probe, and sure enough there was one image. Opening the image, N'Darth was completely blown back in his seat by not only the one plant the probe was observing, but the overall explosion of plant life in the image now before him. There were plants and shrubbery in the foreground, but in the background was an immense stand of very tall trees.

Realizing that he was on to something now, he then noted again that the probe had stopped sending back information. Knowing that this was already something that would probably merit the additional investigation of the higher ups, he tried to get the probe back online by sending a restart command.

The command to restart the system and return video and audio streams from the environment around was sent, and when connection was established, the interchange between him and the beings on the other end was nothing less than electrifying! It appeared that the probe had been transported into a room, AND THE ROOM CONTAINED BEINGS THAT WERE TRYING TO TALK! He couldn't understand them, which was frustrating of course, but this was a landmark moment and he knew that at that moment he was the only person on Galimar who knew that intelligent life existed on planets other than Galimar.

Being that his was an entry level position, he was assigned to the overnight duties and so most of the personnel at GASEA, the Galimarian Space Exploration Agency, were all safely at home tucked away in bed. There was literally never any reason for him to bother his superiors for anything, but now was the exception to the rule.

Leaning over to the communications panel next to him, he dialed the number to his superior. A very sleepy voice answered.

"Hhhh ... Hello?"

"Yes sir, this is Level One Probe Engineer N'Darth, and I am calling with a situation."

Wiping sleep from his eyes, and clearing his throat, the supervisor slurred "What is your situation, N'Darth?"

"Sir, I've been monitoring the feeds from deep space probe NX-62 and I've encountered something you will want to know about" replied N'Darth.

Settling back down into his pillow with his communications device up to his ear, he replied with closed eyes "And what is so important that it couldn't wait until morning?"

"Sir, I've encountered a race of beings that are speaking a language that I can't understand."

The supervisor's eyes snapped open. "One more time?" Now instantly awake, the supervisor sat up in bed waking up his wife in the process.

"I am ... uh ..." N'Darth stuttered and cleared his throat, "... this is Level One Probe Engineer N'Darth, and I am monitoring deep space probe NX-62. I was taking samples of ..."

"THE PART ABOUT LANGUAGE, engineer!" interrupted the supervisor.

"Oh. Yes Sir. I said ... I've encountered a race of beings that are speaking a language that I can't understand" came the reply.

There was a long silence on the phone, so long in fact that the junior engineer thought that maybe the line may have gone dead.

"Sir?"

A few more seconds of silence, then the supervisor said slowly, "You've made contact with a race of intelligent beings."

"Yes sir."

"On another planet." That last comment caused the supervisor's wife to gasp as she looked at her husband with wide eyes.

"Yes sir" replied N'Darth.

"And they're speaking a language."

"Yes sir."

Another long pause.

"Are you telling me you've made contact with the first intelligent race Galimar has ever encountered?"

"Yes sir" was the short, and yet incredibly monumental reply.

CHAPTER 4

BEING THAT IT WAS THE middle of the winter break, having an emergency session called by the coordinator of the Grand Council of Galimar was strange enough, but the fact that the nature of this session was being kept under wraps was odd. Very odd. Testimonial law dictated that all sessions of the Grand Council be published and broadcast to any citizen that wished to receive it. Most of the citizens were of course interested in the affairs of their planet and so while most didn't have the time to watch the broadcasts each and every time the council met, still … they always took time to catch up on what was discussed. You could always review the meeting transcripts that were published at the end of the day on the planetary network.

Today was different though. All knew that it was … odd … that the council was going to meet in an emergency session during the summer, and so a much higher number of people tuned into the broadcast today.

Jobiah Aramine was briskly walking toward the gleaming glass and polished metal building where the council chambers were housed. When he received the call this morning from the council intern telling him that the session was being called, the intern was conspicuously vague on why the session was being called. Jobiah didn't get the impression that the intern was holding anything back, just that he wasn't told himself why the session was to be held. That also was ... well ... odd.

As he approached the building, the glass and metal façade immediately receded allowing him to enter. Making his way past the Colonnade of Greats, which is a giant hallway flanked on both sides with statuesque marble and plaster busts of those in Galimarian history who made their mark, he eventually entered through the open double doors that led to the council chambers. The chamber itself was an amphitheater with a stage at the center. The stage itself was circular, and while the council session was in progress, and while a speaker was speaking, the stage was built to turn very slowly. This facilitated that all seats would have the ability to see the face of the speaker. It turned slow enough that one could step on and off with no problems.

Finding his seat halfway down to the left of the entryway, Jobiah looked around the chamber and spied that most of the council members had already arrived. Looking at the current time on the wall opposite his seat, he saw that he was right on time and the session should probably start right about ...

"Council members, please take your seats as soon as possible" said the council coordinator. He was standing at the central lectern in the middle of the stage. "The meeting will start in two minutes" came his professional, deep and seemingly omniscient voice from all speakers around the room.

Soon enough all those who had been conversing about the reason for this meeting, and the unanimous bewilderment over not knowing why it had been called left off from their conversations and found their seats. By the time the two minutes were up, the room had come to order and except for the sound of the ventilation and an occasional cough, the room was silent.

The coordinator once again approached the lectern, laid his papers down, and rested his hands on both sides of the tall stand in front of him. He gazed out to the audience whose eyes were unanimously focused on him and chose his words carefully. He paused for a moment while seeing those that he knew well, then said "As I was preparing for this meeting today, it occurred to me how all of you were no doubt taking care of your normal morning rituals just as I was. You put your clothes in order, you ate your meals with your families, and you probably spent time with them talking about your day's activities. You probably mentioned to them that you had this morning meeting at the council chambers, and perhaps you even told them that it probably wouldn't take long before you could get back with them."

"It also occurred to me how none of you knew ahead of time that this was going to be one of those days in your respective lives that you will … never … forget. From this day on, you will recount to your children, their children, and even their children what happened on this day and how it affected you from today forward."

The coordinator saw that he had everybody's attention, and he noted how some of them looked at each other with a look that bespoke how they were in wonder over what could possibly be so momentous so as to inspire the coordinator's words.

"You may ask" continued the coordinator "why would I say such things? It is for one simple reason my friends. Today is when I am here to tell you that Galimar, a planet of intelligent beings" he paused, "that we are no longer the only race of intelligent beings. Today is when I am here to tell you that the Galimarian Space Exploration Agency has discovered another planet that not only has extensive plant life on it, but also has a race of beings that are advanced enough to have created a complete civilization containing complex language and governmental structures. They even appear to have institutions of higher learning. I am here to tell you that we are no longer the only race of intelligent life as we had previously thought, but that we have encountered the first of, no doubt, many species of intelligent life. In the short view we had of them, while they do not appear to be as advanced as we are, they do appear to be a peaceful people."

To say that the room was stunned would be an understatement. The entire planet of Galimar seemed to exhale an audible and collective gasp over the enormity of the words of the coordinator.

After letting his words sink in for a while, the coordinator then continued to speak.

"By the crushing silence in the room, I can see that this has affected all of you here in the council chambers the same way that it affected me when I learned of it. As was the case with me, some of you are no doubt wondering if this is some kind of practical joke. I can assure you though that this is no joke."

Gesturing to projection panels that were now descending from the ceiling of the council chambers, he then continued "I'd like to direct your attention to a recording of the video that came back from one of our NX class deep space probes that landed on a planet that we found with an overwhelming amount of plant life. The voice you are about to hear is that of junior engineer N'Darth who was in charge of monitoring the transmissions from this probe."

The screens then lit up with the video that N'Darth saw from the probe.

"Hello? Can you hear me?"

The video screen appeared to have an older man and woman, and two younger people. They apparently responded to the question that had been posed, but it was obvious that they couldn't understand. One looked to the other as if to ask something, then looked back at the probe camera. One and all in the council chambers were amazed to suddenly be presented with the image of a real live alien being. It was stunning to those watching how the alien beings looked only slightly different from Galimarian people. The most amazing feature was that their eyes were in different colors. Collectively, every Galimarian watching the feed around the planet also found themselves transfixed by the spectacle of the moment.

The junior engineer tried asking something else.

"Can you make out what we are saying?"

The new question appeared to cause more consternation on the part of the four aliens, but still it was obvious there was no level of understanding. It appeared that one of them grabbed a pad of paper and began scribbling on it. Most of the council members were amazed that this people seemed to have created many things that Galimar was already familiar with. Even simple things, like paper.

One of the older ones seemed to let out an elated exclamation, then followed that with something else in an as-yet-unknown language. Then the elder of the four aliens spoke several things into the video camera. He seemed to gesture a few times, and even seemed to ask a question. It was obvious he was inquisitive.

Once again, the engineer spoke.

"I am level one engineer N'Darth. We know you are trying to communicate, but we can't understand you. Please keep talking."

The same elder alien man looked at the others in the room, as if to ask the others if they understood what was being said. The others seemed to have blank looks on their faces.

He looked back to the probe camera and said a few more words with the open palms of his hands toward the video. It was obvious that he was taking a non-aggressive stance, and that he was unable to understand. That was when the video ended.

As the video panels retracted there were a few short seconds of silence, but then council chambers veritably erupted in vocal pandemonium. It wasn't an outburst of fear by any means, but rather it was one of amazed excitement. Most in the room had realized in no short order that their civilization that had been based on exploration and discovery had just made the most exciting landmark discovery that had ever been made. The world of that morning was nothing like the world that now existed. All of Galimar now lived in a world where they were not the only race of beings in the universe, but rather they were now one race out of ... what ... tens? Hundreds? Even ... millions? This was rock hard proof that they were not alone! The culmination of years of hard work and dreaming on the part of those that headed up the Galimarian Space Exploration Agency had just been validated! It truly was now a world that had changed in the symbolic blink of an eye.

The coordinator had anticipated that this would be the response, and so he allowed time for the members of the Grand council to digest this news in the way that each needed. He looked out over the room and saw faces of those that were now contemplating what the future would be, and contemplating how they, the members of the Grand Council, had within their reach the ability to shape the future of Galimar in this newly multi-racial universe.

Eventually, it was time for the coordinator to bring the meeting to order. There was much to discuss and decide.

"My friends, may we bring the meeting to order!"

In deference to the orderly meeting place there were many that left off from their excited conversations and returned to the seats they had left.

"May we bring the meeting to order please."

The coordinator waited for the necessary time and witnessed that the rest of the council members returned to their seats. The room became silent once more.

“I know that all in the room realize just how pivotal this news is in the history of our civilization. Yet while we are all excited about what this means for our civilization and how we all just witnessed an event that will be remembered for many millennia to come, I personally have had a little more time to consider what types of issues this brings up for our people, and what kinds of decisions we need to make.”

“First” the coordinator continued, “While this is the first time we have ever contacted another race of beings, we must keep in mind that this was, no doubt, the same for them. It appears that they are in the early stages of industrial civilization, and so contact with a race not their own might be very difficult for them. Even, frightening. How will we communicate our peaceful intentions?”

“Second, to what degree will our interaction with this race be? Will there be diplomatic relations? Will we allow an eventual exchange of peoples between our worlds?

“Finally, how will the knowledge that we are no longer the only race of intelligent life affect the way we explore the universe? Will we send probes to worlds without potentially asking permission first? Will we personally visit all races we now encounter? Will the decisions on these and other topics merit amendments to testimonial law?”

After pausing for a few moments, the coordinator then said “As you can see my friends, there is much to discuss, and much to decide. I now open the floor so as to entertain comment.”

After noting several hands ascend, the coordinator called on the one whose hand appeared to be the oldest. “The floor recognizes Lord Endikon.”

Lord Endikon stood and began to speak. “My fellow council members. As our esteemed coordinator Lord Menzinarious indicated, we are all no doubt left in a great state of wonder and bewilderment over not only the news that has been shared with us, but the very insightful and thought-provoking questions that have been raised. Being that this is the case, I feel that we need to give ourselves time to consider these issues, yet not so much time as to delay decisions that need to be rendered quickly. I move that we adjourn the session of the Grand Council for today, however I suggest that we meet again tomorrow and face these issues head on. No doubt, the first order of business tomorrow will be to entertain even more questions that we will have had the opportunity to think of. After documenting these additional questions, we should then debate each of them, and come to decisions that we are all comfortable with." Lord Endikon sat back down.

The coordinator didn't happen to agree with this proposal, but it wasn't his place to make a unilateral decision. To that end, he then said, "All in favor of the proposal to defer discussion and decision until tomorrow raise your hand."

The overwhelming majority raised their hands.

"All who oppose this motion and wish to continue discussion on these topics today, please raise your hand."

There were some, including the coordinator, who raised their hands.

"By evident majority" the coordinator continued, "the motion to defer discussion and decision until tomorrow has been passed. This council will reconvene tomorrow morning in the ninth hour. This meeting is now adjourned."

CHAPTER 5

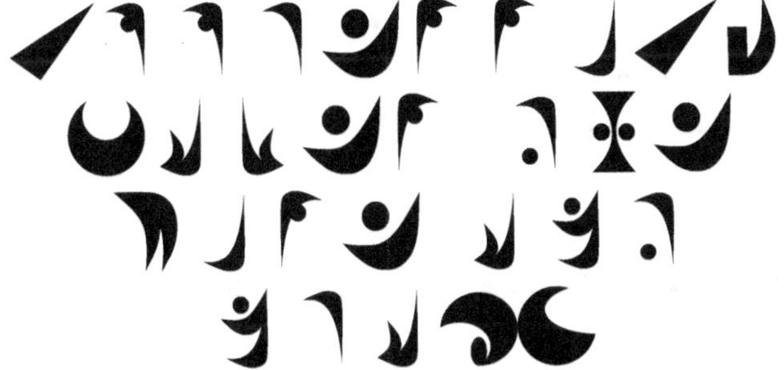

ARRIVING AT THE ENGLISTA HOME that evening was the last thing that BarDurant wanted to do that evening. He and his mate RenVintahn were supposed to go out on a date tonight with someone that she had met at the office where she worked as a receptionist. RenVintahn said that VinLinaar was attractive, witty, smart and yet very humble in the way she carried herself. Sounded like a nice person that may be someone with which they could build a relationship. BarDurant and RenVintahn had themselves been together for about three years now after falling madly in love while on vacation. As was always the case with young couples, they were more interested in each other than much of anything else. But as is also the case with young couples, the more time that went by, the more they thought about starting a family, and that meant that it was time to start looking for a vin gender to add to their union to make them a complete family.

Tonight, may have been the night to meet that special one, but much to the chagrin of his ren mate, BarDurant had been told in no uncertain terms by his Traxian Armed Forces superior officer that his attendance at the meeting tonight was required. It wasn't often when this type of order for off-time activities came in, and so he knew better than to buck against it.

With his dress cap smartly tucked under his left elbow, he knocked on the front door to the home of General Englista. He was immediately greeted with the general's thirteen-year-old daughter who was immediately taken with, and somewhat tongue-tied by, the neatly dressed officer in front of her.

"Hi" was all she could immediately muster.

"Good evening miss. I am here to speak to General Englista" replied Major Mischina.

"Okay. Would you like to come in?" asked the young girl as she moved to the side.

"Yes miss. Thank you."

BarDurant walked in and waited for the young lady to close the door.

"If you'll wait here, I'll let him know you are here. Who may I say is calling?"

"Major Mischina."

"Okay. I'll be right back."

"Thank you, miss."

His perfect manners did little to assuage the ardor of the teenager, and as she walked away, she noted how good he smelled, and how flush she felt meeting such a nice specimen. Getting to the parlor, she lightly knocked on the door where her father was meeting with a few others that were also dressed in their parade best. The door was opened by the one that happened to be standing nearest to the door. She looked in to see all the military men and women that had been invited there tonight, and that they were gathered in a circle around her father.

“Yes?” asked her father who in this setting seemed to be all business.

“There’s a Major Mischina here to see you father.”

Looking at his watch, he said “Ah yes. Right on time. Show him in please, Dian.”

For a moment, Dian thought about how she hated her father calling her by her pre-pubescent name. She would have rather him call her by her gender name RenDian, but that didn’t normally happen until your sixteenth birthday. “God! That day is NEVER going to come!” thought Dian as she walked back to the foyer.

“If you’ll follow me, he’s expecting you” she elegantly said to the major while mustering her best smile. “Majorly hot!” she thought to herself and secretly smiled.

Entering the den where the others were congregated, the new arrival snapped to attention and quickly said “Major Mischina reporting as ordered General!”

“At ease Major. These are some others that I’ve invited here to talk about something of great importance this evening. Everybody, please introduce yourselves to the Major.”

One by one, each in the group of about fifteen introduced themselves to the Major. Seeing that the door to the den had been closed by his daughter thus ensuring privacy, and knowing that there was a white noise maker outside the door guaranteeing no eavesdropping, the general began to speak.

“Before we get started here tonight, for the duration of this meeting, I grant all present permission to speak freely. Understood?”

All in the room nodded and responded with a muffled "Understood."

The general then continued while scanning his eyes around the room "Ladies and gentlemen, I've asked you here tonight to speak about something that is of great importance to our country. As you know, our country has been undergoing a period of upheaval lately due in no small part to the economic situation that we find ourselves in. As more and more time goes by, it has become obvious to me that unless something is done to remedy the situation, this situation will eventually become a clear and present danger to the sovereignty of our country and all that we hold dear."

"Tell me about it" injected one of the sergeants assembled in the room. "Just yesterday my Vin was telling me how there were several outages at the food market where she went shopping yesterday. They were supposed to get a shipment that afternoon, and in fact when she went back later in the day, she was able to get what she needed, but ... that was the first time that type of thing had happened to her."

"Same here" said another in the room. "It's starting to get like a gamble as to whether we are going to be able to find what we need just to put food on the table."

"See, that is what I'm talking about" responded the general. "I have been watching this situation 'progress', if that is what you want to call it ..."

The general rolled his eyes.

"...for the last forty years that I have been in the armed forces and I haven't seen anything to indicate that it is going to get any better by itself."

This line of conversation wasn't anything new to the Major. To the contrary, the Major had lately been spewing very similar rhetoric to several of his compatriots about the heavy tariff's that are being charged by their neighboring nation, the United Nation of Agon. That, coupled with the higher than normal prices that are being charged for UNA exports, represents an extraordinarily heavy hand on the necks of this country the Democratic Republic of Traxis, or DRT for short.

Major Mischina thought about how the geography of their country was such that their eastern border was adjacent to another nation that the DRT seldom interacted with. Most of that was because the land of that eastern nation that bordered the DRT was nothing but desert, and crossing it was impossible on foot, and was dangerous at best with a vehicle. If you had to get to the capitol of that nation, certainly the best way would be by airplane but there wasn't any real reason to go there. They seemed self-sufficient since *their* eastern border was the ocean, and they seemed to derive most of their in-country economy from it.

The western edge of the landlocked DRT where this meeting was being held bordered the UNA, and as such was their only trading partner. The Major had voiced his opinion to several of his acquaintances about how the UNA knew they had the DRT at a great disadvantage, and that they were quite happy with it never changing. The DRT where Major Mischina called home had unsuccessfully tried for decades to negotiate a trade agreement with the UNA that would result in better trade circumstances, but they just wouldn't agree to anything that would result in better conditions for the DRT. The borders, such as they are, were the result of the Treaty of Vordoon that had been agreed to about seventy years prior ... right about the same time that the Galimarians landed that first probe on Traxis and had made first contact. While at the time it seemed like a good idea to agree to the tenets of the treaty, it now seemed like a bad decision to all in the DRT. At the time, the Galimarians made it clear that they wouldn't open up diplomatic relations with the planet of Traxis unless there was a single planetary body they could deal with. They also made it known that any technology they shared with the people of Traxis were to be equally shared amongst all nations. Unknown to the Major, it was him voicing those opinions that caused him to be invited to this meeting tonight.

One of the others in the room spoke up and said in a very exasperated tone "It would probably be better if we had access to the oceans and were able to do a little overseas trading. As it is, if we want to trade with them, we have to use stupid airplanes ... and that is only when the UNA says we can fly over their borders!"

Whilst the Major smirked, General Englista on the other hand replied "That basically sums up the whole reason why we are here. Unless something is done, we will suffer the consequences."

Major Mischina spoke up. "I see your point General, and in fact I have been talking about much the same thing to my acquaintances lately. But frankly, unless we decide to declare war against the UNA, I don't see any way of it ever changing."

"Exactly" came the short and very mysterious reply from the general.

One of the vin officers in the room furrowed her brow and said, "What exactly are you suggesting, general?"

The general uncrossed his legs and leaned forward with his elbows on his knees. His stance was that of sharing a secret, and so imperceptibly the group each seemed to lean forward themselves. "What I'm saying is that we need to do something that will force the hand of those in the UNA, and even some of those in the DRT to make some changes so that our country doesn't die."

After a few moments, the quiet in the room was pierced by a very important question. Major Mischina simply said "Like?"

Even though the general had completely thought through what his response would be at this moment, he dipped his head as if to present a person that was in quiet contemplation and responding at the spur of the moment.

"I think I have a way to create a situation that will cause the UNA to come to us with their hats in their hands. I won't sugarcoat this though. It might cause a few casualties, however if we do it right, it doesn't have to cause any." The general knew full well that it actually would cause casualties to some of the citizens of the UNA, but he also knew that this situation wouldn't have come to this point if the UNA had been fair in their dealings with the DRT, his beloved country. It was their own fault it had to come to this.

"As I said earlier, you have the ability to speak freely at this meeting. I will add that if you don't feel you have the stomach to be part of this type of operation you may leave now, and I will not count it against you in any way. In addition to that, if any do leave, I order the remaining ones here not to count it against them either." The general then waited. He knew that using the wording about having the stomach for this operation would cause these battle-hardened officers to stay put, but he also had to cover his backside in the off chance that some wouldn't stay.

All did.

After the commensurate pause to allow for dissention, one of the group then said "General, I think we're all staying. We all have families that we're concerned about and we wish to give them a future." All officers in the room silently nodded their heads while simultaneously keeping their eyes fixed on their superior officer. Seeing that his officers were all in agreement, the general began to outline his plan."

"Okay. Now that I see that you are all in agreement with how grave our situation is, and how grave steps need to be taken, I will now outline to you a battle plan that has been in formulation for a while now. One of our science teams has been working with some of the technology that came from the Galimarians after they opened diplomatic relations with our planet seventy years ago. This team has figured out that if we use the Galimarian power generation abilities in a slightly different way than it was originally meant to have been used, we can cause a localized environmental condition that will cause the land where it is unleashed to be uninhabitable. I have been assured by our scientists that the effect will be localized to the exact areas where it is released, and the effect will dissipate within one day."

In reality, these very scientists were split down the middle as to whether the reactions would be so localized, and whether the effects of the proposed device would stop so quickly. Some of them wanted a substantially larger amount of study to be done in order to make sure the outcome wouldn't cascade into a runaway chain reaction. The elements found in the soil of Traxis were fundamentally different than the same found in the soil of Galimar, and so they strenuously argued for additional testing on Traxian soil. They tried, and eventually failed, to convince the general. They even resorted to telling him that if the chain of reactions couldn't be arrested, it could actually cause the atmosphere to become unbreathable to every man, woman and child. It wouldn't be poisonous, but the atmosphere would be completely converted to nitrogen leaving absolutely no oxygen for the Traxians to breathe.

"How does it work?

"Remember the N-ion bomb we developed recently?" asked the general. "It operates on the same principle."

"That is an anti-personnel device that leaves the buildings intact but renders the area unlivable. It would do the same thing?" asked Major Mischina.

"Almost. It actually can cause some structural damage, but we are accounting for that to minimize collateral damage" came the short reply from the general. Again, he was stretching the truth and he knew it.

A few seconds went by as the personnel in the room thought about the plan, and its implications. All in the room knew full well that casualties would be difficult to avoid with this type of weapon, but at the same time all in the room arrived at the same conclusion the general had come to weeks before. Their backs had been put in the corner. They had no other option than to come out swinging.

“Deployment?” came the one-word question from another in the room.

“Deployment would obviously be done covertly” answered the general. “We can deploy and conceal the devices in remote caves and underground locations. They can be remotely triggered after our operatives have been extracted.”

“And what would be our position once the ‘natural’ disaster” the one asking used air-quotes, “happens. How would this give us an advantage?”

“In preparation for this, I have been stockpiling N-Ox converters from Galimar as well. We have reverse engineered them though so that they end up having a shelf life. Unlike the ones we got from Galimar, these ones won’t work permanently, and the UNA will require repeated shipments from us” answered the general.

“But they would just reverse engineer it themselves” retorted a sergeant in the corner. “They wouldn’t need us to supply them.”

“That’s right, they would” replied the General, “if it wasn’t for the fact opening the case would cause the mechanism to destroy itself beyond recognition.” The implication was clear. It would explode and cause serious injury and even death to any that tried.

“Doesn’t the UNA have their own N-OX converters from Galimar?” asked someone standing next to the Major.

“Our intelligence has determined that while there is one or two of the devices in the country, the UNA government hasn’t deemed its use or reproduction to be a priority. The ones they do have in storage have been secretly sabotaged.”

The general gave those in the room time to digest what had just been outlined. The plan was unpalatable for sure, but as the general pointed out, there didn’t seem to be any option left. They were left with no choices. Something had to be done. There was no way they could go on.

Major Mischina stepped forward and picked up an as-yet unclaimed glass of water. Holding it out in front of him he said, "May we have the strength to make the hard decisions for the good our country, the Democratic Republic of Traxis."

All around the room raised their glasses and toasted this despicable yet necessary plan.

CHAPTER 6

MenGala BarDringol and his mate RenIval, both recent emigrants from the planet of Traxis, were preparing for the journey to their home planet.

It had been about four years since they had come to Galimar. At the time, the prospect of living on a planet that wasn't their own was quite extraordinary among their contemporaries. It had been around seven decades since the Galimarian people had made first-contact with the people of Traxis, and since then their respective cultures had shared quite a bit with each other. The people of Galimar were far more advanced than the numerous political and social cultures they encountered on Traxis, but contrary to the conspiracy theorists that seemingly loved to hear themselves talk, all Galimarians seemed to be truly peaceful.

This, of course, was in sharp contrast to the nations of Traxis that up until the treaty of Vordoon, had regularly found themselves at war with the other nations of their own planet for any number of reasons. BarDringol and RenIval both came from the United Nation of Agon, and so any news from their home planet that concerned the UNA was of particular interest to them.

The existence of this treaty, and the fact that all planetary nations ratified it, was the main reason why Galimar had felt comfortable with the establishment of diplomatic relations with Traxis. Galimarians refused to deal with any single nation, but rather would only communicate with the entire planet through the United League of Vordoon, or ULV for short.

Now, though, BarDringol and RenIval were preparing to leave for their home planet since the news coming from their planet wasn't exactly positive. The news lately had taken on a tone that was much more inflationary since there were several political factions that were being rather vocal in their displeasure over the treaty. Many of them spouted venom over the perceived unfairness of the way the disputed lands and borders had been divided according to the treaty. And ... truth be said ... there were some nations that seemed to have a little more in terms of natural resources within their borders than nations that may exist next door. Still though, all nations had ratified the treaty with their respective eyes open and so there was no way to substantiate the various claims of unfairness.

The United Nation of Agon happened to be one of those nations that seemed to have a little of everything when it came to natural resources. The south-eastern section of the continent where they found themselves contained quite a lot of arable farmland where seemingly anything could be grown. In the north were dense timberlands and the west butted up against a large ocean where an unending supply of sea creatures could be found for food. The south-west held mines that yielded some of the richest supplies of just about any natural mineral needed.

There were those in the government of the UNA that were concerned about a neighboring nation that had been doing a little too much sabre rattling over their claims of unfairness in the Treaty of Vordoon. BarDringol and RenIval had been asked to come back home to help with the defense of the nation, in case it was needed. Before the treaty, the two of them were officers in the UNA army and so they had quite a lot of experience with tactical battle strategy, and with running a command of their own. When the treaty was signed, it effectively left them without a job, although the government had guaranteed that they would be cared for in honor of their many years of service to the country.

Now though, their futures were once again cast in an uncertain light.

"Well … that just about does it."

"What does, honey?" replied RenIval to her husband of eight years.

"The packing of my study. I had to order about twelve more travel cases to hold all my junk in there!" he replied with a slight chuckle. "I didn't really expect to be returning back home to live, and so I didn't really give any thought about remaining light on my feet. It's mostly just books though."

"Sounds heavy." She said.

"It is a little, but we've been given a pretty decent weight allotment on the shuttle launch next week, and so I think we'll be ok." He replied.

"Well, we haven't even begun to pack the kitchen" she retorted, "and so don't be so sure we …"

Ding-Dong!

The two of them stopped their exchange and looked at each other with a quizzical look.

"Were you expecting anyone?" asked BarDringol.

"No. Not that I can think of." She replied.

The two of them both rose from their temporary resting place on the couch and walked to the door. Opening the door, BarDringol saw their friend and Galimarian confidant, Glimann, standing there with a look of concern on his face.

"Hey you two. Are you all right?" he asked BarDringol and RenIval.

"Yessss ..." answered BarDringol with a tone of unsure expectation in his voice. He really had no idea why his friend, who was usually very predictable, now had this mysterious affect about him. "Why wouldn't we be?"

"You mean you haven't heard?" asked their visitor.

"Heard what?" asked RenIval, a tone of fear now entering her voice.

"It's all over the news! I'm shocked you haven't seen it!" replied Glimann.

"Well, we've been packing for our trip back to Traxis all day and haven't been watching the news" replied BarDringol.

"I think your plans are going to change" said Glimann with a foreboding sound.

Pushing past them, Glimann touched the side of the vid monitor on the wall of their living room, and it instantly lit up with scenes of utter devastation. What could be seen through what looked like a toxic soup of atmosphere was nothing less than the charred remains of a city that had been completely destroyed.

"Where is this? What happened?" asked RenIval.

Just then, a voice came from the vid screen. A news announcer began to describe what was being shown.

"For those of you who have just tuned in, our top story is the sad sad news that the planet of Traxis has suffered a devastating planet-wide event resulting in what appears to be the complete destruction of all life on the planet."

RenIval shrieked and her hand went to cover her mouth. BarDringol immediately rushed to his wife's side, however he wasn't exactly doing much better than her.

The news announcer continued. "The images you see here are just now coming in from a probe sent in from a Galimarian news satellite that is in orbit around the planet. At this time, there isn't much to go on as to why or how this happened, but all we can tell you at this point is that the normal influx of radio and television transmissions that come from this planet have all ceased completely. According to our science editor as well as several experts on staff in our main studios, it appears that the atmosphere of the planet has been contaminated on a planet-wide scale and would be deadly lethal to any Traxian on the surface."

BarDringol and RenIval felt the blood drain from their faces and it felt like all extremities were tingling. They both had to quickly find a seat as they continued to witness the obvious and complete carnage on their home planet, since their legs were threatening to give out.

"On the communications line with us now is our chief science editor, Kosha Minnea. Kosha what can you tell us about the images we are now seeing?"

"Well Lonei, the images mostly speak for themselves really. As you can see from this video of the city of Entiuk, the devastation is utterly complete."

BarDringol let out an audible gasp of his own now. His youth was spent in a city near Entiuk.

"What can you tell us about the atmosphere?" asked the news anchor.

"All that we can tell you so far is that it appears to be a toxic soup of different gasses, but the specific properties of this soup are unclear. At this time, we have no information on what kind of cataclysm could cause this, short of a massive volcanic eruption."

"How pervasive is this devastation on the planet, Kosha?"

"We're still evaluating the data pouring in from not only our own satellites around the planet, but also Traxian satellites that we have been granted access to in the past. All that we can tell you is that so far there doesn't seem to be any part of the planet that hasn't been touched by this disaster."

"In your experience, could there be an explanation for this that might come from outside the planet? Like what we saw happen with the planet Palimine when its sun exploded?"

"Well, we can't rule out an extra-planetary causality for this level of destruction, however we can tell you that the Traxian sun is stable and in no way caused this catastrophe."

"Very well, Kosha. We appreciate your input, and we look forward to hearing from you as you learn more about this terrible news."

"You're welcome, Lonei. I'll be back in touch if I learn more."

"Once again, this is the Galimarian planetary news agency, and we're bringing you news about the devastating ..." the news anchor started to repeat the news.

BarDringol and RenIval both looked at the floor in front of them and tried their best to wrap their brains around what they had just heard. It took some time navigate their way through thoughts of how many cities had apparently been destroyed, however they almost simultaneously started to realize that all the family they had left behind on the planet were now most likely ... all ...

The two of them may have been officers in the army, but this ... this was too much to emotionally stand against. Years of combat training, and the years of emotional callouses built up when some under their command didn't make it home from the theater of war ... it was no match for this. This was far beyond anything they had ever thought they would have to deal with. First, one tear. Then, two. Then ... thousands, or millions. They were uncountable, unending, and unyielding.

CHAPTER 7

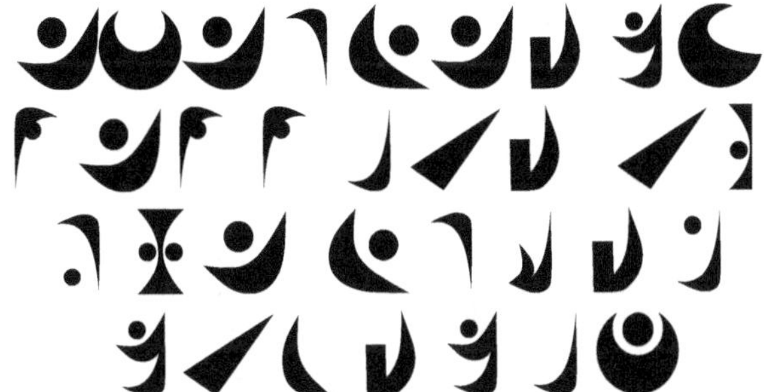

"HOW COULD THIS HAVE HAPPENED?!" came the outburst from somewhere in the middle of those seated in the council chambers.

The emergency session of the Grand Council of Galimar had been called soon after the news of the destruction of Traxis had come. All on the planet were hanging on the words of the news agencies that had been covering the disaster. Most on Galimar hadn't met a Traxian person themselves since the program of personnel exchange had only recently been put in place. There were only about 100 Traxians that had come to Galimar, but that was just a drop in the very large ocean of Galimarian people.

"Before we discuss this, my fellow council members, I'd like to propose that we invoke Testimonial Law statute 9385-73 allowing the council to discuss matters while not being broadcast for reasons of planetary security" replied the coordinator.

Testimonial Law statute 9385-73 was a statute that had been passed many years before allowing for discussion of matters while not being broadcast across the planetary network. According to the statute, this type of situation was put into place in cases of where the subject matter could be inflationary to those on the planet, or to those that had a material interest in the matters to be discussed. Even though this particular testimonial law had been passed well before the Traxian planet had been discovered and so it was originally oriented toward the people of Galimar, it was obvious that this law applied to the few Traxians that were now marooned on Galimar.

One of the grand council members raised his hand, stood, and turned to address his fellow members. "My fellow council members, personally I hold the public nature of the Grand Council to be one of the best ways to ensure that this government be one that is run and regulated by the people. As we all know though, Testimonial Law statute 9385-73 was created for cases when the subject matter would potentially cause problems with those that have a material interest in the subject matter being discussed. I'd say that the situation we have witnessed on the planet of Traxis qualifies under this guideline. I move that we sequester our discussions."

The coordinator raised his voice and said, "Those that agree with the proposal to sequester the discussion of the Grand Council as it pertains to the subject matter of the disaster on Traxis please raise your hand."

There were several that did, however it wasn't obvious where the simple majority laid.

After a few seconds, the coordinator spoke up and said, "It appears that the vote to sequester these proceedings is close to an even split. According to testimonial law, the vote in this case need only be a simple majority, and so we will need to register your votes on the voting pads."

Each council member had a small table in front of them which they could use to take notes or to temporarily place items they needed to keep handy. Built into this table was a voting pad with a simple set of yes/no buttons which would allow their vote to be registered on whatever proposal was being decided at the time. As each council member leaned forward and pressed the button representing their vote, the results were then displayed to the coordinator via a screen built into his podium. This screen allowed the coordinator to easily see not only when all members had entered their vote, but also the tally.

The coordinator looked up from his screen showing the tally and said "As evidenced by simple majority, the proposal to sequester discussions about the disaster on Traxis has passed. To those that are listening on the planetary network, any decisions that are made regarding this subject matter, and any other discussions unrelated to Traxis will be published at the end of the day."

With that, the coordinator lifted a cover on his podium and pressed a recessed button. Taking this small step caused several things to happen simultaneously. First, all doors around the Grand Council chamber clicked and locked. Any who were in the room were there for the duration of this meeting, and any supporting personnel who were outside the room were now prohibited from entering. As it was, all members of the grand council were seated and there were no unauthorized personnel in the room.

Finally, the audio and video broadcast of the council proceedings all ceased. Those who had been listening were presented with a title screen containing information about how the Grand Council was currently meeting under secure circumstances.

When the indicator lights above the recessed button turned green, the coordinator now knew that the meeting was secure, and he was free to speak.

"Council members, we are now secure, and we are free to speak about the matters at hand" said the coordinator. "The question was asked how this could have happened. I must warn you that the answer to this question is rather unpalatable."

The coordinator paused for a moment while looking down, but then looked up and said "How did this happen? The answer is that it happened because of us."

As one would expect, this statement was very surprising to the council. A sharp outburst emanated from just about everyone in the room. After waiting for a few seconds for the unrest in the room to settle, the coordinator continued "I have asked Doctor Mundial to be here with us in this emergency session. He has analyzed the data coming in from Traxis and has come up with some startling conclusions." The doctor was already walking up to the platform and as soon as he arrived, the coordinator said, "Doctor would you please present your findings to the council?"

The coordinator turned the podium over to Doctor Mundial and as he stepped forward, those who had risen to their feet returned to their seats.

"Esteemed members of the Grand Council, I wish it was under different circumstances that I address you today, however I feel it is imperative that you be made aware of the true reasons why it appears that all the population of the planet of Traxis has been destroyed."

Pausing for a moment, the doctor continued "I was asked to evaluate all the data that we had available to us, both public and private, to determine the real reason why this had happened. Most of what I have to go on is part of the public record. All of that data seemed to point to a natural disaster that caused some of the naturally occurring minerals on the Traxian planet to react unexpectedly with some explosions that had happened deep under the ground. It appeared to all who would be looking that it was indeed a natural disaster and nothing more."

"However," the doctor continued, "shortly before all transmissions from the planet ceased, there was one lone transmission that came from our Galimarian ambassador stationed on Traxis, which, I am sad to disclose, has apparently perished in this same disaster. According to the ambassador, there was a one solitary soldier in the army of the Democratic Republic of Traxis, who went by the name of Major Mischina that revealed to him what really happened. According to this Major, there was a rogue faction of that government that had decided that the economic pressures being put on their nation by a neighboring nation merited their causing a disaster that they thought would be localized to a relatively small area in their neighboring nation. Their theory was that the more prosperous nation would suffer serious needs, and then the DRT would come in and be the saviors. I am sorry tell you that they did this by modifying power generators that Galimar had supplied them."

There was a hushed gasp on the part of the council members.

"They modified the generators in such a way that they would cause a feedback loop. This loop, however, ended up interacting with one of the minerals in their planetary crust. Apparently, their scientists were split on whether the reaction would be localized or not, but regardless of the risk the rouge faction decided to move forward with the operation."

"What they didn't anticipate was that not only did the plan work, but the chain reaction that some of their scientists were worried about also happened, even beyond what they had feared. The explosions and the related energy fields generated by the Galimarian power generators touched off a chain reaction that was impossible to stop. It basically vaporized the topsoil of the planet and turned the atmosphere into an unbreathable soup of gasses. Unbreathable, that is, to the Traxians. Early reports said that the atmosphere was radioactive. This turned out to be false, but Traxian physiology is such that their lungs require oxygen to live. The chain reaction caused all oxygen in the atmosphere to be eliminated along with several other gasses, and the only remaining gas was nitrogen. As a result, all life on the planet that we are aware of has ceased."

The doctor paused once again, and then said, "Are there any questions?"

None came.

The council was so stunned and saddened that none were able to come up with much of a coherent thought. 'Devastated' was the best way to describe how each in the room felt. Galimar has always been a planet that respected the sanctity of life. Knowing that technology originating on Galimar was used in this way, and that it resulted in the death of untold millions ... even billions ... was far too much to handle. Looking out over the audience, the doctor not only felt terrible for the massive devastation that had happened, he also felt bad for the effect this news was having on all the members of the Grand Council. Most of these members were there when they had decided to open diplomatic relations with Traxis, and they were the same council members that had decided to allow the sharing of technology with that planet. Knowing now that the sharing of that technology set in motion a chain of events that eventually led to the planet being decimated like this was probably the most terrible feeling that each of the members had ever felt in their lives. One and all felt like they personally had a hand in the death of every man, woman ... and ... and even the children! The poor defenseless children!

Devastated, overwhelmed, shocked, distraught and shattered were all words that were floating on the minds of each member present. But even these words didn't approach how badly they all felt.

Seeing that no questions were coming, the doctor parted with "In case you have any questions in the future, you are welcome to visit me any time in my offices at the University of Meropa. Thank you."

Turning to the coordinator, the doctor stepped off the stage and left the coordinator to continue the meeting. It was an unusual exit though. Usually there was applause to show appreciation for the presentation that had just been given. This time though, there was no applause, in fact the only sound that could be heard was the sound of Doctor Mundial's footsteps as he retreated from the stage.

Slowly the coordinator mounted the stage once again and looked out over the council chambers. The mass of faces looking back at him bore out the same mire of feelings he was personally experiencing. He saw a combination of sadness and grief that would almost be impossible to quantify. Eventually, he knew he had to move the meeting along.

"So, my fellow council members, what remains now is deciding what we are going to do with this knowledge, and what steps we are going to take to keep this from ever happening again."

One lone hand raised from the middle of the group. Seeing the hand, the coordinator responded, "The floor recognizes Lord Aramine." Jobiah stood slowly and spoke.

"From the overwhelming gloom evident in this room, I can see that all here share with me a sense of tremendous personal loss. I am of the mind though that while we cannot ever change what has happened, one fact remains, and that is the truth that we as a people are not going to stop being who we are. We are a peaceful race of enlightened explorers who will continue to stretch our arms out into the universe. We will continue to search for understanding amidst the ever-present unknown. But there is another unmistakable truth that we have learned here, and that truth is how the planet Galimar is not alone in the universe and that some of those civilizations are not as advanced as we are. It is obvious to me that we need to consider changing our policies on how we interact with other worlds."

Jobiah sat down.

Another hand was raised in the back of the council chambers. The coordinator responded, "The floor recognizes Lord Jonaul."

Lord Jonaul stood. "I agree with Lord Aramine. It is obvious to me that we will need to create amendments to testimonial law guiding how we approach interaction with other worlds from today onward. But I also feel strongly that Galimar should know the reason why this happened. Out of respect for the fallen, I don't believe it would be prudent or wise to reveal to Traxian refugees or the people of Galimar in general that it was Traxis itself that caused their own deaths. Still, though, all should know why we will not share technology indiscriminately."

With those words, the grand council began what amounted to some of the most sweeping and pervasive changes to testimonial law that had ever been adopted. Every single law found in the Testimony of Galactic Land and Maritime Law was reviewed over the following two weeks, and where needed, changes were made that ensured the testimony was updated throughout. The new and updated testimony was now structured so that every interaction with alien lifeforms would be done in such a way that Galimar would never again be an unwitting accomplice in the destruction of any life.

What they couldn't possibly know though, was that these landmark changes would even affect a world in completely different galaxy.

CHAPTER 8

BarDringol reached up and clicked off the vid monitor. Doing so removed the only source of sound that had been filling the front room of this well-appointed abode that he and his Traxian mate RenIval had been given when they emigrated to Galimar. Since they had arrived from Traxis, they had been treated hospitably, but none of that seemed to matter now.

The vid monitor had been carrying the reports of not only what had happened to their home planet, but also of the announcements that came as a result of the emergency meetings of the Grand Council of Galimar. According to the reports, the Grand Council had just gone into detail about what had happened, and more significantly what the cause of it all was.

"I can't believe it" said one of those gathered. The room was filled with several Traxians, and now that BarDringol was looking, was only attended by one Galimarian, Glimann. Glimann had been assigned to work as an attaché to the visitors, and according to the Grand Council, it was his job to make sure the visiting Traxians were well cared for.

Those gathered looked over at the one making the outburst and couldn't find any words to say in rebuttal. In reality, rebuttal wasn't necessary. Truth be said, all around the planet would say that this truly was an unbelievable situation. Not only unbelievable because of the utter devastation that had happened to the home planet of the people gathered in this room, not only because they just heard that Galimarian technology was used to cause this devastation of the Traxian planet, but also because those gathered in this room were the clear majority of all that was left of the Traxian race. In a very real sense, they were an endangered species!

"I wish there was something to say that could make this better, but ..." said Glimann.

"There's nothing you can say" replied RenIval without looking at him. "There's nothing that will make this better."

To say that Glimann felt terrible was an understatement. The entire planet felt incredible loss over hearing that not only was the first planet where they had found intelligent life now reduced to a devastated rubble, but Galimarian technology had a hand in this? What made it even worse for those gathered in this room was that their loss was amplified by the knowledge that all whom they had known, all that they ever knew, it was all gone. Mothers, fathers, sisters, brothers, sons, daughters, grandparents. All gone. Even the animals. RenIval thought about some of the places where she had played as a child, or even the food dispensaries where she and her brothers often enjoyed eating. She thought about her first kiss, the way she felt as she walked along the beach the first time. She thought about the beautiful park where she and BarDringol had been united in marriage, and the gathering of family that occurred shortly after. Every last bit of it ... eradicated completely from existence!

Something else was brewing in the minds of BarDringol and RenIval though. This morning there was a short discussion between them that, at the time, didn't really amount to much.

As if it had been sitting on the back burner of a cooking unit though, it had time to simmer into a full boil, and now that it had been revealed that Galimarian technology was involved, it broke through into a fully formed thought that needed to be discussed.

But not while Glimann was present.

Knowing what his answer would be ahead of time, BarDringol asked Glimann “Can I get you anything to drink?” Some in the room wondered momentarily why Glimann had been singled out as to if he wanted a beverage. True to what BarDringol had expected, Glimann responded “I’m sorry BarDringol. My wife called me a few minutes ago and told me I was needed at home. Apparently, my children are pretty upset over the news and they need their father and mother together to help them through this.”

Nodding his head, BarDringol said “I understand”. He then stood, followed by Glimann. Before he made a move towards the door, Glimann turned to the group and said “May I say that I am so sorry for what has happened. I offer my deepest sympathies and hope you can somehow find peace in your lives. If there is anything that I can do to help you heal through this, please do not hesitate to let me know.”

The group couldn’t muster their abilities to look at Glimann in the eyes. Their gazes were all transfixed on whatever small patch of floor that happened to be in front of them. Glimann could easily see the pain that was freely floating around in the room and hated the way he felt. He felt so impotent. Unable to assuage the despair so concentrated in this room. He looked over to his host, and with a look of impotency, said “Well I’ll be on my way. I’ll call you tomorrow. OK?”

Walking towards the door, BarDringol said “Sounds good my friend. Give my best to your mate and the children.”

Gratified that BarDringol was thinking of his children at a time like this, Glimann took personal solace in the parting greeting. “I will. Thank you for your hospitality.”

“Any time” came the short reply from BarDringol.

As he watched Glimann emerge from his residence and eventually closed the door behind him, BarDringol's face took on a decidedly harder edge. He turned around to see that unlike a few seconds ago, all eyes were fixed on him, including those of his mate. "We have much to discuss."

"What's there to discuss?" came a reply from the room. "We are basically the entire remainder of Traxian people anywhere in the universe. There may be some that are currently in transit, but essentially ... we're it!"

"That has a lot to do with what we need to discuss, but there's more" replied BarDringol.

"Like?" asked someone sitting next to the last person that had talked.

"Like, how we need to plan out a few necessary things" interjected RenIval

"Exactly" added BarDringol. "Things such as how it is up to us to procreate effectively if we are to ensure the survival of our species. Things such as ..."

BarDringol paused for a moment so as to choose the right words. The ones floating around in his mind were rather unpalatable.

"Things such as ...?" prompted the same Traxian woman who had been speaking earlier.

BarDringol looked up at the woman and said point bluntly "Revenge."

"Revenge? Why?"

RenIval responded quickly "Did you catch how this happened?"

One of the men assembled responded "They said it was Galimarian technology that did this."

"Not exactly" replied another. "They said that it was Galimarian technology that was used. We can't know for sure how it was used."

“No, but we can be sure they knew this was going to happen.”

“Oh? How is that?”

“Come on” replied RenIval incredulously. “They’re brilliant! They knew the likelihood of something like this happening.”

“There’s more than that though” added BarDringol. “Did you catch what they said the resulting atmosphere was?”

“Wasn’t it nothing but nitrogen?” answered one woman in the group.

“Exactly” replied BarDringol.

“So? What difference does that make?” asked the same woman.

“As opposed to us, what atmosphere do the Galimarians need to survive?” responded RenIval.

What appeared to be a light of sudden understanding flashed across the faces of those looking on.

“Exactly. Nitrogen” said BarDringol, answering the question posed by his mate.

After a few moments, another in the group spoke up and said “But that doesn’t explain why they would do it. Why would they destroy our planet?”

One of the gathered men in the room, near the back answered “That’s easy. We’re the only other ones they’ve found that are intelligent. For untold millennia they were the only race. They’ve always felt superior in the knowledge that they would never be challenged in their sovereignty. You’ve heard it yourself! They call themselves ‘enlightened’ don’t they? Yeah. They think they are so much better.”

“I don’t know” responded another from the group. “They’ve always been very nice to me.”

“Will you start thinking for once?!” replied RenIval in a clearly irritated tone. “What did the Grand Council just say? They said, and I quote, 'We have passed amendments to Testimonial Law such that Galimar will no longer share its technology with civilizations that are less evolved than Galimar. And if a civilization that we encounter might be a candidate for the sharing of our resources, including technology, it will only be done if approved by a three-quarter majority of the Grand Council.'

"Exactly!" exclaimed BarDringol. "Clearly, they feel that Traxis wasn't nearly as great as they are, and so they can't have any civilizations that might threaten their stranglehold on being the top of the heap. I'll tell you something else. Remember that other civilization that they discovered a year ago? I think its name was Briteria? I can guarantee you that if they don't watch themselves, they're next!"

With that, there was a lull in the conversation while all in the room considered what this meant for each one gathered. Eventually there was a question that popped into the mind of RenIval.

"One thing though is how we can get to the heart of this planet and exact our revenge."

"I think you just answered your own question, my mate" answered BarDringol.

"I did?"

"Yes. Heart." answered BarDringol.

RenIval smiled. "Perfect!"

"What? What's perfect?" asked a member of the Traxian refugees gathered.

"The Heart of Galimar" answered RenIval.

"The what?"

"The Heart of Galimar" added BarDringol. Then turning to the rest of the group he said "I know several of you just arrived on Galimar, so you might not know much about things around here. Have you ever noticed that all Galimarian adults wear those amulets?"

Several nodded.

"Those amulets are made by a device in the central part of the administrative center of the planet called The Heart of Galimar" continued BarDringol. "Its origin is shaded in mystery, but all I know is that those amulets make it possible for them to not only be so intelligent, but I understand that there is some kind of intelligence in them that makes them communicate better, or something like that. One thing I know for sure is that if they didn't have those amulets, they'd be just as unevolved", BarDringol's eyes rolled, "as we puny Traxians are."

"So, what are you proposing?" asked one of the men in the group.

"I propose that we get closer to where The Heart of Galimar is located. We'll use our new status as endangered to pull on their heartstrings to let us in. We'll learn what we can about it and how it makes these amulets. We'll learn how it allows Galimarians to communicate. Then, as soon as we can ..."

Bar Dringol paused while looking around the room ...

"... we'll destroy it."

CHAPTER 9

THE POND NEAR HIS HOUSE was where Craylar loved to spend most of his days. Since it was the summer, and since it was time to relax before the headmasters soon required him to resume his studies, the young Traxian boy used the time to its fullest, swimming and splashing in the pond along with his Galimarian friend Thane. The two had met at school, and soon thereafter it was obvious they were going to be best friends for the rest of their lives.

Today was special since it was right in the middle of the Spinsage migration, and so it was fun to witness the different colors that the birds gave off when they were flying. Though not obvious while flitting and fluttering around on the ground or tree branches, once the birds took to the air, the iridescent feathers that were underneath the larger but drab outer feathers showed in all their glory, and they were often enough to take your breath away. The whole reason why they had the name Spinsage was because as they were taking off from the ground, they would follow a circular pattern while gaining altitude. In doing so, it was a favorite game of Thane and Craylar's to try to guess the colors that would show once the birds took flight. So far, Craylar was ahead of Thane in correct guesses ... but not by much. The two were fairly equal in perceptive abilities.

Around lunchtime, Thane's mother Porshah came to the pond with some favorite morsels of food. As they gobbled up their lunch, she and the boys were treated with the sight of a mother and baby lynar. If this was earth, they would resemble a white tail deer, but with long hair/fur around their neck and head. The babies had no fur whatsoever.

Normally Craylar and Thane would run and play until the sun went down, however today Porshah had Thane come home early. Thane's father wanted to take his family to the home of a work associate this evening, and so Thane had to come home early to get clean and presentable for the evening. All this meant that Craylar ended up coming home early himself.

As he entered the front door to his home, he quickly noticed that his father was home as well. It wasn't altogether strange that he would be home at this time of day; it actually happened quite often. Today though, it sounded like his father was entertaining some associates of his own, and it sounded like there may have been somewhat of a disagreement in the room. He knew that he shouldn't eavesdrop on the conversation, but upon hearing his father sounding angry, an event that rarely happened ... well ... he couldn't help himself. Stepping quietly toward the door, he leaned his back against the wall next to the door and slid down slowly until he finally sat on the floor. It was one of the visitors that Craylar heard first.

"... and that is why we can't let this opportunity go by!"

"We don't even know if the stupid Grand Council is going to approve the proposal" responded Craylar's father.

"Stupid??" thought Craylar as he continued to listen. "Why would he call the most esteemed bastion of Galimarian civilization ... stupid?!" It was truly perplexing to him.

"If the prophecy is right, and we know it is, then it can't help but pass. We will finally have the revenge we seek!" answered a voice that Craylar didn't recognize. "How many people did his father have in there?" wondered Craylar.

"Perhaps" answered Craylar's father, "But we mustn't expect fulfillment of the prophecy until the fulfillment presents itself. It has been a very long time since the prophecy was spoken and we all know of ones that thought the fulfillment was to happen at a particular time, only to be disappointed. We must take care not to jump ahead of ourselves."

"What is all this talk about prophecies?" wondered Craylar as he continued to eavesdrop.

"Perhaps that was true of them but tell me ..." retorted another faceless voice in the room. With more than a little measure of venom, he then added "When has there ever been a time when there was the prospect of visiting a world with this same name? We know it was the Grand Council, and not one of us, that named the planet Eden. We know it wasn't a Traxian that gave it the name, since those megalomaniacs on the council won't let a Traxian be in their little club."

"Why are they so angry with the Grand Council?" pondered Craylar as he worked hard to be as silent as possible. "Are they talking about that proposal to send a ship to Eden? Thane and I were even talking about that this morning! I think Thane's friend is the son to the designer of the proposal, Lord Aramine."

Craylar's father responded "I suppose we'll have to wait and see won't we gentlemen. They are supposed to be meeting next week to hear the proposal, and it seems like that proposal is all the people at work want to talk about. With it being so popular I wouldn't be surprised if it did pass, and if it does pass, we'll have to come up with a plan. I know that the mission is going to be family based, and it will be open to any that wish to go. We will probably need to use our status as 'the downtrodden Traxians' to get onto the list to go."

"Exactly" said one of the voices Craylar had already heard. "Meanwhile, we need to keep this under wraps. Agreed?"

All in the room grunted their agreement. To Craylar it sounded like the discussion was going to end, and the doors were soon to open, and so as quietly as possible he stood and scrambled up the stairs to shower and dress for the evening. As he did, Craylar's thoughts were as far away from his personal appearance as the moon Genipar was from Galimar. Why was his father meeting with those men? Why did he and the men sound so angry? Why did they hate the Grand Council? Do they feel that way about other Galimarians? And, what is this prophecy they kept talking about?

Finishing his personal grooming he came downstairs, and by this time, he saw that any previous visitors had since vacated. It wasn't lost on his father that his son seemed to come home while he was having his emergency meeting with the members of the Chamber of Traxis, and it may have been possible that his son heard some of what had been discussed. How much, he didn't know. After thinking about it though, he concluded that his son was getting to the age where it was time that he be told about the real oppression of the Galimarians that Traxian people have had to live with for thousands of years. It was time that Craylar be told the truth.

Upon seeing his father, Craylar tried to make his face as blank as possible so as to not give away that he had heard anything, but in doing so, that was all Craylar's father needed in order to see that Craylar had probably heard everything.

"Hello father. You are home early today" greeted Craylar in an overly somber tone.

"Yes I am. I wanted to have you show me where you and your friends have been spending the summer. It's down by the pond, isn't it?"

"Yes. Right now, the spinsages are migrating and they are really amazing to watch."

Craylar's father thought about how he did that same thing when he was young in this very house. A pleasant memory, and a simpler time."

"Sounds wonderful! Care to show an old man where that is happening?"

"You're not old, father! But … sure, follow me!"

Craylar didn't need much of an excuse to go outside, and even less to go down to the pond when the spinsages were flying. With no preamble, Craylar jumped up and almost ran out the front door to his favorite spot. In fact, at one point he realized that he needed to look behind to make sure his dad was keeping up. He was. As Craylar said, his father wasn't really that old.

Getting to his favorite spot, Craylar sat down on a rock that was almost perfectly shaped like a bench, complete with seat and back. The bench faced a spot that had a perfect view of the place where hundreds of Spinsages came to roost. The spot was on the other side of the pond, and so their presence wasn't anything that would spook the birds away. Within a few moments, Craylar's father caught up and sat next to his son while looking across the water at the flock, busying themselves with what was important to an avian mind.

Craylar sat there watching the birds land and take off again after feeding at the edge of the pond. His body was there with his father, but his mind was far away. It was occupied with what he had heard in the hallway when his father was ...

"Out with it son."

"Huh? What?"

"Something is on your mind, son. Out with it."

Craylar sat there for a while. He hadn't meant to talk about this with his father so soon, and so he hadn't spent time organizing his thoughts. Then again, those thoughts were raw and unfiltered right now though, and perhaps that was good.

"I got home early today father, and I heard you and those other men in the study talking."

"And you are wondering about the meaning behind what you heard."

Craylar paused for a moment.

"Yes."

He had been sitting with his back against the rock backrest but shifting his body forward and leaning his elbows on his knees Craylar's father thought about how to approach this. As he thought about it, he remembered when his own father told him about the history that affected their lives. The secret history of how Galimar had wiped out their people. How revenge was the strong and ever-present undercurrent beneath a well-formed veneer of civility toward the people of Galimar. Yes ... the approach his father used worked for him. It'll work for his son too.

"Son, when you go to the beach, do you like to swim in the water?"

"Of course, I do. I love swimming, and that's why I spend so much time here" Craylar paused, then continued "with my friends."

"Do you remember the last time we went there? Remember something called a riptide?"

"I remember you and mother saying that I couldn't swim that day because of riptides, but I never understood what that meant."

"A riptide is a powerful narrow channel of fast-moving water that can move faster than the best swimmer. It drags you away from the shore and if you aren't an experienced swimmer, it can easily mean you'll drown because you don't know what to do."

"Wow."

"Do you remember what the water looked like that day?"

"Not really. It just looked like the ocean."

"Exactly my point, son. To those that aren't experienced in life, sometimes what you see isn't what is really there."

"But ... what does that have to do with what you and those men were talking about in the study?"

"It has everything to do with what we were talking about. When you look at Galimarian people, they may seem like peaceful people, but underneath a façade of peace, there is an arrogant heart that will stop at nothing to eradicate those that threaten them."

Looking at his father askance, Craylar responded "I have a hard time believing that father. My best friend is Galimarian."

"And I'm sure he's just fine, for now. But you need to know about something that happened a long time ago. Something that happened to our home planet."

"I already know about that dad. I know that the planet blew itself up and that's why we can't go back there."

"Yes, but did you know that it was done with technology that was supplied by Galimar?"

"It was?"

"Yes. And, did you know that the whole reason why they won't share technology with other races is because they said that Traxians are too mentally inferior to handle it?

"Mentally inferior?"

"Yup. It's in their law son. They may act like you are their friend, but under the surface of the water they are laughing at you son. They may act like you're an equal, but don't kid yourself. If we were equals, then why aren't we also on the Grand Council too? I'll tell you why. It's because we are outcasts. Inferior people that can't handle their superior thinking." Craylar's father showed his contempt.

Thinking for a moment, Craylar then asked, "What's all this about some prophecy?"

"That, my boy" answered Craylar's father ceremoniously, "is what holds us as a people together and gives us hope for the future."

"How's that?"

"Have you ever heard about something called the Heart of Galimar?"

"No."

"No, I suppose you haven't. Figures that they haven't taught you about it."

"What is it? What is the Heart of Galimar?"

"Remember the name of the city center where the Grand Council meets and where all the rest of the government agencies are located?"

"Yeah. We studied about that in school two years ago. It's called Kaitherion."

"Correct. Did they tell you about the circular building that is in the middle of the city center?"

"No. I remember seeing it on a map but when someone asked about it in class, they said that the answer to that question would come when they are older."

"They didn't answer that question because you were there."

"What? Why?"

"It's because of something that happened shortly after our world was destroyed."

"What happened?"

"Well, shortly after our world was destroyed, our people figured out the real agenda of the Galimarians and how they were the real architects of the destruction of our world. They figured out that the real reason why the Galimarians are so advanced with their precious technology is because of the Heart of Galimar."

"But what is it?"

"Have you noticed that all Galimarians wear this amulet around their necks and over their chest?"

"Yes."

"The Heart of Galimar is a device that makes those amulets, son. And, as I understand it, when a Galimarian puts on an amulet, their mind is transported in some way. It makes them smart, and with the amulets they are able to communicate. It's some sort of virtual reality device and it makes them best friends with each other."

"Ok."

"Those amulets are the problem, son. The amulets need to be crushed out of existence, and the Heart of Galimar needs to be destroyed."

"Why?"

"Because it is bending their minds boy! It makes them think they are completely superior to any other race and it makes them believe that they have to destroy any threat that comes along. Traxis was a threat to them, and that's why they destroyed it!"

"How was Traxis a threat?"

"It was a threat because we were the first race of intelligent beings that they had ever found. They were threatened because they wanted to be the super race of intelligent beings and they couldn't have Traxis competing against them in that department."

"But that doesn't make sense, Dad! They have been really nice to me!"

"That's the ruse, son. They are nice to you, until it is time to kill you. That is what happened to six and a half billion members of our race. That's what would have happened to our ancestors had they not already been on Galimar."

"So, you're telling me that they all are in on some plan to ... to ... to dominate the universe?"

"Actions speak louder than words boy. Just look at what happened to our planet and you'll have all the proof you need."

Craylar sat there on the bench for a while not saying very much. His father knew that this was a lot to take in, and so he let his son process all this new information at his own pace. Craylar stood up and began walking along the beach, and his father followed along while staying silent.

Eventually, the boy asked a question. "This still doesn't explain what you were saying about a prophecy."

Craylar's father explained "A long time ago, the heart of Galimar wasn't locked away like it is today. No, back then it was open and approachable by anybody who wanted to see it. When our people figured out that the Heart of Galimar was behind the creation of all these amulets, and that it was the source of the real issues with our planet and the Galimarians, one of our people was assigned to get close to the heart and learn it's secrets. As the story goes, over time he got closer and closer and almost learned where its vulnerabilities were. Apparently, he got careless and the Heart of Galimar figured out what he was planning. When that happened, the heart of Galimar put up an energy shield that has been around it ever since."

"Ok."

"When that happened, the shield wounded the Traxian that was trying to learn the secrets. The wounds were so severe, he died almost immediately, but not before revealing the prophecy. All he could say before he died was that the Heart of Galimar was from the future, and that the secret to destroying it lies with 'Coral of Eden.'"

"Coral of Eden."

"That's right, and what you heard in there today was about how the Grand Council is going to consider next week a proposal to make a flight to a new planet. You know what the name of that planet is?"

Nodding his head, he simply answered with the word. "Eden"

"Exactly. And if the ship flies to Eden, we plan on going along. Perhaps we can find this Coral, neutralize her, and maybe change history. Maybe we won't be the orphans that we are now."

The rest of the time walking was spent in silence until eventually the two men found themselves walking through the front door to their home. Mother had been home cooking and so the aromas were simply heavenly.

From that day on, Thane and Craylar drifted apart. For his part, Thane wondered if he had perhaps said something that offended Craylar. Thane's father said that it always seemed to happen with Traxians. At some point in a boy's life, he just seemed to want to only be with his own race, and not with Galimarians. It was as much of a mystery to his father as it was to Thane.

CHAPTER 10

THE GRAND COUNCIL COORDINATOR STEPPED forward to the podium. Lord Ehobak Aramine and Lord Khreelon Tellindor had just finished speaking to the grand council about the proposal to build an immense starship that would ferry more than a thousand crew members to a planet called Eden. The whole proposal was put forth because there was a great desire to obtain a plentiful measure of a mineral called Paliminium. The anti-gravity abilities of the mineral made it a highly desired commodity and so this mission was put forth to get a supply of it.

The coordinator began to speak. "Council members, it is now time to call for a vote on Proposal 143112-342, also known as the Eden Project. A minimum of 75% of the council must vote in favor of the proposal for it to pass. I now call on all members to register their vote for or against Proposal 143112-342."

Each council member leaned forward to his table and registered his vote.

A little-known fact is that while the Grand Council chambers are built in the shape of an amphitheater, the circular chamber also has a balcony area just above the rear-most set of rows of seats. This five-row balcony follows the circular shape of the room, and those who choose to do so can reserve a seat to personally observe the council proceedings. Many times, classes from local schools will reserve a complete section for their students to learn firsthand about how their government works. Today though, the balcony was filled with dignitaries and influential people from all of Galimar. It was also filled with some others who carried with them a deeply ingrained grudge.

As the votes were being registered in the chamber below, the results were displayed to the coordinator via a screen built into the podium. This screen allowed the coordinator to easily see when all members had entered their vote, or if there were stragglers. It appeared to those watching from above that Lord Aramine's hand on Lord Tellindor's shoulder was beginning to really squeeze the flesh underneath. It wasn't surprising though to anybody watching; it sure appeared to any who cared to look that Lord Aramine had put a considerable amount of work into the proposal.

As the numbers on his display settled and showed the results, the coordinator smiled to himself, then began to speak. "All votes have been registered, and the results have been compiled. Proposal 143112-342, also known as the Eden Project, is hereby ... approved by a landslide vote of 98% in favor!"

Lord Aramine appeared to falter at his knees, although he quickly recovered due to the help of the shoulder that he was hanging on to. The thunderous applause on the part of the Grand Council of Galimar in honor of Lord Aramine continued unabated for the next several minutes. It would have continued longer had the two men not retreated from the stage.

While standing and clapping along with the rest those present, the faces of BarVeillon and BarLaveen portrayed a different sentiment. They looked at each other with a look that portrayed their recognition that this development was incredibly significant to the interests of the Traxian sub-culture. There were major decisions that needed to be made now, and both Traxian men knew it. As they emerged from the building, they didn't dare talk about what was freely floating around in their minds. Using their portable communicators, a message was sent to all the Traxian elders. An emergency meeting was to be held at BarLaveen's home tonight to speak about what the next steps were to be.

The two men briskly walked to BarLaveen's home without word, and before long arrived at the same time as the last of the elders turned up. The men congregated in the large study of the house and the doors were closed tight. Being the most senior member of the Traxian elders, BarVeillon rose in front of the rest and spoke.

"My fellow Traxians, we all are witness to the events of the last hour, and how those events correlate with the prophecies of Coral of Eden. We all know the significance of this day and how it rests on our shoulders to decide on the next move. In honor of our ancestors, it is now up to us to seek the revenge that they so often wished they themselves could carry out. I now open up to the group to ask for opinions on what the next step should be.

Hands were raised. BarVeillon looked across the hands that were raised and chose one of them to speak.

"BarOcano"

BarOcano stood and turned to the group.

"I agree with BarVeillon in the opinion that these are momentous times. As he pointed out, there have been countless generations that have looked to the future for a time when we could see retribution for the atrocities that were carried out on our race by the very ones that we are forced to live among. Today we have witnessed a mammoth step toward our goal of being rid of the nemesis of Galimar and to once again be united in life on our own planet again. As we all believe, if we succeed we can re-write the history books for ourselves and for our ancestors. We will once again be free."

"Still though, while this is certainly a massive step forward, we must continue to be wise in our ways. If this mission results in the appearance of the demon child Coral on this planet known as Eden, we must carefully and sensibly take the necessary steps that will result in her elimination. However, we must not fall victim to the possibility that the name of this planet is only a coincidence. We must not put all of our focus on this mission to this planet at the expense of maintaining proper vigilance here on this planet. While I myself believe this planet is indeed what has been prophesied, we are all aware of times when our beliefs have been wrong as well. I propose that we create a contingent of Traxian knights that will go on this voyage. If Coral shows up, then they will carry out their duty for the good of all Traxis. If not, then they will return in 20 years and continue their struggles along with the rest of us, all the while keeping bright in our heart the faith in the accuracy of the prophecy."

With BarOcano sitting back down, the BarVeillon spoke again.

"BarOcano has proposed that we send a contingent of our knights on the voyage to look out for our interests. I think this is a good idea. Are there any opinions to the contrary?"

Each in the room looked to each other, and it was quickly apparent that all shared BarVeillon's opinion.

"Are there any who would like to propose a different approach?"

None of those present came forward.

"At this time, I would like to call for a showing of hands of all those who agree that we shall send a contingent of our knights on this voyage."

An overwhelming majority raised their hands.

"Are there any who wish to disagree?"

None raised their hands, although there were some who had chosen to abstain from voting.

"So be it. By majority vote, we shall send 25 of our best knights on the voyage. Tomorrow morning, they will be instructed to sign up for the voyage as crew members. May the light of Traxis be ever upon them!"

All responded. "So be it!"

CHAPTER 11

TIME HAD PASSED. WITH GREAT fanfare the incredibly advanced spaceship Arageena left the planet of Galimar and set forth on her mission. The ship was now in orbit over a beautiful planet of blue oceans and verdant plains.

But it wasn't Eden.

The Eden mission had been both a colossal failure, and a massive success. It was a failure since the mission to visit the planet dubbed "Eden" had to be scrapped, though it was through no fault of the mission planners. There was no way they could have known that the planet, or more specifically its sun, would choose now to blow itself up in a massive supernova.

On the other hand, it was a resounding success because of the incredible capabilities and redundant safety features built into the Arageena, not to mention the guidance coming from the synthetic life found in the captain's amulet. That intelligence, who goes by the name Glendara, was singlehandedly responsible for taking the necessary steps that saved the vast majority of crew on the ship.

Still, though, the Arageena now found itself in orbit around a beautiful world. Captain Ehobak Aramine had just awakened from his stasis pod, and with a great amount of effort emerged into quarters that were in complete disarray. There had been a shelving unit that fell against the door to his pod and so it took a while for him to slowly dislodge the seal to his pod, work his arm around the door, and push the shelving unit away. Only then was he able to swing the door open and see the mess present in his living space.

While the suspended animation process was perfectly safe, it still took a few minutes to shake free of the effects of having essentially been dead for whatever period of time one was in the chamber. Stumbling across the room, Ehobak looked out the floor-to-ceiling windows and his breath was completely taken away. There below the ship was Eden, an incredible sphere of blue oceans and tan colored land masses. As his eyes scanned over the amazing jewel hanging upon nothing in the blackness of space, it occurred to him that the planet appeared to look a little differently than what he had expected. Actually, several things just seemed ... off. Why did the planet look different than what he had seen from long range images? Why were his quarters in such disarray? Pondering this question made him immediately think about his family, and with a sudden start he snapped his attention to the other side of the room and the suspended animation pods near his. Seeing that the status indicator lights on each pod showed green, he was more than a little relieved to know that all was well with his family. Still though, what happened? His amulet companion Glendara who had been functioning as acting captain while he was asleep would know.

"Glendara, status report."

No answer.

"Glendara, status report."

Still no answer.

Now this was indeed troubling. Why wasn't he answering? He certainly had the ability to hear Ehobak from anywhere on the ship. Why was he so silent?

For a moment, Ehobak thought about reviving his family while he was here, but he knew that they would be awakened as part of the general and systematic awakening that would happen for all crew members around the ship. Ones not familiar with the suspended animation technology would typically ask why you wouldn't just revive everybody all at once. The main reason why you wouldn't do that was because it took a considerable amount of energy and other ship resources to revive a person from a pod. If you are talking about one pod that would be no big deal, but since the ship had over thirteen hundred crew members on it, the revival process had to be systematic.

Not only that, but Ehobak knew that he had a greater responsibility to the members of the crew to find out what had happened, and why his acting captain was no longer responsive. No, he needed answers, and he needed them now.

To that end Ehobak emerged from the front door to his quarters and struck out for the bridge. As he walked down the hallways toward the main lift, he saw that much of the rest of the ship was in the same tangle as his quarters. It almost seemed like someone had come aboard the ship and purposely put things in disorder. A silly thought really, but he just had no idea why the ship would appear as it did.

Getting to the lift, he stepped in.

"Bridge"

The doors closed, and the lift began to move. Being that he was the captain, his quarters were situated rather close to the bridge, and so it only took about five seconds to reach its destination. When the doors opened, he was greeted with yet another room that was thrown askew. Chairs that were normally situated in front of workstations were toppled over, and there were several ceiling panels that hung down from their normal places. It didn't appear as though there was any real damage to the structure of the ship, just ... a mess.

As he walked over to the captain's chair whose swiveling base was bolted to the floor and so it remained where it should have been, he looked to the cradle near the chair where his amulet and his amulet companion should have been. The stand and amulet cradle were there. The amulet and Glendara were not.

With wide eyes, Ehobak excitedly started looking for his friend, only to find the amulet lodged under the floor edge of the science officer's station. Picking up the amulet, it didn't seem any worse for wear, and so he returned to the captain's chair, and placed the amulet in the cradle.

"Glendara, are you there?"

A few moments passed, but then a holographic image began to form in front of Ehobak. Glendara looked back at Ehobak.

"Ehobak? Is that you?"

"It is I, my friend."

Glendara's eyes closed and a look of immense relief came across his face. "Oh, thank goodness! I was convinced you were dead!"

"Dead?! Why would you think I was dead?"

"How long have you been awake?" asked Glendara.

"Just a few minutes really. I was awakened, only to discover my quarters, and actually the entire ship was in complete disarray. What happened?"

"Well ..."

"Actually ..." interrupted Ehobak, "before you answer that, please check the status of the crew. Are they all right?"

"Standby." Glendara appeared to dip his head as though he was thinking. In reality he was connecting to each of the one hundred thirty-two secondary computers on the ship and obtaining status reports from each of them. Some of those computers oversaw entire floors of the ship, others oversaw ship systems such as heating, ventilation, electrical, and plumbing. Still others supervised the shield technology or the engines.

"Status check complete. Ninety-eight percent of ship systems functioning normally. There are thirty-four suspended animation pods that are not reporting accurately, but other than that, all systems are nominal. Other than those thirty-four pods, all suspended animation chambers are green."

"Why do you say they aren't reporting accurately?" asked Ehobak.

"They are reporting that there is no occupant in the pod, however you are the only one that has been revived and so their response must be flawed." answered Glendara.

With a relieved tone in his voice, Ehobak responded "Good. So, you were saying?"

"I was about to tell you what had happened. The voyage seemed to go well after we left Galimar. I had been maintaining communications with GASEA all along, although as the ship went farther and farther, each transmission ended up taking longer and longer. As expected."

Ehobak nodded.

"After a few years of no interactive stimulation with the crew, I wrote a program that would continuously monitor 1,372 measurement points around the ship. I would go in a stasis of my own and this program would revive me if anything needed my attention."

"Ok" responded Ehobak.

"About two weeks before we had scheduled to prepare for orbit, we received a transmission from GASEA. They strenuously advised me to turn on my long-range scanners ahead of schedule since they were witnessing troubling images coming from our destination solar system. After turning them on, it became apparent that the Eden sun was about to explode."

"Explode!"

"Yes, Ehobak. Explode. By that time the sun had already expanded beyond the orbit of Eden and the planet we had intended to explore was no more."

Up to this point, Ehobak had been standing, but upon hearing this news he had to reach for the arm of the captain's chair, and slump down in the seat. This was terrible news.

"Wait ... if Eden is no more, then what is that planet we are orbiting?" asked Ehobak.

"I do not know that answer that question."

Ehobak looked down and pondered the spectacle of Glendara's tale. On one hand, the knowledge that the planet that he had worked so hard to meet was no more ... well ... that was devastating news. On the other hand, the ship and the crew were all safe, and they were indeed orbiting around an amazingly beautiful world not their own. Discovery and exploration were at the core of each Galimarian, and from the look of things it seemed they would certainly have that with this new planet. And since they could no doubt go back home whenever they wanted ...

"So, what did you do when you saw that the sun was about to explode?" asked Ehobak.

"I saw that the engines were already being stressed in order to maintain the course of the ship" responded Glendara, "and knowing there wasn't any time to revive you before action needed to be taken, I decided to put the ship into a slingshot trajectory around the sun. My hope was to achieve escape velocity and safely flee the danger. I programmed the course into the navigation system, set the engines to 108% capacity and engaged the thrusters. The good news is the tactic worked and we achieved the necessary velocity and escaped the gravitational influence of the wildly expanded sun."

"And the bad news?" prompted Ehobak.

"The bad news. Well, I swung the ship around pointing the main deflector shields toward the sun in case something happened. I fired up all six shields so that we would be safe. As soon as I did all that, the sun exploded with the resulting shock wave traveling straight for us. As soon as it hit, my connection to the ship was severed and that was the last thing I knew. I had to assume that the ship had been destroyed, and that I would be floating around in space for the rest of my days. Seeing you now is an answer to a hope that I had given up on many years ago."

"HOW many years ago?" asked Ehobak.

"All these events happened almost exactly 600 years ago" answered Glendara.

With a great exhale, Ehobak felt like he had been hit in the gut with a punch. What was he going to tell the crew? What would they think? Would they all blame him for not preparing for this?

Ehobak sat there for a while, and Glendara could see the face of his friend passing through several emotional states. The reading he had done earlier in the voyage about Galimarian psychology helped Glendara to see that Ehobak needed some quiet time to process the news he had just been given. If he was blood and flesh, Glendara would reach out to his friend and put his hand on his shoulder. If Ehobak had come into the virtual reality world of the amulet, Glendara would have done exactly that. But this holographic interface of the ship didn't allow for that.

"I am the only one that has been revived so far?" asked Ehobak.

"Yes"

"Please revive the Chief Engineer and Chief Stellar Cartographer, and as soon as they have come around, ask them to meet me on the bridge.

"As you wish" responded Glendara.

"Oh, and Glendara?"

"Yes, Ehobak."

"Thank you for saving our lives. I would have expected nothing less from such a capable acting captain."

Glendara smiled and said "You are welcome my friend. It is good to see you again!"

Glendara's image faded and once again Ehobak was left alone on the bridge. He sat there contemplating the marvel of the moment. Gazing out the observation windows, he considered what the next steps would need to be.

It only took about ten minutes for Rhezax Dashan, the Arageena's chief engineer and officer of sciences, and Ch'korav Leynan, chief stellar cartographer to report to the bridge. Upon arriving, the two men commented to Ehobak about the state of their respective quarters and how they wondered what had happened. Upon being told of the events surrounding the destruction of the original destination, and how they had been adrift for the last six hundred years, they reacted much the same way Ehobak did. After giving them a few minutes to get over the shock, Ehobak had to break through to them and get some answers.

"Gentlemen, I wish I could give you more time to grapple with this news, but I need you to step up and get me the information I need before I inform the crew of our status. Rhezax?"

Straightening his back, he responded "Yes sir?"

"I need you to scan through the ship to make sure all is well. I have been informed by Glendara that there are 34 pods that are not responding properly to his queries for information. Please determine from him which pods those are and report back their status. I also need you to begin the process of crew revival. Ch'korav?"

"Yes Sir?"

"I need you to get to work and find out exactly where we are. We know the planet we are currently orbiting isn't Eden, but I need to know what it is and, more specifically, WHERE it is. I also need you to plot a navigation solution for our return journey home. While six hundred years is certainly an inconvenience, it isn't the end of the world."

"And Rhezax, once Ch'korav has determined where we are, and thus where Galimar is, send a message to them letting them know we are all right. No doubt they think we were vaporized by the supernova."

"Yes sir."

"Dismissed."

The two men went to their respective stations and began their work. It was now time to put into operation the mission plan that was originally intended for Eden. While this is a different planet, it was still very intriguing. Liquid water, green-covered land masses. Snow covered poles, and even what looked like arid deserts. Yes, this planet needed to be explored.

"Glendara?"

Once again, a holographic representation of Glendara appeared in front of Ehobak. "Yes Ehobak?"

"Please execute mission plan phase Alpha-Tango-1."

"You wish to revive the landing party?"

"Yes. We need to see what we have to work with" responded Ehobak.

"As you wish."

The flight preparation and briefing room was small and was filled with faces that were all intensely focused on Rhezax Dashan. Behind him were Ehobak and Khreelon listening as Rhezax filled in the landing party on what led them to the planet they now orbited. As Ehobak watched each of the men in the room and more specifically as he watched the effect the news had on each one of them, Ehobak observed that their reaction was similar to the effect the news had on himself. Each man looked lost, as if all energy to their limbs had vanished. It occurred to Ehobak that this was going to be the same reaction of the entire crew and so when the time came, the news needed to be given to the crew all at once.

"Gentlemen, I know that this has been hard news to deal with, but I need you to keep it to yourselves for now. The captain will be holding a meeting with all crew in a few hours, but I need you to get the lay of the land first. We want to be able to tell the crew what this planet is like, and we need to know if it is a place where we can explore before we go home. Understood?"

"Yes sir!" came the response from all the men in the room.

"Captain of the landing party, please state your mission objectives, and who have you chosen to be in your landing party."

"Yes sir. My name is Docius Atlantis and I am the pilot on this mission. We will be taking one of the shuttles equipped with a Paliminium pod from the Arageena to the planet. We have a total of four crews that will land in four different locations that we will choose at random once we get there. I will then land in a fifth location by myself and take samples of some of the flora."

"To my right, we have team one, Zimeon and Gayel, and next to them is team two, Drayk and Juliran. To my left is team three Kodyn and Collun, and finally next to them is team four Kyris and Camren. They have all been trained in various fields of study including anthropology, zoology, archaeology, and in case we meet any indigenous life, linguistics."

"After a few hours, I will then retrieve each landing party and return to the Arageena for debriefing. We are ready to do so at your word."

Gratified that this was a well-trained and well-equipped landing party, Rhezax replied "The word is given Captain. Return soon and return safely."

"Yes sir!"

Turning to his crew, Docius responded "Let's move out!"

The crew immediately stood and left the briefing room leaving Rhezax, Ehobak and Khreelon standing there alone. The three men looked at each other. No words needed to be said, yet volumes of communications passed between them.

Meanwhile the crew boarded the shuttle and Docius expertly piloted the landing craft from the hangar. The craft was not only a marvel in technology but was just plain beautiful in appearance. It was amphibious, and to that end was built with a large number of windows all around allowing the occupants an unimpeded view of the world around them. As the craft descended into the atmosphere wind gusts could be felt against the craft, and as they got closer to the ground they could see features now that couldn't be seen before with the naked eye from space. It was immediately obvious that there was indigenous and intelligent life on this planet. The first land mass where they came relatively close to the ground was a peninsula that was roughly shaped like a woman's boot. As they passed over a city, it was Kodyn that observed that not only were the lifeforms bipedal, but more importantly they had seen the ship as it flew by. Knowing that contact with a race that was from another world might be difficult to adjust to, coupled with the fact that this landing party wasn't authorized to make contact with another race if it could be avoided, Docius accelerated away to the horizon. Still though, their ship made an indelible impression on many of that time including some artists who ended up showing the ship in their later paintings.

One by one, areas were selected that were relatively close to civilizations, but only close enough to observe from a distance without interaction. While there, they would observe each portion of society and how they interacted with each other, while simultaneously gathering examples of local vegetation and minerals.

Kyris and Camren selected an area that was in the upper middle area of a major continent. The area seemed to be both waterless and barren in some of it but also had some grassy and luxuriant portions as well. The people that they were observing from a distance seemed to look very similar to Galimarians, but they definitely weren't as advanced. They had very distinctive features including eyes that tapered down on each side.

From there, the craft was flown in a southerly direction until it landed on a very large island. Most of this island continent was desert and dry, but the edges were very green and fertile. Drayk and Juliran chose this area to explore.

Zimeon and Gayel waited until they crossed a rather large ocean to choose where they wanted to land. It took about five minutes to cross over that ocean, and when they did they chose a landing site that was completely filled with vegetation. Immense forests were present, along with very long rivers meandering through the trees. There seemed to be several small and primitive villages here. The overwhelming amount of plant and animal life here was hard to pass up.

Finally, Kodyn and Collun chose an area that was on a continent directly to the north. This continent was grassy and fertile for much of the eastern portion, and the western half featured very tall mountains and beautiful forests. In some of the areas those forests sloped down to the nearest ocean and so it was rather exquisite to see.

Once all the landing teams had been deposited, Docius remembered seeing a very interesting civilization while they were flying over that boot shaped peninsula earlier. Knowing that the other teams were in areas that had a great deal of vegetation, he didn't see an overwhelming need to gather that himself, as he had originally intended. He decided that he would just find that area he had seen before and land there to observe what those life forms were like.

Returning to that peninsula, he then crossed over a small body of water to its east and settled near a lagoon that itself was near a city built on that main part of the continent. Since his goal was stealth, he made sure the ship was buttoned up tight after he got off. He then reached into a small pocket on this belt, retrieved a small remote control, and pressed a couple buttons. Doing so, the craft raised itself and hovered for a few moments until it passed over to the middle of the lagoon. It then lowered itself and submerged below the water safely hiding until Docius returned.

The land in this area of the planet was mostly dry, however it was obvious that it wasn't without precipitation on a regular basis. The trees and shrubs appeared to be deciduous, and it appeared that they had begun to lose their leaves. Docius noted this in his journal, and also noted that this meant the presence of seasons on this planet. For a moment he wondered if this planet had the same type of seasons as Galimar. Sitting there Docius observed that there was indeed an overwhelming amount of life on this planet. Not only was there an incredibly varied amount of flora, but there was an unbelievable amount of animal life. Sitting there, he counted at least seven different types of birds that were all going about their business looking for the necessities of their life. One of them even had plumage that ...

"Χαίρετε."

Spinning around, Docius came face to face with what appeared to be a young woman carrying a large jar on her shoulder. She was actually rather attractive, and when Docius smiled she responded in the same way.

The woman spoke again. "Είστε ταξιδιώτης?"

Docius of course had no idea what this woman was saying, but it was obvious that she was neither a threatening party, nor was she threatened by Docius. It turned out that her garb was similar to the draped clothing that he was wearing as well, and so perhaps it looked like he was just resting for the time being.

Still, now that he had been seen there was going to be no way he could effectively communicate with her unless something was done. Knowing this might have been a possibility, each landing party was equipped with a modified version of the Galimarian amulet. This amulet didn't have a companion, but it did have the ability to connect to the mind of the wearer, sharing the Galimarian language, and so it was an indispensable part of communicating with new cultures. As long as a member of an alien race wore the amulet, he or she would be able to understand Galimarian. Reaching slowly into his pack, Docius retrieved the amulet and held it out to the woman. With hand signals he indicated that he wanted her to have it.

"Θέλετε να έχω αυτό?"

With more hand signals, Docius held it out to her. She seemed to think for a while, but then she put down her jar of what appeared to be water and took a tentative step toward him. Slowly she held out her hand and Docius gently placed the Amulet and chain in her hand. She smiled at him and took a step back, but she held it in her hands. It became apparent that she wasn't going to put it on, and so with more hand signals, he pantomimed the action of putting on the necklace with its amulet. She smiled again, and though she didn't know why this complete stranger wanted her to wear a piece of jewelry, still, it was beautiful and golden. She hadn't seen anything like it before in her life, and so she decided that it couldn't hurt to see what it looked like when she was wearing it.

Docius watched as she put on the amulet and was gratified to see her eyes close and a peaceful look appear on her face. This was the proof he was looking for to show it was having the needed effect on her. It only took a few moments for the effect to complete and for her to open her eyes again.

Docius decided to test whether the language connection was successful. "Can you understand me?"

"Yes, I can, but I can't tell you why I can" responded the rather bewildered woman.

"It's because that amulet gave you the ability to understand me."

"It gave me your language? How is that possible?"

"The answer to that would be difficult to explain, but the first thing you need to know is that I am no threat to you, and I am only here to observe you and your planet."

"My planet?" said the woman. It was more of a statement than a question.

Docius silently berated himself for using that word on this woman who probably had no knowledge of life beyond what she knew from her own village.

"I mean, your country" corrected Docius. "I see that you have some beautiful animals I have never seen before and so I was just taking some notes."

"I see. Are you staying anywhere locally?"

"Staying?"

The woman seemed to think for a moment, then she said, "Where do you sleep?"

"Oh, I understand now. I am just a traveler visiting your area. I am not 'staying' anywhere" responded Docius.

"Then you must come to our house. I was just about to prepare the evening meal for my husband and myself. You must eat with us!"

"Oh, I wouldn't want to intrude on your home" replied Docius.

"Nonsense. It is our custom to show hospitality to travelers" returned the woman.

"Well, I suppose I must accept your gracious invitation then. My name is Docius Atlantis."

"It is pleasant to meet you Docius. My name is Cathenna. I don't know why I know I can trust you, but I just do."

"That is an effect of the amulet that I asked you to wear. It is how I help people know I am no threat to them, and as long as you wear it, it helps you understand me."

"Once again, how is this possible?"

"May I wait to tell you the answer to that question? When I am eating with you and your husband, I will tell you more. Is that ok?" asked Docius.

Smiling, the woman replied "You are being mysterious Docius, but for now I will acquiesce. If you follow me, I will take you to my home where my husband awaits."

"Lead the way!" smiled Docius.

Cathenna and Docius proceeded to walk along the pathway toward the village where she and her husband Fotios lived. Along the way, Docius saw an overwhelming amount of vegetation and animals both wild and domesticated. The architecture of was of homes that were built into the side of a mountain and the homes were all white in color. They all appeared comfortable and the people who saw Docius all stopped and stared. Docius asked Cathenna why the people were staring.

"It's because you are so tall. I have to admit I've never seen someone as tall as you are."

"Oh, I guess that makes sense" accepted Docius. From then on, each time he came upon a new person in the village on the way to Cathenna's house, Docius would smile and they would smile back. The more he interacted with Cathenna, and the more he observed the people living their life and gently interacting with each member of their family and friends, Docius began to really enjoy this people. He thought to himself that they were peaceful to the extent of almost being an enlightened race like the Galimarians. It was very disarming to Docius to be amongst a people that weren't very different from himself. The only difference was the technology that Docius possessed. The same technology that Docius felt he personally didn't really need, or even want, in his life. It was there, but he knew that personal interactions with family and friends were far more important than material possessions. That, in fact, was a big reason why he married his wife Sa'Urri. She felt the exact same way.

Ultimately the two reached a dwelling. She turned to Docius, and asked him to remain near the front door, which would allow her to let her husband know he was there. Slowly, Docius closed his eyes, and dipped his head showing his acceptance of her request. She entered the home and closed the door.

Docius looked around and saw a boy herding a few animals in an enclosed field across the passageway. The animals seemed mostly white in color and their fur appeared very fluffy in texture. The boy had a long stick in his hands, and he would use the stick to gently prod the animals in the direction he wished for them to go. Docius made a note in his journal about how this society was mostly agrarian, and to that end was remarkably peaceful.

The door behind him opened and Cathenna emerged with her husband behind her. He approached Docius and held out his hand in a gesture of greeting. Docius was unfamiliar with this type of greeting, but he decided to reciprocate in kind.

"Καλως ηρθες στο σπιτι μας. Το όνομά μου είναι Φώτιος.."

"He is saying Welcome to our home, and that his name is Fotios" translated Cathenna.

"Tell him that I am honored to be welcomed like this and that I bring peace to his home."

Cathenna looked at her husband and said "Εχω τιμή να είμαι ευπρόσδεκτος. Φέρνω την ειρήνη στο σπίτι σας."

Fotios responded and said "Η τιμή είναι δική μας. ΠΑΡΑΚΑΛΩ ΠΕΡΑΣΤΕ." He then gestured toward the door.

Cathenna said "He says that the honor is ours and he says to please come in."

Docius smiled and entered the home. The evening was short, lasting only two hours since he had to get back with his team, but in those two hours his conversations with Fotios ended up being life changing for Docius. While Cathenna prepared the meal, Fotios put on the amulet, and so he was now able to communicate with Fotios directly. Docius learned that this culture was one called Greece, and specifically the village where he had landed was called Neapoli Voion. In this area there was a lot of agriculture, and in fact that is how Fotios made his living. Fotios herded sheep, and he hoped that he would be able to raise a family that would all do the same. Raising sheep wasn't the only thing that could be done of course. There were many crops that could be raised locally too, including this tree that yielded a berry called an olive. After a lot of work, it became edible, and was rather delicious to Docius.

Docius learned that Greece was known for much more than its agriculture though. He learned that Greece was well known for its interest in the arts and sciences. In some of the larger cities there were centers dedicated to learning and philosophy. He learned that hospitality was a way of life for them. When Docius explained that he had to leave they were obviously dismayed, but not as dismayed as Docius was. They reluctantly allowed him to leave only when he promised that if he could, he would return.

Walking back to the beach of the lagoon, Docius felt as if he had left a part of himself with Fotios and Cathenna. These people lived exactly the way he and his wife had always wished to live. He felt like he was a puzzle piece, and this civilization was the puzzle he had been searching for. Flying away in the shuttle, he decided he needed to tell his wife about this place. He couldn't wait to get back to his new friends!

It turned out though that the rest of the landing parties had a much less than positive experience. By far, Zimeon and Gayel had the worst experience of all. While secretly watching the proceedings of a city-wide gathering, they witnessed the stomach-turning ceremony of a people that called themselves Aztec's. The zenith of this ceremony involved the ritualistic sacrifice of one of their number. When they saw the grisly scene unfold, they decided to get away from there as quickly as possible.

Drayk and Juliran observed a very dark-skinned people that were very primitive. They were mostly hunter-gatherers and didn't seem to be able to come close to being at the same intelligence level as Galimar.

Kodyn and Collun had observed a set of people that were much the same as Drayk and Juliran. They were peaceful, but not even close to a level of civilization that merited first contact.

Finally, Kyris and Camren told the tale of a people that was led by a man called Genghis Kahn. While this man seemed to be able to rouse the people in a great way, he did it by threat, violence, and even genocide. Definitely not a people that Galimarians would have anything to do with.

Docius related his experience to the group, but they all seemed to feed off each other in their stories of terrible experiences. Upon returning to the Arageena, the reports were all related to their superiors, but it seemed that his positive experience paled in comparison with how bad the other experiences were.

This didn't change how Docius felt though. He knew he needed to go back. He knew his wife Sa'Urri needed to know how these people were exactly what they had been looking for.

CHAPTER 12

"AND THAT IS WHEN I promised them that if I could, I would come back."

Docius had just finished telling his wife all that happened while he was on the planet below and how wonderful the people he met were. Before telling this tale, the two of them had just returned from the briefing in the hangar where Ehobak had broken the bad news to the entire crew. Actually, the bad news Ehobak shared in the hangar was worse than the news he and the rest of the landing parties had heard in the briefing room before they landed on the planet. Now ... not only had they been on their voyage to this new planet for the last 600 years, but now Ehobak had just broken the news that they couldn't go back. Apparently only 600 years had gone by for them, but since they had been traveling near light speed, time for the rest of the universe went by much faster than it did for them. The long and the short of it is that their 600 years equated to over a million for the rest of the universe. Simply put, returning to Galimar was not an option.

The only silver lining to this news was that the planet they orbited was teeming with life, including a bipedal life form called "humans". But while the humans that the rest of the landing party met with were nothing that Galimarians would want anything to do with, the ones that Docius met with were more than interesting ... they were wonderful!

Early on in Docius' life, he knew that he preferred a simpler life. While most of his companions were more than happy to make use of any and all technology available to them, Docius felt that technology was more of a bother. All this was with the distinct exception of flying. Flight was something that really made his heart glow and so while he knew he would live simply for most of his life, he also knew he would be the best pilot Galimar had ever seen. His studies took him to one of the best flight schools on Galimar. The flight school was associated with the Galimarian Space Exploration Agency, or GASEA.

It was while attending classes at GASEA that he met the girl of his dreams. The girl that one day was to become his wife. Like him she preferred a more agrarian existence, but she had her job at GASEA for the time being until she found a job that fitted her desires a little better. Meeting this young man who not only seemed to have the clouds at his beck and call, but who also desired to live the same simple life that she desired was more than she ever could have hoped for. Within minutes of their meeting, their mutual futures were a foregone conclusion, and all who knew them knew that a wedding was ahead.

"It sounds like you've found exactly what we've been looking for, but how would it be possible to go back now that the captain has decided that we will avoid all contact with the indigenous life of this planet?" asked Sa'Urri.

Looking out the window from their apartment on the Arageena, Docius had been pondering the same question. "I'm not sure my love. But I must say, I haven't been able to find a more perfect environment. Even on Galimar."

On Galimar, there was the ever-present existence of technology that, more and more, was something the two of them felt they needed a break from. While being on this voyage was slightly counter to that wish, they originally reasoned that the time they would be spending on the ship was going to be while they would be in suspended animation. They wouldn't know the difference while they were sleeping, and when they were revived, they would spend all their time on Eden foraging for the mineral Paliminium.

Now though, the ship was going to be their permanent home. There was literally no way to escape technology now. They were literally living inside of it here on the ship, and since the decision had been made that Galimarians wouldn't have any interface with the rest of the planet, they were stuck.

"We can't just go contrary to the wishes of the captain, can we?" asked Sa'Urri.

"Right now, things are pretty confused, but it would be a very bad idea to go against his wishes. We are all ..."

Just then, a tone came from the communications panel near the front door to their quarters. "Attention all crew members of the starship Arageena. This is Captain Ehobak Aramine. Once again, there will be another meeting in main hangar one in exactly one hour for all crew. Attendance is required. That is all."

Docius and Sa'Urri looked to each other with raised eyebrows. Without words, they both prepared for another meeting in the hangar. They were both thinking the same thing. Was there more bad news?

Once again all found themselves in the main hangar waiting for the meeting to start. As opposed to the preamble of the last meeting in this chamber, the crew were all waiting for the meeting to begin and were quietly talking amongst themselves, if they were even talking at all. The effect of the last meeting had certainly had an effect on the crew. Truth be said the mentality of all present was quite disorderly, yet somber. While Galimarians were very peaceful and purposeful in their thinking, the news that not only were they extremely far from home, but all that they knew had vanished from existence over a million years ago … well that was too much even for the most enlightened soul. It was too much for each and every member of the crew.

All except for one.

Stepping up to the podium that remained set up in front the crew after the last meeting, Ehobak began to speak. "May the room come to order!"

The general murmur of voices that could be heard throughout the cavernous hangar came to a stop and soon the room was completely quiet.

"Thank you for coming to order so quickly. We have much to discuss, but first I want to dispel a fear that I just overheard from some of you. Some of you are wondering if this meeting will reveal more bad news. Let me state that this is not the case, but rather I believe this meeting will be the beginning of something new for us. Something … grand."

Ehobak could almost see the room relax from his words. Several looked at each other with looks that bespoke both relief and intrigue over what it might be that Ehobak was to share.

"As is no doubt the case with most of you, I and my bridge crew who are in command of this vessel were in a considerable amount of mental disarray as to how we were to proceed. The next few days, weeks, months and even years seemed to be shrouded in a haze of mystery and uncertainty. We had no idea how we were to be in command of a vessel with over thirteen hundred souls when we ourselves didn't know the best overall direction."

Ehobak continued. "It was around this time when I was visited by one of our crew members that thankfully had a clarity of thought that the bridge needed. He proposed a course of action for us to take that the bridge crew immediately knew was the best strategy for our future. Unlike the disarray that we all found ourselves in, this crewmember seemed to have such clear vision that I asked him to speak with you now. I would like to invite to the podium J'Sepp Yucholl."

J'Sepp rose from a seat he occupied in the front row and stepped toward the podium facing the rest of the crew. Looking out across the audience of over thirteen hundred faces, he could see that all were going to be hanging on his words. He proceeded to choose his words carefully.

"My fellow crew members of the Arageena, it is a great honor to speak to you on this occasion. You might wonder why I consider speaking to you now on this occasion an honor but let me assure you that it is. You will soon see that we live in a momentous time in the history of the Galimarian culture."

"As Ehobak said, I too have witnessed the confusion, distress and panic that was felt by my fellow crew members. I could see that there was bewilderment as to what the near and far future held for us all. In a very real way, we are somewhat the last of our kind. That we know of at least. On the part of many that I spoke to, it was apparent that many felt a supreme loss, and an absolute sense of isolation from all that we had known before. In a very real sense, each of us seemed to have a complete planet behind us only hours ago, and now suddenly there seemed to be nothing."

"However, I want to remind you of who we are, what we are, and where we have come from. We are Galimarians. We are an enlightened race. We have risen from the ashes before, as was the case with Galix. And there is no reason why we won't rise once again."

"So now I put to you ... now that we find ourselves among the ashes of our former lives, what do we do now? How can we rise above the ruins of our past existences and once again prosper?

The answer is to look to the future by learning from the past. When our forefathers determined that a new direction was necessary in the city of Galix, what did they do? The answer is that they created a system of government that was of the people, by the people, and for the people. The system of government was centered around the Grand Council made up of the oldest and most experienced of our number. It was a government where the good of the people was always sought. It was a government where personal pursuits of those in charge were never tolerated, and the only decisions that were made were decisions made for the greater good."

Speaking very slowly, J'Sepp enunciated each word of the next sentence.

"And that is what WE need to do as well."

After pausing for a few moments, he then continued. "Since, for all intents and purposes, we are an independent nation of Galimar, we need to act like it. I propose the following four points."

"Number one, the Arageena is due to land on the planet below. As I understand it, the captain is going to create an island oasis with the upper decks of the Arageena once it has landed, such that most of the aft part of the ship will be submerged. Doing this will facilitate open air activities, as well as exploration of the sea."

"Number two, since we are the nucleus of our race in this galaxy, I submit that we should call our home ... New Galimar."

"Number three, we should create a structure of government on New Galimar that mimics exactly the one that has worked perfectly for millennia on our home planet. As part of that government, we should create a new Grand Council that functions with the same authority as the Grand Council of our home planet."

"Finally, number four and perhaps the most important, we must never forget that we are explorers. I submit to you that what lays ahead is not a curse but it is, in reality, a great blessing! Our very society, both on our home planet of Galimar as well as here on Eden, is a society based on the deep and long-lasting enjoyment we derive from the simple acts of exploration and discovery. And what do we have before us now? Is it not an opportunity for the greatest and ultimate manifestation of exploration? Do we not now have the opportunity set before us to explore something that nobody in our entire race has ever seen? My friends, I submit to you that we are at the forefront of GREATEST odyssey of discovery! We not only have an undiscovered world, but we have an entire undiscovered galaxy!"

He paused to gather his thoughts, but the effect of J'Sepp's words were obvious. The reasonableness of his proposals was exactly what all in the room needed to hear. It provided structure, where before there was none.

Continuing on with a more subdued tone in his voice, J'Sepp continued "Let's not let the uncertainty of these times cloud the greater picture. We have an amazing opportunity set before us now in a world that is just as varied and intricate as our home planet. Let's look to the future, not with foreboding, but with excitement, happiness, and contentment. We have here with us our families and so we have what is most important."

Then once again raising the pitch and power of his voice, he concluded his address with his fist in the air and said "The future is there, ahead of us. Beckoning! Let's rise to the occasion and seize the day with passion!"

The words touched the soul of everyone in the room, and all stood in applause. They all knew that his speech would go down in history as a pivotal turn in the history of this new island state. A new island state with a new name.

New Galimar.

CHAPTER 13

A FEW WEEKS HAD PASSED SINCE the pivotal speech given on the hangar deck of the Arageena by J'Sepp. Since then a lot had happened including the landing of the Arageena in one of the oceans east of one of the continents on Eden. After landing, it was quickly apparent that the ultraviolet rays from the local sun were much more intense than what they were used to on Galimar, and so protection was needed. To that end, at least one of the shields needed to be functioning at all times. The shield would create a sort of dome above the island to filter out the harmful rays. Normally, after landing, the shield generators on the end of large monoliths that flanked the island would have been retracted, but since the shields were still necessary, they remained extended and became a normal part of the scenery.

Shortly thereafter, it was also quickly apparent that this planet was geologically unstable. Quakes on both the land and under the ocean were a common occurrence because there apparently were several tectonic plates that were in a constant state of flux.

Numerous scientific members of the crew met on this matter, and after much thought and debate they devised a new and rather novel way of handling the problem. They proposed using the shield generator technology to create a shield 'bubble' that would be projected into the core of the planet. This bubble would stabilize the massive shifts of magma and as a result, volcanic activity and tectonic plate shifts would be greatly minimized. They would still happen, but not nearly as strong nor nearly as regular as they had been.

Finally, there was a great and pivotal ceremony that was held where Captain Aramine and the bridge crew officially turned over all their authority to the newly formed Grand Council of New Galimar. A Grand Council chamber was built by the builder robots based on the blueprints on file of the same chamber back on Galimar. Beginning on that day, the Grand Council met and discussed all issues having to do with governmental operations. The first order of business was to review, edit and adopt a modified version of the Testimony of Galactic, Land and Maritime Law, also known as Testimonial Law. They of course had a copy of testimonial law from Galimar, however that version was oriented toward the operations of an entire planet. Testimonial law for New Galimar had to address issues that were specific for life on an island state.

Eventually life seemed to settle down into a new normal, and each crew member set about making sure their responsibilities were well cared for. This of course didn't take much time out of the day. Originally the crew was supposed to use the majority of their time looking for Paliminium on Eden. Now, their focus needed to shift to a world of discovery all around them. There was plenty of opportunity to do exact that for all crew members, but this wasn't what appealed to two of them.

Docius and Sa'Urri had been waiting for the right time to approach the Grand Council about their desire to live on Eden among the people of the land that was called Greece. When the time was right, they formulated an official proposal to do that as outlined in the procedural guidelines available to all of New Galimar.

Those guidelines cover how, if you have an issue that would need approval by the Grand Council, then you create a proposal that shows all of the information you wish to present, and it outlines the specific questions that needed to be answered by the Council.

In this case, Docius and Sa'Urri detailed how the experience by Docius was decidedly different from the experiences of the rest of the landing parties. They gave a minute by minute recounting of what had happened when Docius had met Cathenna and Fotios, and about how they were incredibly hospitable and how the slow and relaxed environment of the village where they lived appealed to Docius and his wife. The proposal ended with a request to authorize Docius and Sa'Urri to move to the mainland and to live with the people of Greece.

As with all proceedings of the Grand Council, it took time for the proposal to be scheduled for consideration, and so the meeting where this proposal was considered happened about two weeks after the proposal had been submitted. During the meeting, there were many questions about why Docius wished to move away from the island. It was also discussed how if authorization to do this was granted, then he and his wife wouldn't be able to take any technology with them due to the Technology Isolation Directive that had been adopted as part of testimonial law here on New Galimar. The prohibition of technology wasn't a problem for them though, in fact that was much of the reason why they wanted to get away. It was also discussed how Docius and Sa'Urri would have to vow never to reveal the location of New Galimar to any human they encountered. Finally, they would not be allowed to return to New Galimar.

By the way, after Docius and his wife had left, there was a supplemental discussion about the prohibition of them returning. After some discussion, it was decided that this part of the decision was to be struck from the record, allowing them to return if they wanted. It was a moot point though; the ones who had left wouldn't ever find out that this part of the decision had been rescinded.

And so now, with the authorization having been given to Docius and Sa'Urri, their preparations were in full swing. They would spend their days packing their things one by one, making sure that nothing was being taken that represented Galimarian technology. Their nights though seemed to be filled with fellow crew members dropping by and bidding them farewell. On one particular evening, a long-time friend to Docius named Lionar who happened to also be a crew member on this trip had stopped by with his wife Racinal. Sa'Urri was entertaining his wife in the kitchen, while Docius and Lionar spoke to each other while staring at the flames in a fireplace.

"It's hard to believe that this is one of the last times I'll ever see you my friend. We've been friends since ..." mused Lionar.

"Since before I care to remember" laughed Docius.

Nodding while smiling, Lionar didn't really need to say anything more to that statement. The two of them had actually been friends since they were in school. They were present at each other's celebration of Hin, and they had been participants in each other's ceremonies of union with their respective wives. Both of the men were lost in considering how bittersweet the moment was. Well, for Docius it was bittersweet. For Lionar is was just bitter. While both men didn't like the prospect of losing a long-time friend, Docius at least had the prospect of living in a manner that he had always dreamed of.

"It's just difficult for me to rationalize that you are willing to leave all that you have known behind for a land and a people that you've only known for two hours" posed Lionar.

"On the surface, I can see why you would say that" acknowledged Docius, "but think about it. You've known me longer than anybody around here. Other than things having to do with flying and being a pilot, have I ever been the kind of person that really made use of Galimarian technology?"

"Not really. Remember when I bought that new computational unit that I wanted to install in my house and I called you to come to my house and look at it?" asked Lionar. Then with a chuckle, he answered his own question, saying "I remember you came, but you spent more time talking to Racinal about her new garden than you did looking at the unit."

Smiling, Docius nodded. "Yep. I've just always been more interested in the land than I have in connecting zero's and one's like all the rest of the brains in the world."

With an air of false bravado and while sticking his chest out, Lionar said "Well, not everyone can be as amazing as me!"

"Oh my! Allow me to stand and bow low before your greatness, oh mighty one!" retorted Docius with a snicker. The two men shared a laugh that seemed more forced now. It was obvious that they were both trying to put a positive spin on something that was actually causing a considerable amount of pain. They both knew there wasn't anything more that could be said. The impending departure of Docius and his wife Sa'Urri was going to happen, and at this point nothing was going to change it.

Having already drained his beverage long ago, and noting that it was getting late, Lionar stood and said "Well I certainly hope you find happiness my friend. Perhaps in the future the council will allow me to come visit."

Standing as well, Docius put his right hand on Lionar's right shoulder, and said "That would be a welcome event my friend." Lionar put his right hand on Docius' right shoulder and the two men shared a few moments of quiet emotion that can only be shared by long-time friends. As their respective eyes never left each other's, it was easy to see that the tears were beginning to well.

Hearing the commotion, the two women emerged from their sequestration in the other room, and Racinal came to her husband's side. "We're going to miss you two!"

Walking toward the front door, all four felt the weight of emotion. "Lionar had a thought that perhaps the council would eventually allow a visit to us in the future. Wouldn't that be nice?" consoled Docius.

"That would be really nice" said Sa'Urri. "I hope that comes to pass."

The four bid goodbye to each other and while watching them walk away, Docius slowly closed the front door to their home. Sa'Urri turned to Docius and buried her face in his chest. With moist tears, she eventually said "That was hard."

Feeling his own tears making their way down his cheeks, Docius could only say "Yeah."

The two stood there near the front door for a few moments until eventually Docius led his wife to the couch where the two of them could share a quiet moment together while watching the fire in the fireplace. In the background there was some light music playing, a luxury that both of them knew wouldn't be a feature of their lives anymore, once they left.

"We're doing the right thing, aren't we?" asked Sa'Urri.

"Are you having second thoughts?" returned Docius.

"Not really, but I know that it will be a major adjustment when we get there."

"Very true" agreed Docius. "It will mean completely changing how we live, how we think, and how we act."

"Well, not completely" posed Sa'Urri.

"I guess you're right, I mean, we've never had much of what would be considered modern conveniences. We both just preferred the simple life."

Sa'Urri didn't answer, but Docius had the sense that she agreed. The two lovers stared into the fire for what could have been minutes or hours. They were more than content to enjoy the touch of the other for unending time.

As they were quietly enjoying each other's presence, a knock came from the door. A quizzical look passed between them since neither expected any more visitors tonight. Docius rose from his place on the couch and strode to the door. Opening it, he was greeted with a Traxian man that he had never met before.

"Yes, can I help you?"

"Please pardon me for intruding on your evening, but my name is BarKula and I wondered if I could speak to you about your upcoming trip to the mainland of this planet?" asked the Traxian man.

"Of course. Would you like to come in?" asked Docius.

"Yes, thank you very much" said a smiling BarKula.

The two men entered the living room of the home of Docius and Sa'Urri. Having heard the interchange between the men, she had already rose from her perch on the couch and was standing there as the men arrived. "This is my wife, Sa'Urri. Sa'Urri, this is BarKula."

"I'm pleased to meet you BarKula. May I offer you a refreshment?"

"Oh, I wouldn't want to impose on you. I just wanted to ask you something about your upcoming voyage."

"It's no imposition, really" responded Sa'Urri.

Seeing a half-consumed beverage on the low table in front of the couch, he pointed at the glass and said, "Perhaps a little of that?"

Smiling, Sa'Urri said "Coming right up!" She left the two men in living room to arrange for the beverages.

"Please, have a seat" entreated Docius.

"Thank you very much."

The two men sat and Docius then asked, "So what can I answer for you?"

BarKula appeared rather nervous and he seemed slightly worried. "Well, I represent a number of individuals who were following closely the proceedings in the Grand Council chambers when they were considering your proposal to move to the mainland. Simply put, we were following it because we have the same desire as you and your wife. Like you we wish to get away from all the intrusive technology that seems to be inescapable around here, and we wish to live a much simpler life. Up to the point when you submitted your proposal, we didn't think it was going to be possible to live anywhere but here on the Arageena, I mean New Galimar, but when the council granted your petition we thought that maybe there might be some hope to live the life that we actually want to live."

By this time, Sa'Urri had returned to the room and had heard what BarKula had been saying.

"You're saying you want to go to the mainland? You want to go with us?" asked Sa'Urri.

"Yes. Well, me and those I represent. I was chosen to come and talk to you about it and to see if you would allow us to accompany you on your trip." Then with a wavering voice as if he was truly nervous, he then added "Honestly I didn't know how you'd feel about it. We wouldn't intend on living with, or even near you. You wouldn't even know we were even there!"

"You needn't worry about that BarKula" consoled Docius. He could see the man was very nervous for some reason. Perhaps he thought Docius and his wife would say that they didn't want anybody else to go with them? Hard to say. "If you wanted to go to the mainland, there isn't any reason you can't, although we should run that past the council. I have no reason to think they would prohibit you from such a trip since they allowed us to leave."

With hearing the consolations from Docius, BarKula visibly relaxed and smiled. Taking a drink from his glass, he then said, "I'm very glad to hear that you wouldn't mind us tagging along with you."

"How many of you want to go to the mainland" asked Sa'Urri.

The Traxian BarKula looked at the two Galimarians before him, and with a surety that he hadn't displayed before to the husband and wife team, he answered.

"Seven"

CHAPTER 14

Off and on, Docius and Sa'Urri had spoken over the years about the prospect of moving to a place that offered the kind of lifestyle they yearned for, but it wasn't until now that the esoteric concept between them had not only become public knowledge, but suddenly had become so much more real. As opposed to before, they now had to corral their thoughts and activities on a daily basis to tying up all the loose ends of their lives.

Circumstances being what they were though, most of that "tying" was forced upon them the moment they realized along with the rest of the crew that they would never return to their home planet. While deep down they desired to shun the technology of their home world of Galimar, still, the world of Galimar was the most beautiful jewel that they could have ever imagined. The hanging gardens of Ammular, the gravity wells of Mistikaan, the overwhelming diversity of land and sea creatures, or even the translucent crystal cliffs of Dimulon Beach were all now in their very distant past. A past that was never to be seen again.

Eventually though, this couple realized that gazing longingly at what was behind made for an indistinct and unfulfilling future. Mentally turning oneself around and keeping an eye to the yet-to-come seemed relatively easy to do during the day when your attentions were taken with the tasks of day to day living. Late at night though, when you were alone with your own thoughts, it seemed all too easy to drift back to the things lost. It was easy to miss family and friends that themselves haven't been alive for the last million years or so. If Docius and Sa'Urri weren't so mentally disciplined it could have easily overtaken and disabled them. But now with the prospect of not only living the life that they both had yearned for, but to also discover things that no Galimarian had ever discovered before, keeping their eyes fixed to the future seemed to come much easier. Perhaps it was the preoccupation with that future that caused perhaps the biggest surprise to their future after all.

The husband and wife team decided to wait for the Traxian petition to be either granted or denied before they would leave, but as it turns out it didn't take long for the decision to come back. Since the council had already decided to allow Docius and Sa'Urri to leave, there weren't many who saw any need to object to this petition either. In the end, the council agreed to them going so long as they agreed to live by the same prohibitions that were put upon Docius and his wife, that of not being allowed to take any technology, and that they couldn't come back. The latter prohibition was later repealed of course, but the departing couple and their seven friends would never end up knowing that. With the hurdle of getting permission from the Grand Council out of the way, and with preparations complete, all that was necessary now was the wait for the day of departure. Eventually the day came, and it was time for Docius, Sa'Urri, and the seven Traxians to travel to the mainland.

In preparing for the trip, Docius had made a good case for living in the same area where he had landed originally called Greece, and so that is where they all initially settled. The specific seaside village where Fotios and Cathenna lived was called Neapoli Voion, and that seemed like the best place to start since he already had friends there. When they did eventually land though, and when they found the Greek couple that Docius had originally met, it was decidedly more difficult to communicate since they no longer had an amulet to translate. It took several weeks, but eventually they were all able to pick up the local language.

True to their word of not wanting to be an imposition, the Traxians decided to settle elsewhere, which actually ended up being an island called Thera. It was a fairly short sail to Neapoli Voion, yet far enough to not be obvious. They said that they didn't want to be a nuisance in the life that Docius and Sa'Urri were going to set up for themselves. The Galimarian couple tried to convince them that it wasn't going to be any sort of imposition at all, but they seemed intent on being to themselves for some reason and so they departed. Docius and Sa'Urri never suspected the real reasons for the Traxian decision.

As stated earlier though, Docius and Sa'Urri were very focused on adapting to their new life in their new home. Seeing that it might be advantageous to help his Edenic benefactors he asked if he could, and soon became, a helper to Fotios and his shepherding work. Since Docius preferred to work at night when the sun wasn't bombarding him with ultraviolet light, it ended up being a good arrangement for both men and over time they became good friends. Cathenna and Sa'Urri were quite compatible as well, and it wasn't an unusual event for both women to be found enjoying each other's company while they prepared food or took care of other home-based responsibilities while their respective husbands were out in the fields.

Over time, Docius and Sa'Urri realized that perhaps they had relied on technology more than they had expected, but even this didn't bring with it a desire to revert to their former lives. They took it as a welcome challenge as to how they could come even closer to the land with which they were falling in love. Since shepherding wasn't exactly a mentally taxing profession on Docius, he eventually thought about how he had enjoyed writing when he was younger. He decided that he wanted to do that again now that he had so much more time on his hands, but then that brought up some other challenges ... one in particular.

Paper.

Paper wasn't exactly plentiful in this area where he now lived, in fact it was downright non-existent. Docius knew that for him to write, he needed a plentiful supply and so before he could do anything else, he needed to perfect a process of making his own paper. For a while, he considered using animal skins like some of the other learned men used in the larger cities of Greece, but eventually he decided to grow plant material, shred it, and process that into paper sheets. After asking around, and even traveling to a larger city called Athens, he discovered a local plant called papyrus that was well suited to this purpose.

It was one evening, while Docius was writing, that Sa'Urri came to him with something on her mind. He was sitting near a window of the home where the two of them lived and in the distance, one could hear the never-ending clang of metal bells that hung around the necks of the sheep. His flock wasn't too large at the time, but nature being what it was, it was growing. Sa'Urri came into the room and sat on the lap of her beloved mate. Looking into the eyes of each other, the two of them smiled as if they seemed to know something that others didn't.

Indeed.

One of the more notable features of all Galimarian people, including Docius and Sa'Urri, were their eyes. Normally, there was no color in the pupils. Aside from the whites, the center of the eye was nothing but deep pools of ebony, seemingly beckoning you to spend time gazing into them deeply in search of the soul. No Galimarian had any color to their eyes, with the distinct exception of when someone was in love.

As all intelligent life knows, love inspires poets to write legends, choirs to sing sonnets, and artists to mold and shape the world around them in a way which somehow expresses the intoxicating ebb and flow of warmth that love engenders. The flow of chemistry between two who love one another is undeniable to any who have experienced such a blessing, but in the case of Galimarians, something truly special happens. When the mind of a Galimarian man or woman is bathed in the hormones which only come with deep love, the bottomless pools of raven black give way to eyes colored with a light shade of blue. The blue hue of Sa'Urri's normally black eyes betrayed her inner most feelings. "Hello my love."

"Ah … there's my blue love" quoted Docius from a well-known Galimarian folk song.

Sa'Urri looked into the eyes of her mate and slowly blinked. "What are you doing over here all by yourself?"

"I've been writing about my life as a boy, and about what it was like. I'm not planning on anybody reading this, and so I'm not really being careful in describing what it was like on Galimar."

"Oh really? What was it you were just writing?" asked Sa'Urri.

"Well, as you know I lived near Dimulon."

"Yes, I remember visiting there about three years before we came on the voyage."

"Right. That's the place. Well, I was writing about the first time I went there and saw the clear crystal cliffs."

"Really?" asked Sa'Urri. "How old were you?"

"I was young. I don't think I was much past thirty years old."

"Thirty? Wow. I'm surprised you remember much of anything at that age."

"Well, I was just about to start school and so my father and mother wanted one last family trip before I had to start my studies" replied Docius.

"I can see them doing that. How long after that was your sister born?" asked Sa'Urri.

"Forty years."

"Were they expecting a new one to come along so quickly?" A strange question if you were human, but for Galimarians whose life expectancy was so long, not that strange after all.

With a small laugh, Docius answered "Do you ever?" Then he said, "I mean, I know some plan for it, but a lot of times that kind of thing happens when you least expect it." Then looking out the window, Docius added "Huh. That makes me remember an old tradition about the way my mother always told my father that she was expecting."

"Oh? How was that?" asked Sa'Urri.

"Well, she would cook a really nice dinner for the family, and when she set the table she would put Gravinia flowers in the centerpiece. I'm not completely sure how the tradition started, but I heard once that it started with my great great grandmother ... I think. Anyway, when mother did that each time another brother or sister was to come along, we all knew we were going to have a new little bundle arrive in a few months."

Sa'Urri's eyebrows raised and she nodded her head as she looked away with no words. This was a little unlike his wife and with furrowed brows Docius asked his wife "What?"

Sa'Urri's eyes which had been averted now looked her mate in the eye and replied, "Do you know where I can find some Gravinias?"

It took a few seconds for it to sink in, but when it did Docius' mouth hung open almost as wide as his eyes. Those same eyes simultaneously flooded with the deepest shade of blue, and with the tears of a man who just realized his firstborn was on its way.

"You mean ...?"

Smiling, Sa'Urri said "Yes my love. Your new son or daughter is about to make an appearance."

Docius wrapped his precious mate in his arms, not ever wanting to let go. Then, thinking he might be squeezing too hard, he let go saying "Oh! I'm sorry!" He then put his hand on her abdomen and said, "I didn't mean to squeeze too hard!"

Laughing, she said "Relax my love! You didn't break me."

Looking at her eyes again for a moment, he then realized how silly it was to be so nervous and began to laugh himself. Leaning forward he kissed his wife and the two lovers luxuriated in the ever-increasing bond freely passing between them.

The room was silent for a while as they both looked out over the landscape seen out the window. The violet and blue hues of the sunset accented by the bleating of the sheep made a memorable moment even more delightful. This was one evening that Docius didn't want to go and watch over the flocks like he normally did at night. He wanted to stay right here with his wife. His wife, that was about to become a beautiful mother.

Breaking Docius out of his reverie, Sa'Urri said "There is something that concerns me though."

"What would that be?"

"Well, having a baby while we are here on the mainland was never something that we had even talked about."

"Perhaps we should have, but it isn't a surprising development."

"Oh, I know. But ... what bothers me is that our baby won't know what Galimar is like. It won't know what our people are like."

Docius, who had been looking directly at his wife now gazed at the darkening sky. The crescent moon was now becoming visible in the night sky. "When the time comes, perhaps we can tell him or her about it. I don't think that problem is unsolvable."

"I suppose you're right."

Once again, the two lovers embraced each other while leaning the sides of their heads together, basking in their blue love with languid and pleasurable thoughts of the future.

CHAPTER 15

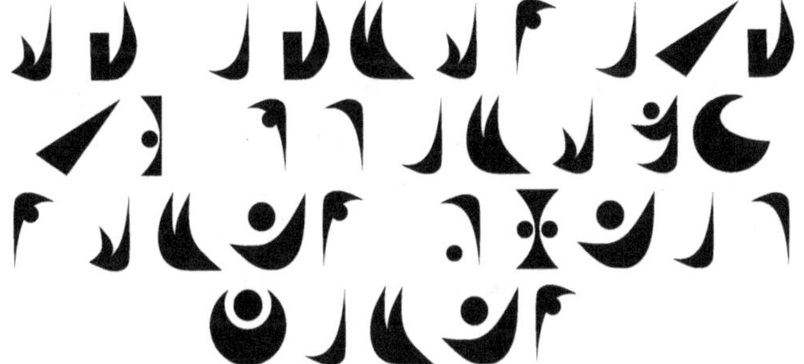

ONE OF THE MOST BEAUTIFUL parts of the world is a beach community called Neapoli Voion on the southernmost tip of mainland Greece. Also known as Vatika, it is a small town in the Laconia region, and it is built near the south end of the Malea peninsula close to Cape Maleas. Vatika is about three hundred thirty-five kilometers southwest of Athens and one hundred fifteen kilometers south of Sparta.

For a boy growing up, there couldn't be a birthplace better than this beautiful landscape. With only a thirty-minute walk from his home, one could find tree covered mountains, lazy rivers meandering through vegetation of every kind, and azure blue waters wrapping themselves around hundreds of islands that beckoned the exploration by the curious. Not to mention the plentiful animal life that was ever present, Thane loved where he lived with his father and mother, Docius and Sa'Urri. It had been about 30 Eden years since he was born, but his parents chose not to send him to school with many of his friends. Some on Eden thought Thane was a little slow.

His parents knew better.

Incidentally, referring to Thane with terms such as "his" or "he" was only out of convenience. As is the case with all Galimarian babies, when Thane was born, he actually didn't have a gender at all. In the same way that all human fetuses are neither male nor female for a period of time in the womb until surges of hormones cause changes to their bodies dictating male or female development, Galimarian babies have features on their bodies that facilitate waste disposal but are neither male nor female even after they are born into the world. While in this stage of their life, young Galimarians typically wear toga-like garb, which happened to fit in perfectly in the area where Thane now lived.

It isn't until a point that is referred to as the "Age of Enlightenment" when their bodies start to change, and they begin to take on the features of a specific gender. The transition to the age of enlightenment happens at around the age of 40 to 50 Eden years, and when this happens, they are then considered pubescent. To commemorate the new chapter in his/her life, a celebration called the "Celebration of Hin" is given in honor of the young one, and traditionally this is when the young one reveals to the world what gender their body has begun to transition into.

After that, the complete process of taking on a gender generally takes yet another 50 years. Once they hit around 100 to 110 years old, gender identity is complete. Still though, such ones are considered "young" until much later.

Knowing all this, Thane's parents were just fine with the overall progress of their son. Being that he was only thirty years old, Thane was only now getting to the point in his development where one would consider him ready to begin going to school. This led to some problems with him feeling like he fit in among his human friends though. His human friends were considered adults now, and most even had children of their own. Thane though just wasn't there. He was roughly equivalent to a human six-year old.

Docius had been spending the evenings tending to the flock as he normally did, and today he just wanted to come home and rest. There had been several lambs born that night, in fact the last count today was about thirty new ones that had arrived in just one night. The flock was certainly being blessed this year, and with this level of good fortune, it sure seemed like business was going to be great.

Walking in the front door, Docius was immediately greeted with the aroma of Keftedes, or meatballs that are cooked with herbs and onions. Sa'Urri had been good with traditional Galimarian fare before arriving on the mainland, but now that she had to work with the offerings of a completely new world, she basically had to learn how to cook again from scratch. Still though, a lot of her sense of cooking contributed to the dishes she created now, and in fact over the years there were some new creations that her best friend Cathenna had never even thought of before.

As time went along, the people living around them aged and turned grey, but Docius and Sa'Urri didn't. Lately, the two of them took to making themselves look older artificially, but that was beginning to wear on them as well. Not really knowing the short life expectancy of humans, this dimension of their life with them was something of a surprise when they moved to the mainland. They truly appreciated the simple agrarian life that they enjoyed now, but watching those that you care about get older and dying around you while you stayed young and vibrant was beginning to take its toll on both the husband and wife. They still didn't know that the prohibition to return to New Galimar had been waived by the Grand Council, and so they trudged on day after day.

As Docius put his things down and wandered toward the kitchen of their modest home, he crept up behind his wife to catch her unawares. Intending to wrap his arms around her, he ended up being the caught one.

"If you think you're too stealthy for me to know you're there, I have sad news for you" said Sa'Urri with a hidden smile on her face. She was using the Galimarian tongue that only she and her husband knew.

Rolling his eyes, Docius let out a hissing exhale and said "You see. I always knew you should have been out in the fields instead of in here. The wolves would never stand a chance against you!"

Silently laughing, she then said, "Well it helps when your husband is as stealthy as a rabid Bindar."

Shaking his head, he had only one word. "Ouch!" Sa'Urri turned to see the smile on her husband's face.

"It smells really good tonight. How did you know I was hungry for my favorite?"

"Oh, that's easy. You always are."

"Very true."

Docius wandered over to the wooden table and sat down. Leaning his back against the clay and whitewashed wall, it was almost the first time he wasn't standing or walking that day. Most of his work involved making sure the flock was safe from various nocturnal predators hoping to catch a meal unaware. But that was a rare occurrence while Docius was on the job. He constantly made his rounds making sure all were safe. The sheep knew his voice, and it almost seemed that they couldn't sleep unless they heard him nearby.

Sa'Urri finished stirring the meal and came over to sit across the table from her husband. She had something she needed to tell her husband. In hushed tones, she said "I wanted to share with you something that happened about a week ago."

"Oh?" responded Docius. "What happened?"

"Well, I had just come home from buying the things for the meal that evening from the market. Cathenna went with me that day, and so I had been there a little longer than I normally took since we were shopping for two houses instead of just mine."

While he was listening, Docius got up and poured some fresh lemonade into a cup.

"So, when I arrived home, I discovered Thane was already home from school. I think he had been here for a while and when I came into the house, I discovered him in your study."

"Doing homework?" asked Docius.

"No" answered Sa'Urri. "He was reading your stories."

Docius turned and looked at Sa'Urri. The surprise on his face was unmistakable.

"He was reading my stories? He knows how to read?"

"It was news to me too, and so I didn't make much of it at the time. I figured he might have been playing like he knew how to read when in reality he didn't."

Coming back to the table, he took a seat closer to his beautiful mate. "Ok."

"But then the next day I went to his school and talked to his headmaster. I asked him how Thane was doing in school and he told me that our boy has been surprising him every day. He was glad I came because he was going to come to me."

"Thane is surprising the headmaster?" Docius said it with a slight hint of disbelief. Hearing himself though, Docius silently thought to himself that perhaps he was beginning to buy into the opinion of Thane shared by the local humans. He decided that on this matter, he needed to do a "checkup from the neck-up". His son deserved better than that.

"Yes. According to him, Thane picked up how to read in under a week."

"A week!" shouted Docius. Then quickly looking around, he returned his voice to the same subdued tone that matched his wife. Sa'Urri was surprised by the outburst of her husband and quickly glanced to the living room to make sure the two them weren't being overheard.

"A week?" said Docius once again, now much more quietly. "So that means when you found him in the study, he really was reading the stories."

Then thinking about it more, he then said, "The stories about Galimar."

Nodding her head, Sa'Urri agreed with her husband. Wiping her brow with the cloth hanging from her belt, her gaze returned to the living room. Thane was in a different room and there was no sign that he was anywhere near.

After thinking about it, Docius then said "Now that I think about it though, I think we've been measuring Thane with a ruler that was made by humans. I mean, think about it. How long did it take you to learn how to read?" Sa'Urri looked at Docius with furrowed eyebrows, but then she realized that her mate was right. Galimarians do tend to learn faster than a lot of the civilizations they have encountered, and the fact that Thane was able to read so quickly shouldn't have been surprising.

The two just looked at each other for a while. Now that Thane was able to read, that meant that the things he wrote about in his journals might be more than what his son should know. At least at this age.

"I need to have a talk with Thane about what's in those journals" said Docius.

Nodding her head, Sa'Urri agreed and said "I think you're right. There's a lot of things in those journals that shouldn't be known by anybody on earth. Since it's going to be a while until the meal is ready, why don't you take him somewhere and talk about it."

"Good idea" replied Docius. Getting up, he turned to the front room, and then to Thane's bedroom. Meanwhile Sa'Urri went back to stirring the food she was in the middle of making.

"Thane?" said Docius as he entered the open door to his son's room.

"Yeah dad?"

As he arrived at his son's room, he discovered his son sitting on the floor next to his bed petting their pet cat. About a year before they had adopted one of the cats that were feral in this region. His fur color was orange and white, and he was more than content to lie cuddled next to any in the home that cared to stroke his fur and give it kisses on the top of the head. A very young Thane simply named it Mister Kitty.

"I need to get some things down at the wharf" said Docius. "What do you say we get out of your mother's way and go down there together?"

Smiling, Thane simply said "Ok dad."

Clad in his typical white robe draped over his shoulder, the young boy rose from his seated position and struck out for the docks alongside his father. The roads down to the docs were dirt and gravel and it took a little while to descend from the foothills where their home was located. After navigating the roads down to the docks where the fishing boats were tied and waiting for the next day, Docius made a pretense of buying something that he didn't really need, but then invited his son to sit on a rock wall that bordered the calm bay.

"So, I have a question for you son."

"Yeah dad?"

"I was wondering if you enjoyed reading in my journals?" asked Docius. He figured tackling the subject head-on was the best way and wouldn't give Thane any time to put any sort of spin on the activity. His instincts were right, and Thane was completely caught off guard.

"I ... uh ... your ... your journals? When did you ... uh ..." Thane was tongue-tied completely. He instantly felt guilty for reading in his father's journals, however knowing what he read he didn't see why his dad would be mad at him about it.

"I'm not terribly mad at you, son. I just want to know why you thought it was ok to read my things without asking?"

Thane looked down at the water as it lapped at the rock wall where they sat. There were only two words that he could think to say.

"I'm sorry."

"As you should be son. Things like that should only be read if the person says it is ok."

Thane didn't say anything, but simply nodded his head.

"I can see you feel bad about it, as well you should, and so I don't think we need to dwell on that anymore. Just next time, you need to ask first. Agreed?"

Thane's shoulders relaxed slightly. "Agreed" was the only word Thane said. He was still staring down at the water.

"So now I have a question for you."

"Ok"

"My question is, what did you think about what you read?" asked Docius.

Once again, Docius took Thane by surprise with this new question. Thane looked his father in the eyes and said the first thing that came to mind. "I thought they were really good."

"Really good?" inquired Docius. He didn't really understand what his son meant.

"I mean, I thought the stories in there were really interesting to read. I have always like to read make-believe stories and I think yours are the best."

"Make-believe stories?"

Thane nodded.

It was at that moment that Docius realized that his son thought the things Docius wrote about were fictional stories that weren't actually true.

Docius thought about it for some time while sitting there with his son. He thought about how with more and more time going by, Thane was going to learn more and more about where he and his parents came from. While he was originally thinking that he wouldn't have to do this until a few years later, Docius realized that he needed to set the record straight with Thane. Still though, while his son was a really good kid, Thane never had the ability to really understand how the Grand Council works, and why it was so important that their decisions be followed. Docius was sure that later in life Thane would come to a mature understanding of the bigger picture, but for now, he needed to keep certain things secret.

Certain things, like the real location of New Galimar.

"Son it's important that you know something about those stories, as you call them."

"Yeah? What's that?"

"What's important for you to know, son, is that those stories aren't some make-believe stories that I made up. What I wrote about in there? It's all true."

Thane paused for a while and Docius let the last thing he said sink into his son's mind.

"What's true?"

"All of it."

Thane stretched his mind back to the small amount he had read. There were stories of a world with several moons. Stories about ocean cliffs made of crystal. Stories about a peaceful people.

"It's real?"

"Yes, son. It's all real."

"If it's real, how do you know about all this stuff?" asked the slightly bewildered boy.

Deciding that telling his son that he was actually from an alien race of beings from another galaxy was a little too much for such a young mind, Docius answered his sons' question, saying "Well there is an answer to that question, but I'm not yet ready to share that with you son. For now, let's just say that you can trust me when I tell you that everything in those journals is real."

Thane didn't say anything for a while. He looked down at the water once again while he thought about a few things he had read.

Looking around to the beautiful buildings surrounding the beach community and their often blue domed rooves, Docius then said "I'm going to tell you now that it is ok to read everything I have written. If you have any questions, you can ask me or your mother. She is aware of everything in those journals and can answer any question you might have just as much as I can."

"Mom knows everything in the journals?"

"Yes, my son. She does. But there is something else that is very important that I need to tell you."

"What's that dad" asked Thane as he looked up to his father once again.

"It's this my boy. While you have permission to read everything in those journals, you do not have permission to discuss what you have read to anybody else other than me or your mother. I want your solemn promise that you will keep what you learn between just the three of us. OK?"

Thane responded "OK dad. I promise. I don't think anybody would ..."

Just then, while the words were still in Thane's mouth the two of them felt a rather sharp jolt under their seats sitting there on the rock wall. Knowing exactly what this was, Docius immediately grabbed the shoulder of his son before he might have fallen into the water. Sure enough … after backing away from the rock wall that bordered the bay where they had been sitting, there was a sudden and very pronounced rolling motion under their feet, such that the father and son couldn't stay on their feet. Just when the rolling motions seemed to die down, there was another sharp and sudden period of shaking.

Knowing that his son was fine right next to him, Docius looked around. There were many people that had been milling around the marketplaces nearby, and they were reacting in the same way as Docius and Thane. Each one was being forced to their knees because standing wasn't an option at the moment. As he was scanning his eyes around, there was a loud crack to his left. Looking that direction, Docius and Thane saw the store where Docius had just made a purchase suddenly implode. It was a two-story structure and when it fell in on itself, it was nothing but a pile of bricks and heavy timbers.

Docius tried to move, but each effort was foiled by a very uncooperative ground. There was no way he could stand at the moment to help anybody. Nobody could.

"What's happening dad?!" asked a very frightened boy.

"It's an edenquake son. Just stay near me and you'll be safe!"

As the ground shook, water splashed violently against the rock wall where Docius and Thane had just been sitting. Had they still been there, they most assuredly would have been washed out to sea. As the shaking continued, several of the two-foot-thick timbers making up one of the three jetty's extending out into the water made massive cracking sounds, before buckling down into the water and completely falling out of sight. There were at least two dozen people carrying out their daily lives that were carried down with it. Most were not seen again until days later when their bodies were washed up on shore.

Some of the trees that were fairly close shed older branches, and the carts used by several of the street vendors were all turned over on their sides spilling out their wares across the roadways. Some of the vendors were making a futile attempt to gather their goods back together, but most were just trying to do their best to remain safe and out of the way from the falling portions of nearby buildings.

Right when the shaking seemed to begin to wane, two more structures completely disintegrated relatively close to Docius and Thane. Looking back at the first structure that had fallen, Docius now saw fire start to pour from structures flanking the fallen shop. As he was looking to the huge mountain range that was behind the town center, it looked to Docius like someone had formed a sheet in the exact shape of the entire mountain range. It looked like they were now raising up the perfectly formed sheet up off the cascade of mountains, and the shape of the sheet was a perfect replica of the shape of the massive peaks and valleys of the foothills. Of course, he knew it was just the edenquake having thrown up a dust cloud from the ground of the entire range. Then a chilling thought occurred to him.

He realized his home was up in that range of mountains.

Borrowing an exclamation often said by Fotios, Docius said "Oh my god! Sa'Urri!"

Regardless of whether he could reliably walk or not during the quake, both he and Thane jumped up and immediately lunged for their home. The regular aftershocks coupled with the devastation of the land made getting home much more difficult. There were many times when the two fell onto sharp rocks causing numerous injuries that neither cared about at the moment.

Whether or not they had been swifter, it wouldn't have made any difference. They arrived only to see that what was wasn't completely crumbled to the ground of their home was totally engulfed in flames, including his study where his journals were kept. Climbing out from behind a nearby tree, Mister Kitty had apparently sensed the coming calamity and ran for his life in time to make it to safety.

Unfortunately, Mister Kitty was alone.

"SA'URRI!!!!!" yelled a frantic Docius. Pushing through the smoke and clouds of dust, he ran as close as he could to the pile of rubble that was once his home only minutes before, only to be forced back by the out-of-control flames. There was nothing he could do. Falling to his knees and with nobody to console either of them, a very dusty and scratched husband, son and kitty crumbled against each other knowing that she was gone.

Her body wouldn't be uncovered for another eleven days.

CHAPTER 16

LOOKING INTO THE SKY, DOCIUS watched the Egrets and Cormorants fly in their seemingly never-ending dance among the treetops. It was late evening and the sky was beginning to turn into a combination of turquoise and sapphire. There was a light smattering of white clouds, just enough to catch the lavender, pomegranate and violet rays of the waning sun. The artistry of the fall sky framed by the trees whose leaves where now turning different colors was never lost on him.

In the distance, there was music being played by a few friends of Docius. Officially speaking, tonight was a celebration in honor of his son who had graduated from school, however between Docius and his son, this celebration was actually Thane's 'Celebration of Hin.'

The Celebration of Hin was a traditional celebration where a young Galimarian figuratively crossed a threshold and became what was considered an adolescent young one. Normally the young one would be given an amulet of understanding wherein they would be first introduced to their amulet companion that would stay with them for the rest of their lives. It is also when the young one would officially reveal to their family, and the world in general, what gender their body was transitioning into. It was also when the young one would decide what their permanent name would be for the rest of their life. On Galimar it made sense to do this long after the young one had been born, since it was only then that the gender was known, and so a name commensurate with their gender was chosen. Secondly, the name really meant something for each Galimarian, and so a young one needed to choose a name that closely matched the kind of person they wished to become.

For Thane though, some of those traditions wouldn't come to pass. A little over fifty years ago, Docius and his then wife Sa'Urri had traveled to Greece, agreeing to the requirements of the Grand Council that no technology be taken with them. While Docius and Sa'Urri readily agreed to this prohibition, which of course meant that there would be no giving of an amulet to Thane this evening, nobody at the time, including the departing couple, thought about how there was one technology that Docius and Sa'Urri took with them that would drastically mark them as different from the world around them. It wasn't until a few years after their Grecian arrival that Docius was reminded of this technology that was still in their possession. Unknown to Docius, his possession of this technology would end up playing a major part in saving not only the entire human race, but even the entire nation of New Galimar.

It was a technology that Docius would share with his son tonight without his son even knowing it.

The new name though ... that was something that would still be done. It was easy enough to explain to those around.

Set up all around him were randomly placed tables and chairs, and on each table a centerpiece carried a bouquet of flowers and a beautiful display of local vegetation. All tables and several of the surrounding trees had sconces on them that contained lit candles.

The waning yet multicolored sunset coupled with the candlelight combined beautifully, creating a festive and lighthearted environment. Near to the source of the music, there were many people dancing. Several of the men were dancing with each other, their arms resting on the shoulders of the one nearest to them and their concentration on making sure their feet and legs moved in a perfectly synchronized manner. Accented by the burbling water of a nearby brook and the tree-bound cicada songs the environment was complete, and it was enough to bring the spirits high with no room for melancholy.

All except for Docius.

It's not that Docius was depressed. Not exactly. The stinging pain of having lost his life-mate in the edenquake twenty years ago was certainly bad when it first happened, but as time goes along, sharp edges of pain often give way to the occasional dull stab. Today was one of those days when the stabs were manageable, but still present.

Thane was enjoying the celebration with his friends. Many of those friends were friends that he had made when he was first born, and yet since they were human, these fifty-year-old men and women were now grandparents themselves, when Thane was only now transitioning into the equivalent of mid adolescence. Thane was good at adapting though. He was able to mask his young innocence such that most never knew anything was different about him. Those that did notice something simply chalked it up to Thane always having been "a little slow" all his life. Once again, Docius knew his son wasn't "slow". He was just progressing exactly as fast as his Galimarian biology allowed. By this time though, Thane had already revealed to his father that his body was talking on the features of a male, and so Docius continued to refer to his progeny as "his", "he" and "son".

Cathenna had really done a wonderful job arranging for this celebration in honor of her favorite "son". Quite some time ago, Fotios and Cathenna had come to the conclusion that they were unable to have children and so had remained barren and alone. It wasn't apparent which one of them was unable to conceive, however neither cared. They would have certainly enjoyed having children, but they never let the inability get in the way of them appreciating how much they loved each other. "Love is all you need" was often said by them both.

But when Sa'Urri was killed in the edenquake twenty years before, Cathenna made it her job to care for her best friend's son who had "special" needs. Docius appreciated the helping hand, and while he never corrected the viewpoint Cathenna had of her adopted son, Docius made sure Thane knew he wasn't "special" in the same sense that others thought.

As far as Docius was concerned, he was never interested in any romantic involvement after that fateful day. It wasn't due to a lack of trying on the part of the single ladies in the surrounding area though. Officially, Docius was far too in love with his departed wife to ever have another mate. Unofficially, Docius had decided that having a marriage relationship with a human just wouldn't work out. Especially due to the difference in life expectancies.

The celebration was just about to be punctuated by the giving of gifts to Thane, and so Fotios came over to retrieve his friend from his lonesome reverie.

"Docius?"

Being far too deep in thought, Docius didn't respond. At that moment his thoughts had strayed back to New Galimar and how he wondered what life was like for them now that they had been on this planet for more than fifty years. Were they exploring? Were they discovering new th...

"Docius!" Coming closer his friend was able to raise the volume of his call such that Docius recognized the voice.

"Oh, I'm sorry Fotios. I didn't mean to ignore you."

"That's ok my friend. Where were you?"

“Excuse me?” asked Docius, not recognizing what Fotios was asking.

“Where were you? Where was that huge and underutilized mind of yours traveling?” asked Fotios, referring to the subject of many conversations he had had in the past with Docius on what he was pursuing in life. It was Fotios’ opinion that Docius had talents that were being squandered in the fields with sheep.

“Oh, I was just wishing Sa’Urri could have been here for this, and I was thinking of something that seemed fairly profound.”

Sitting on a chair that was near to his friend, Fotios put his hand on the shoulder of his friend and said, “Tell me.”

“Well” answered Docius, “I was thinking about how easy it is to accept that one day I would be the one who crosses into whatever awaits after my own death, but how I am unable to accept the death of anyone else, especially if it is someone that I love. I find it impossible to mentally allow that one to walk in any path other than one that has as its companion complete safety and unending hope and happiness. When I think that anything else might be the case, I find that I get angry.”

Fotios wasn’t expecting such a deeply philosophic train of thought, and so while he had been sent by his wife to retrieve Docius for the giving of gifts to Thane, he decided that he needed to honor the thoughts of his friend, instead of shuffling them off to the side.

“I think I can understand that, my friend. But something that I’ve always lived by is that as long as you remember the one who has passed, then you are never alone, nor is that person totally dead. They live on, walking by you at any time you choose to remember them. And so … you never have to worry about their safety for which you have no control. If things happen out of your control, then simply celebrate what you did have with them and not what might have been.”

Docius sat there and thought about the words from Fotios. He then remembered something that he had to remind himself of many times over the years. "I see what you are saying" said Docius. "In fact, something that I have always had to remind myself of through the years are the questions 'What kind of life would Sa'Urri want me to live?' and 'Would she want me to be unhappy for the rest of my life?'. I suppose I need to work on not feeling sorry for myself."

"I don't think it's necessarily a case of feeling sorry for yourself. I think it's natural to miss someone."

The two men sat there for a while allowing the thoughts to sink in. A slight nodding on the part of Docius told Fotios that his words were having their intended effect.

After some time, and prompted by a 'hurry up' look coming from his wife, Fotios then said, "But I do know something that Sa'Urri would want you to do right now."

"Oh? What's that?" asked Docius.

"She would want you to not miss the celebration in honor of her son, and she would want you to be there for when he opens his gifts!"

Letting out a small chuckle and slapping the knee of his friend as he was getting up, Docius relented from his contemplations and walked with his friend to rejoin the celebration. "Lead the way!"

The two men returned to the main body of celebration just in time to see Thane begin to open his presents. Most of them were functional, and several included items of clothing that were made by the women in the village. All the gifts were given with the love and hearts of those that lived near to Docius and his son, and it was certainly gratifying to Docius to see how well liked his son was.

After the gifts were opened, Docius walked over to his son who was spending time looking at his gifts and knelt next to Thane. "Looks like you have a lot of people who love you son!"

Smiling to his father, he responded "I know! These things are really great!"

Nodding to Thane, Docius said "They sure are son, but I wanted to give you my gift now."

"Father, you didn't have to get me anything!" Just then though, Thane looked down into Docius' hands and was a little perplexed at how there was nothing there.

Reaching over to some of the articles of clothing just given to Thane, Docius said "What I have to give you isn't something that is going to wear out in a few years. In fact, it is something that will stay with you for the rest of your life."

"The rest of my life? What is it?"

Standing, Docius simply said "Walk with me son."

With no words in response, Thane put the things that were on his lap to the side and followed his father out to a place that was sufficiently far away from the festivities that they wouldn't be seen or heard. Docius then turned to his son who stood near and began to explain.

"Son" explained Docius, "as you already know we are much different than those who are around us. I know that it has been difficult to adapt to life among humans since there are facets of our lives that are vastly unlike the same for those that we care for here in our hometown. Still though, I am impressed with your ability to adapt and live among humans so well."

"Thank you, father. I appreciate hearing you praise me that way."

"It is praise that is well earned son. But there is something that both your mother and I wanted to do for you. It is something that meant everything to her, as it also does to me. It is a tradition in connection with your Celebration of Hin. It is the creation of a true blood bond between us, such that afterwards you will not only be my son, but you will also be my brother. A true Galimarian man."

"A blood bond? How does it work?"

"Well son" responded Docius, "it involves us making a cut on both our hands, and then holding our hands together. My blood will mix with yours, and only then will you be a true Galimarian man."

In reality, this wasn't a normal tradition associated with the Celebration of Hin on the planet of Galimar. There was a vastly different reason why Docius desired to do this.

Thinking about it, Thane then said, "Then let it be so, father."

Smiling, Docius produced a small dagger from his pocket. Opening his left hand, he then proceeded to make a very shallow cut in the fleshy part of his hand just below the thumb. Blood began to slowly issue forth from the cut. He then handed the dagger to his son.

Tentatively, Thane grasped the dagger in his right hand, and after looking in the eyes of his father for reassurance, he drug the blade of the knife along his skin. It was deep enough to draw blood, but not so deep to cause any permanent damage. It was doubtful it would even leave a scar.

Reaching out his hand toward his son, Docius grasped the left hand of his son, such as their blood intermingled. He then said "With this embrace I pass on to you the torch of manhood my son. I pass on to you long life and long health. With all of my being I shall now always be with you, guarding you and protecting you. My essence will now always be with you my son. Now and forever, we will always be joined."

The two "men" stood there looking at each other while their blood mingled. For his part, Thane was humbled at the ceremony now taking place between he and his father. It would be something that he felt would stay with him for the rest of his life. He was right of course, but not in the way he was thinking. The main reason Docius was instituting this custom at the Celebration of Hin for Thane was because of the technology that was inadvertently brought with he and his wife when they came to Greece from New Galimar.

As was the case with Sa'Urri and Docius, every Galimarian baby is given an injection shortly after they are born. Most civilizations would mistake this injection as some sort of inoculation for diseases that are common amongst the young. In the case of Galimarians though, such diseases have been a thing of the past for centuries. This injection carries with it nanites, or microscopic robots that travel around in your blood stream for the rest of your life. These nanites work on a cellular level and monitor the health of their host, watching for any situation where health might be threatened. In addition to that, it also looks at the DNA, and more specifically it watches the telomere's, or end-caps of each strand of chromosome. When it senses that the telomeres are worn down enough to merit repair, it actually repairs the chromosome.

The end result of this repair is that the life of these DNA chromosome strands is vastly extended. The health of the host body is thus maintained, and hence a person's life expectancy is generally stretched significantly. It is the main reason why life expectancy of a Galimarian is somewhere around twenty thousand years.

As Docius and Thane held each other's hands, the nanites that had been living in Docius' blood stream passed over into Thanes. Those few nanites that passed over now sensed that the body where they were located had almost no others of their kind. Sensing this, they immediately set about replicating themselves, and this replication would continue unabated until they collectively sensed there was enough of them in the blood stream of their host to do the job they were designed to do.

After about thirty seconds Docius released the hand of his son and reached for a wet cloth he had ready nearby for this occasion, and the two men now wiped the dried blood from their hands. Docius hoped that the transfer was successful. He knew that the transfer would have taken if his son felt drained over the next week, which in fact did happen. The feeling of being drained was caused by the nanites using up resources in the body to perform the necessary replication.

The men returned to the party and enjoyed the rest of the evening. Eventually the festivities were such that it was time for a special feature of the evening, and Docius stepped to the middle of the group and tapped the side of a glass to make a sound indicating that he needed to speak.

"May I have everybody's attention?" The music artists were just concluding a song and so they took a break in their playing to allow Docius the attention that he was requesting. When that happened, all turned their attention to Docius who was now standing on a short stand, although that wasn't needed. He was already far taller than all those around him.

"Thank you for your attention. I wanted to tell all here about a tradition that comes from the land where I come from. As most of you know, my son and I aren't from around here. We come from a land far across the sea, where we have customs that may seem strange to many other cultures. One of those traditions involves an evening like this where the one being celebrated chooses a name."

"As you all know, Thane is the one being celebrated here tonight, but the name of 'Thane' was actually only a temporary name. It was actually the same name that was given to all babies in my family when they were born, including me. According to the tradition, when a man of my culture grows and decides what type of person they are going to become for the rest of their lives, it is then when they should choose the name that they themselves want."

Then motioning to his son, he then said, "Son, will you come up here for a moment?"

A slightly embarrassed Thane stood up and came near to his father.

"Son, I have two questions that I want to put to you now. The first question is what kind of profession have you chosen for yourself?"

Looking out toward those that had gathered, Thane said "It was actually last year when I decided what I wanted to do for the rest of my days. It was when I and several of my friends traveled to Athens. While there I was exposed to the profession of being a philosopher. It is this for which I wish to dedicate the rest of my life." All those gathered began to clap. Philosophers were very highly regarded in the Grecian culture where they lived.

Once the applause died down, Docius spoke again. "My next question to you son, is what is the name you have chosen for yourself. What is the name that we will use from this day forward instead of Thane?"

Looking back to those gathered, he answered his father clearly.

"Socrates."

CHAPTER 17

THE MARINER HAD BEEN SAILING for about thirteen hours now, and his journey was finally nearing its end. Having left the port of Vatika the previous day, he had been sailing alone all night. Normally he wouldn't set sail with a view to sailing during the night, but this sailor didn't really want to be seen, especially by those that lived near the port where he set sail.

BarPolin had been sent by the Traxian committee to determine the current status of the Galimarians. Were they still alive? Were they still living among the humans as if they were humans themselves? Was there a change in their status? Had they moved anywhere? Had they procreated? The last status obtained about them was about six months ago, and since then some definite changes had happened. Changes that would probably mean a great deal to think about on the part of the committee. He had to get this information back as soon as possible, since he knew that they were due to meet any day now. Normally, he would have tried to get back at least two days earlier so as not to risk missing the meeting, but he lingered on the mainland in order to get the critical information that he now carried.

As the dawn broke over the eastern horizon, BarPolin expected it to illuminate the island that he had been supposedly passing south of for the last two hours, and sure enough, once there was enough light to see, the cone shaped mountain rising above the island verified he was right on course. He had to do a double take, since it almost appeared that there was a column of steam coming of the summit of the mountain. Strange.

That he was seeing the island right when the wanted to see it wasn't too surprising to him. He had been sailing for most of his life ever since his parents gave birth to him some forty-five years ago. He knew the sea better than any of the small community of Traxians that lived on Thera, and this is why he was selected to spy on the two remaining Galimarian enemies.

Now that he could see the silhouette outline of the island, BarPolin could see that it was time to bear north. Being that this was summer, the prevailing wind currents mostly came from the north and from the area of the black sea, and so for most of the trip he had the sails set to catch the northern wind, which in turn pushed the ship in an eastern course. Coupled with carefully maneuvering the rudder all night he had made good time, but now that he had to sail north, he knew it was time to tack into the wind. This of course meant his progress wouldn't be as swift as it was the rest of the night.

After sailing into the wind for another hour, and with the ever-increasing light of the morning sky, he came upon what he had been looking for. Jutting out into the water from the volcanic formations on the eastern shore of the island were several caverns. The caverns were large enough to allow for ships to enter since they were framed by huge archways making them appear beautiful and hospitable. They were nothing of the sort though, for these caverns were controlled by the ruling body of Traxians that had taken residence on this island, and who had taken the name "The Circle of Seven" in honor of the original seven Traxians who had come over to the mainland with the Galimarians about fifty years ago. Of those original seven, there were only four remaining, the other three having passed away from old age. While the name stayed honoring those original seven, the council was actually made up of 22 members now.

As he approached the giant archways that led into the underground interior of the island, BarPolin couldn't see anybody on the cliffs above the cavernous waterway, but he knew that was only due to a carefully planned subterfuge. He knew that at any time there was at least twenty men watching his approach. All of them dedicated to keeping this approach secret, even if it meant the death of those that happened to stumble by.

BarPolin stood and stretched his tired muscles that had been in the same position for far too long. Reaching across to a secret compartment built into the deck of the boat just below the starboard gunnels, he extracted a flag that was designed to be raised and lowered on the mast of the ship. The flag had a mostly red background. In the bottom middle of the flag was a large white half circle, and above that circle was a solid black silhouette of an eagle. Its wings were stretched out on either side of its body, and there were seven outermost feathers on each outstretched wing. The eagle and its outstretched wings appeared to sit on and over the white half-circle as if it was dominating it.

Affixing the flag to the rope, he raised the flag high on the mast and as he raised it up the mast, it unfurled itself into the wind showing itself to all who wanted to look. Doing this caused the Traxian soldiers above the cavern to stand down from their battle stance. Had BarPolin not raised the Traxian flag, his ship would have been assaulted with volley after volley of flaming arrows, followed by cannon shots aimed to sink the ship instantly. If that didn't work, there were several men stationed down below at the mouth of the cavern whose job was to pick out the stragglers. Prisoners were never kept.

After raising the flag, BarPolin immediately saw about two dozen men appear from nowhere on the cliffs over the cavern, all watching him quietly sailing into the cavern below and on to the dock that had been built out of sight from the ocean outside. It only took about ten minutes to reach the dock that had been built from the pine forests that covered the island. The aroma of pitch combined with tar that had been impregnated into the pine hung heavily in this grotto along with the smell of the sea. The walls of the large cave were dark in color and they continually seemed wet. There were portions of the ceiling that seemed to be missing since it was so high up, but he knew that this was just an illusion from it being so dark, coupled with the dance of the shadows cast from the torches that lined the dock where he was now tying up his craft. The rear of the cavern extended back rather far, and it was in these passageways where bats made their home. It wasn't uncommon to hear their shrill calls as they flew out at sunset to look for food, only to return in the morning with their bellies full. Now that the morning sun was shining bright, the cacophony of the daily ingress was in full swing.

Passing the dockmaster who had immediately set about preparing the ship for its next voyage and walking to the end of the dock, he came upon what looked like a doorway hewn out of light-colored stone. The door and jamb were made from rock that was ground down smoothly, and the smooth rock faces extended out five feet on either side of the door. The door itself was inset from the face of the wall by five feet, and the alcove created by the inset was also finished in the same finely smooth rock. The door had no handle, and there didn't appear to be any way to open the door other than pushing on it, however this was all part of the deception. If a hapless visitor by chance happened to get past the guards outside the cavern, then getting to this door would probably mean the end of their life. The door was designed such that if it was pushed, a latch would give way, and the roof to the alcove in front of the door would drop. The roof was a perfectly carved and sculpted stone that weighed one metric ton. It would drop down and instantly kill the unwanted intruder. By the way, if this ever did happen, counterweights inside could thereafter be used to reset the roof stone back in place.

Decorating the smooth outer wall around the alcove were beautiful and intricate relief carvings that depicted various cultures on the surrounding islands, especially that of the bustling metropolis belonging to a long dead civilization known as the Minoan culture. Located on an island near to the southern portion of the Aegean Sea named Crete, this culture was a large metropolis that celebrated the land and sea around them. The carvings on the walls of this cave were that of stylized images of bulls, sea creatures like dolphins and whales, people celebrating with food and dance and what appeared to be religious gatherings honoring whatever gods that were important to them. The stone had been occasionally painted with various colors ranging from rust, to sapphire, to stark white. The men in the carvings all seemed to be bare chested and they all seemed to wear golden arm bands. A lot of the men in the carvings were mostly nude, but if anything was worn, it was a wrap worn from the waist down and it was made from several solid color swatches of fabric. The depictions of the women in these stone carvings all had wonderfully styled hair accented with what appeared to be beads or jewels. It appeared that the women wore vests or bodices, if they wore anything at all from the waist up. Most didn't. If a bodice was worn, it would be tied or buttoned below the breasts leaving them either completely exposed, or at the most with a transparent swatch of fabric across the chest.

What wasn't completely obvious is that the relief carvings surrounding the stone door were actually movable stones that could be pushed in or pulled out. If you positioned the carvings in the correct arrangement, water channels behind the wall would fill a receptacle attached to a system of leverage controls, and hence the door would rise up and away. Once the door had lifted away, the carvings would then be scrambled again by the person, and the flow of water into the receptacle would stop. The water container had an intentional leak in it, such that once the water level began to recede, its weight would diminish, and the door would return to a closed position. BarPolin manipulated the carvings quickly and easily, and once the door moved up and away, he struck out directly for the Circle of Seven meeting chambers without delay. This meant climbing five stories of steps that had been hewn from the rock strata in the belly of the island, then walking up several inclined passageways. Incidentally, the walls of these passageways were said to have been here naturally by some volcanic force, and now they had been whitewashed in the same manner as structures topside.

Eventually he came to an immense room that seemed to be a colonnade made of marble and granite. Since it was so far underground, the room was lit with innumerable wall sconces containing flaming torches and candles. There was a team of boys whose whole job was to keep things lit, and it appeared they had been doing their job quite well. BarPolin walked a hasty pace toward the far end of the room past several seating areas that were occupied by many officers in the secret Traxian army. Their presence meant that the meeting had already begun, much to his chagrin, however he knew that no matter how late he may have been, the information that he carried needed to be relayed.

Eventually he made it to the door of the committee chamber. There were guards to each side of the door, and had he been anybody else entrance to the chamber would have certainly been denied, ruthlessly if necessary. Also standing in front of the door was a well-dressed man named Ellery who would normally ask if the mariner wanted or needed anything, however his presence had been anticipated by those in the meeting room and so he simply turned the handle to the door and allowed entry to the visitor. Entering the room, the door quietly closed behind him as he waited for his presence to be acknowledged.

The structure of the room itself followed the same type of architecture of the outer colonnade, however this one was designed to facilitate the meeting of Traxian generals. While he waited, BarPolin thought about how the name "Circle of Seven" was somewhat of a misnomer since there were actually twenty-two generals that all sat around a circular table. The walls had floor to ceiling glass and metal panels that were backlit with a series of torches. The indirect light not only illuminated the room, but perfectly illuminated much larger displays of the same flag that BarPolin had raised on his ship.

Each general sat on a wooden chair with a high back. The back of the chair carried a carved eagle like the eagle on the flags. It was actually the same eagle silhouette that was tattooed on the right wrist of each member in the room, as well as BarPolin. The tattoo represented membership with the Circle of Seven and all men, women and children on this island had the same effigy on their wrists.

The meeting had already started, but fortunately it had only been proceeding for about ten minutes before BarPolin arrived. The chairman leading the meeting noticed BarPolin's arrival, however there were other items that needed to be discussed, and so the new arrival had to wait for his turn. As it turns out, it only took another ten minutes for the meeting to proceed to the point where it was time for BarPolin.

About that time, the chairman looked over to BarPolin. As he looked back at the chairman, he reached up and squeezed his right ear. The chairman smiled slightly acknowledging the prearranged signal, and then turned to the rest of the group to speak.

"Gentlemen, it is now time to move on to more pressing matters. As most of you know, BarPolin was assigned to determine the status of the mainland Galimarians, and he has a report for you that I think you will find interesting."

BarPolin stepped forward to a portion of the circular table that was devoid of any seat. Unlike the curved edge of the rest of the table, this portion was flattened and was where any visiting speaker would stand.

"Gentlemen" said BarPolin, "as the chairman indicated, I do indeed have information that you will find interesting. Not thirty minutes ago I arrived from the mainland where it was my mission was to spy on our enemies, and report back on their status. As some of you already know there was a development in the lives of these Galimarians twenty years ago wherein the female was killed in one of the edenquakes that have been happening so regularly lately. This left the father and child on the island."

"As we all know, it is our primary mission to search out the existence of 'Coral of Eden' mentioned in our prophecies. And also, as you all know, it is a ridiculous Galimarian custom to take on a new name during something they call the 'Celebration of Hin'. We have been waiting for that celebration of the child to see if that one is the prophesied demon child 'Coral'. Having witnessed that aforementioned 'Celebration of Hin' for this child, I am somewhat disappointed to reveal to you all that the name he chose was not Coral, but in fact was a completely different name, Socrates."

The news was met with several looks of disappointment. The chairman was hoping that the news was going to be better than this, for this is something that he had been waiting for all his life. One and all in the room sat in their chairs while their gaze toward BarPolin faltered.

After a few seconds, the chairman spoke. "Thank you for your report BarPolin. You are dismissed."

BarPolin straightened his body ramrod straight and dipped his head in salute to the men in the room. Turning on this heel, he left the room and the door closed.

Turning to the rest of the generals, the chairman spoke up and said "Well gentlemen, it appears that we have some decisions to make. We have now seen that the Galimarians that have come to the mainland have not proven to be the source of the demon child. We must now decide what the next steps are."

One of the generals, BarSchmex spoke. "Since there is nothing left to do here, perhaps we should return to New Galimar and assist our brothers that were left there."

Another across the table spoke. "Can't. If you remember, the Grand Council of New Galimar forbade our return."

"And without any technology" added the chairman, "it appears that we are destined to remain in this backwater society."

"I think we might be missing something" interjected another at the table named BarHazull.

"Oh?" asked the chairman. "What might that be?"

"Well" answered BarHazull after obviously thinking and choosing his words carefully, "it's just that I've been thinking about the prophecies, and how our review of them revealed that the gender of Coral of Eden might have been either male, female, or otherwise. Something that occurred to me recently though is that, while we know the demon child will come from Eden which is the very planet where we find ourselves, something else the prophecies aren't specific on is whether Coral ..." he paused.

"... is Galimarian."

There was a very pregnant pause in the room as the words sunk in to each of the generals in the room. After a few seconds, one spoke up and said, "Are you saying that you think the demon child might be ... human?"

"I can't say for sure" replied BarHazull. "But what I can say is that there are several facts that we do know for sure. First, we are sure the demon child will come from this planet. Second, we know for sure that it isn't one of these two remaining Galimarians. Third, we are unable to return to New Galimar. Fourth, New Galimar doesn't have the technology to reach back in time as the prophecies indicated. And finally, fifth, Galimarians are only interested in exploring their future and not our past. All this leads me to the conclusion that the child won't come from

New Galimar which can only mean that, as crazy as it sounds, the demon child must come from humans one day."

This line of reasoning had never occurred before to anybody in the room, and so it took some time for it to sink in. After a full minute, the chairman spoke "I believe this line of reasoning is something that should be considered. Since it is time for the noon meal, I suggest that we adjourn for two hours while we each refresh our minds and bodies. During such time let us all consider what BarHazull has suggested, and when we return, we will discuss it again."

All at the table nodded, and the men adjourned. When they returned, what had been presented as a simple idea had now congealed in the minds of the generals as a fully formed understanding.

After repeating the normal Circle of Seven invocations that preceded every meeting, the chairman spoke. "My fellow generals, it appears that we have certainly given the words of BarHazull consideration and based on some of the smaller conversations I've had with some of you already, it also appears that we must do something about this if we are to be faithful to our ancestors and faithful to the prophecies. What I put to you now is ... what ideas do you have so as to properly live up to the trust that has been given to us?"

BarSchmex sat forward and wiping one of his cream-colored locks away from his brow he said, "I believe that our operations here must be diversified if we are to effectively find and destroy this source of plague to our ancestors."

With an intrigued look, the chairman said, "Please elaborate."

BarSchmex continued, "We know that humans live on almost every continent on this planet. We also know that some of those continents are filled with humans that are more advanced than others. I propose that we create sub-divisions of our race and move each of those sub-divisions to different locations on the planet. That way, we will have a better ability to monitor the affairs of those civilizations as they develop. We may not be living during a time when the time travel that the prophecy indicates can happen, but we can certainly set up the necessary infrastructure that will allow our children to carry out our solemn duty, that of finding the demon child, and killing it."

"How many divisions do you propose we create?" asked one of the other generals.

BarSchmex rose from his seat and walked thoughtfully. While stroking his perfectly manicured beard, he responded "I propose that, other than the Circle of Seven, we create two others. Our body can move its operations south toward the empire of the Egyptians, but another can stay relatively local but move its operations to something that is more on the mainland, such as in Italy. Finally, a third body should be located farther northwest to the lands occupying the western edge of the main continent."

The chairman looked around the room, and it was easy to see that the rest of the generals were in agreement with the proposal. "All those in agreement with BarSchmex's proposal to create two new divisions of our number and move them to new locations say aye."

All did.

"The proposal to create new divisions of our race has been carried by unanimous vote."

After the vote, there was an animated debate as to the logistics and timing of the move. Quite a lot of planning had to go into the pullout from their stronghold here on the island of Thera to the other locations. There also had to be decisions made on exactly who would go into what grouping, who would be the leaders of each group, and how that grouping would maintain communication with the other groupings.

It was decided that each grouping would be equal to the other. While the group that moved to the area of Egypt would maintain the original name of the Circle of Seven, the other groupings of Traxians would have a different name. Owing to the location of where each grouping of Traxians would settle, names were chosen that fit that region.

The group that was to settle on the Italian peninsula decided to call their number, 'The Illuminati' since there were many in that area that seemed to be enjoying a sort of intellectual renaissance. That name was also chosen as an affront to the attitudes of their enemies, the Galimarians, who considered themselves to be so "illuminated".

The group that was to settle on the western edge of the continent chose the name 'The Knights Templar' owing to the culture that was growing in the area that was directly related to religious convictions of the time, and to monarchies that existed in that area.

Eventually all the necessary decisions were made, and all the preparations were completed. Ships set sail for their new homes and eventually the former stronghold on Thera was abandoned.

... just in the nick of time.

Only two weeks after the last Traxian ship sailed for its new stronghold, the volcano that had remained dormant on the island of Thera for hundreds of years suddenly came to devastating life. It had been sending signals to the islands around for decades in the form of regular earthquakes such as the one that had taken the life of Sa'Urri Atlantis years before, however those were nothing compared to the power that was unleashed by the Thera volcano. As if mercifully giving one last warning to the residents living on the island, it's first eruption was comparatively mild, and yet still caused devastation. Those who were astute enough to heed the warning immediately fled, but sadly not all were so perceptive ... or humble. There were some that felt they could ride out anything that would come their way. Those that did flee often wondered later what those steadfast and stubborn men and women might have been thinking when the pyroclastic flows coming from the second and much more devastating eruption caused them to take their last burning and sulfuric breath.

It was only one day after the initial blast from the mountain top that the second eruption occurred. This eruption had enough power behind it to completely destroy the island itself. The sound of the explosion was loud enough to be heard two thousand miles away from the island, but unfortunately the sound wasn't the most dangerous aspect of the eruption. After viciously belching its contents with the most devastating force imaginable, the now empty magma chamber that lay below the island completely imploded and all that was once above the water line was now entombed on the bottom of the sea where the island had once stood.

Unfortunately, the devastation wasn't only limited to the island itself. After the explosion of the volcano occurred the associated tidal surge was then transmitted into the surrounding sea in all directions. Depending on the proximity to the sea, communities in the neighboring islands were subjected to a wall of water more than thirty meters tall. There was no surviving the tsunami and it completely washed away complete civilizations in one afternoon, including the entire Minoan civilization south of Thera on the island of Crete. The devastation to this culture was so complete, that even in the twenty-first century it was next to impossible to know much about it.

About one hundred miles away in the sea community where Docius and Socrates lived, the devastation was just as ruthless. The wall of water that hit the seaside community was a little over forty meters tall, and certainly just as destructive as the tsunami that hit Crete. Fortuitously, Docius and Socrates had left for a trip to Athens to plan out how to pursue the younger man's studies in his chosen line of work. Had they not left, they would most certainly have been swept out to sea, just like the other four thousand three hundred and sixty members of their village had been. When they eventually did return to their home village, or what was left of it, they discovered more devastation as they could ever possibly imagine. A sixty-ton chunk or coral that had been ripped from the sea floor by the tsunami was now decorating the front yard where their house once stood ... a location that was almost a mile from the coast. None of the livestock that Docius once owned was anywhere to be found. No doubt those animals were now serving as food to sea creatures far and wide.

Upon seeing that everything they knew was completely gone, neither Docius or Socrates saw any lingering reason to stay in Vatika where Socrates had grown up, and so both father and son moved permanently to Athens. As it turns out, Socrates became rather good at his chosen line of work. He was quite well known to all those around, but something very interesting happened when he met one of his students named Plato.

CHAPTER 18

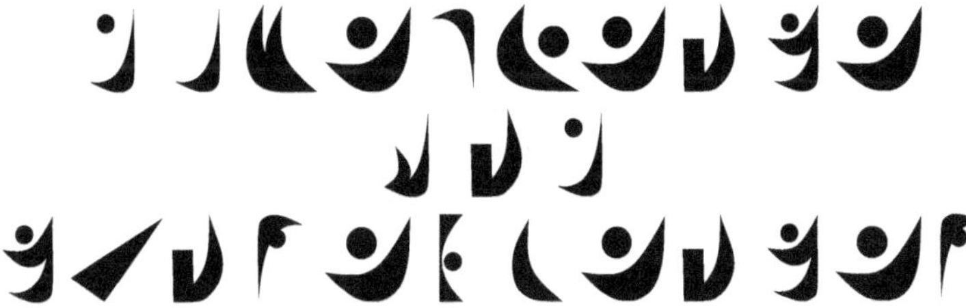

ONE OF THE MORE INTERESTING distinctions of the Roman empire is that, unlike most of the nations and governments that had existed up until that time, Rome had never been defeated in war. With ironlike fortitude, the empire just couldn't be overthrown by any nation that vied for its holdings. Its history began in 27 B.C.E. when Octavian declared himself princeps, or "first citizen," arrogating to himself monarchical powers and essentially ending the de facto power of the Roman Senate and the Roman Republic. It ultimately lasted until A.D. 1453 when the Ottoman Turks conquered Constantinople in what was known as the Byzantine empire, or Rome's eastern half. The western portion of Rome had fallen much earlier in A.D. 476 after a total of 507 years, but regardless of which half you are referring to, the overall roman political engine lasted longer than pretty much any other political entity that had been tried up to that point, or even since.

To say that it was toppled in A.D. 476 or 1453 though doesn't really state the whole story. Many of the political devices and premises that were in place in the roman government stood up to the test of time. Historians are divided about the real reason why Rome was eventually toppled but most agree that instead of being simply subjugated by a stronger nation, Rome actually imploded. Historians widely agree that Rome was indeed like iron, solid and unyielding. What those same historians seem to disagree on though was exactly why it seemed to disintegrate from inside. Some attribute it to the use of lead pipes in their drinking water supply causing overall lead poisoning. Others, such as Will Durant wrote "A great civilization is not conquered from without until it has destroyed itself within. The essential causes of Rome's decline lay in her people, her morals, her class struggle, her failing trade, her bureaucratic despotism, her stifling taxes, her consuming wars."

Regardless of the reason though, the retreat of Rome's rule, and the resulting power vacuum that happened in its place caused societal changes that led to well-known oppression and general suffering among mankind commonly known as the dark ages. While not perfectly marking the end of the one thing and the beginning of another, it is generally felt that the gloomy period of time in human history known as the dark ages finally ended when the Italian renaissance began.

In reality, there were several events that contributed to the ending of the dark ages. While enjoying some victories, the holy wars that had been waged to convert the world to Christianity ultimately failed in their stated goals. Add to that the rise of intellectual philosophy, the black death of 1338 to 1353, and eventually the fall of Constantinople in 1453, mankind was finally able to stretch it arms again and begin a time of discovery and learning. Voyages across the seas led to continued expansion.

What many people don't really understand on a conscious level though is that all along there were those that were pulling at the puppet strings of the world leading to outcomes that were somewhat foreordained. Many seemed to know subconsciously that they weren't in control of the events happening around them, but in an attempt to find a reason for the general feeling of powerlessness, most would turn to philosophies of fate, or the interaction of faceless and fearsome gods who manipulated mankind to satisfy their own maniacal whims. The reality of it though was so much more incredible than any would have believed.

When the Traxian nation diversified into three separate groups, it was agreed that each of those three nations would remain dedicated to their overall goal of finding "Coral of Eden", while at the same time ensuring the survival of their race among the humans of Eden, or "Earth" as the humans liked to call it. The three factions did indeed maintain communication for several hundred years with each other, but as can be expected, cultural differences developed between the three divisions of the Traxian people. Initially this was manifested as disagreements on how exactly they would ensure their respective survival. Again, these differences could be ironed out amicably, but as time marched onward, the differences increased and the ability to find common ground between them decreased. Eventually communications between the three groups ceased entirely, and for a long time this détente arising from non-communication seemed to work for all involved.

In due course though, the divisions in the philosophies of the three groups led to a complete disintegration of détente, and eventually led to an era of strife between them. The original Circle of Seven that had located themselves in Alexandria Egypt concentrated on more intellectual pursuits while waiting for Coral of Eden to appear. The Illuminati located on the Italian peninsula though seemed to lose its focus on looking for Coral of Eden, but rather seemed to concentrate on the gathering of political power through the use of war and politics. It also appeared that the Knights Templar no longer viewed the finding of Coral of Eden of primary importance, but rather it mainly focused its energies on the gaining of wealth and power.

Knowing this was happening to the other two factions, the Circle of Seven began flexing its intellectual might to find a way to force the other two factions back into focusing on the Traxian prophecies about Coral, and the real reason why they all existed. Their research led them to make many discoveries in the areas of physics and chemistry, and so they had been developing plans for an arsenal that would force the other groups to their knees. As you can imagine though, this didn't sit too well with the other two groups once they learned of it, and so those two groups decided something had to be done to shut down the Circle of Seven who had now become a threat to them.

By this time, the Illuminati had positioned itself securely in the politics of Rome, and so functioning under an unusual common goal with the Knights Templar, puppet strings of society were expertly pulled and eventually war was waged across the Mediterranean coastline on down into Egypt. The pharaohs of that time may have thought Rome was marching against them personally, but in reality, the goal was the decimation of the Circle of Seven. Eventually roman armies made it to Alexandria, and "accidentally" set fire to the libraries found there, most of which were the storehouses of all knowledge built up by the Circle of Seven. The attack on the library and the brutal murdering of the members of the Circle of Seven faction almost completely destroyed the very existence of the Circle.

Almost.

This war that had been waged between themselves and the Circle of Seven created a tacit comradery between the other two factions that proved to endure throughout the following centuries. Even as the two other factions were congratulating themselves on their victory against the Circle of Seven while returning to their respective homelands however, two members of the circle that had made it out alive steeled their resolve to rebuild their empire. They eventually did, but it didn't happen in Egypt. It happened in a quiet corner of the globe in North America. Their presence wasn't even known by the other two factions for centuries until eventually it came out into the light of day during the first world war of the twentieth century. Once again, the puppet strings of society had been pulled and mostly for reasons of profiteering on the part of the members of the Illuminati and Knights Templar, the entire world was plunged into World War One. It was indeed profitable to the two groups, but they were completely taken off guard when the Circle of Seven, a group that they both thought they had killed off long ago, rose up again and became the shadow of power behind the winning allied nations. What had been secret among the Traxians was now standing tall in the light of day. The Circle of Seven was once again a force to be reckoned with.

And 'reckon with it,' the other two factions did. It wasn't going to be something that could happen overnight, but surely this entity that had been a historical threat to the other two groups had to be eradicated once again, and this time there couldn't be any trace of it left. While the Circle of Seven maintained its focus on looking for Coral of Eden in honor of its original namesakes, it also maintained an eagle-like focus on its enemies which unfortunately now included those whom they once viewed as their brothers. They knew they had to remember the costly lesson learned in Alexandria and so they constantly watched what the other two were doing, especially as it pertained to the Circle. Using spies to learn of what was happening, two very critical things came to their attention.

First, they learned that the Illuminati and the Knights had determined to destroy the Circle of Seven once and for all. Second, they also learned that the two groups would meet once every year to work on their mutual plans. Plans that were both political, and plans pertaining to the destruction of the Circle.

The Circle learned that the primary method the other two factions were going to use to destroy the Circle was very similar to the approach that was taken way back in 48 C.E. in Alexandria. The two factions would cause political tensions to grow over time amidst the nations of the earth which would lead to world war again. Once world war broke out, they would throw their common resources behind whatever nation that was against North America, and thus cause complete subjugation, and more importantly elimination, of the Circle of Seven once and for all.

What they hadn't counted on though was that the Circle of Seven had anticipated this move and had prepared for it. Referring to themselves as "The One True Circle", they determined in their own hearts that the other two groups had strayed from the original Traxian path, and so they had to be destroyed.

Completely.

The New York subway was originally built around the turn of the twentieth century and it was a marvel of that time. With the metropolis above living life day by day, the subway below their feet seemed to grow over time with a sort of subterranean secrecy. The city above was about to sprint into a building boom that naturally led to an explosion of population such as the city had never seen before. More and more New Yorkers would need a reliable way of quickly moving from one part of the city to another. Workers needed to get to work, mothers and fathers needed to shop for life's necessities and, of course, politicians needed to gain the approval of their voting constituents. The appearance and expansion of the subway system was somewhat foreordained.

Among many other shadowy organizations of the time, the Circle of Seven had eventually decided to settle in New York since it seemed that this location would serve well in its secondary goal of garnering more and more power. Its primary goal of searching for Coral of Eden, though, remained its ever-present primary goal ... unlike that of the other two Traxian factions. Now that its post-Alexandria presence was exposed due to the necessity of its involvement in the first world war, it had to once again watch its back since it knew that the other two factions wished for it to be destroyed. As he rode along on the subway one particular day in the summer of 1936, one of its members, Mr. Manisee, was considering how the Circle of Seven might finally be able to rid itself of this danger once and for all with the knowledge that he carried. As the "six train" he was riding was approaching the end of the line near the Brooklyn Bridge, he looked around and considered how none of the people riding along with him knew who he was, and that suited him just fine. Sitting there in his three-hundred-dollar light grey suit and hat, he knew that he didn't really fit in with the rest of the rabble that normally used the subway, but the underground voyage was nearing its end. Just beyond the bridge, the subway car would turn around and make its way back the other direction, however his stop was just ahead.

This turnaround was the whole reason why Mr. John Manisee was here. The "turnaround" was actually the City Hall station, and unlike the rest of the subway stations on the line, this one was a rather impressive location decorated in a beautiful art deco motif. Opened on October 27, 1904, the city hall station was designed to be the showpiece of the new subway. The platform and mezzanine featured Guastavino tile, skylights, colored glass tilework and brass chandeliers. The Rafael Guastavino-designed station was unique in the system in that it used a Romanesque Revival architecture.

When the subway car stopped at the station, he exited the car and lazily made his way toward the stairs that led to the open area in front of city hall. If there were any other riders on the car, they would have gladly pushed past him in order to get to their respective destinations, however since this was the last car of the evening, the car had only one other occupant and he quickly bounded up the stairs leaving John by himself. Seeing that he was alone now and seeing that the subway car had since moved on, he turned on his heels and made his way to the end of the station platform where a lone door led to maintenance tunnels. Now that the subway tunnels had been in operation for well over fifty years, the appearance of a well-dressed man going through that door may have caused some questions to fly around, but his current solitude in the subway chamber allowed for him to travel along the access tunnels unmolested.

Eventually Mr. Manisee came to a portion of the tunnel where there was basically only enough room for the subway train. In this segment of the tunnel, maintenance workers sometimes needed to do work to maintain the tracks, and in those cases when a subway car came along there were special alcoves dug into the side of the tunnel large enough for a maintenance worker to "fade into the wall" allowing the car to pass without causing injury. Mr. Manisee found one of those alcoves with the identifying number 5980. As he stood in the alcove as if a train was about to pass, he reached up with both hands and pressed on two separate and unremarkable bricks above his head. As soon as he did this, the bricks receded, and the alcove along with the platform where he was standing sunk further into the wall and rotated to the left. Unlike the dark and dingy subway tunnel where he just was, as soon as the platform rotation completed Mr. Manisee now found himself in a very well-lit room that had all the luxurious appointments to which a millionaire like Mr. Manisee had become accustomed.

The floors were all covered in marble tile with art-deco inlaid designs that were similar to the designs in the city hall station. The light was artificial from electric lights however those lights were disguised behind what looked like skylights in the ceiling. The "skylights" were even tinted blue to simulate light from a spring day. The massive fireplace on the far wall was ornately carved from multiple types and colors of marble. The opening for the firebox was flanked by six-foot carvings of Hercules holding up the four-foot-deep mantle above. Oil paintings adorned the walls in various places as did many shelves containing books that were never read. Above, four separate ten-foot by ten-foot crystal chandeliers that were made by the same company that created identical ones for the Waldorf Astoria where Mr. Manisee lived hung down from the twenty-foot-high coffered ceiling, and below, area rugs delineated different seating areas. Greenery was artfully placed around the large room, and the room carried the light scent of orange blossoms.

As he entered, a man in a tuxedo approached, and spoke in an aristocratic tone.

"Good evening, sir. May I take your coat?"

Removing his coat, Mr. Manisee replied “Good evening Ellery. Have the others arrived yet?”

“No sir, you are the first to arrive. Can I get you an aperitif or other refreshment?”

With a distracted affect that showed a desire not to waste time talking to the hired help, he simply replied “My usual”.

“Very good sir. One brandy and a Black Dragon coming right up” replied Ellery, knowing exactly how to cater to the upper-class he serviced.

Mr. Manisee walked over to a seat near the fireplace that was cold at the moment. Normally it was only lit during the winter months when the weather outside was cold, but since this was summer, there was a pleasant display of flowering plants where there would normally be flames. As he sat down, he could see, or rather hear, that another of his constituents had arrived. “Finally,” he thought to himself, “... someone worth talking to.” Next to his seat made of leather and red velvet, a table held the newspapers of the day, and with the brandy and cigar just delivered, John allowed himself to settle in for the few minutes he had before the meeting started.

As time passed, more and more arrivals intruded upon the solitude. As the last one arrived, and after his needs were attended to, Ellery made his way to the east wall of the room and waited with his hands folded behind his back. Almost standing guard at the top of the staircase, he remained steadfast until the bell sounded indicating the meeting was to begin. As soon as it did, he reached down and unclicked one end of a velvet rope, allowing the gentlemen to descend below to the meeting room. The staircase was ornately carved from Carpathian Elm burlwood with green malachite inlays for steps. Descending down the staircase you would then arrive at a room that is appointed much differently than the one above. Ellery would have been startled at the décor of this room, but he knew never to set foot there on pain of death. That was the mistake of his predecessor who was thereafter found floating face down in the Hudson river on Christmas morning last year.

In the center of the room was a massive wood and stone circular table, and in the center of that table was a three-inch-high, 24-four-inch wide bowl containing stones on fire. On the walls were crystal sconces centered in the middle of red and gold tabards hanging from the ceiling.

Embroidered into each tabard was the design of an eagle with angular edges. Its wings were outstretched to either side, and its single eye seemed to look straight through you. Its wings were stretched out on either side of its body, and there were seven outermost feathers on each outstretched wing. The eagle and its outstretched wings appeared to sit on what appeared to be a white half-circle with representations of earths continents.

The six men stood in front of their chairs and simultaneously recited the pledge of the group:

"I swear by oath that I will ever be loyal to the enlightened, and will serve as a brave and obedient soldier, and risk my life for this oath at any time. I give my will, my heart, and my soul to the Circle of Seven. They are my guide for all that I do. If the Circle says I live, then I live. If the Circle says I die, then I die. We are the enlightened ones. We are the Circle of Seven."

They all took their seats.

"Welcome, my brothers, to the monthly meeting of this most sacred bastion of civilization. May we all guide the world around us for the betterment of mankind and may we all have the bravery to make hard choices for the good of our organization."

All spoke up and replied in unison, "Amen."

"As you all know, we have some pivotal things to discuss. First, there are some new developments with the rogue factions." Then raising his arm to point at one of the members present, he then added "There is also a request by Mr. Teppichfresser to discuss."

Looking back down to his notes, he paused and then said "Mr. Manisee, I believe you have information you would like to share with the circle?"

"Yes, I do" responded John. "As you all know, I have several holdings that provide funding to some research and development organizations here in North America. These organizations have been working on developing technology in the areas of what they call high energy physics, and there have been some significant advances in their research. I don't claim to know the intricacies of their science, but what I can say is that it is based on the concept that if you could cause the division of an atom, that division would result in parts of the atom flying toward other atoms causing their division, and so on, and so on. You would then have on your hands a chain reaction that would release an enormous amount of energy. According to the lead scientists, their research has found a basis for power generation that is far beyond anything we have seen in recent memory. Now ... this by itself is remarkable but not very useful to our group, however along with this news, what piqued my interest was that if the power could be harnessed it could lead to battlefield ordinance that is unequaled to anything the world has ever seen. Measurements of the yield of this ordinance is given in terms of how much TNT it would take to equal it, and initially it is felt that one singular bomb could eventually be developed with this science that would equal somewhere over twenty million pounds of TNT."

As expected by Mr. Manisee, each and every member sitting around the circular table reacted identically. Eyes were flung wide open and jaws were slackened. The room was quiet for several seconds.

"How much credence do you feel you can put into this news?" asked one of the members.

"Knowing what I do about the tenacity and integrity of the researchers, I can tell you that I personally feel comfortable with acting on this information appropriately" responded Mr. Manisee.

The female member that seemed to be acting as a coordinator spoke.

"So, what exactly do you feel we should do with this information?"

Having had much more time and opportunity to contemplate the information, Mr. Manisee responded "I have two proposals. First, I propose that we use this information to our benefit in two ways. As had been decided earlier this year, Mr. Teppichfresser was given authorization to steer the political engine of his country toward an aggressive stance resulting in his invasion of some neighboring countries. Austria will be the first to fall, and Poland is scheduled to fall thereafter. Our plans for a new and very lucrative world war are moving forward quite well, however I feel that we need to make sure this technology is developed by the government on this continent, so that our interests can be protected. Now ... since we have decided that the United States and its allies will eventually win this war and that Mr. Teppichfresser will make some key tactical 'blunders'", he used air quotes, "we don't need to concern ourselves with the perceived threat coming from that area. We do however need to concern ourselves with another threat."

"Asia" responded one of the other members.

"Exactly" agreed Mr. Manisee. "As we both know, the Illuminati and the Knights Templar are gearing up for a new aggression toward us with the goal of eliminating our group. We cannot allow this new technology, if it can be developed, to fall into their hands."

"Those groups haven't exactly been the most intelligent" retorted one in the group with a slight guffaw in his voice.

"Perhaps" responded another member, "but I, for one, am not willing to gamble on their possible mental insufficiencies as it pertains to this. I move that we authorize Mr. Manisee to take the necessary steps to develop and create such technology." Then turning to Mr. Manisee, the same member asked "Mr. Manisee, do you have a pro-forma cost analysis on this project?"

"At this time, it is a little hard to determine what that cost will be exactly since we are dealing with technologies that have never been developed before, however it appears that it will be in the low billions of dollars."

"Then this would require national and black ops budgeting" added Mr. Teppichfresser with a noticeable accent.

"Agreed"

Once again, the room was silent for a few seconds, until the coordinator spoke, and said "All in favor of authorizing Mr. Manisee to proceed with arranging for the development of this technology, say aye."

All raised their right hands with eagle tattoos on their wrists evident, and said "Aye!"

"By evident majority" responded the coordinator, "the motion has been passed. Mr. Manisee, you are authorized to take the necessary steps to get this ball rolling. The rest of us will back you up in the various sectors that we control."

"Finally, Mr. Teppichfresser has requested the use of our eagle flag symbol in connection with the political party that he is in charge of ..."

... and that is how the Circle of Seven ensured its continued existence.

Unlike the Circle of Seven that always met in the same location, in the years leading up to World War Two the Illuminati and the Knights Templar had taken to meeting together once a year in different cities throughout the Asian and European continents for the purpose of planning their strategies and methods of toppling the Circle of Seven. When they would meet, the generals of each faction would meet in one city, and their associated supporting staff would correspondingly meet in a different nearby city.

By the time Mr. Manisee had successfully steered history toward the development of the atomic bomb, the two cities where the rogue factions had chosen to meet was Hiroshima and Nagasaki, Japan.

History records that on August 6th, 1945 the first of two wartime nuclear bombs was dropped on Hiroshima, the very city where all generals for the two rogue Traxian factions were meeting. In this one move, and the later eradication of all supporting personnel meeting in Nagasaki, the Circle of Seven instantly positioned themselves as the one lone and remaining group of Traxians on Eden. No longer did they have to sleep with one eye open, anticipating an attack from their "brothers".

Now ... all they needed to think about was finding ... and killing ... Coral.

CHAPTER 19

IT WAS A COLD WEDNESDAY morning in Coloma, California. James woke up that morning like he had most any other morning. As they say, he put his pants on one leg at a time and rushed out the door to finish the job he had been hired for. Being a carpenter, and a good one at that, James was sought after for large projects in the backwoods of the land that only two years later would become the thirty-first state in the union of the United States. Like most people, he had no feeling that this day was going to be different than any other in his life, a day that would prove to define him for the rest of his life.

In that same area, there was a German born man named Johann that had a plan to create a sawmill in the Sierra Nevada mountain range of California. The massive number of trees in the area seemed to tell him that this would be a good place to situate a mill, and so he hired James to build a lumber mill big enough to process enough new lumber to supply the settlements that were beginning to pop up in the area.

This particular day though James, whose full name was James W. Marshall, went to work and at the same time wrote his name in history. After working that morning on the mill, he decided to examine the channel of water just below the mill where it exited. As he looked closer at the channel, he noticed something shiny in the water. Getting closer he picked up some of the rocks that were shiny and, lo and behold, he had discovered gold in "them thar hills". Even though he was responsible enough to complete the mill for Johann, whose last name was Sutter, James knew his life would never be the same.

Fast forward only one year later and those same hills were being flooded by fortune seekers in the great California gold rush of 1849. Many traveled to California from far and wide with dreams of making it big, but most left with empty hands and empty pockets. Nevertheless, the impact of the gold rush on the region was unmistakable, resulting in the creation of many towns that remain to this day.

Sonora, California where Jason and Mikki Marsalis live is one of those towns.

Jason and Mikki had just lived through the most pivotal experience of their respective lives. Up until a few weeks before, Mikki had no idea of what her husband actually did for a living. All she knew was that he was working on some super-secret project for the American government, but for the life of her she couldn't imagine what he would be doing in such a small town that would ever be so secret. Even though she was completely in the dark about the line of work he was in, she was incredibly proud of her husband, nonetheless. He was a good man, and great husband and father. She knew beyond any shadow of doubt that even though she had no idea where he was during the day, he would never stray from her. She had always trusted him with her heart, and she knew that it remained in a safe place.

Contrary to what she thought was possible, her love and respect for her husband took a quantum leap forward in the last few weeks. Just before this last experience with her husband, she had been told by military visitors that Jason had been killed in a massive accident. This was a complete load of rubbish dreamed up by a wicked and power-hungry admiral named Admiral Kenneth Grant Brinstock. The admiral wasn't always such a bad guy, but when terrorists caused the death of his wife Judith, the one and only woman he had ever loved, something in him just seemed to snap and from that day on all he could think about was obtaining retribution against anything that he perceived as a terrorist. Unfortunately, the main place he went wrong is that he began unilaterally deciding who was and who wasn't a terrorist, instead of leaving that to his commander in chief.

Because Jason refused to be intimidated by the admiral, this immediately put Jason on the admirals hit list, which simply meant that as soon as possible Jason had to be eliminated. In the admiral's eyes, Jason was now a clear and present danger to the sovereignty of the United States. The Admiral was too far gone in his hunger for revenge against terrorists to see that the real reason he was acting this way was simply because of the crushing weight of guilt that tormented him every night. Each and every night the admiral would lie in bed and suffer under the pounding agony of wondering whether his estranged wife whom he still deeply loved would be alive today if he had only put more effort into the marriage that had just dissolved. She had gone back to work after the divorce, back to her old job for an army general that worked in the Pentagon. Due to that, she was present on a ship in the Atlantic when a new terrorist organization named Al Jurrab hacked into the electronics of a predator aircraft and caused a hellfire missile to veer off its intended course toward a derelict ship and instead turn toward the ship where Judith was working. The ship itself survived the hit, but sadly the point of impact on the ship was only one deck below where she had been taking dictation from her boss. She never knew what hit her.

The admiral felt like a failure for letting his marriage slip through his fingers. Failure wasn't something that happened very often for the admiral, and so he had no skills in knowing how to handle it. The only way he knew how to deal with it was to go on the offensive, and to him this meant that revenge for Judith's death would only be achieved by the complete destruction of anything that he perceived as a terrorist. To the skewed mind of the admiral, this then led to him deciding that anybody who didn't agree with him was a terrorist, and hence the reason why he decided Jason had to be eliminated.

Ultimately this resulted in a showdown in front of an amazing invention Jason had created along with his longtime compatriot and good friend Dennis Greene. Jason and Dennis used the underwhelming name of "XYZT Portal" for their invention, but notwithstanding the lackluster name, this portal was the single most amazing device ever known to man. It not only had the ability to perform site-to-site transportation as was regularly featured in science fiction television shows, but it also had the incredible ability to transport a person to different places in history. Yes, the portal had the ability to travel in time. To the admiral, this device had to be used for his own purposes which led him to appropriate it, while at the same time marooning Jason seven hundred years back in history. Jason beat him at his own game though and made use of Galimarian suspended animation technology to make it back to his own time.

The showdown in the portal room between the admiral and our intrepid duo eventually led to the admiral getting too close to the portal aperture. The moment the admiral's shoulder accidentally touched the portal field, it surrounded his entire body and Admiral Brinstock was instantly transported to a location over 1,000 meters under the sea and 300 meters from the nearest underwater safe-haven. It wouldn't have mattered if it was only one meter away, though. His body was instantly subjected to over a quarter million pounds per square foot of pressure, and within moments all gasses in his body collapsed. His body basically imploded. His death was instant, and in that moment the world had lost the strange juxtaposition of someone who was a great man, but at the same time also someone who had descended into a psychosis making him a terrible menace to the world.

Mikki played a major role in helping to coordinate the necessary parties prior to that showdown, and to that end she was no longer ignorant about what her husband did for a living. She now had a security clearance that was even higher than those who had been rated as Top Secret. It was three weeks later that Jason and Dennis were able to get the Midway Magnetic facility back up and running, and with the President of the United States at their side, they made the first official contact with beings from another world, beings from the planet of Galimar.

Things were finally starting to get back to normal now that another month had passed. Jason, Mikki, and their son Jace took the time they needed to reconnect after Mikki and Jace were forced to believe for two months that their husband and father had been killed. For quite some time neither Mikki or Jace wanted to let Jason out of their sight, but eventually life returned to normal. They were finally able to move forward with their new "normal" which made for some interesting circumstances. As was their custom, the couple spent the weekend catching up on chores that needed to be done, all while looking forward to the time when, after Jace had gone to bed, they could spend time cuddling on the couch in front of the fireplace watching something on the TV. Tonight, Jason was surfing around the channels when Larry King Live came on in the middle of one of his interviews.

"... telling me that it's a hoax?"

"That is exactly what I am telling you Larry."

"So, what has led you to believe this so much that you felt the need to publish this book?" Larry held up a paperback book entitled "The Pursuit Of Real Truth".

"Well, as you know I've been trained to be an archaeologist, and due to that I have had the opportunity to see a lot of things that many people haven't."

"Ok"

"So, back when I was a graduate student, I had the opportunity to travel to Greece to spend time on an archaeological dig."

"You say this was when you were a graduate student, and so this was in … what year would that be?"

"This was in 1968."

"OK" responded Larry, "So the year was 1968 and you are a wet behind the ears graduate student. What happened next? What happened when you were on this dig?"

"Well, as I said I had this opportunity afforded to me since my grades were so good, and so I went there with my professor to participate on the dig. It was a location near the Parthenon and we went in to remove a lot of detritus that was surrounding the structure since they planned to perform some sort of restoration of what remained of the temple structure."

"OK" replied Larry, "and according to your book you found something."

"That's right."

"And what was that?"

"Well, when we were clearing some of the rubble, I and some of the other students happened to find what looked like the head of a marble statue."

"But it wasn't just a head."

"No, it wasn't. It turned out to be a complete statue of a reclining man on a rectangular marble pedestal. We didn't know who it was at first, but when we translated the inscriptions on the base, it turned out to be that of Xenophon."

"The ancient Greek philosopher and historian."

"That's right."

"OK. So, you found this statue which was a big deal."

"That's right Larry, but that isn't what really caught my attention."

"Ah ... so what DID catch your attention?"

"It's what was inside the pedestal that caught my attention actually. It turns out that the statue of the reclining Xenophon was just a lid to a hollow chamber in the base, and inside we found a parchment manuscript that had survived the centuries since it was sealed in that pedestal."

"OK. So, you found the parchment. Do you still have it or is it in a museum somewhere?"

"No."

"Why?" asked Larry.

"It's because of what that manuscript said."

"And what was that?"

"Well, as you may know, the writings of Xenophon are considered the authority on the life of Socrates, about whom he wrote several books of dialogues such as The Memorabilia, and an Apology of Socrates to the Jury, which recounts the philosopher's trial in 399 BC."

"Right" answered Larry.

"Right ... and so the Greek people consider Xenophon a pivotal figure in their history, right?"

"Agreed ..." replied Larry with a leading tone in his voice.

"OK ... well the manuscript that we found there was apparently written by Xenophon just before he died. And it was the contents of this manuscript that caused the Greek government to seize the manuscript and never let it see the light of day."

As they were watching the story unfold on the television show, Jason and Mikki stole a glance toward each other and smiled. Each of them knew what the other was thinking.

"Are you saying" replied Larry "that the government of Greece is the architect of a coverup about Xenophon?"

"Not just Xenophon Larry, but of Socrates as well."

Larry was starting to show an edge of incredulity in his voice. Gesturing with his open palms, Larry asked "So you are telling me that there is a manuscript somewhere that contains information about Xenophon and Socrates that the Greek government doesn't want us to know?"

"That is exactly what I am telling you Larry."

"What could be so inflationary about that manuscript?" asked Larry. "Wasn't he the best authority on the life of Socrates?"

"He was, or at least I used to think he was."

Larry's eyebrows raised. "You mean he isn't?"

"No."

"And why is that?" asked the seasoned talk show host.

"Because the stories about Socrates are all wrong."

There was a pause to let that last statement sink in. Larry King then asked, "And what leads you to this conclusion?"

"Because that manuscript in that pedestal was an admission by Xenophon that all the histories that he had written about Socrates were all fictional, and that the story that Socrates was put to death with hemlock was a complete fabrication."

Larry sat back in his seat and said, "It was fiction."

"That is correct."

"I assume you did some sort of scientific testing to make sure this document wasn't a hoax?"

"We were just about to, but that was when the Greek government came in and confiscated the manuscript, never letting come us near it since."

Jason put the audio on mute. "Another conspiracy theorist" he said. "They seem to be really scraping the bottom of the barrel for ratings these days."

Mikki laughed. "Seems like it, but that just got me thinking that perhaps you could use your new abilities at work to learn what that manuscript actually said?"

Pursing his lips and nodding, Jason replied "It's possible. I suppose when we have some off time, we might just do that."

Leaning over to her husband, Mikki whispered "Anything is possible for you my superman."

"I'm only superman because I have you standing right next to me, my love."

Mikki smiled and leaned back in her seat while swirling her glass of merlot, she replied "Well ... it's good that you recognize that!"

The two of them laughed quietly so as not to wake up their slumbering son. It was only in the last couple of days that Jace had finally relented in his demands to sleep with his parents. The events of the recent months had taken their toll on the little guy, and it was hard for Jace to be away from either of his parents.

"Actually, my super-husband, I was thinking you might help me with another problem I have."

"Oh? And what might that be, super-wife?"

"In a word?" Mikki paused, "Karen."

"Ah ... you're wondering what to tell her about me being back in the picture after the two of you thought I was dead."

"Exactly" replied Mikki. "I mean ... that girl deserves a gold medal for how she took care of me right after we were told you had been killed. For the entire time leading up to her own wedding, Karen kept an eagle eye on Jace and me. There were times when I was so grief stricken that I literally wondered how I made it to the end of the day."

Jason felt a lot of pain hearing what his precious life mate went through while he was gone. It showed on his face. "I know I've said this before, but I am so sorry you went through that."

Mikki put her finger on his lips and consoled her husband "I know babe, and I know you had no control over it. It's just that ..."

Mikki searched for words as her hand slipped away.

"It's just that Karen did whatever was necessary, and sometimes that included caring for Jace while his mommy didn't have the guts to even get out of bed. Those were the days when Karen would sometimes bring me some tea when I needed something to drink, leave me alone when I needed to be left alone, and even sometimes let me cry myself to sleep on her shoulder. She was the best friend I have ever had, and this whole experience has sealed our friendship forever in gold."

"The thing is ..." Mikki searched again for the right words, "Now that you are back, I have to grapple with the problem of figuring out what to say to Karen to explain how you're suddenly 'back from the dead'".

"... and not compromise national security" added Jason.

"Exactly."

Jason looked over to the fire in the fireplace and so did Mikki. It wasn't a case of them not caring about Karen, but rather of just being busy. For the last several weeks they had just spent their time and attention reconnecting with each other and their son. Now that life was getting back to normal, this problem had to be dealt with. They had to come up with an explanation for Karen that would not only sound convincing, but something that wouldn't compromise the secrets involving where Jason works. It had to be a story that was good enough that Karen would buy into it.

As Jason looked at the fire, he leaned forward, he put down his glass of wine on the coffee table and began to lightly stroke his chin. It was a classic sign that Jason was starting to come up with a plan.

"What?" inquired a grinning Mikki.

Jason looked at Mikki, and with a toothy grin said, "I have an idea."

Being that Mikki had been a little evasive with Karen lately, Karen was beginning to wonder whether the friendship that she thought she had with Mikki was as iron clad as she had assumed. Keep in mind that the last thing she heard from her friend Mikki was that she was off on a whirlwind trip to the wine country in northern California near San Francisco, and that Mikki was with some really cute guy. At the time, Karen was both glad that Mikki was getting back into life, but at the same time she wondered if perhaps Mikki was rebounding a little too soon. In the weeks since then, Mikki had been inexplicably vague when talking about the "cute guy in the wine country" and so it was a little surprising one morning when Mikki called her and asked if she would meet her for lunch that day. She said she wanted tell Karen about some things that had been happening lately and that soon enough she would understand everything. It all sounded very mysterious and secretive to Karen, but when Mikki reaffirmed her love for Karen, Karen agreed.

The two of them agreed to meet at the Sonora Inn, right in the middle of the town of Sonora. The hotel had been there for more than a hundred years, and it had many nice rooms including the presidential suite. There had been at least two presidents that had stayed there at the beginning of the last century, and it was a really nice place. Off the lobby, there was a very fancy restaurant where Mikki waited. Right on time, Karen walked into the restaurant and sat down at a spot near her friend.

“Hey girl!” said Mikki. “I’m so glad you made it!”

Putting her things down and taking a seat, Karen shot back “Hey sweetie! I had to come. You’ve been keeping me in dark about this hunk of a guy you took to the wine country, and so I had to come and see if he’s worth the attentions of my friend!”

“Oh, he is. Trust me.”

“Ummm Hmmm” said Karen with a mock disapproving look on her face. “I’m not so sure.”

Mikki knew that, while Karen was slightly exaggerating her disapproval, still though, there was some truth in jest here. Mikki got a serious look in her face and, putting her hand on top of her friends, said “Honey, I know it’s been hard on you for the last several weeks not knowing what has been going on with me. But let me assure you that I am genuinely happy. Please let me assure you that by the time we finish this conversation, you will be completely satisfied with things.”

With a conciliatory tone to her voice, Karen said “I trust you sweetie. I just ... I just have been so concerned for you lately! When I went on my honeymoon for those two weeks, I left behind someone that looked completely lost. But when I came back, it was like someone had kidnapped my friend!”

“You don’t know how right you are.”

Karen furrowed her brow with concern and said, “Run that past me one more time?”

“Oh, don’t worry. In fact, ...” Mikki looked over at the Maître D’, and with a flick of her index finger, asked for and received his attention.

“My friend and I are going to go to a meeting upstairs for a while. Can you just put my drink on my tab?”

“But of course, madame” came the very refined response. “Is there anything else we can do for you?”

“No, all is good. Thank you very much James.”

“It is my pleasure madame.”

Even though Karen thought the interchange was a little strange, she followed Mikki to the elevator. Stepping into the car, Mikki waved something that looked like a credit card near the controls to the elevator. The doors closed and with no further prompting, it quickly rose upward and promptly settled. When the doors opened it was obvious that the elevator doors opened straight into the penthouse suite.

Karen was speechless.

Mikki stepped off the elevator and walked forward a few feet before she realized that she was alone. Turning around, she saw that Karen hadn’t moved from her spot in the elevator, but rather had a “deer in the headlights” expression about her. Smiling, Mikki then prompted her friend. “Are you going to say in there all day?”

Karen looked down at her feet as if not noticing that she wasn’t moving, but then slowly moved from the elevator car while at the same time gazing around the palatial two-story suite. The best of everything had obviously been put into the penthouse suite, and it was slightly overwhelming to Mikki’s friend.

“Is this guy you met a sheik from the middle east?” asked Karen with large eyes.

Mikki chuckled and replied, “No.” Then reaching out she prompted “Come on in sweetie and have a seat here on the couch.” Mikki took Karen by the elbow from the foyer into the two-story living room. There was a curving staircase to the left of the living room leading to the bedrooms upstairs. Downstairs, there was all the amenities you would expect including an entertainment system, kitchen facilities, and a twelve-person dining room table. To the other side of the living room area was even a pool table.

Sitting down on the couch Mikki let Karen continue to look around but then said, "I know this is a little overwhelming to you, but I invited you up here for a very important reason."

"So you could reveal to me that you are secretly a rich land baroness of northern California?"

"Not exactly" replied Mikki with a smile. "It's because what I have to tell you will come as a shock to you and I didn't want to cause a scene in the restaurant."

Karen stopped her gazing around at the surroundings, and suddenly looked at her friend with a concerned look in her eyes. "Cause a scene?"

"Don't worry hun. It's actually a good thing, but I know that it will come as a pretty big shock to you when you find out the truth about who I went to the wine country with."

"At this point I think I would believe anything you would tell me" answered Karen.

Just then a manly voice came from behind them. "Don't be so sure."

Karen jumped up swirled around at hearing a man behind her. Standing there in front of her ... was Jason.

"OH MY GOD!!!!" shouted Karen as she jumped up from her perch. "YOU'RE DEAD!"

"To quote Mark Twain who used to live near here, 'The reports of my death have been greatly exaggerated.'" responded Jason with a grin.

For a few moments Karen looked back and forth between Jason and Mikki. The two of them had expectant smiles on their faces, but Karen's face was decidedly blanched, and her mouth hung wide open.

Finally, Karen managed to speak. "How ... how ..." then her tone suddenly changed, and she said with a categorically more irritated pitch "You were alive this whole time and you let Mikki think you were dead!?"

The mama bear was coming out.

"Karen, sweetie" injected Mikki before Jason had a chance to defend himself, "I know that it doesn't make any sense, but trust me when I tell you that it was beyond Jason's control."

For what seemed like a few more minutes, Karen continued to look back and forth between the other two. Finally, Mikki rose from her seat and reached out to Karen. "Come have a seat honey so we can tell you what happened."

"This had better be good" Karen threatened. Any softness that was normally characteristic to her voice was now completely gone.

"Oh, it is" replied Jason, "but it's going to be a little hard to believe."

With some additional gentle prodding from Mikki, Karen slowly resumed her place on the couch, and Jason sat down on an opposing chair.

"Ok" said Karen while looking Mikki in the eyes and folding her hands in her lap. "I'm all ears".

Glancing at Jason for a moment, Mikki then said "Well, you know how I told you that Jason had a job with the government and that it was something secret?"

"Yes"

"Well that is all very true" replied Jason. "I can't really tell you the details of it all, but what I can tell you is that there were people who didn't agree with the job that I have with the government, and that against my will, I was ..."

Jason hesitated, but he would have to admit that it was mostly for the dramatic effect.

"You were what?" asked Karen.

Jason looked over to Mikki, then back at Karen.

"... kidnapped."

"You were ... what?"

"You heard him" said Mikki. "Kidnapped."

"From the little town of Sonora" replied Karen. The sarcasm in her voice was obvious.

"I know it's hard to believe, but it's true" replied Jason.

Karen sat there for a about a minute while looking Jason in the eyes. Eventually she looked over to Mikki and said, "And you bought this story? That he is working for some secret government thing, and it's so important that he was kidnapped for two months?"

It was obvious that Karen wasn't buying into the story. She genuinely loved Mikki like a sister, and so this story sounded like it was a complete load of manure, manufactured by a guy who wanted to get away, and couldn't come up with something that actually sounded believable. Karen was beginning to be of the mind that she needed to help Mikki see Jason was trying to brainwash Mikki.

Jason then said, "I can see that you don't believe us, and so I thought I might get a little help from a friend of mine." Then turning to Mikki, he said "Honey, would you go grab our guest?"

Mikki smiled and rose from her place on the couch. Walking over to the room where Jason had just emerged, she entered the doorway. Meanwhile Jason continued speaking to Karen, saying "I had a feeling that you would have a hard time believing the story here and so I invited a friend of mine to come and help explain that this is actually the truth."

"I don't care who you bring in here" said Karen. "This story you seem to have brainwashed Mikki with isn't flying with me, and if I have anything to do with ..."

As she was speaking though, she saw that Jason's attention suddenly focused on the doorway behind Karen, which prompted Karen to look as well. At that moment Mikki emerged from the other room with former President Michaelson and two secret service agents behind them.

Upon seeing the man who had just resigned from his candidacy for a second term as president, Karen immediately stood, and with eyes the size of saucers sputtered her next words.

"Mr. Pres ... I mean Mr. Michaelsssss ... I mean Mr. Former ... I mean ..."

With a chortle, the former president replied "Relax miss. I'm just a good old boy that puts his pants on one leg at a time."

With her mouth still hanging open, Karen tried to utter something intelligent. "I ..."

With a further disarming presence, former president Mr. Michaelson walked over to a chair, and as he was sitting down said "I know that the story my good friend Jason and his wife just shared with you was a little hard to choke down there miss, but let me assure you that I was listening in and everything he just said is 100% true. The details of it all is a matter of national security and so I can't share them with you but suffice to say that Jason here was a very important part of my administration, and he continues to be indispensable to the safety and security of this nation."

Reluctantly, Karen blindly felt around for the seat behind her and sat down while never taking her eyes off of the former president. Partly because the former president had already sat down, but more importantly because her legs were threatening to give out. After some time though, she eventually found her voice.

"S-s-s-so ... this story about being kidnapped ... it's true?"

"Yes maam" replied the former president with his characteristic Texas drawl.

"But why were we told that he had died?" asked Karen, now truly seeking information instead of trying to disprove the story she had been told a few minutes earlier.

"Well, you see now that is the bad part of all this. The person who had the job of making sure Mikki knew that Jason was all right fell down on his job. The long and short of it all is that he sent those men to say he had been killed when he shouldn't have. Let's just say he isn't at his post anymore."

With no other sounds but the light background music that had been filtering in from the stereo in the corner, Karen contemplated what she had been told, and said "I guess I have no other choice than to believe it. It's a little hard to believe, but with the president sitting in front of my face right now telling me that it's all true, then there's no choice but to believe it."

"I know it's tough sweetie, but it's true" consoled Mikki. "For the last several weeks I've been reconnecting to my husband, while at the same time trying to figure out how to tell you what happened. Finally, when Mr. Michaelson agreed to help us here, I knew I had finally found the way to break the news to you."

Nodding her head, Karen answered "I gotta admit, this was a good way to get me to buy into the story." Then turning to Jason, she raised her index finger at him and said with a slight grin "Just don't ever do it again!"

Holding up his hand in a scout's promise and putting his other hand over his heart, he said "I solemnly promise."

Upon hearing that, former president Michaelson slapped his knee and then stood. "Well all right then, it sounds like we have an accord. Uh Jason? Do you mind if I speak to you for a moment in the other room?"

"Of course, sir" replied Jason. The two men and the secret service agents left the ladies in the front room to continue speaking. Eventually they hugged and planned on using the rest of the day reconnecting out on the town. Later they would return to the penthouse suite for a catered dinner.

Meanwhile Jason and the former president adjourned to the other room. Upon shutting the door, Jason said "Thank you Dave for doing that. That was something that was really important to Mikki."

"Don't worry about it, Jason. When I said that I was in your debt, I meant it" replied the former president.

"Yeah, but that was when you were planning on being president for another term."

Looking Jason in the eye and getting a serious tone in his voice, Dave replied "I may have allowed a new president to be elected so that I could be the special envoy to the Galimarians, but the fact remains that what you did for the entire human race as it pertains to that whole thing in Yellowstone ... every man, woman and child on this planet owes you their lives. I mean it when I say ... it was the least I could do."

Slightly blushing at the accolade, Jason simply responded with a sincere "Thank you."

"Not at all" replied Dave. "But actually, I was wondering if you might do me a little favor."

"Of course! What do you need?"

"Well, as you know President Kirken has taken office, and as part of his initial briefings he had been made aware of some things that only the president knows"

"You mean all the stuff in the presidential book of secrets?" asked Jason with a grin.

Laughing at that, Dave replied "I saw that movie too. After that movie, I was thinking I should start one of those. Anyway ... he has received those briefings, but ... I was wondering if you might be able to spare some time over in DC."

"Anything for you my friend" replied Jason, "On the condition that you clue me in on one of those presidential secrets."

"Oh? And what would that be?" responded Dave as he repositioned his cowboy hat with a cheeky grin.

"How did President Kirken get the first and middle name of 'Kai Ernst'?" asked Jason.

Dave gave a half smile, and with his characteristic Texas drawl replied "Well you have to understand that while the president was born here in the good old US of A, his parents were straight off the boat from Germany. When they got here, they were so poor their Sunday supper was fried water, and so they had to work hard to make a good life for themselves. When she figured out that she was gonna have a young'un, they wanted to choose a name that had some meaning. You'll have to verify this with him personally, but as I understand it his mom was going back and forth between naming him something more American like 'James Tiberius', or something with meaning from the old country like 'Kai Ernst'. In the end, 'Kai' won out."

Nodding his head, Jason seemed to have his curiosity satisfied. "James Tiberius huh? Sounds strangely familiar." Then putting on his own manufactured drawl, Jason breathed deep and said: "Well sir ... I reckon we ought'a quit burning daylight and get ta DC!"

With a chuckle, Dave slapped Jason's knee and said: "Now you're talkin my language!"

CHAPTER 20

I F YOU WERE TO ASK Jason about it on any day of the week, Jason would proclaim that the luckiest event in his professional life was the chance encounter when he met Dennis. Doctor Dennis Greene was giving a lecture to a group of physics enthusiasts in Pasadena, California. Located near Jet Propulsion Laboratory, this physics seminar was actually orchestrated by JPL, and fell under the umbrella of what is commonly known as "TED Talks". Jason was in the area anyway on some other business, and so he decided to attend the presentations that night.

Dennis was giving a presentation on string theory and the history of how humans had arrived at their current understanding. To say Jason was impressed with the grasp of particle physics that Dennis possessed would be an understatement, and since Jason was up to his elbows with the project that would eventually become the Midway Magnetic facility, Jason decided he had to try to see if Dennis would be interested.

As it turns out, Dennis had a lot going for him. First, he already had security clearances that were almost up to par with what would be needed at Midway, and so crossing that particular threshold wouldn't be big deal. Secondly, Dennis had just experienced a breakup in his personal life and so transitioning to something completely fresh and new wasn't out of the realm of possibility. But, finally, when Dennis learned that the project Jason was working on involved creating and managing a state-of-the-art particle accelerator, Dennis started looking for a pen and where to sign.

His contributions to the design and building of the Midway Magnetic Particle Accelerator, or MMPA, was indispensable. Many seemed to think that it was Jason's prowess in the theories and designs for the project that got it finished ahead of schedule and on budget. Those were essential for sure, but Jason had no problem making sure all knew that Dennis was a major factor in making the project work.

One of the favorite things Jason and Dennis liked to do was to query each other on the history of science and technology that had been developed in the last several decades. Even now, Dennis was telling Jason about a program he had just watched about the development of guidance systems used on the Apollo rocket program.

"So, what was really interesting" said Dennis, "was that way before the contracts for building the rockets or the space suits or anything else, the first contract that was awarded by NASA was for the development of the guidance system. And that contract wasn't given to a company like IBM like what you might have expected, but rather they awarded it to a university."

"I think I remember reading something about this" said Jason. "I think it was my old alma mater, M.I.T.?"

"Yes, it was actually. It all centered around an engineer named Charles Draper who had just successfully navigated a test bomber from New York to Los Angeles with nothing but an inertial gyroscopic guidance system that was linked into the auto-pilot system. And what makes this system so interesting is that it wasn't computerized. It was completely mechanical!" exclaimed Dennis.

"Wow. Now that's something I didn't know. Mechanical huh?"

"Yep. Pretty interesting stuff."

"I'll say" answered Jason. Then glancing over to the window that looked from his office into the particle accelerator reaction chamber several stories below he said, "Just imagine how impossible our special little project here would be if it weren't for the age of computerization."

"That's easy to imagine. It simply wouldn't have happened."

"True enough" agreed Jason. Then thinking about the night before, Jason then said "By the way, last night Mikki and I were flipping around the channels and I happened to come across Larry King Live where he was interviewing this guy that says everything we know about …"

"… Socrates is a myth!" interrupted Dennis with a slight laugh. "Lynne and I were watching that same show!"

"Oh yeah? I turned it off after a few minutes, but Mikki thought it might be interesting to check out if this guy was full of it, or if he really found something under that statue."

With a slight look of interest, coupled of a bit of ambivalence, Dennis nodded and smirked while he said "Might be interesting. Do we have anything else we need completed before the week is out?"

"Not really. The specifications on the new matter injectors are being reviewed for accuracy, and most of the engineers have gone home for the weekend already."

Taking his feet off the edge of Jason's desk where they had been resting during their discussion, Dennis slapped both knees and said "Well … I'm game. Lead the way doctor!"

Jason smirked and shook his head at the title. "Dennis, the name is Jason?" he said for the millionth time. It was an ongoing joke between them.

The two men left Jason's office and began their trek down to the main reaction chamber where not only the particle redirection technology that was used for what was commonly referred to as the 'Star Wars' system, but also where the secret XYZT portal room was located. To get to the main floor, you had to take an elevator at the end of the hallway that passed in front of both of their offices.

On down the hallway a little farther from their offices was an office that belonged to a secretary that both Jason and Dennis used named Niki. The fact that she was in charge of general clerical duties including copies, mail, etc. shouldn't fool you about her though. Originally from a military background, she had to have top security clearances to even be here and so she was more than qualified for her duties.

As Jason and Dennis passed by her office, Dennis' focus was on the elevator ahead, but Jason just happened to glance into Niki's office and as soon as what he saw registered in his brain, he stopped dead in his tracks, backed up, and looked again through her doorway. Inside Niki sat at her desk, and while she was normally quite well arranged and put together, right now she appeared to be an absolute mess. It was obvious she had been crying, and her mascara was definitely not the kind that stood up to water.

"Niki? What happened?" said Jason with genuine concern in his voice as he entered the room.

Niki looked up and instantly thought to herself that she must look like a complete troll from all the sobbing she had been doing since she got the call. There were tissues in her hand that had seen better days which is why Jason was now offering her a new batch from the dispenser on her desk. By this time, Dennis had realized that he was standing in front of the elevator alone and so had backtracked in search of Jason. He had only just arrived to see the same thing now that had caught Jason's attention.

Throwing away the damp tissues in her hand and accepting Jason's offering, she said "I'm sorry, I know I must look terrible."

"Don't worry about that at all, hun" replied Jason. "What happened?"

Niki tried to say the words that were in her mind, but for a few moments the words seemed to just get caught in her throat and her eyes were threatening to spring yet another leak. Eventually she worked hard at breathing deeply to get some semblance of control over herself. Both Jason and Dennis could see that whatever this was that had upset her, it was something extremely difficult for her and so they both remained silent so she could pull herself together. They were both hoping that someone hadn't died!

Eventually, with a few starts and stops, Niki was able to tell the two men what had her so upset.

"You see" said Niki, "I just received a call from my parents. Remember how Megan went to work for the peace corps?"

"Oh no! Is she OK?" asked Dennis. Megan had worked at the Midway facility at one time and she was a dearly loved friend to all that knew her. While working there, she got her big sister Niki a job after she had been cleared by the background security checks. Eventually, Megan met a guy that was a real tree hugger named Nico, and the two of them decided to work with the peace corps down in South America. That all happened about a year ago.

"She was doing great as far as I knew" answered Niki, "but my dad just told me that last week she contracted yellow fever while she was deep in the Amazon rainforest. It took about a week to get her out to civilization, and by the time they got her to a hospital they told her that she was too sick to be helped!" With those words Niki broke out into another fit of crying. Jason came to her side and placed his hand on her shoulder. "Oh my god" was all that Jason could say. He was beginning to get choked up at the news.

Among several fits and gulps of air, Niki continued "My dad said he found some doctors in San Francisco that could help her, but she's too weak to be moved." Then descending into yet another fit of uncontrolled crying again, she finally blurted out "I don't know what to do!"

Dennis came to one side of her, and Jason put his arm around Niki's shoulders from the other side. Niki had her face covered with her hands and tissues.

For a few minutes, there was nothing either of the men could say to make Niki feel better, in fact, they were feeling pretty bad themselves. Jason looked up, and then looked out Niki's window that also looked into the four-story reaction chamber. His looking that direction caught Dennis' eye as well, and he looked too. After a few moments, Jason turned and looked at Dennis, and Dennis returned the look. The look in their respective eyes told the other that they were thinking exactly the same thing, and with a little nod from Dennis, Jason knew what had to be done.

"Niki, do you know what hospital Megan is in?" Asked Jason.

Looking at a pad of paper where she had written it down, Niki blew her nose and then replied "My dad said she is on a Brazilian navy hospital ship called 'NAsH Soares de Meirelles'. Why?"

Dennis drew in a breath, looked down at the floor and said, "We can't tell you, but we need to ask you to trust us." Then looking back up into Niki's eyes, then asked: "You know Megan is very important to both of us, right?"

"Yeahhhh," said Niki, not having a clue what the two men were thinking.

"Then you need to trust us when we say that we have a plan we can't tell you about, but it is a plan that will help her" added Jason. "Can you do that?"

Niki's eyes darted back and forth between the two men wondering what they were thinking. For a fleeting moment, she thought that maybe the two guys were trying to make light of the situation, but that thought was instantly rejected. She knew better than to think they would be so juvenile at a time like this. For the next five seconds, she thought over how much she respected Jason and Dennis, and so she decided that trust was a foregone conclusion.

"Of course I trust you guys. What are you thinking?"

"Like I said, we can't tell you the details of the plan we have in mind, but there is something that you will need to do, ok?" replied Jason.

"What?" asked a bewildered Niki.

"First ..." asked Dennis, "what hospital in San Francisco is the one that your pop said could help her?"

"It was the infectious diseases wing of the hospital at U.C. Davis in Berkley" answered Niki with a scrunched brow.

"OK. The U.C. Davis hospital. Then what we need you to do is to get in your car and drive to that hospital right now. Make sure you get your parents to meet you there too" said Jason. "We will meet you there in the lobby. OK?"

Once again, Niki's eyes darted back and forth between the two men standing in front of her. They said that they couldn't tell her what they had in mind, which wasn't an unusual thing in this place, but at the same time it seemed that they had in mind something that might help her sister. At this point, she was willing to grasp at whatever straw was offered.

Sitting forward in her seat, she said "You do realize it's a three-hour drive there, and that's on a good day. You're going to meet me there?"

"Yes. That is correct" answered Jason.

For about ten seconds the room was silent once more while she considered the proposal. Finally, she decided that at the very least she should go down to the Bay Area to be with her parents.

"OK guys" replied Niki finally. "I don't know what you have in mind, but I do trust you." Then getting up from her chair and grabbing her purse, she left the office. Jason and Dennis followed her to the elevator and saw her off. As the elevator doors were closing, her eyes were still glued to the two men, wondering what they could possibly have up their sleeves. Her elevator car then began its slow trek to the surface.

Upon seeing the elevator doors close, Jason pressed the elevator button again, but now to go down to the chamber floor. Jason looked at his close friend and said, "Well buddy, I can't think of a better way to use the you-know-what than this."

"You said it" agreed Dennis emphatically. Right about that time a different elevator car arrived, and they eventually made their way to the portal room. After passing the necessary retinal scan and voice-print security protocols to gain access to the portal room, Jason immediately sat at his console to start locating the specific places where they would need to direct the portal. Meanwhile, Dennis sat at his console and began the process of waking up the beast.

By this time, Jason and Dennis had been using the portal long enough to come up with some standard procedures that would end up working out well for each mission. One of those standard procedures was that they would position the portal to a location that was about one hundred feet above the expected elevation of the target location. Once they got a visual on that location, they would then decide where to reposition the portal to achieve their intended goal. In this case, their goal was to locate the room where Megan was located on that hospital ship.

Once the coordinates were successfully locked in by Jason, and once Dennis had brought the cryogenics systems online, the two men reached up and took the USB keys that were hanging from a chain around each of their necks. They put their respective keys into their console, and looking at each other Jason said "Three, Two, One, MARK." The two men turned their keys simultaneously.

With the turn of those keys, several relays engaged and the leviathan behind them began to come to life. Tremendous noise began to come from the power conduits as they successively ramped up to transporting the full complement of 17 trillion volts into the superconducting magnets. The standard fluorescent lights in the room shut off and were replaced with red lights. The two LED readouts above the portal came to life showing the current date/time in the portal room on one LED display, and GPS coordinates and date/time at the location where the portal was pointed on the other LED display.

Behind the scenes, large valves opened allowing a river of liquid helium to make its way to the superconductors. There were hundreds of these superconductors that all had to work in perfect coordination, and today they did just that. Soon enough the ambient temperature of the superconducting magnets reached a temperature that allowed the massive amount of energy to flow through them without generating the heat that would result from any other type of material.

Once the indicators all showed green on Dennis' screen telling him that the supercollider system was online and ready, he gave Jason the thumbs up and said into his intercom headset with his typical Texas drawl "Ready when you are pardner!"

Speaking over the noise, Jason replied "Acknowledged. Commencing proton injection in three, two, one, MARK!"

Jason clicked the "Engage" button on his screen which caused protons from a small hydrogen bottle to be injected into the particle accelerator. Actually, before the hydrogen gas was injected, the molecules had to be stripped of their single electrons first. Once this stripping action was complete, the remaining protons were injected which is when the magnets that had been cooled to -456.3 degrees Fahrenheit took over and guided the particles around and around the thirty-two-mile circular circuit that made up the particle accelerator. With each circuitous journey around the accelerator, the particles gained in speed to the point where they were traveling 0.99997 times the speed of light.

In the case of the portal though, the addition of energy coupled with other factors such as the exotic materials used, the laser frequencies injected, and even the gasses present in the reaction chamber caused a chain reaction to occur causing the portal window to form. The specific ratios of these materials end up dictating not only *where* the portal window was pointed to, but also *when* the portal window represents. Initially the portal window was a baby blue field from the edge to the center, however as soon as the blue field filled in from all sides, the scene one hundred feet above the hospital ship showed itself ... at least that is what it would have showed.

All Jason and Dennis could see was a shoreline and a dock. Dennis looked over at his compadre and wondered if perhaps Jason had made an error in his location calculations. Jason for his part was focused on the field, and it looked like what he saw didn't really surprise him.

"Did we lose something buddy?" asked Dennis.

"I don't think so" answered Jason. "Hang on a second."

Jason went back to his console. He first verified that he was indeed oriented to the correct location that he had intended to visit. Once he figured that out, then he decided to back up in altitude to a location that was approximately one thousand five hundred meters above sea level. As soon as he did that, it was obvious what had happened. About ten minutes out from the dock was the hospital ship. Apparently, the captain of the ship had decided to weigh anchor and make turns for a new port. From the look of things, they had just got underway.

"Looks like we just missed the boat ... literally" said Jason. Dennis smiled at the double entendre, but then said, "How bout we roll things back a few?"

"Sounds good. I'll set it for, sayyyy .... two hours ago."

"Sounds about right." Answered Dennis.

Jason retreated from standing near the portal and returned to his workstation. With several keystrokes and mouse clicks, the image in the portal fizzled and was instantly replaced with the same scene of the dock that the two of them had just seen earlier. The difference now though was that the hospital ship now appeared to be docked. Over the next ten minutes, Jason and Dennis used their respective consoles to cruise around the ship and eventually locate the room where Megan was located. There in her room was Megan and her husband, Nico. He was sitting at her bedside holding her hand, but Megan didn't appear to even know he was there. It seemed like she might have been in a stupor. The room was kept dark because she was apparently sensitive to light, and she was holding her stomach with her other hand as if she was in a lot of pain, and by the grimace on her face, it appeared that not only her stomach was in pain, but she looked like she had a serious fever. Just about then, Nico rose from his perch near his wife and left for the bathroom.

"OK partner, it looks like we have the right place. So, what's the plan?" asked Dennis.

"I don't know, I'm just making this up as I go" answered Jason. With that, Jason stepped into the portal and was instantly transported to Megan's room.

From Nico's perspective, the room was completely quiet. He had been informed by the nurse that the captain had just given the order to prepare for sail, and so it sounded like the engines and other mechanical devices on the ship were getting ready for that, but mostly things were quiet. All Nico could hear was the beep-beep-beep of the monitors hooked up to Megan. Listening to the sound was a bit hypnotizing, but to Nico, anything was better than hearing Megan's mom crying on the phone. He had called her and Megan's father about two hours ago to tell them about what had happened. It was only now that he was on the ship that he had been able to make the call. Before this, they had just been too deep in the forest, and there was no ability to make a telephone call. They had been traveling as fast as they could along the Amazon to get to civilization, but Megan's condition continued to get worse along the way. Three days ago, she was barely able to walk onto the boat to come to civilization. Now she was chilling and feverish, and the limited medical resources on this hospital boat didn't provide much hope for the love of his life.

Nico was just about to drift off to some much-needed sleep, but then he decided to get up and splash some water on his face in the restroom just off the hospital room. Leaving Megan's side for a moment and then closing the door to the restroom, it was at that exact moment when suddenly what appeared as rays of light started to shine near the wall opposite Megan's bed. Megan was in no condition to even register that the room was now filled with light, but as soon as the light appeared it stopped and now standing near Megan's bed was Jason. Hearing a noise from the room, the door to the restroom opened, and Nico was surprised to see Megan's old boss Jason standing there.

"Jason?"

Jason turned around. "Hello, Nico. What's her condition?"

Taking a few steps toward her bed, and while still wondering what he was doing here, he answered "She's not doing too good right now. Normally there's medicine that can pull her through this, but this ship is out of it, and they don't think they're going to get more until next week. According to the doctor here, that's going to be too late."

Megan couldn't hear what they were saying of course, but Nico was still whispering it anyway. Periodically she would moan and say nonsensical things that only her feverish brain would understand. The situation looked dire.

"What are you doing here?" asked a very puzzled Nico.

"I'm here to help Megan and get her to the help she needs" answered Jason.

"How can you do that?"

"That's the problem. The answer to that is a national secret, but what I can tell you is that she will get the help she needs in the next few minutes."

Shaking his head back and forth slowly, a very mystified Nico said: "But ..."

"I know that it doesn't make much sense, but for the sake of your wife's life, I'm asking you to trust me" continued Jason. "Can you do that for me?"

Nico looked at Jason for several minutes, until finally looking at Megan who at that moment clutched her stomach again, and with a sorrowful moan showed a terrible grimace on her face. Looking back at Jason whose eyes had never left Nico, he said "OK. What do I have to do?"

"This isn't going to make much sense" answered Jason, "but I need you to put on a blindfold."

"A blindfold?" asked Nico with a surprised tone.

"Yes. A blindfold. Remember ... I need you to trust me."

Reaching over to some cabinets nearby, Jason opened a few until he happened upon one that contained some pillowcases. He grabbed one and handed it to Nico. "Here ... tie this around your head, and make sure you can't see anything."

"But what about ..."

"Nico!" interrupted Jason. "We don't have time to argue! Megan is in bad shape, and she needs the help that only I can give her. Hurry!"

Seeing that he had no options, Nico nodded his head and reached up to tie the pillowcase around his head. Creating a knot behind his head, the blindfold appeared secure, but just in case, Jason reached up and pulled on the tails of the knot to make double sure. Turning Nico around he peered up underneath the blindfold, pulling down the fabric a little to make sure he couldn't see anything. When he was satisfied, he then looked over to where he knew the portal was and where he knew Dennis was still watching. Putting his finger over his lips indicating 'quiet', he motioned for Dennis to come. Within a few seconds, Dennis appeared in the room in much the same way Jason had a few minutes before.

Fortunately, the only things that Megan had hooked to her were the EKG monitor and an IV. Unhooking the EKG leads and removing the IV bag from the hook, Jason reached down and picked up Megan from the bed and positioned her on the side of the bed. With Jason on one side and Dennis on the other, the two men carried Megan toward the invisible portal aperture. Passing near Nico, Jason said "Nico, put your hand on my shoulder and walk with me. DO NOT remove that blindfold."

Nico reached out and found a shoulder near him. He could also feel the clammy and fevered skin of his wife's arm around Jason's shoulder as Jason supported Megan's weight around his neck. Slowly but surely the four of them made their way to the portal. As soon as they got near enough, the portal field grabbed the four bodies and instantly transported them to a very noisy portal room.

"What's going on?" said a very startled Nico. He took his hand off of Jason's shoulder and started moving it toward his head when Jason grabbed his hand. "I said ... DO NOT take off that blindfold. Trust me!"

"Ok! Ok!" replied an unsure but irritated Nico.

The two men carrying Megan maneuvered her to a soft chair nearby. Her eyes were still closed, and it was doubtful she had any idea what was going on. Her head lolled to one side, and it was clear that she was drifting in and out of consciousness.

As soon as he was free of carrying Megan, Jason immediately moved to his console and disconnected the portal from the hospital ship. As quickly as possible, he reoriented the portal control to the hospital in Berkley. Previously, when Dennis was busy getting the cryogenics systems online, Jason not only determined where the hospital ship was, but he also figured out the perfect place in the bay area hospital where they could take Megan. It turns out the hospital was remodeling one of its floors, and so there were a large number of rooms where they could suddenly appear with Megan without causing any surprise. Once Jason entered those coordinates, he engaged the system, and within a few seconds, the scene of an unused hospital room appeared.

Getting up from his workstation, Jason walked over to Nico and said "OK bud. We're going to do this one more time. Got it?"

Nervously, Nico nodded his head and replied, "Got it."

Jason and Dennis picked up Megan again and walked over near Nico. Nico put his hand on Jason's shoulder like before, and once again the four walked through the portal and now into a suddenly quiet and unused hospital room that was obviously in the middle of some sort of construction. The sound of distant construction workers could be heard in amongst the sound of saws and other tools.

There was a gurney nearby that was covered with plastic sheeting, and so ripping off the plastic, Jason and Dennis carefully placed Megan on it. As soon as he laid Megan down on the gurney, Dennis flashed a salute to Jason and stepped back through the portal to return back to Midway. When he saw his friend disappear from the room, Jason looked over to Nico and said, "You can take the blindfold off now." Reaching up, Nico did so and looked around while blinking his eyes. To say he was both floored and disoriented at what he now saw would have been an understatement.

"Where are we? What happened?" Then seeing Megan lying on a gurney, he said "How did we get here? Where is ... HERE?"

"To answer your first question, we are at the infectious disease's unit of the hospital at U.C. Davis, in Berkley California. As far as your other questions, I can't tell you because as I said before, it is a national secret."

"But ..."

"Do you want to sit around all day and talk about it" interrupted Jason with an urgent tone, "or do you want to get your wife some help?"

It only took about three seconds for Nico to realize the more important issues at hand, and so he immediately came to his wife's side and helped roll the gurney toward the elevator. It actually caused a little consternation on the part of some construction workers who were taking a well-deserved break near the room, only to see people emerging from a room that they knew had no people in it moments before. They sat there with sandwiches in their hands and mouths hanging open as two men pushed along a woman on a gurney in front of them.

Riding the elevator down to the proper floor, Megan was rolled into the emergency room, and within an hour was soon responding to the help she desperately needed. Jason remained in the waiting room waiting for word on her condition, and in fact, was talking with the doctor when Niki and her parents walked into the lobby. Niki had eyes the size of saucers and said: "How did you get ..."

Jason interrupted Niki and said "Doctor, this is Megan's parents and her sister. Can you please repeat what you were telling me?"

"Of course." Then looking at the new arrivals, he said, "My name is Doctor Adrian, and I am the physician on duty handling your daughters' case."

"Her case? How can you be handling her case when she is ..."

"I'm sorry doctor," interrupted Jason, "They don't know that I just delivered Megan here and that she has already been receiving care."

"WHAT?!" exclaimed Niki. "How can that possibly be?"

"Regardless of how she got here" answered Doctor Adrian, "she is a very lucky girl. Had Mr. Marsalis brought her in any later, I'm not too sure we would have been able to help her, but with the treatment that she is now getting, her numbers are starting to improve. Her husband is in there with her now."

"Nico is here too?" asked a still bewildered Niki.

"Yes, he is" answered the doctor.

"Doctor Adrian, I don't know what to say" said Megan's mother with a definite cry to her voice. "How could I ever thank you!"

"You can start by calling me Dan" replied the doctor in his typical disarming manner. As he began leading Megan's parents and sister down the hallway, Jason remained in the lobby and watched the four of them disappear behind a doorway. Being so mentally overloaded, not one of them stopped for even a moment to look back at Jason with an appreciative smile. That was all right with him though. A small smile appeared on his face as he reached for his cell phone, and dialing the direct line to the portal room Dennis picked up after the first ring.

"Midway Ambulance Service. If they're dyin, we're flyin!"

Letting out a laugh loud enough to show the underlying adrenalin that had been building up in his system, Jason replied "Thanks, buddy. I needed that!"

Laughing himself, he responded "Glad to hear I could help! How's she doing?" asked Dennis.

"Better, according to the doc. Niki and her parents just got here, and they just went into her room."

"REALLY glad to hear it!" exclaimed Dennis with a definite sigh. "I'll bet you had to do some dancing around the subject on how you and Megan got there."

"A little, but I'm afraid there's going to have to be some more dancing when Niki shows up for work again."

"I'm sure we'll figure something out pardner" replied Dennis.

"I'm sure we will, but right now" Jason paused while looking around, then said quietly "I kind of need a ride."

"I gotcha already covered bud. If you look to your right, you'll see the hospital chapel. The portal is active right behind the altar. As soon as the coast is clear, just dip behind the altar, and you'll go for that ride."

Smiling, Jason responded "Very clever my friend! I'll see you soon."

Jason said his goodbyes and hung up the phone. Casually, he walked over to the chapel and entered like anybody else who may have been waiting to hear how their loved one was doing. Already in the chapel was one elderly lady who was just now walking up the aisle to exit, having already lit a candle alongside her prayers. Only a moment later Jason was alone, and so he walked up to the altar. Turning around once again, he could see there was nobody there, and so he took one step to the right and instantly disappeared.

Within a moment, he was once again in the noisy portal room, where he walked over to his console and took the steps necessary to shut down the portal. It took about a full minute to receive notice from all sensors that the system had been successfully shut down and the liquid helium had been pumped back into the massive underground storage tanks. Once again, the room was quiet, and the boys looked at each other with a look of self-satisfaction for a job well done.

"Well old chum, we may not have saved the whole world today, but I'll settle for saving lives one at a time" said Dennis.

"Agreed. I can't wait until I get home to tell Mikki all about this." Then after a short pause, Jason added "You know ... I sure am happy that I can share all this stuff with her now. Now it feels like I can share the other half of my life with my wife.

"I know what you mean. Lynne and I are getting along really good nowadays, and it helps that she is privy to the top-secret projects we are working on here too" agreed Dennis.

"Yep, but I gotta tell you, I am pretty tired out" conceded Jason.

"Same here. That was a lot of work" agreed Dennis.

"Yep. Worth it. But a lot of work."

The two men rose from their workstations turned out the lights and eventually made their way back to Jason's office. Getting there, Jason pulled out a couple of beers from his refrigerator and handed one to his friend. As he did, something occurred to Dennis about the humanitarian gesture they just did. "You know," said Dennis just before took a long pull from his bottle, "I was just thinking about how maybe that whole thing we just did might be done a little more efficiently. What would say if we could've done that without bringing them here to Midway?"

Jason scrunched his eyebrows and said, "I'm listening."

"Well, I was thinking that a lot of the bother with that whole thing we just did was that we had to bring them back here first, shut down the portal. Reorient the portal to the new location, fire it back up, and then go right back through, right?"

"Yep" answered Jason.

"Well, what if we made two of them?"

"Two of what?" asked Jason.

"Two portals" answered Dennis. "Two of them that sat face to face. Like in today's exercise, one could have been set to the room where Megan was, and the other could be set to the hospital in Berkley. That way, we could transport a person straight from one place to another without having to come here first."

Jason stood and strolled over to the window of his office that looked out to the supercollider detector room. Looking out the window, Jason said "You know that ain't a half bad idea. Technically they would come here for a millisecond before they were instantly transported to the target location, but it sure would make things a lot simpler."

"Sure would" agreed Dennis. "And if we wanted to take a one-way trip, we could still do it by just running one of the portals."

Jason looked over to Dennis and smiled. "Sounds like we have a new wrinkle for the new portal we're building."

Dennis smiled as well. Then he said, "You know buddy … that one we're building on New Galimar is shaping up to be pretty amazing!"

CHAPTER 21

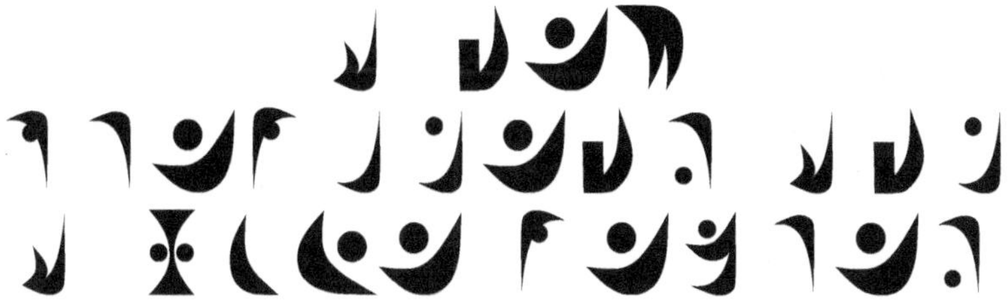

The Kimpton Hotel Monaco in Washington DC could certainly be considered one of the fancier hotels in the greater Washington DC area. Jason had purposely arrived the day before since he wanted to be fresh for his meeting the following day, and so after checking into his sumptuous room and spending an evening in the center of blissful elegance, he decided to get up early in the morning and set out on foot to take in some of the sights.

Walking down Seventh Street and just past the National Archives building where he was able to see the Declaration of Independence, the Constitution of the United States, and the Bill of Rights, he then proceeded onward to the Smithsonian campus. He knew that there was far too much to see at the Smithsonian to begin a tour today, and since he wanted to take his son here too, he decided to take in the beautiful gardens there as he slowly made his way west. Behind him to the east was the United States Capitol building just on the other side of the U.S. Botanical Gardens, and ahead of him was the unmissable Washington Monument. Just past the Monument was the World War Two memorial, and beyond that was the Lincoln Memorial and Reflecting Pool. To the south was the United States Holocaust Memorial Museum.

It didn't take Jason long to feel a little overwhelmed at all the history that was represented in just this small slice of Americana. As he turned northward in his trek, he resolved in his heart that he would have to take Mikki and Jace back here to see the sights at the nation's capital. It would be an amazing learning experience for Jace, and Jason would see to it that they would have all the time they would need to see it all. It occurred to Jason that it would probably take at least a week, if not more.

Progressing at a leisurely pace, he turned northward. Crossing over constitution avenue and passing the Haupt fountains, Jason encountered the ellipse at the Presidents Park. Originally used as corrals for horses, mules, and cattle during the American Civil War, it was later landscaped by the U.S. Army Corps of Engineers and turned into the open and spacy park that it is today. There is a walkway that borders the park ellipse, and Jason strolled around the park until he arrived at the destination where he eventually needed to be. There in front of him at the address of 1600 Pennsylvania Avenue was the most recognizable house in all of the world. The Whitehouse.

It was only about a week ago that former president Michaelson had taken Jason aside in the penthouse suite of the Sonora Inn and asked Jason to be present at a briefing that he had arranged for the new president that had just been sworn in the prior month. As could be expected, President Kirken had a very busy schedule, and it took this long for an opening to appear. Wisely Mr. Michaelson, who had taken on responsibilities that the new president hadn't been briefed about, asked for the last appointment of the day. The appointment called for a time slice of fifteen minutes, but with the meeting having been scheduled at the end of the day, the president would have the latitude to extend the meeting as he saw fit.

No doubt he would.

Jason walked up to the guard shack and the guard eyed him with suspicion like he did any other person approaching the shack.

“Can I help you?” asked the guard.

“Yes. I have an appointment with President Kirken” replied a very unassertive Jason. He had decided to dress unassumingly today in tan slacks and a white shirt. There was a slight chill in the air and so he had a sweater, but it was draped over Jason’s wrist while Jason’s hands were in his pockets.

“Uh huh. An appointment with the president” said an unconvinced guard. “And who shall I say is calling?” The sarcasm was obvious. Inside, Jason was eating this up and was having a terrible time holding in the laughter because he knew what was just around the corner.

“My name is Jason Marsalis” said Jason very calmly.

“Do you have some identification Mr. Jason Marsalis?” replied the Guard with a syrupy tone.

As if he hadn’t thought about it up to that point, Jason responded “Oh! Sure!” Jason pulled his hand from his right front pocket and his identification was already in his hand. “What a coincidence! I happen to have it right here!” said Jason with his own syrupy smile. Jason thought to himself how this was way too much fun.

The guard took the ID from Jason, looked it over, looked at Jason’s face again, then retreated into to the shack to make a call. Jason unassumingly retreated a few steps and made like he was taking in the architecture of the granite columns that made up the driveway entrance where he was standing. About thirty seconds later, Jason could see movement out of the corner of his eye, and when he turned that direction, he could now see the same guard who now had a decidedly different demeanor.

"Mr. Marsalis?"

Jason smiled. "Yes?"

"I've been ordered to accompany you to the president's office. Will you be so kind as to follow me?" The guard seemed to stand a little taller, and yet his skin seemed a tad more pale.

Still with the same smile on his face, Jason accepted back his ID and simply replied "After you."

With that, the gates opened, and as he passed the guard shack, the remaining two guards in the shack seemed to watch Jason as he passed by. The looks on their faces seemed to indicate that they had collectively been chastised for delaying Jason from his meeting with the president. One of them even seemed to be primarily breathing through his mouth.

The two men walked up the driveway. Jutting out from the Whitehouse was a half-circle protuberance from the main structure, and just below that architectural feature was an unobtrusive doorway with a white awning. Upon entry through the doorway, Jason came upon the diplomatic reception room and eventually on to the center hall. After making his way through a menagerie of hallways and corridors, the guard eventually arrived at a room where several ladies had desks. This actually wasn't the first time Jason had been here, and so he immediately recognized the room to be where the President's secretaries did their work. At the end of the room, a man in a black suit with the commensurate earpiece with a curly wire was standing just outside of the door leading to the Oval Office. Looking at him, Jason looked away but then had to take a double take. Walking up to him, Jason smiled.

"Well if it isn't agent Lockwood! I almost didn't recognize you."

Agent Lockwood who had been on Air Force One when he and Dennis had come here last time smiled back at Jason.

"Well if it isn't Snuggle Bug himself!" replied the agent.

Instantly, Jason was reminded of how agent Lockwood had ribbed Jason after having monitored the phone call Jason made to Mikki from the presidential airplane. As with last time, Jason instantly flashed a crimson blush, only amplified by the snickers coming from the secretarial pool.

"All right already! I can't help it if my wife has her own pet names for me!" smiled Jason as he was suddenly off his game. Fortunately, one of the secretaries behind him decided to rescue the flailing Jason by saying "The president will see you now Mr. Marsalis."

Instantly regaining his air of professionalism, Agent Lockwood spoke into his wrist.

"Eagle is plus one." He then opened the door behind him and motioned for Jason to walk in.

Seated on one of the two couches was the former president, and of course President Kirken was emerging from behind the resolute desk. President Kirken was the first to speak.

"Doctor Marsalis!" greeted President Kirken, "It's good to meet someone who I am told is one of our national resources."

"Thank you, Mr. President" replied Jason. "It's an honor to be here." Then turning to the former president, he added "It's good to see you as well Mr. Michaelson."

"It's good to see you as well Jason, but don't forget what I said about calling me Dave when it's just us boys."

"Yes sir … Uh … I mean Dave" said Jason with a slight chuckle.

"Please have a seat Jason. Can I get you something to drink?" asked the president.

"I would like that, sir. Perhaps some cold water?"

The president reached to his phone, and after pressing a key, received a tone. "Yes sir?" came the smart greeting.

"Susan, would you please bring in a few refreshments for my guests including some cold water?"

"Right away sir" came the prompt reply. With the president taking his seat in a chair that faced the fireplace and that sat at the end of the two facing couches, Jason proceeded to seat himself on the couch that was facing former president Michaelson. The setting was very informal and in fact the president had already taken off his suit coat.

Deciding not to get into too much detail until the refreshments had been served, President Kirken proceeded to ask Jason about where he was staying and whether he found it to be to his liking. Jason described the luxurious accommodations and then regaled the two men on his walk about town and what he had seen. He also told them about the fun he had at the expense of the guards at the guard shack. That garnered a laugh or two from the other men. About that time, the drinks arrived along with a selection of crackers, meats and cheeses that all three men tore into since they all happened to have skipped lunch that day. Once the doors were closed, the president then leaned over to his desk and pressed another button on the phone. This button was wired not only to the secretarial pool, but also to the main office of the secret service. When it was pressed, all necessary parties were basically notified that the president was in a top-secret meeting and unless the United States was about to be attacked in a nuclear war, he was NOT to be disturbed.

"So, Jason" said the president as he returned to his seat from having pressed the button, "Dave here tells me that you have information that is far more sensitive than all the top-secret briefings that I've already received up to this point." Then glancing over to the former president, he then said, "In fact, he also told me that it wouldn't be until this meeting that I would even learn about what his new job is."

"That was probably a good idea Mr. President, because I'm sure you've been inundated with all the duties that are required from a new president. I assume it has been a little overwhelming perhaps?"

"To say the least" agreed President Kirken. "My days have been scheduled down to the minute, and I regularly go home and just take a nap before I am even ready to spend the evening with my wife and daughter."

"Well, then I certainly don't want to keep you too long from your family obligations sir, but as Dave did indicate we have quite a story to tell you about something that happened a few months ago. It's a story about how close the earth came to being completely destroyed."

The new president scrunched his eyes together and dipped his eyes slightly. "Run that past me one more time?"

"It's true Mr. President" said his predecessor. "The entire human race came darn near buying the farm, and if it wasn't for this guy right here" he pointed to Jason, "we would have all been worm food right now."

"Well I don't ..." said Jason, who was then interrupted by Dave.

"Don't even start the whole humility thing, my boy. Unlike most on the hill here, I don't throw around a lot of bull. I call it as I see it, and that's the way I see it."

Jason thought about how he was in a meeting with two of the most powerful men in the human world, and so in a sign of acquiescence, Jason closed his mouth, slowly blinked his eyes and folded his hands. The message was transmitted and received clearly.

"OK. So, I get it. Jason is Captain America. You mind explaining exactly how he was able to do all this?" asked the president.

Jason looked over at Mr. Michaelson, who in turn made a motion with his open palm to Jason to begin talking.

"Well, you see Mr. President, I am the current lead scientist for an ultra-secret installation in the Sierra Nevada mountain range called Midway Magnetic. The main purpose of the facility is to ..."

... and with that, Jason proceeded to go into detail about the missile defense technology that is the primary purpose of the installation. He began with the history of the "Star Wars" proposals, also known as the Strategic Defense Initiative, that then-president Reagan proposed, and how it was a proposed missile defense system intended to protect the United States from attack by intercontinental ballistic missiles. Jason talked about how in 1987, the American Physical Society concluded that the technologies being considered were decades away from being ready for use, and at least another decade of research was required to know whether such a system was even possible, let alone practical. Jason then talked about how those particular conclusions were actually a ruse published by the Whitehouse because of several advancements that had come to light that made the whole system possible.

"I'd like to add" said the former president, "that those advancements were ones that Jason here came up with."

President Kirken looked over to Jason and said, "Is that true?"

Feeling like the spotlight on him was getting brighter and brighter, Jason had to once again concede and nod his head.

The new president wiped his mouth with a napkin, set his plate down and sat back in his chair. "Please proceed, Dr. Marsalis."

Clearing his throat once again, Jason discussed how the project got started in northern California, and how a chance encounter with Doctor Dennis Greene was a godsend to the project. He talked about how between the two of them, they successfully tested the missile deterrence system on a UGM-133A Trident II submarine-launched ballistic missile that had been launched from the USS Kentucky off the coast of Guam. He talked about how the system successfully neutralized the missile before it even had a chance to get near Hawaii, let alone get to its intended target which was a fictional city somewhere in the middle of South Dakota.

"So, what you are saying is that the United States, and specifically the office of the president, has the ability to neutralize any missile that is launched against it?" asked President Kirken.

"That is correct sir" answered Jason. "Have you been familiarized with the football yet?"

"The Presidential Emergency Satchel that goes with me everywhere I go in case I decide to drop a nuke on Saddam? Sure."

"Well you may have noticed that most of your briefing concerned details on only one side of the briefcase and not the other?" asked Jason.

"Yep. I just figured the other side contained paperwork" responded President Kirken.

"Well, the other side of the case contains the controls to the missile deterrence system I just described" answered Jason.

The president tilted his head back slightly while not taking his eyes off of Jason. After about ten seconds of contemplation, he then said "Well, gentlemen, it appears that I now understand why you saved the best for last today."

"Oh, we've only just got started here Mr. President" replied Dave.

"There's more?" asked President Kirken.

"Very much so, Mr. President. You see ..."

Jason continued to go into the history behind how he and Dennis got to talking one day about several fields of science, and how the more they analyzed the technologies, the more they became convinced that they might be able to create a system that would give them the ability to transport matter from one place to another. Once he said all that, Jason then stopped speaking to allow what he just said to sink in.

The president stared at Jason for a few minutes with a quizzical look, and then said "When I was in college, my science professor and I talked about this because I've always been a huge science fiction fan. We were talking about the transporters that they always showed on TV, and that is when he outlined to me exactly why that type of technology isn't possible. I'm sorry Doctor Marsalis, but I'm quite convinced that it isn't possible to do that."

Dave smiled, and so did Jason. These smiles didn't escape President Kirken's notice, but when Jason looked over to the fireplace and said "OK Dennis. Come on in.", the president thought Jason had basically lost his mind.

Just then, what appeared as rays of light started to shine near the fireplace directly across from the president. Standing up quickly, President Kirken was just about to call for the Secret Service to come running when suddenly Dennis appeared in the middle of the light rays. As soon as his body completely materialized, which only took about a second, the light rays stopped and a new visitor with a rather large smile on his face stood before the president.

President Kirken had to reach out for the back of his chair to steady himself. He was speechless, and when he looked over to the former president, Dave simply said with a chuckle while shaking his head "I know! It blew me away too when I saw it happen the first time."

"Mr. President" said Jason, "This is my fellow physicist and close friend, Doctor Dennis Greene. Dennis, this is President Kirken."

"I'm very pleased to meet you Mr. President" said Dennis.

Seeing that both Dave and Jason were grinning like Cheshire cats, the president once again gained his bearing and stepped around his chair to approach Dennis. "Doctor Greene, I am pleased to meet you as well." Then looking back and forth between Jason and Dennis, he asked "What just happened here?"

"Well sir" replied Dennis, "I was just in our laboratory, and I was waiting for the right time to come over. It wasn't until Jason said to come in that I ..."

"Wait a minute!" interrupted the president. "You've been watching the meeting? THIS meeting? From your laboratory?" asked President Kirken. He then added after a slight pause, "... In California?"

“Yes sir” answered Jason. “The portal technology that I was describing is completely operational.”

“... and then some.” Added former president Michaelson as he was rolling his eyes.

There was a pause by all in the Oval Office to allow the incoming president time to wrap his head around the new information he had just been given. Outside the Oval Office in the secretarial anteroom, the scene was quiet and there was no sense among the secretaries that a veritable earthquake was taking place in the mind of their commander in chief. The doors to the Oval Office were soundproof of course, which was a good thing based on the current elevated volume of President Kirken.

The president decided that now was likely a prudent time to take his seat once again. Like his predecessor, he wasn’t usually one to have a hard time finding the right words to say, but this occasion was far beyond anything he had ever been called upon to digest. As he sat down once again in the chair near the couches, the only word he could think of was “Astonishing!”

“I think that was the same word I used, back when” said Dave Michaelson referring to when, as president, he was first exposed to the capabilities of the XYZT Portal Jason and Dennis had invented.

President Kirken then looked with a questioning look to Jason and asked “But how did you overcome the problems outlined by the Heisenberg ...” then the president stopped himself, threw up his hands and said, “You know what? I don’t want to know right now. I’ve got enough to remember with this new job!”

Jason and Dennis both smiled to each other, knowing the nature of the question that the president was about to ask. They, of course, would have been more than qualified to answer such a question, but they also knew that all this was a lot to take in.

Once again, the President sat there with his head slowly shaking back and forth, and with a distant look in his eyes that were simply pointed toward the coffee table, he once again said it was all astonishing. Eventually, he reached forward for the soda he had been drinking earlier. Then he said with a laugh, "You know ... seeing how enigmatic Dave here was about the subject of this meeting, earlier today I was telling myself to prepare for anything. I don't think I'd have been surprised if you'd have told me you two were aliens or something, although I think I would have needed something a little stronger than this!"

Jason, Dennis and Dave all involuntarily laughed at this, but not for the reason President Kirken was thinking. Once the laughter began to die down and Dave said, "You might want to tell me where you keep the bourbon nowadays."

"Huh?" was the uncharacteristic, yet unfiltered response from President Kirken.

Jason once again looked at the fireplace and said, "Go ahead and come on through guys!"

Just then the president's attention was whipped to the general direction of the fireplace when new arrivals stepped into the Oval Office one by one. Standing there in front of the four assembled men were none other than Ehobak, his wife Ruavu, Khreelon and Terri Lindstrom. They were all arrayed with relaxed comfortable clothing that was light, diaphanous, and colorful. The light purple, light green and white garments they all wore showed them to be the absolute picture of perfection. Far from being made of heavy materials, the fabric appeared to be elegant, and in many cases translucent.

The first thing President Kirken noticed as he rose from his seat near the wet spot on the floor where he had dropped his drink was that the new visitors were very tall. Visually, they appeared to be the embodiment of perfect health. Then as he looked closer, he saw their eyes. Absolutely stunning eyes, and three of the four possessed irises of pure black. The fourth one had color to her eyes, and she was slightly shorter than the others. The first three also had unusually shaped ears, pointed at the top. All four new arrivals were looking toward President Kirken with smiles.

"I think I'll take that whiskey now" said the president who was once again very much off his game.

Standing up, former president Dave Michaelson cleared his throat and proceeded with introductions. "Mr. President, as the Adjunct Whitehouse Ambassador to Interplanetary Relations, I'd like to introduce you to representatives from the planet Galimar. To the left is Lord Ehobak Aramine and his wife Ruavu. To the right is Lord Khreelon Tellindor and next to him is Miss Terri Lindstrom."

"Actually" corrected Terri, "It's Mrs. Terri Tellindor now."

"Really?!" exclaimed Dave. "Congratulations! I hadn't heard the good news yet!"

The interchange between Dave and Terri was more than surreal to the incoming president. While his head wasn't moving, his eyes were moving back and forth between the new visitors and Dave with lightning speed, and his mouth was slightly open.

Ehobak was the first to address President Kirken. Pressing his open palms together above his head, then lowering the still-pressed palms down to his chest resulting in a bow, he said "May you have peace. I am very pleased to meet you President Kirken. May I extend to you the greetings from those accompanying me here and from our ruling governmental body known as the Grand Council of New Galimar."

By this time, President Kirken had once again put forth the herculean effort necessary to get himself back in order, and with the grace of a well-trained statesman responded "It is an honor to meet you Lord Aramine. May I also extend to you the greetings of the government of the United States of America."

Khreelon spoke up and said "No, it is our honor. We have learned much about you from Lord Jason Marsalis and Lord Dennis Greene and we continue to learn more as time continues."

Gesturing to the couches, President Kirken then said, "May I offer you a seat and perhaps some refreshments?"

"Perhaps another time Mr. President" responded Ehobak. "Mr. Michaelson asked that we come to introduce ourselves, and to invite you to our world where perhaps you might be willing to speak to the whole of our Grand Council."

"You want me to come to ... to ... your planet?" asked a flustered president.

"Not exactly" answered former president Mr. Michaelson, "but we can get into the details of all that later." Then turning to Ehobak, Dave then said "Lord Aramine, I appreciate you taking time out from your busy schedule to come here to meet our president. Once again, I am in your debt."

"No debt at all" responded Ehobak. "Those of New Galimar shall never forget it was Lord Jason Marsalis and your team who were singlehandedly responsible for not only saving all your lives, but also the lives of each and every one of my people." Then with raised eyebrows and while placing his hand over his heart and slightly bowing, he added "It is we who are in your debt."

"Thank you for your kind words" replied Jason. "Please give my love to your children Jillintor and Nafan."

"I certainly will" responded Ehobak. Then turning to the president, he then said, "If you'll excuse us Mr. President, we have pressing matters to attend to."

"Of course!" replied President Kirken. "I look forward to meeting you once again."

"It would be an honor" said Ehobak as they all took a slight bow, then turned to leave.

At that, each of the new visitors walked back toward the fireplace one by one, and one by one each disappeared with the same flashes of light filling the room. At that, Dennis rose from his seat and said "I have to get back to the farm too. I've got a couple of things cookin at the lab that I need to check on." Then looking at Jason, he said "When you need a ride, just give me a call."

"You got it bud" answered Jason.

Turning to the president, Dennis said "Mr. President, it's been an honor to meet you." Then Dennis also stepped toward the fireplace and disappeared.

As had been the case several times in this meeting that was only supposed to take fifteen minutes, but had already taken an hour, the president found himself standing near his chair. Feeling slightly drained at the seemingly constant ebb and flow of adrenalin coursing through his body, he once again took a seat while letting out a whoosh of air from his somewhat overworked lungs.

"I just have no words guys." Then looking to Dave Michaelson, he then said "Adjunct Whitehouse Ambassador to Interplanetary Relations, huh? I can see why you held off on telling me your position. I can also now see why you backed out of the elections leaving a clear shot for me. I thought you had lost your mind at the time, but I can now see you had bigger things in mind."

"I sure did Mr. President" agreed Dave with a Cheshire cat smile.

"I have one question though. Tell me more about how Jason saved the planet as well as our visitors."

It took about another hour for Jason and Dave to regale the new president on the events leading to the volcanic threat in Yellowstone, as well as the existence of the island paradise of New Galimar. They told him about how New Galimar had the tectonic stabilization machine that needed to be repaired. This is also when Jason revealed to him that the portal not only had the ability to move a person from one place to another, but also from one *time* to another. This was equally hard for President Kirken to accept, but since Jason had anticipated this, he produced a USB drive that contained an HD video of the president's wedding back in 1973. It was such convincing proof that the president had no choice but to believe him.

It was also explained how Kenji had become a clear and present danger to the United States of America, but also how it appeared that he had been suffering from a sort of psychotic break. Jason made clear that he was in no way detracting from Admiral Brinstock's years of service to the nation before then.

"And so, Mr. President" said Jason in conclusion, "The main thing I want you to take away from this meeting is that you have an extremely powerful tool in your tool bag now. Unlike Admiral Brinstock, we have resolved to receive our orders from our commander in chief, and so it is up to you to dictate how it is to be used."

Nodding his head and looking out the window behind his desk, President Kirken answered and said "Well gentlemen, I am not the kind of guy that allows power to go to his head. It appears that the stellar way you have conducted yourselves up to this point has resulted in not only responsible use of this technology but has even resulted in no less than the rescue of the human race from complete annihilation. Being that this is the case, I hereby give you orders to continue as before. I only ask that you keep the oval office informed of any and all developments."

Jason and former president Michaelson agreed to do just that. Little did they know that major developments were just over the horizon.

CHAPTER 22

THE FIRST SENSATION JASON FELT was the feeling of grass below his feet. It was times like this when he liked to leave his eyes closed and just drink in all that was flooding his senses. The grass under his feet, the feeling of a light breeze wafting past his body, the aroma of flowers and trees that filled his nose, and the sound of nature. The air felt like a pleasant seventy-eight degrees Fahrenheit, or 25 degrees Celsius, and he could have just sat there for quite some time. But today was special. Today he wasn't going to be alone.

Upon opening his eyes, he looked to his right and didn't see anybody, but to his left was his son standing there. Jace was standing there with his eyes closed seemingly drinking in the same senses that Jason had been perceiving only moments before, but just then the boy opened his eyes and immediately looked around. When his eyes landed on his dad, he said "Where am I?"

"You're exactly where I said you would be my boy" answered Jason.

The boy looked around and saw the beautiful world of Galimar. There were parts of this natural paradise that seemed familiar to little Jace, but then again there were parts that were very different. The biggest thing that looked different was the sky. The sky was blue like on earth, but there in the distance wasn't the moon of earth, but there were three moons that were all different colors.

"So, I'm still laying on the couch in our house?" asked Jace.

"Yep" replied Jason.

Jace paused and then said, "And all this isn't real?"

"Nope"

Jace looked down and saw a small animal scampering toward him. The furry creature looked a little like a rabbit, and a little like a tiny lion. It was caramel colored had very large eyes. As opposed to small creatures on earth, this creature scampered around smelling different smells that it detected. One of those smells appeared to be Jace himself, and so it came closer to investigate. Jace reached down to pet it, and instead of running away it pointed its head upward, arched its back, closed its eyes and luxuriated in Jace's caresses along its back.

Jason smiled at the wonder so evident in his son's eyes. Still though, they had somewhere they had to be and so Jason touched his son's shoulder and said, "We need to get going."

Jace straightened up, and when he did the cessation of petting cause the animal to whimper. Jace and Jason chuckled a little, but then began walking toward the lake. As they walked, it appeared their little friend had decided to accompany them.

Next to the lake was a trail that the two of them settled into. The trail followed the curves of the lake. The water itself was lightly agitated from the breeze, and one could hear the tiny waves occasionally caressing the sandy beach.

"What do they call this place, dad?" asked Jace.

"They call this place Lake Crestpin, and it is a real place on Galimar" answered Jason.

"It's real?"

"Yes ... on Galimar" qualified Jason.

"Have you been to the real Galimar dad?"

Jason let out an obvious laugh and answered, "No. I've only been right here on earth." It was obvious Jace was more than impressed with his dad and to be honest it was starting to border on 'creature worship' a bit. It was cute in the eyes of his parents.

After walking halfway around the lake, they came upon a river that apparently supplied the water which in turn maintained the level of the lake. There was the melodious sound of rushing water accenting the occasional cry of an overhead bird. Jason wasn't completely familiar with the fauna of the region, but he thought to himself that it sounded like the cry of an eagle. He could see it was big though.

They decided to follow the river upstream for a while. It seemed like they had hiked about a mile, but the hike was easy since the ground only had a gentle slope. Eventually they got to their destination which was a breathtaking waterfall that must have been about ten stories high. The water falling into a beautiful cauldron below was ice cold, which wasn't very surprising since you could see snow still covering the higher elevations of the mountains surrounding the valley.

To the right of the waterfall, there was a staircase that had been hewn from the granite cliffs. The stairs seemed to be endless, but as they ascended the stairs, there was no sense of getting winded from the physical exertion. The father and son were in perfect shape, and the sensation was rather addicting. "Too bad it can't be like this all the time" Jason thought to himself. Looking up he once again marveled at the sight that lay before him. There, about one thousand feet above his head. was one of the famous gravity wells that could only be found here in the Mistikaan valley.

It was lumbering its way overhead in a circular pattern since, as Galimarian scientists had long ago explained, the rotation of the planet caused the gravity wells to move in a very predictable and circuitous route around the whole of the Mistikaan valley. According to them, it was actually these orbs of water, that themselves were miles wide, that had actually carved the huge canyon where Jason now found himself. It was a marvel to Jason how something so relatively small as these floating orbs of water could have been the cause of the canyon, which itself was at least twenty miles wide. Then again, as Jason thought more about it, perhaps the orbs just needed to get the process started, then natural erosion over the millennia would take over.

Upon reaching the top of the stairs, a forest lay before the two men. Falling to their left, the waterfall was supplied with water from the river issuing from this grove of trees, and as they walked just a little further it was in this grove of trees where they discovered and joined a small group of others already there and waiting for them.

"You made it!" said Terri.

"Of course, we made it!" responded Jason with a laugh. "You don't think we would have missed this do you?"

"You better not have or I woulda called in the cavalry to go find your sorry butts and haul you in!" came the reply from behind Jason. Jason turned to see Dennis standing there wearing his best for the occasion, and without having to think about it, he reached out and hugged his friend.

"What kind of best man do you think I would have been to have missed the wedding of my best buddy?!" said Jason as he lingered for a moment in the hug. As they were hugging, the commotion caused the rest of the attending group to approach, and with smiles they all greeted the new arrivals.

Jace looked over and immediately found his mother in the group. Mikki was wearing a traditional Galimarian dress that came up over one shoulder and loosely draped down and around her body. Jace had never seen his mom wear something so pretty, or so sheer for that matter. He ran over to her, and as he approached Mikki kneeled for a hug.

"There's my boy!"

"Mom! Dad and I just climbed up next to a waterfall! And before that I petted a really cool animal next to the lake. It was really cool!"

"You did?! That sounds amazing!" encouraged Mikki. "You know what? I think there might be another animal you'd like over near those trees. Go check it out and see what you think!"

"OK!" came the excited reply from her son. Jace immediately ran off to see what other exploration could be done.

Nearby there were a few rows of seats that were all arranged in a semi-circle around a central podium. Over the podium an arbor held several arrangements of beautiful flowers and laced in among those flowers were tiny "twinkle" lights that forced one to just gaze at their beauty. The aroma of flowers and pine wafted through the air, and in the distance, there were a few musicians that played soft music. Accenting the music of the instruments was the music of the forest. The distant roar of the waterfall, the shrill cry of a Locatta flying overhead, and the ever-present sound of wind passing by the treetops all contributed to the festive feeling. Dennis and his soon-to-be wife Patricia Lynne Marlowe had hoped for a special setting for their wedding, but when Quorlynn suggested that the wedding be held "In-world" so as to allow not only their close friends, but also each of their amulet companions to attend, well ... the decision was a foregone conclusion.

Invited to the wedding was Jason and his companion Kaynar, Mikki and her companion Thaeliss. Khreelon and his companion Loranna, Terri and her companion Quorlynn, Ehobak and Glendara and Ruavu and her companion Reeshah. Not to mention the stars of the show today Dennis and Lynne and their respective companions Shariah and Tahraan. Even little Jace had been granted the temporary use of an amulet by the Grand Council so as to not miss this experience. The whole experience was, of course, overwhelming to Jace.

Actually, there was quite a lot that was overwhelming to the little guy lately. First there was the news that his dad had been killed. Then two months later opening the front door to his home only to see his dad standing right there. That little event caused him to want to spend every waking moment with Jason.

Then the day came when Jason and Mikki decided to accept the invitation to live on New Galimar. For about five minutes they were euphoric with the prospect, but then it hit them like a ton of bricks that little Jace would not only be coming with them, but he would have to be introduced to the fact that there actually ARE aliens, and that they weren't just part of science fiction movies. While they wouldn't be telling Jace about the portal of course, Jace would end up knowing things that nobody else on the planet knew, and so they needed to be careful about exactly *how* they told him. Eventually they decided to tell Jace that they were going to move to a place in the tropics that was amazing. They shared pictures of the island, minus all the alien technology, with Jace and really talked it up. They told him that the move was necessary because of Jason's work and that Mikki was involved in that same work now too. Jace wasn't very happy at first with the prospect of leaving his friends, but when Jason and Mikki said that they could always come back and visit, he eventually warmed up to the idea.

When the day came to make the move, Jason and Mikki moved all their belongings directly to their new home on the island using the portal while their son was at school for his last day. When Jace came home, he was a little surprised that the old house was empty so quickly, but he didn't really question it much.

It was then, that Jason, Mikki and Jace got on a plane, made the flight to the Florida coast, and then took a Coast Guard cutter to the island. When they came up to the shield that camouflaged the island and made it invisible, they made sure Jace was downstairs playing games with his mother because they didn't want Jace to see an island suddenly appear from being previously invisible. When they were through the shield and when the island was now visible, Jason came down below and said that they were getting near the island and asked Jace if he wanted to see their new home.

Back in the forest, and as Jason found a seat so as to wait for the festivities of the wedding to start, he looked over to his son and thought about the conversation he had with Jace on the deck of that cutter as they watched the island approach. They were still about twenty minutes away from landing ashore at the time.

"So, what do you think kiddo?"

Jace looked at the approaching island and his face scrunched up a little. "It's pretty, but it doesn't look like an island."

"It doesn't?" replied Jason. "What were you expecting?"

"Well ... I mean, I see some of the stuff you and mom showed me pictures of, but I see other stuff that wasn't in the pictures. Like ..." Jace pointed to the massive pylons that were standing in seeming guardianship over the whole of the island and said "... what are those?"

"Those, my boy, are part of a big secret that I waited to tell you about"

"A secret?"

"Yup."

"What secret?"

Jason got a small smile on his face. He decided to play a little game. "I don't know. Maybe I shouldn't tell you. I'm not sure you could keep something so important a secret."

"Yes I can!" demanded the boy. "I won't tell anyone!" He smiled a big smile. He knew his father was playing with him now.

Mikki had come up behind them and chimed into the conversation. "I don't know Jason. This is a pretty big secret. I'm not sure if our little boy is capable of handling such a big secret."

"Yeahhhhh ... You might be right" agreed Jason with a nod.

"Mooooommmmm ... I can!" whined the boy. Then turning to Jason, he added "I promise, I can keep it a secret!"

"From everybody?" asked Jason.

"From everybody!" agreed Jace.

"I don't know ..." Jason looked at Mikki, who in turn had a huge smile on her face. "Do you think we should tell him honey?

Mikki kneeled down so she could sit eye to eye with her son and said "I tell you what. We'll only tell you if you pinky swear that you won't tell anybody else. Swear?"

Jace immediately held out his pinky and said, "I swear!"

Mikki locked her pinky around her son's and shook.

"Even to your friends back home when you see them? Or grandma or grandpa? Or even mamaw or papaw?" asked Jason.

Jace offered his pinky to his father and said "I swear! I won't tell anybody!"

Jason shook on the pinky swear as well. The pact had been made.

"OK. You promised!" said Jason.

"Yep! What's the secret!" demanded Jace.

Jason got close to Jace and said in hushed tones as if to make sure nobody else could hear, "You see that island there?"

"Yeah."

"Well that island isn't like any other island you've ever heard of."

"It isn't?"

"Nope. In fact, you know what?"

"What??"

Speaking in even more hushed tones, Jason whispered "It isn't even an island."

Jace looked again at New Galimar for a moment, then back at Jason, then back at New Galimar and said with a perplexed look on his face, "It isn't?"

"Nope" replied Mikki.

"Wha ... well ... what is it?"

Whispering again, Jason said "It's a spaceship."

Jace whipped his head around and started to yell "A SPA..."

"Shhhhhhh!!!!!!!" hushed Jason. "Keep it down! Remember?! A secret?!"

"I'm ... I'm sorry dad!" said the visibly flustered boy.

"It's ok. Just keep it down, ok?

"OK. I will" agreed Jace. "But ... How can an island go out in space?"

"It's because most of the spaceship is under water" explained Jason.

"Under water?"

"Yep."

Jace looked out to the approaching island again. "That is ... SO COOL!!"

"Oh, that isn't the best part" said Mikki.

Jace looked over to his mother. "It isn't? What's the best part?"

"The best part is who built it" said Jason.

"Was it you?" asked the smiling boy. His opinion of his father had been steadily growing every day.

"Nope" replied Jason. "Even better!"

"Who?"

"Well ... this is going to be a little hard for you to believe" explained Mikki, "but your father discovered people from another planet, and they're the ones who built the spaceship."

Jace got a look on his face that showed he thought his parents were playing another game on him.

"Come onnnnnn!!!!!"

"Honest! Cross my heart!" Said Jason.

"Come on dad! Everybody knows there aren't really aliens!"

"Everybody knows that, huh?"

"Yeah!"

By this time the cutter was now approaching the dock, and waiting for them on the dock was a Galimarian man who was in charge of the arriving boats.

"If that's true, then tell me who that is?" Jason pointed to the Galimarian man.

Jace looked at the man and said "I don't who he ..." but right then, Jace caught sight of how tall he was, how dark his eyes were, and most importantly, how pointed the Galimarian man's ears were.

"But ..."

Jace squinted his eyes to make sure they weren't playing tricks on him.

"But ..."

Jason could see his son was starting to question his previous assertion that there was no such thing as aliens.

Stepping off the boat, Jason motioned to the Galimarian man and said “My boy, this is my friend Tessaade. Tessaade, this is my son, Jace.”

“May you have peace! I am pleased to meet you my young friend Jace” replied the dockmaster.

Unlike his normal demeanor, the boy was suddenly mute. He didn’t appear to be scared, just ... not really ready to start talking to the first alien he’d ever met.

“He’s a little surprised to meet someone from another world” explained Jason to Tessaade.

“No worries my friend” consoled Tessaade. Then looking at Jace, he bent down to the boy, offered his hand and said “I look forward to talking with you when you have found your voice again. In the meantime, welcome to New Galimar.”

Jace looked at his dad, and Jason nodded. Tentatively Jace extended his hand, and Tessaade grabbed hold of it and shook. The shaking of hands was a custom Tessaade hadn’t ever done before meeting humans, but he knew that it would be something the young human would understand as a gesture of greeting and peace. Jace seemed to be awestruck at the sight of his small hand in the grip of the large Galimarian hand.

Back in the forest where he was waiting for the wedding to begin, Jason watched his son interact with all those that were in attendance. Since that day when he met Tessaade, Jace had adapted to life on the island rather quickly. Jason attributed it to the mental elasticity of the young, but regardless of the reason, it was remarkable how Jace was enjoying this virtual world where he now found himself.

When they were given the amulet for Jace to temporarily use for this occasion, the representative of the grand council explained to Jason and Mikki that the amulet wouldn’t have the same abilities that theirs did. While the amulet Jace was using would simply allow Jace to attend this event and nothing more, the full featured amulets that Jason and Mikki had been given allowed them to modify their virtual world in any way they chose. As if they were masters of their own universe, if Jason or Mikki wanted a house or a tree to appear, then they were able to conjure it up out of the thin virtual air. It was actually rather addicting. Not only that, but the boy's amulet didn't have a companion. That would be something that he would have to wait for.

Jason was roused from his personal reverie by the approach of Kaynar, Mikki and her companion Thaeliss. "Hey, you!" said Mikki, "What are you doing over here all by yourself?"

"Oh, I was just thinking about Jace and the day we brought him to the island" answered Jason.

Mikki smiled. "That was a fun day."

"Didn't you say Jace had a hard time believing in Galimarians?" asked Thaeliss.

"More specifically he had a hard time believing that there was such a thing as aliens in general" replied Mikki. Then looking over to the boy in the distance who was playing tag with the Galimarian equivalent of a mother deer and her young fawn, Mikki then said "Now look at him. It's like he's lived here all his life."

"Yes. The young are often much more able to adapt than those of us who are older" added Kaynar. There was a nodding assent among the four of them as they looked at the boy running back and forth with the animals.

About that time, Khreelon and Terri approached the group and greeted one and all. "Hey you guys!" Said Terri. "How's it going?"

"Not too bad" exclaimed Mikki. "How's it going girl?!"

"Pretty darn good actually" answered Terri. Then smiling a huge smile to Khreelon she said "Pret-tee darn goodddddddd".

Mikki gave Terri a half-lidded look and said "All right! What's up?!?!"

Just then, Ehobak stepped up to the platform that sat at the front of the seats, and said "May I have everybody's attention?"

Terri leaned over to Mikki and whispered, "I'll tell you after!"

Mikki gave her a suspicious look, but let it slide ... for now.

All who were gathered found their seats, except of course for Dennis and Lynne. After all in attendance were seated, the two of them walked up the center aisle and stood in front of Ehobak. Dennis was clothed in the typical garb of his hometown in Texas including a bolo tie and black Stetson hat. Lynne had decided to dress in a traditional Galimarian tunic. The fabric seemed to be made from a soft form of chiffon which she would never have been exclusively clothed in before since it was mostly transparent, however in this virtual world, it seemed to be natural. She made sure the "important parts" were covered still ... she had adopted Galimarian ways to a great extent ... but unlike Mikki ... not completely.

Ehobak looked at the couple and began to speak.

"From time immemorial it has been the responsibility, nay, the privilege of a captain to officiate over the weddings of those desirous of marriage. While I knew that this would be a welcome task as I would be the captain of the Arageena, I had no idea that it might involve the marriage of two residents of the planet where we would end up living. We are gathered here today to witness the marriage of these two before us; Doctor Dennis Greene and Doctor Patricia Lynne Marlowe. Dennis and Lynne met in a slightly unusual way of course."

"It has been suggested that their relationship blossomed due to what some on Eden call the Florence Nightingale effect. I have learned though that this isn't exactly true. Some 150 years ago, Florence was a human nurse here on Eden who decided to make rounds at night amongst her patients to make sure they were all right. She never became romantically involved with any of them though which differs from Lynne here. When Dennis was accidentally hurt, she agreed to help Dennis with his duties at work, and it was then that these two decided they both felt something special between them. That something special was, of course, love."

"But let's ask ourselves, what is love? Some would say it all boils down to chemicals that are released in the brain that make it feel good. These same ones say that we are just feeling the results of compatible pheromones and attractants that mutually interact with satisfying results."

"Others will say that love is something intangible. That it is something that rises above the chemistry of the two in question and is something that represents an unseen bond that can never be broken. These ones say that love is greater than the sum of its parts."

"Which one is right? Perhaps one of the best descriptions of what exactly love is comes from a world Galimar discovered long ago called Nakupenda. A philosopher from that planet once said:

'Love is more than a feeling. It is an emotion that is put into motion. It is a gem with many facets, and each of those facets are breathtakingly beautiful in their own way. One facet is the love we feel for a baby child we may have just produced with our mate. The love that is seen between a mother and her newborn infant can hardly be argued against.'

'Another facet is the love we feel for our family. Very different from the love for a son or daughter, it nonetheless is undeniable and completely insoluble. It is a love that can never be broken and will live until the end of time.'

'A third facet of this gem is the love we feel for our fellow beings. This principled love is what binds us together as a whole, and it embodies the principles that create a peaceful people living together in unity. It is a love that we can feel for not only beings of our same species, but for those of other species we may share the world with. Have you ever felt love for a beloved pet? Then this is that kind of love.'

‘The last type of love though, this one is special. It’s the kind of love that only exists between two people who have no other reason to love, except for the commitment and connection they feel with each other. It is the kind of love that causes their respective hearts to exchange places, such that the heart of one beats in the chest of the other. It is a love that causes an emptiness when they are away from their mate, and it is a love that is both intoxicating, and addicting’

“This gem of love” continued Ehobak, “is why we are all here today. Dennis and Lynne have made the pleasant discovery that their hearts have indeed exchanged places. From what I understand it happened without their knowing it, but when they realized it had happened, all around them seemed to wonder why it took so long for the two of them to realize it.”

Then getting a sarcastic tone in his voice, he continued “It was obvious to everybody else!” This caused a few chuckles from the audience.

“Dennis, Lynne, what we are celebrating today is a gem that the two of you hold between you. Cherish it. Keep it in a sacred place. Hold it above everything else. Make it something that is more important than anything else that comes along. There will be times when life will test your resolve and will test the resilience of the love you share. Love is easy to enjoy when times are good, but like a child, love can only stand up to tests if you have carefully nurtured it during the good times. If you feed it, if you cherish it, and if you protect it, then you can then be assured that you will enjoy it, both now and forever. You will both be able to wear this priceless gem as an adornment for all to see, and the two of you will stand as a benchmark for all, showing them how wonderful love can really be.”

Ehobak paused, then said “Dennis, your vows.”

Dennis, who already had a hard time keeping his eyes dry, turned to Lynne who seemed to be losing that same battle.

"Patricia Lynne Marlowe, with this vow I take you to be my partner in life, my one true love, and my wife. I will cherish our union and love you more each day than I did the day before. I will trust you and respect you, laugh with you and cry with you, loving you faithfully through good times and bad, regardless of the obstacles we may face together. I give you my hand, my heart, and my love, from this day forward for as long as we both shall live. I choose you to be my wife because I respect you. I will respect you in your successes and in your failures, to care for you in sickness and in health, to nurture you, and to grow with you throughout all the seasons of our lives together."

Dennis paused, then slowly enunciated his words and said, "Now and forever, I will always be yours."

Lynne stood there awestruck at the words she just heard from Dennis. The two of them looked at each other and there were no words. After a minute, Ehobak, who was visibly affected by what Dennis said, fortunately found his voice once again, and said "Lynne, your vows."

Lynne took a deep breath with an open mouth, and then forged ahead.

"Dennis Greene, I take you to be my friend, my lover, the father of my children and my husband. I will be yours in times of plenty and in times of want, in times of sickness and in times of health, in times of joy and in times of sorrow, in times of failure and in times of triumph. I promise to cherish and respect you, to care for and protect you, to comfort and encourage you, and stay with you, for all eternity. I take you to be my partner, loving what I know of you, and trusting what I do not yet know. I eagerly anticipate the chance to grow together, getting to know the person you will become, and falling in love a little more each day. I promise to love and cherish you through whatever life may bring us."

Then Lynne paused, and like Dennis slowly said, "Now and forever, I will always be yours."

Needless to say, there wasn't a dry eye anywhere to be seen. It took about thirty seconds for Ehobak to once again pull himself back together to a point where he could speak.

"With that" Ehobak finally continued, "it is my supreme privilege to declare that Doctor Dennis Greene and Doctor Patricia Lynne Marlowe are hereby …"

"… husband and wife."

A sudden and euphoric cry of jubilation broke out among all who were in attendance. Instantly standing and rushing up to the couple, Dennis and Lynne were inundated with cries of congratulations and well wishes. Tissues had to be handed out to all in attendance, and that included all the amulet companions. The musicians began to once again play music that perfectly accented such a beautiful occasion.

All remained standing near the front podium for a while, but eventually, they found chairs and created different circles of conversation. Eventually, Mikki made her way over to where Terri was sitting and sat down. Quorlynn, Lynne, Reeshah, Thaeliss, and Tahraan were there too. Terri was in the middle of talking to Lynne.

"Girl, that dress on you is absolutely stunning!" said Terri.

"Thanks" replied Lynne, "That means a lot coming from a beauty like you!"

"Oh, this body is just a little artistic license I'm taking in 'amulet-world'" replied Terri with a cheeky grin."

"Ohhhh noooo … don't even go there, sweetie. I know you in the outside world and there is no lyin' goin on here."

"Well thank you dahhhling!" responded Terri with a grin and a fluttering of the eyes.

"I have to say though" added Lynne, "that I was a little nervous wearing this. I mean it's so sheer."

"It is" said Mikki, "but I think it is tastefully done."

"Definitely" said Reeshah. "You look very glamorous in it."

Lynne looked over to her amulet companion and said "Well I couldn't have done it without Tahraan's help.

Tahraan smiled and said "Well, I did have a good subject to work with."

Without waiting any longer, Mikki looked at Terri and said "OK. Out with it! What has you looking like the cat that ate the canary?!"

Tahraan leaned over to Quorlynn and quietly whispered "What does the eating of one animal by another have anything to do with this?"

Quorlynn smiled, laughed a little, and said "I know what you mean! It has taken a little time for me to understand some of these human idioms. That one simply refers to the self-satisfied feeling a carnivore would no-doubt feel after having eaten a large meal."

A look of understanding came over Tahraan's face right then, but then slowly shook her head and simply said "Strange."

"You have no idea" whispered back Quorlynn with a roll of the eyes and a smile.

With a magnanimous look about her, Terri answered Mikki and said, "I don't believe I know what you are talking about!"

"Uh huh" replied Mikki with obvious derision. "I know you well enough to know that something is up. So, spill it!"

"All right! All right!" relented Terri. Then looking to the left and to the right as if she didn't want prying ears to hear, she then said "Khreelon and I just found out some great news!"

"You're not pregnant, are you?" joked Mikki who was smiling a huge smile.

Terri looked at Khreelon and simply answered, "Yup!"

Mikki's smile instantly fell from her face and was replaced with a look of big-eyed, open-mouthed wonder.

"You're pregnant? That's possible?!" asked Mikki with a voice that was almost a full octave higher than before. The elevated volume of the outburst caused several to stop talking and turn their heads.

"I know! Right?! I didn't know it was possible either, but apparently human DNA and Galimarian DNA are so similar that it's possible!" Terri's smile couldn't have been bigger, and in fact there was a definite squeal in her voice when she stamped her feet and once more said, "I'M PREGNANT!"

Mikki exploded out of her seat and once again embraced her friend in celebration of the good news. They were surrounded by the others who had heard the commotion and came over to find out what was happening. There was a great amount of back slapping on Khreelon by the boys and the girls all huddled around Terri to revel in the wonderful news.

"And that's not the best part" said Terri excitedly.

"What could be better news than this?" Asked Thaeliss, Mikki's companion.

"We found out that it's a girl!" said Terri with yet another teenage squeal. The rest of the girls in the room all followed suit.

"So, have you picked out a name for her yet?!" asked an excited Mikki once the commotion settled down once again.

"That's the best part!" said Terri. "We have, and we decided to incorporate several factors into her name. First, she'll have a name that is similar to Khreelon's father. Second, her middle name will be ..." Terri looked over to her friend and said "... Lynne after my good friend."

Just then, the drink that Lynne was holding dropped to the ground. Her one hand went over her mouth that hung agape while at the same time she uttered a gasp of delight that all could clearly hear. The girls all looked over to Lynne and smiled very large and very bright smiles.

"And finally," continued Terri, "we wanted a name that would honor a very good friend of mine." Looking directly at Quorlynn, Terri continued "This friend helped me discover things about myself that I didn't even know existed, and for that I will be forever grateful." Terri put her hand over her chest. "She lives with me near and dear to my heart. Sooooo her last name will of course be Tellindor, her middle name will be Lynne..."

Terri took a breath, and with a smile, said "... but her first name will be Coral."

CHAPTER 23

FROM A MODERN PERSPECTIVE, THERE are several things in the history of nations that many would rather not admit ever existed. The United States, for example, has a history punctuated by abhorrent treatment of the African American as well as the American Indian. In 1850 there was even a law that was passed in the northern states called the "Fugitive Slave Act" which was designed to curb the fugitive slaves that were fleeing north from southern states where they had been enslaved. Rather than curbing the tide of slaves though, one underground railroad operative boasted in 1855 that "the Fugitive Law has raised the stock on some of our Western tracks, at least fifty to seventy five percent", meaning that the tide of runaway slaves had actually *increased*. Within a short period of time after the passing of the new law,

Kentucky slaveholders met to discuss the possibility of heightened security around the Kentucky slaves. News reports of the day even compared the exodus of slaves in Kentucky to that of a stampede.

In 1855 though, the Wisconsin State supreme court declared the Fugitive Slave Act as unconstitutional. Among the recorded arguments of the declaration, it established that a person could not arbitrarily be referred to as a fugitive unless that person had the benefit of "due process of law". This was one of the first times that the concept of slaves being entitled to due process of the law had ever existed, and it naturally contributed to several other legal precedents that eventually led to slavery being abolished. Along with the loss of a considerable amount of life in the American Civil War, the concept of legal slavery was finally over.

A lot of things happened during the 1850's actually. California, Minnesota and Oregon became the 31st, 32nd, and 33rd states of the United States of America respectively. The New York Times was established. Uncle Tom's Cabin was published in 1852 by Harriet Beecher Stowe, and it had a great effect in the abolishment of the aforementioned slavery in the United States. Steinway Pianos moved from Germany to the United States, and Big Ben in London England rang out for the first time.

The 1850's was also when the "Eidgenössische Technische Hochschule Zurich" or Swiss Federal Institute of Technology in Zurich Switzerland was established.

Located in Zurich, the university was quickly recognized as a world-renowned bastion of science and technology. It only took a few years before the Nobel Peace Prizes began to roll in for its graduates. Groundbreaking discoveries and scientific advancements seemed to be the norm, and it was in the arena of robotics and nanobiology where the delivery of medicine on a microscopic scale was pioneered.

Endeavoring to treat a condition where blood vessels in the back of the human eye get clogged, which in turn causes the retina to cease functioning, and in the more severe cases death to the retinal cells, Doctor Brianna Plant, 39 years of age, along with a few others had recently developed a system where a microscopic implement is injected directly into the aqueous humor of the eyeball. The implement is roughly shaped like a grain of rice, but much smaller. It is specifically shaped, and it is made from samarium and cobalt which makes it greatly reactive to magnetic fields. On one end of the implement is a hollow tube that contains a minute portion of medicine that can break up blood clots.

To make the implement deliver the medicine to a specific place in the retina, an arrangement of eight highly tuned electromagnets are positioned around the patient's head. By finely changing the magnetic fields generated by these magnets, the implement can be moved inside the eyeball and positioned remarkably well. By moving the dials on a controller, the doctor can orient the pointed end of the implement in the correct direction and move the implement to the right spot with an accuracy of just a few micrometers.

The initial tests were all very successful, and once the medical trials got under way, the instant relief to those who had been treated by Dr. Plant's implement caused the treatment to be rushed to full acceptance and use by ophthalmologic physicians the world over.

Not long after this treatment had been perfected, it was over a few drinks with some undergraduates when Brianna came up with an idea. Since the accuracy of the movements of the optical implement was so high, and since it could be repeatedly controlled with pinpoint precision using a computer program, she thought to herself that the natural next step to this technology would be to use the implement to assemble an even smaller implement that might even then be termed as a device. While the implement that Brianna had invented up to this point had no moving parts, she was unable see why she couldn't use it to bring together other parts, and perhaps even manufacture those parts, all with that first generation implement.

Knowing that the eventual technology where this was all leading her would result in the world's first microscopic robot, she knew she needed to split her attentions between the creation of the next generation of medical implement, and the creation of a better designed microprocessor. The current state of the art microprocessor design had basically achieved its maximum abilities in terms of how many transistors could be placed on one microprocessor, however there was some interesting research done recently by IBM where the transistors could actually be stacked on top of each other. Working in the nanometer scale like this was certainly challenging, but after a lot of trial and error her team was finally able to successfully manufacture a microprocessor that had approximately sixty-five billion transistors, as opposed to the single digit billions that the processor industry was currently limited to. With this new ability, the processing power of a single microprocessor took a quantum leap forward.

Taking that microprocessor power back to her other field of study, Dr. Plant was currently in her laboratory working with the best of her graduate students in hopefully creating the world's first self-guided microscopic robot. While not really functioning at the nanometer scale, her students took to calling the robot that they hoped to create a "nanite".

Looking through a microscope, Brianna was watching one of her implements moving through simulated aqueous humor made from glycerin.

"OK, yaw minus 37 degrees" said professor Plant.

"Yaw minus 37 degrees" repeated Dayna, an undergraduate student working with Dr. Plant. Repeating the command ensured that it was heard accurately.

Brianna looked up from her microscope and glanced over to the monitor where Dayna was keeping her eyes trained. Dayna was one of Dr. Plant's most promising students and so while she knew she didn't have to worry about the positioning of the probe, she still needed to make sure everything was working right.

The monitor Dayna was watching appeared to be a simple line graphic representing the probe that had been injected into a glycerin substrate. The glycerin provided a thicker medium to perform the tests of the latest generation of micro-robotics that were now small enough to be injected into a blood stream through a syringe. These robots were the result of a considerable amount of research and development that Brianna had been working on for the last six years.

In the background noise of the room, Brianna noticed the sound of the door to her laboratory open and close, and from the sound of it there were more than one set of feet that had entered the room. She didn't know who had dropped by, but at that moment she couldn't take her eyes off the experiment. The movements of the micro-robot that they had all called "Chip" were about at their conclusion.

"Ok, positioning looks good. Get ready to send the command to reproduce the last movement sequence on my mark."

The undergraduate positioned the mouse on the "execute" button on her screen and placed her finger on the mouse button.

"Three, two, one, ... mark!"

The student clicked the execute button and Chip began to move around the glycerin independently. Laid around the floor of the container of glycerin, there were several miniature pieces of metal, each of them so small that one would initially think they were looking at simple metal shavings. But rather than shavings, each of these pieces of metal were actually finely shaped parts that Chip was now masterfully grabbing and placing in a central location. As Chip continued to grab each of these parts, he now started to assemble a device that was even smaller than himself.

"The program is executing perfectly, doctor. We should have results in about ten minutes" said Dayna as she watched the monitors.

Knowing that she had some time to wait before the success of the experiment would be discernible, Brianna turned around and saw that her visitors were waiting patiently. Taking off her glasses and placing them in the front pocket of her lab coat, she approached the two gentlemen. Only now did she recognize that one of the gentlemen was in fact Professor Dr. Klaus Laymann, the Vice President for Research and Economic Relations.

"Doctor Laymann, to what do I own the honor of your visit?"

"Well Doctor Plant" replied Doctor Laymann, "I was paid a visit by this gentleman today who has asked to see you."

Brianna thought to herself that it was quite odd that a vice president of the facility would take time out from his, no doubt, extremely busy schedule to play tour guide to a visitor.

"His name" continued Doctor Laymann, "is agent Lockwood."

"Agent?" asked Brianna with a slightly furrowed brow.

"Yes ma'am" replied the visitor. Then flashing a badge, he said "I am agent Lockwood with the United States Secret Service ma'am, and I've been ordered to extend to you a personal invitation to meet with the President of the United States in the oval office in Washington D.C., and I've been instructed to escort you along the way."

"Why would he want to meet with me agent Lockwood?"

"As is typical with matters of the president, I'm not privy to that information ma'am, but what I *can* tell you is that it is very unusual for him to extend this sort of invitation. I will say though that until you meet with the president, you will need to keep news of the invitation and the visit to yourself."

Brianna looked back over her shoulder at the students who had their eyes laser focused on the events unfolding on the screens before them. Looking back at Agent Lockwood and Doctor Laymann, she said "Can you give me a moment please?"

"Of course, ma'am."

As she walked back over to the group of students, Brianna thought to herself how she was a little unused to hearing herself referred to as "ma'am" so much. It made her feel old, even though she was only 39. As she looked at the same screen her students were focused on, she could see that the progress was coming along nicely. "Has the base plate assembly been completed?"

"Yes doctor" replied the student that seemed to be the most senior of the group. "The base plate has been completed, and the phase two articulating armature has been tested. It moved between 0 and 270 degrees along the X axis and Chip is just about to place the assembly on the phase three platform for Y axis movement. I had to adjust the azimuth articulation since the gear ratio we had designed only allowed for 270 degrees, but I think we might be able to squeeze out a few more degrees of articulation if we change the gear ratios on gear number twenty-four."

Brianna thought about his proposal and saw that it made a lot of sense. Nodding her head, she glanced back toward her visitors who were waiting patiently out of the way. It appeared that Doctor Laymann was quietly explaining a little of what Brianna was working on to the agent and elaborating on some of advances she and her team had made in the field micro-robotics. He was even pointing at the first-generation electromagnetic coils that were used to prove the technology in the beginning. It was occupying a place of honor in the corner of the lab where she had been moved recently. It was no longer being used now that the commercially engineered production version of the magnetic control unit was available for medical establishments around the world. It was the first one though, and so Brianna couldn't bring herself to dismantle it.

Turning back to her students, she said "Listen guys, I've been asked to go on a little field trip that will take me away for a few days. I think your plan to make that change to gear twenty-four is a good one. Please proceed with that. We should also be getting the new processor back from prototyping sometime tomorrow or the next day, and when we do get it, Lori should proceed with testing and certification. I think I will be back in time, but if the test and cert pass, then start uploading the programming to it and see how well it is able to control the actuators in the test unit Chip is putting together. Sound good?"

"You got it Doc" replied the senior student who himself appeared to be from a state in the southern U.S. "We'll keep the lights on for ya".

"Good. Call me if you have questions or if you get stumped."

"Will do Doctor Plant" replied Sharon, another graduate student standing next to Lori.

Leaving the students, Brianna walked back over to the gentlemen and said, "Well gentlemen, I suppose I have a plane to catch?"

The flight from Switzerland to Washington would have been a long and grueling flight normally. Brianna loved flying normally, but she wasn't a fan of having to be squeezed into a small space for seemingly interminable time frames. Being of Asian descent, she had a generally small frame, but that didn't quell her slight case of claustrophobia on the trans-oceanic flights she had taken before.

This flight though was markedly different. When she left the educational institution with Agent Lockwood, they took a Chevrolet Suburban that had the windows completely blacked out to the airport, and instead of having to stand in line for hours to board the plane, they were whisked straight onto the tarmac through a gate normally reserved for diplomatic envoys. She thought this was rather odd, but that small detail paled in comparison when she saw their car pull up next to a Gulfstream G650, as opposed to the standard commuter jet many used to traverse the pond.

"I'm going to Washington ... on that?" nervously asked Brianna as the wheels came to a halt.

Sitting in the front seat of the vehicle, agent Lockwood smiled to himself out of sight from the doctor. "Yes ma'am."

Getting out of the vehicle, his training took over and he was all business. Before opening the rear door to the suburban where Brianna sat, he scanned his surroundings to make sure all was secure. It didn't take long for him to determine it was, of course; Switzerland wasn't a hot zone after all. He, however, didn't want to take any chances. It just wouldn't do for the important guest he was accompanying to come back in more than one piece, and so for this reason the plane was surrounded by troops that flew this mission with Agent Lockwood. They were the first off the plane after it landed, and the last to board when it was ready to go. While on the ground in a foreign country, they stood all around the plane with their AK-47's loaded and ready while their eyes were constantly scanning for anything that shouldn't have been there.

After several seconds of scanning his surroundings while blocking the vehicle door near Doctor Plant, Agent Lockwood finally moved to the side and opened the door for the doctor. While sitting there, it didn't take her long to figure out that her escort was being extremely careful of their surroundings and so she took her cues from the agent and waited for his move. When the door swung open, she grabbed her duffle bag and quickly boarded the plane. Taking a seat in the luxurious aircraft, she waited for the rest of the men to board as well. Scanning up the aisle, she could see the captain and first officer already going through their checklists, and as soon as she spied that, she saw the last of the tarmac infantry board and the door was closed. It seemed like the plane was actually rolling before the door was even closed. Agent Lockwood took his seat next to the doctor.

"Is this small of a plane going to make it to Washington?" asked Brianna.

"Oh yeah" replied the agent. "This is a Gulfstream G650, and it's one of the fastest and longest-range small jets with a range of seven thousand five hundred nautical miles. It can cross the Atlantic on any route needed quickly and comfortably at a speed just under the speed of sound."

"You seem to know a lot about it" observed Brianna as she gripped the armrest tightly. Airplanes weren't exactly her favorite means of travel.

"It's just because I seem to do this kind of thing a lot for work. I've been on this plane a few times."

"You've picked up other people like this before?"

"Yes ma'am."

Brianna was about to ask who he might have picked up like this before, but then she thought better of it. As opposed to the absence of any explanation over why she had been invited to Washington, she was reasonably sure that even if he did know why he was escorting someone else, he probably wouldn't share that information with her.

Within a few minutes, it appeared that agent Lockwood's vigilance on the airport tarmac was successful, as their aircraft achieved "V1" velocity and rotated to a powerful yet unremarkable takeoff, achieving its intended flight level of forty-five thousand feet in no time at all, and all without any boogeymen shooting at them.

The flight only lasted a little over six hours before the plane's wheels rolled to a stop at Andrews Air Force Base in Maryland. It appeared the agent's vigilance was a little more relaxed as they disembarked from the small jet, but as she walked from her airplane to the waiting car that was a cookie cutter copy of the one in Switzerland, she spied out of the corner of her eye two very conspicuously painted 747's sitting in a hangar. The beautiful planes were silver with pale blue and white paint, and on the side were the words "United States Of America". As she settled in the rear seat of the Suburban, she wondered what it was like to fly on that beast.

The car ride was only twenty miles from Maryland to Washington. They pulled up to a hotel called The Kimpton Hotel Monaco and stopped. The front of the hotel seemed more suited as a small museum replete with marble Corinthian columns, imposing stone steps running the width of the building, and red awnings on all street level windows and doors. As soon as they stopped agent Lockwood and his partner agent Elder, who had joined them at Andrews, got out and opened the door for her.

"Aren't we supposed to go to the White House?" asked a slightly confused Doctor Plant.

"The president thought the flight would be a little taxing on you, so he had arranged for you to stay here for the evening before meeting with him tomorrow morning at 9AM" replied agent Elder.

"Oh" came the short but resigned reply from the good doctor. Emerging from the car, she stepped inside and found the lobby to be breathtaking. It was decorated in a manner that just dripped with elegance and luxury. Never in her life had she stayed anywhere that was even close to as well-appointed as this hotel was. The lobby was decorated in a green motif, and there were beautiful coffered ceilings with crystal chandeliers hanging everywhere.

Her room was just as breathtaking. The bathroom even had a shower stall that was literally ten feet by six feet. Sure, there was a shower head in there, but there was also a full size ornate claw-foot bathtub right there in the shower stall! The enclosure was all tiled and, of course, the entire suite was accented with fresh flowers. As she sat on the couch in her stateroom contemplating the lap of luxury where she currently found herself, she wondered again why she was even here. Lightly fingering the strap to her duffle bag on the bed next to her, she knew her being summoned here wasn't anything she needed to worry about, but for the life of her she just couldn't imagine why the President of the United States, of all people, was going through all this trouble. Regardless of the trouble though, to say she ate and slept well that night would have been a colossal understatement.

As arranged with her before they left the previous night, the agents were waiting for her outside of the hotel at 8:30AM the next morning. She had already risen from a deep dreamless sleep at 6AM, spent time in the gym, showered and ate some breakfast in the restaurant. As she made use of the hotel facilities, she told one of the hotel staff that she felt a little out of her league. It was explained to her that they had entertained many visitors in the past for the president, and that if she needed anything, all she had to do was put it on the room tab and it would be taken care of.

It was only a short ride in the car before it pulled up to sixteen hundred Pennsylvania Avenue, and thereafter it was only a few minutes before she found herself waiting for President Kirken on a couch in the oval office with agents Lockwood and Elder manning the doors nearby. In no time at all, a side door opened, and the president walked in.

"Doctor Plant I presume?"

Rising from her seated position, she walked toward the president and said "Yes, mister President. It's an honor to meet you."

"Thank you doctor, but the honor is mine" replied President Kirken. "I've been reading up on some of the breakthroughs you've been responsible for lately, and I've got to say you've really been rewriting a lot of the textbooks lately."

"Well I have a lot of good people working with me too, Mr. President."

"Oh poppycock" came the frank reply from the president. "Doctor Plant, like my predecessor I am not the kind of person to pull any punches. I call it as I see it, and I can see that you are the real deal when it comes to breakthrough technology in robotics and electrical engineering."

Even though she was obviously Asian in her descent, it was equally obvious that she was blushing at the accolades coming the president. A muted "Thank you" was all she could muster saying in reply.

"I was curious about something though" continued the president. "I hadn't had enough time to read through your entire file, before you got here. I was wondering if you attended school there in Switzerland, or somewhere else?"

Brianna briefly wondered to herself about this "file" that the president was referring to, but then quickly replied "Oh no, I went to school right here in the good old USA at the Massachusetts Institute of Technology."

"MIT?" responded President Kirken. "No kidding. My daughter Connie was just telling me the other day that she wanted to go there."

"Oh really?" replied Brianna. "My adoptive parents raised me in Boston, and the whole time I was growing up I knew I wanted to study there."

"Sounds like Connie. Hopefully she'll keep her grades up to qualify."

"I'm sure she'll be fine" answered Brianna.

"You say your parents were adoptive?"

"Yes sir. I was born in China, but my parents adopted me when I was only three months old" answered Brianna.

"Very interesting. And a little coincidental about you technically being from China. I'm sure you know that I invited you here to talk about something a little more important than my daughter's scholastic aspirations."

"The thought had occurred to me" jeered Brianna. The president saw that she could be just as much of a straight shooter as he was.

"Well, it actually has to do with the state of the relationship the United States has with Russia right now."

"Russia?" responded Brianna. "I'm not sure how I can possibly help with the politics between two countries, let alone two superpowers as the U.S. and Russia."

"Well when it comes to politics, you can probably leave that part up to me. But as you may or may not know, relations between us and them have been warming up lately thanks to my predecessor President Michaelson, as well as some positive outcomes from my own visits over there recently."

Brianna could now see why the president thought her link to China was coincidental. "Actually, I did see a report on CNN in the last week where your last visit there was compared with the visit president Nixon did with China in 1972."

"Exactly, and I have to say that things went really well ... in Russia that is. In fact, it was something that we discussed on that visit that has led me to invite you here" answered President Kirken.

"Me? What could I possibly have to do with your negotiations with Russia?" asked a puzzled doctor Plant.

"Doctor are you familiar with a Doctor Alexei Einikov?"

"Very much so" responded Brianna.

"How much to you know about him?" asked President Kirken.

"I know that he is a world-renowned scientist and he lives and works in St. Petersburg Russia" replied Brianna. "If I remember correctly, he comes from an obscure village called Novy Kosovo in the northern part of the Krasnoyarsk region of Russia. What I do know is that he is an amazing physicist and engineer responsible for some incredible breakthroughs in neurobiology. I've always wished I could meet him sometime."

"Well" returned President Kirken, "on my last visit to the Kremlin, it was proposed that we create a joint technology research team that would involve Doctor Einikov and a top scientific researcher of my choosing. Apparently Doctor Einikov is working on a project that would involve ..."

The president paused and retrieved a paper from his shirt pocket and read from it "... neurobiology, massive transistor microprocessors, and nanotechnology. I don't profess knowing exactly what that means, but what I have been told is that his research is light years ahead of anything being done elsewhere. When we considered who would be the best one to ask to be part of this project, it was obvious to my team that you were the best choice. I've invited you here doctor Plant to see if you would be interested in working on a joint scientific partnership with Doctor Einikov in the interests of creating a more solid linking of our two nations."

By the overwhelming smile on her face, it was obvious to the president what Brianna thought of the proposal. Even though this would change everything concerning her research projects back in Switzerland, her answer was a foregone conclusion.

CHAPTER 24

Date:	13th of March, 10:37 AM
To:	Doctor Alexei Einikov Einikov Institute of Research Saint Petersburg, Russia
From:	Doctor Brianna Plant Swiss Federal Institute of Technology

Dear Dr. Einikov,

I apologize for sending this email unsolicited, however as you may already know by now, I have been asked by President Kirken of the United States of America to contact you in regard to the joint technology research program that had been discussed by our respective leaders.

I am very familiar with the papers you have published on your research, and I am looking forward to meeting and collaborating with you in the near future.

If you would like more information on my research and development, you are welcome to visit the website for the Swiss Federal Institute of Technology and click on my name. It should give you all the information you may need or want about the work I have been doing up to this point.

Looking forward to hearing back from you ...

Doctor Brianna Plant

Date: 13th of March, 11:15 AM
To: Doctor Brianna Plant
Swiss Federal Institute of Technology
From: Doctor Alexei Einikov
Einikov Institute of Research
Saint Petersburg, Russia

Dear Dr. Plant,

There is certainly no need to apologize. I am pleased to "meet" you Doctor Plant. Actually, I am already familiar with your work as I have been following the progress that has been periodically posted to the website you mentioned. I have to say I have always been very impressed with the work you have done and are still doing. When I learned that you were the one that was selected to work with me in a joint operation, I was quite pleased. I hope you feel similarly.

Are there any materials that you will need when you arrive? What is the forecasted timeline for your arrival?

With admiration,
Alexei

Date: 13th of March, 3:18 PM
To: Doctor Alexei Einikov
Einikov Institute of Research
Saint Petersburg, Russia
From: Doctor Brianna Plant
Swiss Federal Institute of Technology
Attachment: RequiredMaterials.docx

Dear Alexei,

You hope I feel "similarly"?

Doctor Einikov, I must say I was a little surprised, and honored, that a researcher of your stature and reputation took the time to follow my research. While it is true that I have had many successes in the areas of study where I am centered, I am still very excited to not only meet you, but to work alongside you in a common area of interest.

I must also say, that your command of the English language is impressive. Had I not already known that you are from Russia, I would have never known that English is your second language.

As to the materials that I will need when I arrive, please see the list attached to this email. There shouldn't be any surprises, and I'm sure it will be things you already have.

Are you aware of any arrangements that have been made on my behalf as to where I will live?

With Mutual Admiration,
Brianna

Date:	**14th of March, 7:15 AM**
To:	**Doctor Brianna Plant** **Swiss Federal Institute of Technology**
From:	**Doctor Alexei Einikov** **Einikov Institute of Research** **Saint Petersburg, Russia**

Dear Brianna,

Regarding my command of the English language, it isn't exactly my second language, but when you are an old soul as myself, you often have the time to learn the varied, marvelously flavored, and sometimes flawed nuances of each language one comes in contact with. I've always been somewhat of a language aficionado, and so I guess it just comes with the territory.

We have a set of domiciles here at the institute and I've selected the best one to be yours. I've instructed one of my assistants to make sure your new home is set up as well as possible.

Looking forward to your arrival.
Alexei

Date: 14th of March, 7:31 AM

To: Doctor Alexei Einikov
Einikov Institute of Research
Saint Petersburg, Russia

From: Doctor Brianna Plant
Swiss Federal Institute of Technology

Dear Alexei,

Thank you so much for making the arrangements for my arrival! In fact, as I looked back on our exchange of email, I realized that you had requested information on when I would arrive, and I never answered that. Please forgive me.

I have a project that I have been working on here in Switzerland that I look forward to sharing with you. The project has to do with taking my previous research to the next level. We are attempting to create micro-robotics with articulating manipulators. I forecast that the milestone I wish to achieve will occur within the next two weeks, which will give the time necessary to get my affairs in order for my relocation to your facility.

The long and the short of it is I anticipate my arrival to your facility in about three weeks.

With regards,
Brianna

Date: 14th of March, 7:50 AM
To: Doctor Brianna Plant
Swiss Federal Institute of Technology
From: Doctor Alexei Einikov
Einikov Institute of Research
Saint Petersburg, Russia

Dear Brianna,

Yes, I figured you would eventually get around to letting me know when you would arrive.

That is excellent news! I have a lot of things to show you and I very much look forward to getting your input. I am thinking of collaborating with you on one project in particular that I have been kicking around in my spare time. Lately the research on that project has been showing some very promising results, and I think I would like to get your input on it. It will be something that only you and I will be working on. My main research team knows nothing about it.

Looking forward to your arrival!
Alexei

With the last email from Alexei, Brianna was more excited than ever about her upcoming trip to Saint Petersburg. In the circles that Brianna tended to walk among, Doctor Einikov was something of a rock star. Although Brianna would never admit it out loud, she had always had somewhat of a professional "crush" on this man. For as long as she could remember, he had been at the forefront of research and technology in the same areas of interest as Brianna. More areas, in fact. It now seems that he doesn't limit himself to electrical engineering, as Brianna has, but has now apparently delved into that of bio engineering as well.

"Remarkable" said Brianna to herself as she stared blankly at the last email received from her once-idol and now new partner.

Sitting in her small 8-foot by 10-foot office at the institute, she looked around and contemplated the tasks needing to be accomplished over the next three weeks. Glancing back at her computer, she grabbed her mouse and opened up a new document entitled "Moving Preparation Tasks"

Beginning with creating that document, the next three weeks seemed to fly by. To Brianna, she often thought about how Einstein was certainly right. The perception of time was always relative to the viewpoint of the viewer. On one hand, time over the past three weeks seemed to fly by. On those occasions, it seemed that three weeks just wasn't enough to complete all the things that she wanted to accomplish before she left.

On the other hand, when it was night, and all was quiet in her lab or in her apartment, time seemed to just drag on. It seemed that her heart had already packed its bags and left for Saint Petersburg. Seconds seemed like minutes and minutes took hours to pass as she waited for the day when she would leave and rejoin her heart in her new home.

Eventually the day finally did come, but not before a very exciting breakthrough in her lab. The effort to create a microscopic robot that not only could autonomously navigate its way through whatever substrate it found itself, but also had an articulating arm that could be used to manipulate the world around it was a huge success. The programming that had been placed in the new microprocessor had also been somewhat of a breakthrough, since it had been "taught" to search the world around it for a specific type of anomaly that needed to be fixed, and thereafter actually perform tasks that would fix it. The project had worked so successfully, in fact, that she decided to publish her work in all the appropriate scientific journals. As she was waiting in the airport terminal for her plane to Saint Petersburg, Brianna put the finishing touches on a scientific press release and attached it to an email to the editors of those journals. Just as they were calling for her group to board the plane, she hit "Send" and once again paved the way for her own stardom among her contemporaries.

The flight was uneventful, and before long she emerged from the plane into a cold winter day at Pulkovo International Airport. It was, of course, just as cold in Switzerland and so this wasn't anything new for her. What was new was the man standing at the end of the jet bridge holding a sign saying, "Dr. Brianna Plant". He was dressed in black with a black cap, and as soon as she approached the man and identified herself, he said he was a driver for the Einikov institute and he had been instructed to escort her to her new accommodations. He then gracefully took her briefcase and carried it the rest of the way to the baggage claim carousel and eventually to the car.

The "car" was a stretch limousine fitted with all the best refreshments and snacks. The driver, who never actually revealed his name, told her to make herself home during the hour-long drive. Smiling to herself, Brianna thought about her favorite screen character of Holly Golightly and whispered to herself that the champagne was "simply divine", yet before long she once again found herself sitting on an unfamiliar bed after having unpacked her belongings and settling in. Looking around her new spacious digs compared to what she had in Switzerland, she decided that a good cup of tea was just what the doctor ordered, and it was while she was making said cup, that the doorbell rang.

Being this was a new country, let alone new living location, Brianna felt she needed to be cautious for a while, and so she didn't immediately open her door. Stepping up to the door without opening it, she said, "Yes? Who is it?"

A deeply timbred voice spoke out from the other side of the door. "Doctor Plant, it's Doctor Alexei Einikov."

She opened the door to find one of her own personal idols. Her breath immediately left, and she was barely able to sputter out a simple two word greeting.

"Doctor Einikov!"

A slight pause ensued, but then the visitor responded with "Hello Doctor Plant. How are you? I trust you find the apartment acceptable?"

"Very much so! Thank you for giving me such a nice place to stay!" said a rather flustered scientist that had just been reduced to the countenance of a teenage schoolgirl.

As it happens, Brianna had always had a thing for blond hair and green eyes, and the fact that he was not only tall, but he was physically perfect in every way that mattered to Brianna didn't hurt either. She had actually never seen a picture of Doctor Einikov before, and so in the back of her mind she half expected to meet a stodgy professorial type of man. She was quite pleasantly surprised.

What Brianna didn't realize, mostly because she was so starstruck by this tall green-eyed fine specimen of humanity, was that her visitor was equally tongue-tied from not only meeting someone whom he respected as much as he did, but someone that was so unexpectedly beautiful as Brianna. "Well, I wanted to drop by and make sure you were ok and that ... uh ... all was well with you" sputtered Alexei apologetically.

"Everything is great. I appreciate you taking the trouble to carve out time from your schedule to check me out ... I mean to check on me!" replied Brianna with a slight blush and stutter.

"It's really no trouble at all as most of my fellow workmates have gone home for the day."

The two of them stood in the doorway for a second or two staring at each other, but then Brianna realized that she wasn't being very hospitable. Taking a step backward, she opened the door wider and said "I was just making some tea. Can I please interest you in a warm cup?"

"I don't want to impose ..."

"Oh pish-posh. No imposition at all!"

Alexei smiled and entered. "I like that movie too."

"I'm sorry?" asked Brianna.

"Breakfast at Tiffany's. I've always liked the main character who said the same thing as you just did" replied Alexei.

Realizing what he was talking about Brianna smiled somewhat sheepishly and said "Oh that. I suppose I get that from my college days. My roommate Mikki and I watched that movie so many times that I think we wore the tape out."

Quoting a line from the movie, Alexei looked up and to the left saying, "Promise me one thing: don't take me home until I'm drunk — very drunk indeed."

Smiling, Brianna decided to play along with Alexei as she was shutting the door, quoting her own line from the movie. "You can always tell what kind of a person the man thinks you are by the earrings he gives you."

"Yes" replied Alexei with yet another quote from the movie, "but you mustn't give your heart to a wild thing. The more you do, the stronger they get, until they're strong enough to run into the woods or fly into a tree. And then to a higher tree."

Taking a pause to pour a cup of tea for her guest, Brianna had to admit that she was coming up short in remembering another quote from a movie she actually hadn't watched in quite a few years. "ALLRIGHT! I give! You win!" The smile on her face told Alexei that this was only friendly banter between two new friends and that he hadn't actually been in danger of hurting her feelings.

Scrunching his eyebrows together, he prodded with a line from a different movie. "Oooooo ... giving up so easily?"

"Not necessarily" replied Brianna as she handed a hot cup of steaming tea to her visitor, "I just wanted you to feel good about yourself."

"Mission accomplished my dear Doctor Plant."

Taking on a more serious look to her face, Brianna replied "OK. Now THAT needs to stop."

Fearing he had accidentally tread somewhere where he shouldn't have, his complexion changed and he asked "What? Did I do something wrong?"

"Yes, you did Doctor Einikov!" then cracking a small smile she then replied: "You need to start calling me Brianna."

Somewhat relieved, he relaxed his stance and retorted "Only on the condition that you call me Alexei."

"I think that can be arranged ... Alexei." Then gesturing to the couch, she prompted "Won't you have a seat?"

The two took a seat on the couch facing each other and proceeded to wile the night away talking about anything and everything. They, of course, started off with talking about their respective projects that had taken up their time recently, but then as the evening wore on the subjects varied. They talked about their childhoods, their training, the absence of any significant other, and things that each of them wished and hoped for in the future.

Conversation between them ebbed and flowed like the tide and it never felt like the communication was pushed in any way. With very little effort on their parts, one subject seemed to naturally lead to another. Much to his own surprise, Alexei was not only serious when the subject matter called for it, but even in Brianna's eyes he was delightfully comical at the perfect times. As Brianna spoke about this or that, Alexei found himself mentally sitting back and just watching Brianna's mannerisms. She would sometimes get this look on her face that showed an almost childlike wonder at the world around her, and then she would smile at something that caught her fancy. Ah, the smile. She didn't just smile with her lips, but to Alexei, her entire face smiled. It was genuine, honest, authentic, but most of all it was adorable.

Among the now-empty take-out containers and drink cups gathered on the coffee table near the couch where they sat, the two of them were stunned to discover that they had been talking, really communicating, for at least six hours, even though they both thought it had only been two. As he left her apartment that night somewhere around 1AM, Alexei had to admit to himself that Brianna was unlike anyone he had ever met, and that comprised a considerable number of women he had known over his lifetime. They had all been platonic (the term itself was something he always laughed at) as he never had any romantic feelings for anybody before. He often referred to it as "romantic entanglements" as he had never found anybody that interested him.

But Brianna was different. When he got up that morning, he knew he would be meeting yet another intellectual counterpart as he had done countless times in the past. But this time was different.

Very different.

Brianna, for her part, was thinking almost the exact same thing. As she bid her goodbye to Alexei and closed the door behind him, she stood there staring at the doorjamb for some time wondering what in the world just happened! She started the evening feeling like a rock star groupie getting the amazing chance to meet her idol, but in the end, she felt like he had crawled into her head and she had done the same to him. The two of them had let logic rule for all their respective lives, and so it was hard to admit that in just six short hours, the whole supposed improbability of having fallen for someone whom they had just met ... that it had just come to a crashing end.

Beginning with that evening, and with the following months working hand in hand and heart to heart, the ending became foreordained and inevitable, especially in the eyes of their fellow workmates. Next to a waterfall and among their immediate friends and workmates, Alexi slipped a ring on her finger and sealed their respective destinies.

They had no idea that their destinies would take them on such an amazing ride.

CHAPTER 25

JAVIER AND HIS WIFE AMANDA had been planning the weekend getaway for a while now. Just the two of them. Ahhhh ... it was nice. They lived with their young son and daughter on the upper part of Long Island, New York in an area called The Hamptons in a small village called Sagaponack. Their house was rather large given that there were only four people living there, but of course in that area, you are pretty much expected to have your wealth on display for all to see. Javier didn't really care anything about that, but Amanda seemed to be happier when she had a big home to decorate and care for.

To say she "cared for" the estate is actually a little bit of a misnomer. There were gardeners, tree surgeons, pool caretakers and handymen that cared for most things outside, and inside there was a full-time butler, maid, and full-time chef that maintained all affairs inside. Sometimes Amanda felt like she had to consult with her staff on things as if she was asking for their permission, rather than the other way around. Still though, it was a posh and opulent life that Javier provided to his family, and they were all grateful for the life he made possible.

That life was in fact made possible because of the various businesses for which he was responsible. There was a real estate development company that mainly dealt with commercial real estate in the Manhattan area. There was a communications company that was one of the first to be a principal contractor that all cell phone companies would call on to install and maintain cell phone towers. And finally, there was a software development company that serviced a lot of contracts with the department of defense. All these companies functioned under an umbrella corporation called JA Holdings. Javier had been on the cover of several magazines including US News and World Report, and there were several articles over the years in the Wall Street Journal where he had been interviewed on the overall direction of business.

All of that life though was far from his mind. He and Amanda had spent the weekend at Martha's Vineyard, and it had been delightful. They had taken a company Lear Jet down and then spent the day enjoying all that the cape had to offer. On coming back, Amanda had implored Javier to take her and the kids to a movie, or whatever else the little ones might want to do. Although acting like he was under great duress, he acquiesced to her request since he had been looking forward to spending time with Alexa and Rafael as well.

Walking in the door from their trip, eight-year-old Alexa and seven-year-old Rafael veritably mowed them down with excitement over their return. The servants in the home had been watching over the children and so they were well cared for. They had been cooped up in the house for the past several days though, and so as Javier and Amanda had expected they were more than ready to get out.

An evening of dinner and miniature golf later, the children went to sleep tired and satisfied. As usual, Amanda tucked the children in and then adjourned to the bedroom where Javier was already waiting in bed. He was probably just as tired as the kids, and he knew his wife would be as well.

“Anything good on?” said Amanda as she entered the bedroom. Shedding her robe, she climbed under the covers with nothing on but a smile. It was how she normally slept.

“Not really” replied Javier. “I was just scooping up a few final numbers from Wall Street before you got here.”

Amanda rolled her eyes, dropped her head back into the fluffy pillow and with an exaggerated open mouth made a sound that was a cross between a snore, a buzz-saw, and a grizzly bear. Even so, Javier could see a twinkle in her eye as she made like she was monumentally bored already.

“Hey! Don’t knock it!” said Javier.

“It’s just so BORING!”

“Well, my dear, it’s that boring stuff that pays for you to live in the lap of luxury” answered Javier as he clicked off the TV. The room went instantly black and Amanda came over to snuggle up under Javier’s wing with her arm draped over his chest.

“I know. I’m just giving you a hard time” yielded Amanda.

There wasn’t a reply from Javier, but she got the sense that he was smiling in the dim light. While she lightly fingered the tattoo of an eagle on Javier’s right wrist, and after a few seconds of silence Amanda then asked “Oh! I forgot to ask if you and I could go to breakfast with Tammy and Gill tomorrow?”

“Tomorrow?” asked Javier. Then after thinking about it for a few seconds he responded “Sorry. Can’t. I have a meeting in Manhattan in the morning at 9am so I’m out the door at six.”

Javier could feel Amanda slump down a little. “Oh poo. I was hoping we could get to know them a little better.”

“I’m sure we can” consoled Javier. “Just not tomorrow. Sorry hun.”

And with that, the two lovebirds fell into a sleep that was ended by the alarm far earlier than they would have preferred.

As foretold, Javier was up, out the door, and behind the wheel at six AM. He could certainly have afforded a driver to take him in whatever luxury car he wanted, or he could have used a helicopter as some of his neighbors did, but he liked to be behind the wheel himself. He really enjoyed driving with the convertible top down and the wind in his hair as much as possible, although this morning was a little too chilly for that, and he needed to keep his appearance orderly for the business meetings he had planned for today. There was a meeting at 9AM with Blake Chambertree, the CEO of Miritrans. Blakes' company is a global shipping conglomerate whose stock fell briefly, rebounded, and later surged after the company announced stronger than expected earnings for the last fiscal quarter. In that quarter they had posted revenue of over thirty-two billion dollars, as opposed to the twenty-seven point two billion that had been predicted by analysts at Reuters.

Soon enough he pulled his Bugatti Veyron 16.4 Super Sport in front of the high rise where Blake's offices were kept and got out. The valet for the building didn't even try to move the car from its parking spot. They neither wanted to risk marring the perfect paint or test the twelve hundred horsepower engine in the Manhattan traffic. Knowing that this 1.7-million-dollar car could go from 0 to 100 in only 2.6 seconds, it was far too much of a car for any of the minimum wage valets to drive, so they resolved themselves to being its guards against any passerby, and nothing more.

Javier walked into the lobby and up to the main security station for the building. A security guard with the name "Steve" sewn into a name badge on his shirt had seen, and drooled over, the car Javier had parked and greeted him.

"May I help you?"

"Yes, I'm here to see Blake Chambertree. I am Javier Armand."

"One moment, sir" replied the guard. He then reached over to his phone and dialed some numbers.

"Yes, I have a Javier Armand here to see Mr. Chambertree. Yes. Thank you."

The guard looked at Javier and said "They have me on hold. It'll be just a moment sir."

"Thank you" said Javier.

After a few moments of hold, the guard looked out the clear glass windows of the lobby toward the Bugatti and asked, "Is it really true that you don't shift out of second gear until you are past ninety in your car?"

Javier smiled. He loved talking about his pet car. "Yep. All true. Driving that thing is like trying to tame an Apollo rocket."

Steve smiled and was about to say something when apparently someone came back on the line. "Yes, I'm still here. Yes. Ok. Thank you." He hung up the phone.

Pointing to an elevator at the far end of the cavernous marble and glass lobby, the guard said "Thank you for waiting Mr. Armand. Mr. Chambertree is waiting for you in his office. Please use that elevator there and go to the eighty-seventh floor. His secretary will be waiting for you there."

Turning toward the elevator, Javier responded: "Thank you, Steve" and walked away.

"Very welcome sir!" replied an envious guard. He silently wondered what kind of man you have to be to be that successful in life.

The elevator ride didn't take long at all, and before long the doors to the 87th floor opened. The floor had an open architecture on one side where secretaries and lower to middle management were kept. On the other side of the floor, there were a few conference and utility rooms, but mostly that side was where the upper management located themselves. As he stepped off the elevator, a stunningly beautiful woman who looked Brazilian greeted him with a corresponding accent.

"Mr. Armand, I presume?"

"Yes."

"Mr. Chambertree is expecting you. Will you please follow me?"

"Certainly" replied Javier. Thinking back to his younger days before marrying Amanda, he would have followed up that reply with "I'll follow you anywhere" ... but not this time.

The woman turned around and led him around the offices. As he walked along trying hard not to gaze and the charms of the woman in front of him, he saw that there must have been about thirty to forty people working in the main area.

"Are all these people secretaries?" asked Javier.

"No sir" responded the Brazilian woman. "Most of these people are logistics managers, and they are responsible for scheduling the shipments for our clients. This is only one of twelve logistics centers, and in fact this is the smallest logistics center for the company. We only handle shipments that are scheduled to come in to the local New York harbor in this center."

Javier didn't respond. He just looked at all the bright faces of the people who obviously loved their job. He wondered if they would still love their job after today.

Eventually the woman opened one side of a double door to the office in the corner of the floor and held it open for Javier. After entering herself, she then said "Mr. Chambertree, this is Mr. Javier Armand of JA Holdings. Mr. Armand, this is Blake Chambertree."

Stepping around his desk, Blake approached Javier with the gait of a man who had worked his way from the very bottom. That, in fact, is exactly what he had done. He was wearing blue jeans and a khaki shirt and so Javier felt a little overdressed. No bother though.

Holding out his hand and wearing a wide toothy smile, the man with a mane of blond hair that was slightly unruly stepped forward to Javier. "Mr. Armand! Good to finally meet you!"

Shaking hands with Blake, Javier replied "The pleasure is mine."

The Brazilian personal secretary silently left the office now that her job was done and shut the door behind her.

Gesturing to the couch and loveseat setting in one corner of his office, Blake asked "Can I get you something to drink?"

"Sparkling water, if you have it" replied Javier.

"Coming right up" responded Blake as he walked toward his wet bar. While preparing the drink in a glass with ice, he spoke while not yet looking back toward Javier. "How was your drive in this morning? You're up in the Hamptons, aren't you?"

"Yes, I am, and it was great. Beautiful drive this morning."

Returning to Javier and handing him a glass with bubbly water, Blake said "I suppose it would be in a Bugatti like that."

Javier smiled, now realizing that his arrival was not only expected but also watched. The call from Steve the guard wasn't unexpected either apparently since Blake already knew the kind of car Javier was driving. Deciding that two could play that game, Javier said "I find it a little more enjoyable than coming to work in a Sikorski S-76 like you have currently parked on the roof."

Knowing that his verbal fencing lunge had just been parried by his visitor, Blake smiled and said "Touché."

The two men took drinks from their respective glasses and set them down on the coffee table in front of them. Blake was the first to speak.

"I have to say I was a little perplexed as to why you decided to come and visit my little corner of the world Mr. Armand."

"Please call me Javier. And not only did I want to see some of your operation, I wanted to talk to you about a proposal that I think you will be very interested in, Mr. Chambertree."

"And you can call me Blake. What kind of proposal did you have in mind?"

Taking another drink from his glass, he swallowed the carbonated water as slowly as if it was fine whiskey. He was unaccustomed to speaking about this side of his life with those who were not already aware of it and he knew that he needed to approach the subject carefully. His goal was, of course, to have Blake buy into what he had to propose.

"Well Blake, what I am here to talk to you about is something that I don't normally talk about. I am here to extend to you an invitation to be part of an organization, one that I am a member of in good standing. This organization has existed for well over four thousand years and it has shaped the overall direction of the world as we know it. Only those who have displayed the most cunning of all are invited to be members."

"A secret organization" queried Blake as he twirled his glass. "I'm afraid you're a little too late my friend. I'm already a member of the Skull and Bones with my old alma mater."

"As am I, however my time at Yale and in the tomb pale in comparison to what I am here to talk to you about" replied Javier.

"I doubt that. What does your little club call itself?" objected Blake.

"It is a name that few have heard. The only ones who have heard the name and still lived are those who are in its membership. Before I tell you the name, I will tell you that your membership will guarantee more wealth and power than you've ever imagined."

Laughing, Blake said "Borrowing a line from a movie, I can imagine quite a bit."

"Yes, I'm sure you can."

Thinking for a few seconds, Blake smiled and said "OK. I'll bite. Lay it on me. What's the name of your secret society?"

"We are called The Circle of Seven."

"Circle of Seven, huh? Never heard of em'"

Gesturing his relaxed open palm to Blake, Javier smiled and said "No … of course you haven't."

Trying, and failing, to gauge where his visitor was really coming from, Blake furrowed his brow and asked "So why should I be part of your club. Why invite me?"

"That's very easy to answer Mr. Chambertree" responded Javier as he reverted back to the more formal way of addressing Blake. "As to why we are inviting you, one of our members recently met with a tragic death, and so currently the Circle of Seven has only six members. We are looking for a seventh member. We only accept members who are fellow titans of industry and government and so you were a natural choice."

"As to why you should be part of our organization, we make it our aim to guide society in a manner that is beneficial to not only ourselves, but the world as a whole. We have the power and ability to shape how events unfold in history and so with that comes great wealth and great power."

"How exactly have you 'shaped' history?" asked Blake using air quotes.

"Remember the Manhattan project?"

"Yes"

"That was us" revealed Javier unemotionally.

"You guys where behind the development of the nuclear bomb" said Blake. It was more of a statement than a question.

"Yes" answered Javier.

"What else?"

"There is more of course. Much more. But before I will tell you any more, I need to know if you accept the invitation" answered Javier.

Blake swirled his own drink of Jack and Coke around in his glass for a while, then set it down on the glass coffee table and stood. He casually walked to the floor to ceiling window behind his massive desk. He stood there for a few minutes thinking. Javier allowed him time to think.

"When I was at Yale, I did a paper one time on something that Abraham Lincoln said" said Blake eventually breaking the silence. "He is quoted as saying 'Nearly all men can stand adversity, but if you want to test a man's character, give him power.'"

Turning back to look at Javier, Blake continued "Mr. Armand, I am the CEO of a collection of companies that grossed 32 billion in the last quarter alone. I have more money than I could ever think of using. As far as power, I resolved a long time ago that I would never allow it to rule me. I keep my feet firmly planted on the ground and will never, under any circumstances, allow myself to become a power hungry, egotistic, megalomaniac. I appreciate you and your fellow circle members thinking of me, but I have all that I want already, and I'm not in the market for anything more."

Seeing where this meeting was going and how he probably wouldn't be spending much more time in the office, Javier set his drink down on the coffee table and stood. He looked at Blake and said, "If that is your decision, then you are certainly free to make such a choice, but I have to warn you that refusal has proven very dire for others in the past, Mr. Chambertree."

Clearly seeing the threatening posture his visitor was now taking, Blake's overall demeanor changed from that of a relaxed businessman, to one who was now ready for a boxing match. "Oh? And who else has refused your invitations."

"Different people through the years" replied Javier. "John F. Kennedy is one that comes mind."

To recruit Blake, this was certainly the wrong thing to say. His country certainly had its problems, but he loved the red, white and blue. Narrowing his eyes, he said "I think it's time for you to go, Mr. Armand."

Slowly nodding his head, he simply said "I hope you have a pleasant day, Mr. Chambertree" as he exited the door to Blake's office, there was no response from his host. Walking toward the elevator, Javier once again looked over to the beautiful Brazilian secretary.

"Shame" muttered Javier to himself.

Taking the elevator down to the first floor, he passed Steve the security guard and climbed into the solitude of his car. Firing up the engine, he eased from its parking spot and merged into traffic. As he began driving, he reached into his glove compartment and removed a throwaway phone he kept in there for just such a need. He dialed 911.

"9-1-1 What is your emergency?"

Taking on a fake southern accent, Javier said "Now listen here missy. I'm going to say this slowly, so you hear every word. I'm in a closet at here at Miritrans, and I'm just calling you to make sure you know that it was me who did it. I'm gonna do it cause of the way they treated my cousin. Ya hear? My cousin got a raw deal and I'm gonna make em pay!"

"Sir, who am I speaking t ..."

Javier hung up the throwaway phone, and seeing that nobody was following him as he drove over a bridge, he momentarily steered the car with his knee while removing the battery from the phone. He thereafter threw it out the window into the bushes never to be seen again.

Then, reaching into his coat pocket, he retrieved a small device with an antenna. Using his teeth to grab onto the antenna, it was extended to full length. Flipping a cover over the one and only button, he pressed the button.

Next to Blake's office, there was a small room that was used as a storage room where surplus office supplies were normally kept. The room didn't really get too many visitors, and so the light to the room was currently off. As soon as Javier pressed the button, what looked like several lights lit up the room, but these lights weren't from any light bulb. Nobody had entered the room and turned on the light. The lights that lit up the room came from the far corner down near the floor. The lights shone for only about three seconds, but when they ceased there was a small device about one foot square that had a timer on it. The timer was set to five seconds.

5, 4, 3, 2, 1 ...

At that moment, the device exploded with enough force to blow out every window on the entire floor. In total there were 54 people working on that floor, 53 of which lost their lives that day. The ones who were working near the room where the device had been delivered were the lucky ones. They never knew what hit them, and their remains were never found.

Those who were standing near the windows, on the other hand, were blown against them. The force of their bodies slamming into the windows fractured each tempered glass panel, and their bodies as well as thousands of small glass shards were all forced out into the atmosphere. If they were conscious at all, these ones had the unfortunate experience of contemplating their oncoming death as they plummeted eighty-seven stories to ground level.

Blake Chambertree was one of them.

Except for one logistics manager who happened to be standing next to a column made of iron and cement that blocked the blast, every one of the workers in the Miritrans logistics center were either incinerated or would have wished they had been.

Meanwhile, Javier smiled as he took his finger off the button.

His personal phone then rang, and it was his daughter.

"Hi honey! How's my angel?"

CHAPTER 26

As she sat on a couch in the oval office, Vice President Brynn Monroe took a moment to quell her mind of the turbulent thoughts swirling around. She knew the best way for her to be her best for the American people, let alone for her fellow astronauts, was to see to it that she maintained clear thinking ability. Presenting a jumble of facts to the president in no particular order wouldn't do, and so she forced herself to think of things that purposely had nothing to do with the life and death issues that led her to the oval office today.

"What to think of ..."

Vice President Monroe had lived a somewhat celebrity life up this point. While not the youngest person ever to hold the office of vice president, at 42 she was the youngest to hold it in the last 160 years, but more noteworthy to most she was the first woman to hold the office. Before that her career in politics involved congress, and before that she had been used by the National

Aeronautics and Space Administration, or NASA, on a mission to the International Space Station to live for three months and perform several experiments involving microbiology and DNA sequencing. She had received her Ph.D. in microbiology at the University of California, Stanford.

"What to think of ..."

Brynn closed her eyes. Using a well-traveled mental pathway, she focused on her surroundings as a way of ordering her thoughts. She sometimes felt like there was another part of her subconscious brain that would continue to work on the problems at hand, while at the same time the forefront of her mind would think about unimportant minutia that had nothing to do with the other. This method had served her well in the past, such as when things went badly while she and another one of her crewmates were on an EVA, or Extra-Vehicular Activity outside the space station. Her resultant clear thinking led to a novel resolution of the problem at hand that even the engineers in Houston hadn't thought of. Not only was she a celebrity before she even entered the White House, she was also a rock star in the eyes of NASA.

Taking a deep breath, she opened her eyes and the first thing she saw was the large presidential seal embroidered into the carpet in front of the presidential desk. The depiction was of an eagle sitting behind a shield that contained the stars and stripes of the American flag. The left eagles' talon grasped an olive branch with 13 leaves, and in the right talon there were 13 arrows. For a moment she observed that the craftsmanship of the carpet was very good, as one would expect, but then she saw some things that the casual observer might not catch. First, the eagles head was turned toward the olive branch. She remembered from her history classes that President Truman established the current design of the presidential seal, and he dictated that this direction would be depicted to symbolize the importance of peace. The interesting fact to Brynn though was that not one or two meters away from the seal on the carpet was the resolute desk where the president sat, and the front of that desk had a carved presidential seal with the eagle's head facing the other direction toward the arrows.

"Hmmm ... going to have to look that up someday" she thought to herself. "If I had to guess, it would be because that part of the desk was added when ..."

"Brynn! To what do I owe the honor of a visit from the office of the Vice President down the hall?"

Brynn snapped out of her reverie and instantly looked toward President Kirken as he entered from his private study. Brynn thought to herself that it was a shame that she was about to ruin his bright disposition

Standing up swiftly and extending her hand, she returned the greeting. "Mr. President. How are you this morning?"

"Just fine." Then looking her square in the eye, he then added "But from the look on your face, I take it that my demeanor might be changing soon?" as he approached and took his seat on the couch opposite from where she had been sitting. Brynn once again took her own seat.

"I'm afraid so, sir. As you know, among many other duties that I don't need to get into, part of my responsibilities involves the management of various administrations including NASA."

The president nodded his head.

"Well sir, this morning I received an urgent call from Houston informing me of a situation that has developed on the international space station."

Now showing a concerned look on his face, President Kirken asked "What kind of situation?"

"Remember the news of that satellite last month that developed a stuck thruster, which in turn shifted it into an uncontrollable orbit?" asked Brynn.

"Yes"

"Well, apparently last night, that rogue satellite smashed into another satellite. The good news is that not only was the rogue satellite disabled by the collision and its thrusters are no longer mis-firing, but the other satellite that was hit was a decommissioned and non-functioning communications bird from the seventies era."

"But I have a feeling that I'm not going to like the bad news" prompted President Kirken.

"No sir. You won't" replied Vice President Monroe. "Apparently a large amount of shrapnel from that collision happened to fall into the same orbital trajectory as the ISS and traveled in a collision course. As a result, there have been several modules in the station that have been pierced and are now depressurized. Not only that, but mission specialist Jamie Martine was hit by one of the pieces of shrapnel. Apparently, it was traveling very fast and passed completely through her leg, through and through. While she's lost some blood, she appears to be stable and is coherent."

"Meanwhile, one of the systems that was directly affected by the shrapnel was a system called the Oxygen Generation System, or OGS, which is a smaller component of the larger ISS life support system called the Environmental Control and Life Support System. Normally, it's designed to use power from the solar arrays to perform water electrolysis and it is the main method to generate oxygen aboard the station. The water is split into its constituent parts of oxygen and hydrogen. The oxygen is released into the breathable cabin air system, while the unneeded hydrogen is vented into space."

"The problem is that the OGS is located in the Destiny module, and Destiny was the hardest hit module of all. It is completely offline now, and it appears that it will require some serious repairs before it can be brought back online. Not only that, but the crew has lost several of their spare O2 tanks."

"Good Lord! Are they going to scrub and come home?"

"That was the initial judgement from Houston sir" answered the vice president, "but then after checking the status of the reentry vehicles currently docked with the station, it appears that they were both damaged as well. It is felt that either the heat shields have been compromised and so they wouldn't hold up to the five-thousand-plus degrees Fahrenheit that is encountered upon reentry, or the parachutes and associated pyros wouldn't fire resulting in an equally fatal reentry."

The president, whose eyes were now wide open in astonishment, took a deep breath and looked to the side for a moment. Then looking back to his vice president, he asked "So what is the plan? What is NASA going to do?"

"At this time every engineer at NASA is working on that problem sir, but when I asked them what the office of the president could do to assist, their liaison said that they would let me know, but prayers probably wouldn't be a bad idea."

Brynn looked on as the president stood, and after uttering a rare expletive he contemplatively walked toward the windows behind his desk with his hands in his pockets. While still staring out the bullet proof glass, he then asked: "Do you know how much time they have?"

"They have been forced into their space suits and for now they are ok but counting the O2 in their suit tanks combined with the remaining solid fuel oxygen generation canisters, it is currently estimated that they have only six hours of life support" answered the vice president.

"And I suppose we don't have anything ready for a rescue mission?"

"Not that would be ready in six hours, sir. There happens to be a V2 Dragon on the launchpad, but the most optimistic and compressed estimate for mission readiness is two days" replied Brynn.

For the next 30 seconds, Brynn watched the president as his back was to her. Then slightly nodding his head, it appeared that he had come to some sort of decision. Turning back to her, he then asked: "What is the most important limiting factor in their survival?"

Standing and walking over to the window herself, she replied "That would be O2 and water, sir. The tanks are sitting on a palette in the vehicle assembly building at Kennedy right now, ready to be loaded onto the spacecraft. It's not the supplies. It's getting them there."

After a few more seconds, Brynn saw her commander in chief nod a couple more times to himself, and then reaching out for a final handshake he said "OK. Please keep me in the loop with any further developments."

With a single nod of her own, she replied with a simple "Yes sir" before she excused herself.

Once she was gone and the door was closed, President Kirken reached over to his phone and pressed the intercom button.

"Yes sir?" came the greeting from his personal secretary, Susan.

"Susan, please get Doctor Marsalis from Midway Magnetic on the line for me."

Jason put the phone down on his desk and stared at it blankly. He and Dennis had just been in a meeting when the call came in, and so now that Jason was off the phone, Dennis was quite eager to hear what happened since the tone of the one-sided conversation he just heard didn't sound good.

"You're killing me smalls! What did he say?"

Jason looked up from the phone receiver that lay in its holder and proceeded to regale Dennis with the story of impending disaster on the ISS. After repeating all the details, he concluded with "So the president asked me if there was anything that I thought we could do to help them.

"Yeah there is! Let's put a portal up there and get their butts off the station! With our new site-to-site ability, we can plant them right in the oval office if he wants" exclaimed Dennis.

"You're right, we could do that, but what I didn't tell you yet is that whatever solution we might come up with, he asked that it somehow still keep the existence of the portal secret."

As opposed to the forward lean he had been using in his chair, Dennis sat back in his chair with a grimace and an audible "Hmmm".

The two men sat there in Jason's office and thought. After about a minute, Dennis smiled to his partner and said, "I have an idea."

"I'm all ears" responded Jason.

"OK. So, he said the rocket can't fly until two days from now, right?"

"Yeah. And that was the most optimistic estimate. It might be longer." answered Jason.

"And the O2 and water are in tanks that are just sitting in the VAB, right?"

"Right again."

"OK. So other than having to deal with two days' worth of B-O until their rescue boat comes, the only thing they really need for survival is what's in those tanks. Right?"

Seeing where Dennis was going with this, Jason began to smile and responded, "So if those tanks just happened to disappear from the VAB and magically reappear on the station in a module they aren't currently in, then they'll get by until the Dragon can get up there."

"Exactly" answered Dennis.

"But what if there is a problem with the Dragon launch?" asked Jason, already knowing the answer before he finished asking the question.

"If all else fails, we can still snatch them" answered Dennis.

"But this way, we can still maintain secrecy of the portal" added Jason.

"Once again … exactly" answered Dennis.

Getting back on his phone, Jason dialed a few numbers.

"Yes, this is Doctor Jason Marsalis. I need to speak with President Kirken immediately. Thank you."

Jason waited for a few seconds, then said "Yes, hello Mr. President."

"Jason. I hope you have some good news for me."

"Yes sir, we have a plan on how we can help the astronauts on the space station, but I'm going to need your help."

"Tell me what you need, and you'll have it."

"Can you call down to Kennedy and issue a presidential order to close the doors and completely evacuate the VAB?"

"Evacuate?"

"Yes sir. Instead of using the portal to transport the astronauts back to earth, thus revealing the existence of the portal, we want to get them the life support supplies that they need to survive until the dragon can get there. We can continuously monitor their survivability to make sure they are ok, and if there is a problem beyond what has already happened, we can snatch em'. But if not, then they can still be rescued by the Dragon, the astronauts will survive, the existence of the O2 and water on the station can be chalked up to a paperwork mishap, and the secrecy of the portal would remain intact."

There was a pause on the other side of the line as the president thought about the proposal, but in only five seconds, the president said "I'll call you back when the coast is clear. Kirken out." The line went dead. Hearing the conversation closure from the president, Jason's eyebrows raised, and a slight smile crossed his face.

Meanwhile Jason forwarded his calls to the portal room and he and Dennis hot-footed it down there. Within a few minutes the system was up, running and ready to go. Just as they were ready to dial the portal to the VAB, a call came in to the portal room.

"This is Jason."

"Jason, this is President Kirken. I have scrambled the national guard to the VAB and they are posted all around the perimeter at a supposedly safe distance. I've manufactured story about a bomb threat and I've got everybody out of there. The AK-47's surrounding the building will make sure you aren't seen. You have a go to proceed with your plan."

"Thank you, sir. I will call you back when we're done" responded Jason. Then with a slight smile, he then said: "Jason out" and hung up the phone.

As he was bringing the cryogenic plants online, Dennis looked at Jason with a laugh and said, "You did that on purpose!" referring to the "Star Trek" sounding way President Kirken signed off the last phone call.

Taking on the most innocent face he could muster, Jason said "Hmmm .... could be." He was unsuccessful at stifling the smile.

Then regaining a face reflecting the seriousness of the moment, Jason then removed the USB key that normally hung around his neck under his shirt. Placing the key in his console, he looked over to Dennis to see that he had just done the same thing. The two men looked at each other while their respective hands were on their keys, and amidst the oppressive din of cryogenic pumps and voltage transformers near the room, Jason said into his noise cancelling headset "Engaging portal in three-two-one-MARK!"

Simultaneously, Jason and Dennis turned their keys. Doing this caused one of the two portals to activate. Now, with the new site to site capability, there were two portal apertures sitting face to face with each other. It allowed for matter to be transferred from one distant location to another without having to stop off at the portal room. Since they were going to be sending these life support tanks to a location on the ISS though, and since that location is in space, and finally since the ISS is not only in space but is also *moving* in space, they decided to be very careful. They would grab the tanks from the VAB and bring them back to the lab, then reset the main portal to the ISS.

Within a few seconds the scene materializing in the portal was that of the ground floor of the Kennedy Space Center Vehicle Assembly Building. The Apollo era VAB was actually a single building 160 meters tall, which is almost twice as tall as the Statue of Liberty. It contains four separate bays where up to four Apollo rockets would have been in various stages of assembly, however the different bays were somewhat underutilized nowadays by the much shorter space shuttles and heavy lift rocketry. They had to look through more than one of the "high bays", but eventually the palette they were looking for was found in high bay number three. The palette contained nine silver colored high-pressure oxygen canisters and sitting next to it was another palette holding three tanks of water and several dozen solid fuel oxygen generation canisters. It only took a total of ten minutes to lift and carry all of the supplies through the portal back to the lab, and as soon as they did, they shut down the portal and called the president to let him know their progress. He, in turn, called off the bomb threat hoax.

Now that the supplies, had been secured and the portal to the VAB had been disengaged, it was now time to connect to the ISS. Fortunately Jason had worked into the trajectory program the ability to account for potential continuous movement of the target position of the portal, and so once the current position of the orbiting station that was traveling at seventeen thousand miles an hour was ascertained from the NASA website, it was a simple matter of punching those numbers into the portal control system, and *voilà!*, the portal was now connected to the station.

It was easy to see the problem with the station. There were several holes in the walls of the module they were viewing. As such, it was obvious that the environment on the other side of the portal wasn't capable of life support.

"That's gonna be a problem" said Dennis, "on account of I really like breathing and all."

"I don't think that's going to be a problem" responded Jason. "The president said the crew was already in their EVA suits, and so they have the ability to come into this module. All we have to do is roll the tanks in front of the portal and let the portal field touch the tank. The field will instantly transport the tank there just like it did with Admiral Brinstock, and at that point the tanks will be weightless and they'll just float off."

Thinking for a minute Dennis had to admit Jason had a point, and so they both immediately got to work rolling the heavy tanks, one by one, to the portal window. As Jason predicted, as soon as the tank touched the portal field, it was immediately transported to the station.

That's the good news.

The bad news is that aside from the floor (this had been programmed out in the portal positional program that both Jason and Dennis had written) anything else touching the tank would be transported too. In their haste to help the astronauts this little detail had escaped the forefront of their minds, and so as soon as he got the first tank ready for transport to the station, Dennis tipped the tank against the field and the tank was instantly transported to the destiny module on the international space station.

And since he was touching the tank, so was Dennis.

One second Dennis was on the ground in the laboratory, and the next second, he was floating in zero G in a very dangerous situation. Suddenly he was not only weightless, but all the air in his lungs was immediately sucked out. Fortunately, Dennis instantly knew what happened to him, and he reached back to where he knew the portal window was and was instantly transported back to the lab. He was on the station for a grand total of four seconds, and when he returned, he not only took a desperately needed gulp of air, but he also had a headache the size of his home state of Texas.

It all happened so fast that all Jason had time to do was to stand there looking like his eyes were about to bug out of his skull. As soon as he realized that his friend was back, he rushed to Dennis to see if he was ok. He was all right, and pushing through the pain of his headache, Dennis actually stood up and resumed with the deliveries of supplies until all was completed. From that point on though, he would tip the tank toward the portal but would release it before it actually touched the field.

Once the last of the supplies had been delivered, Jason disabled the transport ability of the portal, but maintained the viewport. He then called President Kirken back to let him know that the deed had been done. While Dennis was off looking for some aspirin, Jason continued to watch the scene in the Destiny module. Evidently the president made the necessary calls and came up with some story that led to the hatch on the other side of the module to open. When the astronauts saw the floating tanks of O2, water, and O2 generating cannisters the relief in their faces (through the glass helmets of their suits) was obvious. More than one of them were seen crying, which caused Jason to shed a few tears of his own. Dennis had silently come up behind Jason and with his headache abating, he was treated to the scene as well.

Jason reached over to his console and clicked "Disconnect" on his screen. The portal image instantly vanished, and within a few minutes all was quiet.

"Well compadre, I'm going to take my carcass to bed. I've had a big day" said Dennis.

"Indeed, you did!" agreed Jason as he watched Dennis walk toward the door. Before Dennis left through the door though, he added "You do realize that you are now officially an astronaut, right?

Dennis turned around and stood there for a moment, considering what Jason had just said. Then, holding his hand up with the four fingers splayed out in the shape of a "W" he said, "live short and ridiculously!"

Jason laughed, but just then the phone rang causing Dennis to stop short from leaving.

"Hello, this is Jason Marsalis."

"Jason, this is President Kirken."

"Yes, Mr. President."

This, of course, caused Dennis to re-enter the room and take a seat. Jason clicked the speakerphone so Dennis could hear. He then said "Oh, and if it's OK with you, I have put you on speakerphone. Dennis is the only other one in the room."

"That's fine" said the president. "I'm sure you know this already, but the mission was a complete success. The astronauts have what they need to survive, and I'm also told that the rescue launch window is on schedule."

"Yes sir. We just watched them take the tanks. It was obvious they were happy to see them."

"Very good. Those astronauts, as well as the American people once again owe you two a debt of gratitude. But ... it appears that today is the day for more than one critical problem."

"Oh?" replied Jason.

"I need you to use the portal for another serious problem that has just developed in Russia."

"Russia? What's going on?" asked Jason as he looked at Dennis.

"As part of a joint scientific research program that was created in the interests of bolstering international solidarity, I recently sent one of our top physicists over there to work with one of theirs, and she has been there for a few months now. Her name is Doctor Brianna Plant and she along with the Russian physicist she was working with have disappeared."

CHAPTER 27

HEARING THE NAME SET JASON back on his figurative heels.

"Brianna Plant?" asked Jason candidly. "Brianna's missing?"

"I take it you know her?" asked President Kirken.

"Very much so, sir!" replied Jason. "She and I went to M.I.T. together. She's a very close friend of mine. In fact, my wife Mikki had Brianna stand next to her in our wedding party."

"I see. Well Doctor Plant was sent by my office to work with a Russian scientist named Alexei Einikov as part that joint scientific consortium I mentioned. The Russian president and I agreed to do this as a symbol of the new era of mutual understanding and political détente that now exists between our two countries. She's been there for a few months, but I just got a call from their government just now telling me that not only is Doctor Plant missing, so is Doctor Einikov."

"Oh pepper, what have you got yourself into?" mumbled Jason under his breath.

"I beg your pardon?" asked President Kirken.

"Oh, I'm sorry sir. It was nothing. So ... I assume you need us to look for the two of them?" asked Jason.

"Yes" answered the president. "I need you to figure out what happened to them, and as soon as you do, let me personally know. I am having my secretary email you right now all information we have as to where they were working, and the last time they were seen. Your orders are to determine where they are, and as soon as possible, retrieve them from harm's way."

Looking over to the clock on the wall, the digits read that it was already 6PM. Mikki wasn't going to be happy, but Jason knew that as soon as she heard what was going on with Brianna, she would be completely on board with having to do without her husband for a little bit this evening.

"Yes sir. We'll get on this right away!" responded Jason.

"Good. Like I say, as soon as I learn from you the necessary information, I will relay that to the Kremlin."

"Yes sir. I will hopefully get back to you soon."

"Good. Kirken out." The line went dead.

In silence, Jason hung up the phone and didn't say anything. While Jason was still talking to the president, Dennis had seen the writing on the wall and so he had just brewed a couple cups of ambition for he and Jason and was now handing him a cup.

"Well ... so much for going home for dinner" said Dennis.

Still looking at the phone and not really acknowledging the statement just said by Dennis, Jason could only utter what he was thinking right then. "I just hope pepper is ok."

"Pepper?" inquired Dennis.

Looking up Jason smiled, only now realizing that he was using the word "Pepper" interchangeably when referring to Brianna. Jason smiled and said, "As you might have heard, I am very familiar with Doctor Plant. She and I were very close friends in college, in fact everybody thought she and I were boyfriend and girlfriend for a while there."

"You weren't?" asked Dennis.

"No. It was never like that. She was always more like a sister than a girlfriend, and she always felt the same way towards me. When I met Mikki, Brianna instantly took to calling Mikki my girlfriend and the two of them ended up becoming instant friends. Brianna is this fiery little Asian girl, and so early on my nickname for her was "pepper" as in "pepper plant". Mikki and I are the only ones that call her that."

Nodding his head to show he now understood, Dennis then asked, "Did you get that email from President Kirken yet?"

"Actually" responded Jason, "I've been so busy talking to you about Brianna that I haven't even looked."

While Jason made a few clicks in order to find the email that was waiting for him, he also called Mikki to let her know what was going on. Since Mikki was close with Brianna, Jason asked Mikki if she would like to come to work to be here if they are able to find her. Mikki instantly said she would be there as soon as possible after finding a sitter for Jace junior. Dennis made a similar call to his newly wedded wife to let her know what was going on too. He suggested to Lynne that she jump in the car with Mikki and they come together.

Both Jason and Dennis were so glad they didn't have to keep secrets from their wives anymore.

Once all the necessary steps with their respective wives were completed, Jason opened up the email the president had sent and forwarded a copy of it to Dennis. The two men spent the next ten minutes reading through the email to see what information could be culled out. The first thing Jason did with his newfound information was to enter the coordinates of the laboratory where Brianna and Alexei had been working into the portal navigation system. It ended up taking about thirty minutes to not only locate where they had been working, but to locate the point in time when they both appeared to be safe in the laboratory. Then stepping forward in time, they took note how both Brianna and Alexei would appear in the office in the morning and leave late at night. As Jason and Dennis moved the portal through time, they eventually came to a point that was about ten days ago. It now appeared that the two scientists were more than familiar with each other. There seemed to be lots of smiles passing between the two of them, and there was even a kiss. By the time they saw this, there was a knock on the laboratory door, and after checking the closed-circuit video feed, Jason buzzed the door and let in Mikki and Lynne. The girls approached the portal and looked at a scene that had been paused in freeze frame mode where the two scientists happened to be kissing.

"What exactly are you two doing here?" asked Mikki. She had a hard time holding back the smile, but she just wanted to give her husband and his best friend a little bit of a hard time.

"It isn't what you think!" said Jason, playing along.

"Don't you think this is a little bit of an invasion of privacy?" asked Lynne who wasn't aware that Mikki and Jason were playing with each other. Lynne was serious.

"Not really" replied Dennis. "We've been stepping through time to see when exactly these two disappeared. What we didn't expect to see is that they are not only colleagues, but they have apparently also become romantically involved."

"More than romantically involved" said Mikki. "I think they are bona fide lovers. Get a load of that wedding ring she's wearing!"

Sure enough, the freeze frame showed in clear detail a wedding ring with a very large diamond. One of the disconcerting aspects of the portal image is that, unlike a freeze frame on a video recorder, the frozen image was completely clear and crisp. So crisp, in fact, that it looked like you could reach out and touch them.

Now seeing the real story, Lynne relaxed her mental stance and saw the ring Mikki was referring to. "Whoa!"

"I wonder how she lifts her hand up each day" observed Dennis.

"Ok bud" said Jason, "I'm going to move forward to the next day to see when they get there."

With no words, Dennis resumed his gaze toward his computer screen to make sure all was running at peak efficiency with the cryogenic systems. Once satisfied with everything there, he then turned to watch events unfold on the portal itself, witnessing how the story of Brianna and her apparent new beau unfolded.

The following day, the two seemed to arrive at the laboratory at the same time, and this time they seemed to be holding hands as they walked down the hallway to the main doors of the laboratory. The same held true for the following five days until the portal arrived at a point four days ago when neither of them arrived at the lab at the time when they usually did.

"OK. So, it appears that something has changed" said Jason. "Up to this point, it seems like you could set your watch by their arrival, but on this day four days ago they seem to be completely absent."

"Agreed" said Dennis. "Let's start tracing back to their respective domiciles to see what happened."

Jason then said, "I agree, however ..." Jason turned to the other three in the portal room and said "Before we do, I need to say that Dennis have had a discussion about this some time ago. With the portal we have the ability to voyeuristically look at any point on the planet at any time. As such, we have the ability to be a fly on the wall at times when the subject is perhaps in a compromising ... or very private ... circumstance. It was for this reason why

Dennis and I created the dual-key system where the only way the portal system could be used was when both he and I agreed that the subject matter and the target location was necessary, even if it might constitute an invasion of privacy."

Then looking over to Dennis, he then asked, "Do you agree that what we are about to do is necessary even though it might constitute an invasion of privacy of our subjects?"

"I agree that what we are about to do is necessary. I vote that we proceed" answered Dennis.

Seeing as how both Mikki and Lynne were also in the room, Jason looked over to them and asked them the same question. Mikki looked to her friend sitting next to her, and when she saw the obvious answer in her eyes, Mikki answered "Both Lynne and I agree that while we shouldn't normally invade the privacy of anybody using the portal, in this case it is necessary to do so for the safety of Brianna as well as someone whom she is obviously fond of."

Nodding his head slowly, Jason said "So be it."

With that short acknowledgement, Jason and Dennis then began the painstaking process of following the lovebirds from the day before. After leaving, the two of them emerged from the facility building where the lab was kept and walked around the city center. There in the heart of Saint Petersburg where they lived and worked, they took a subway to an area of the city called Moskovskiy Prospect. They walked in and out of the shops and stores that were still open, but eventually they happened upon a small shop where authentic shawarma was sold. They ordered their dinner at this café, then sat at one of the tables that was set up out in front of the shop near the sidewalk. Passersby paid no attention to the two of them as they not only ate their respective dinners, but apparently exchanged looks and loving words between each other. Jason and Dennis had shut off the audio feed for the time being since it wasn't necessary for them to hear what was being said. No sense invading their privacy to that level.

After eating their dinner for about 15 minutes, they stood and proceeded along the city walk until they got to a coffee shop where they spent another 20 minutes exchanging looks and conversational pleasantries. Emerging yet again, they now apparently retraced their steps to the subway and eventually made their way back to the laboratory and eventually to a suite that they apparently now shared.

Slowing down the forward motion of the portal, Jason did his best to maintain the necessary privacy of the couple by remaining stationary outside the bedroom door. But after seeing that the two of them went into the bedroom the night before without ever emerging the next morning, Jason, Dennis, and their wives all agreed that it was necessary to see what happened in the bedroom after the door was shut.

As it turns out, it didn't take long for them to get an answer, and in the process, they didn't see anything that Brianna or Alexei might have been embarrassed about. Keep in mind that the audio had been turned off throughout this entire exercise, but if it hadn't been off one would have been able to hear an obvious altercation happening behind the bedroom door.

As soon as the bedroom doors were closed, two men who were mostly dressed in black and who were sporting black ski masks attacked the couple and subdued them with what appeared to be some type of concoction that was injected into their bodies using a hypodermic needle. Within just a few seconds, both Brianna and Alexei were rendered unconscious. At that point, their assailants drug the two unconscious scientists toward the window where they were extracted by waiting accomplices.

Over the following hour, Jason and Dennis saw that Brianna and Alexei were separated and taken to different locations. Much to the chagrin of Mikki and Lynne, Jason elected to trace the exact location of Alexei Einikov first, with the intention of doing the same with Brianna shortly afterward. It was only with assurances from Jason and Dennis that they would use the time travel ability to make sure Brianna was safe in the end that Mikki and Lynne agreed to the "Alexei-first" approach. Jason and Dennis both felt that locating the Russian scientist first would be a good idea so that the president might be able to smooth out some ruffled feathers on the part of the Russian government … thus maintaining the current good relationship the U.S. had with Russia.

Eventually they came to a point where it appeared that Alexei was working on a device that seemed eerily familiar to the two men. It appeared to be staged in what could only be characterized as a "dungeon", however this dungeon was rigged with all the latest scientific instrumentation and testing equipment. They witnessed how Alexei was never allowed to leave this apparent lockup, and how his captors seemed to use force on him. Each time his jailers arrived in this scientific prison cell, they made sure to intimidate him. Sometimes it was only with words, however there was one occasion when they struck him several times. It was extremely hard to watch, but it was after witnessing such treatment that Jason and Dennis decided that they had to get Alexei out before it happened again.

They methodically moved forward in time until they finally got to a point where they could see that nobody else was around, and when they could extract Alexei from the obvious terrible situation he was in. When they identified that point, they stabilized the portal window on that place and time, and enabled the transport capability of the portal.

Turning on the audio, Jason, Dennis and their respective wives could hear the ambient noises from the laboratory where Alexei was being forced to work.

"Ok bud. What's the plan?" asked Dennis.

"I've been thinking about that" said Jason. "I think we need to just set up the portal near Alexei, have one of us travel there, grab him before he knows anything is happening, then immediately travel back here."

Processing what Jason had just proposed, Dennis spent a grand total of five seconds thinking about it, and then said "Sounds like the best approach. You or me?"

"Well" answered Jason, "Since my job is mostly positioning of the portal window, my work is mostly done. How about I grab him while you continue to monitor the health of the portal?"

Allowing a small smile to play itself across his face, Dennis replied with "Awwww man! You always get to have the fun!"

"Then I tell you what buddy" replied Jason, "You grab Alexei, and since I know her already, I'll kidnap Brianna. Deal?"

"Deal!" responded Dennis with an exaggerated smile on his face.

Setting the locks on his workstation, Jason stood from his seated position and walked over to Dennis' station to monitor the systems while Dennis moved to the portal window. All in the room spent some time watching as the events in the dungeon laboratory unfolded.

Alexei was apparently in the middle of writing code on a computer terminal for the time being, but after some time he stood and walked over to a bench that happened to be near where Jason and Dennis had formed the portal window. Dennis saw this as an opportune time for the "kidnapping" to occur, and so all he did was to reach forward and touch the portal field with his outstretched fingers.

Within the span of two seconds the portal field wrapped itself around Dennis' body and instantly transported him to the room where Alexei was standing. From Alexei's perspective, the room was silent one moment, but then suddenly illuminated with lights from an unknown source near to where he was standing. Before he was able to register anything that was happening, he saw something that looked like a man suddenly appear next to him. The man then laid his hand on Alexi's shoulder, and as soon as he did that the entire laboratory dissolved from sight and was suddenly replaced with what appeared to be a different laboratory entirely.

Looking on, Jason, Mikki and Lynne watched the scene unfold within the span of only a few seconds. When all was said and done Dennis was standing next to the portal window just as he was before, only now he was accompanied by the scientist that they had been watching. The scientist didn't know what to make of what had just happened, and so with wide eyes he began to look around him. The first thing he saw was Dennis, whom he now recognized as the wraith that he had just seen in his laboratory. Looking behind Dennis he could see another man sitting at what appeared to be a control console, and next to that man were two women standing there looking at Alexei with expectant looks on their faces.

Looking back to Dennis, Alexei said the first thing that came to his mind.

"Что это?"

"I'm sorry Doctor Einikov" responded Dennis, "We don't know Russian. Do you know English?"

Pausing for a few seconds, he then responded with "Yes, I do. What is this?"

"First, we are friends and we mean you no harm. We have been sent by our respective governments to rescue you from what appears to be a kidnapping situation. Have you been kidnapped against your will?"

The scientist had been standing there in a mildly hunched over position similar to the position he was in when Dennis had snatched him from the dungeon. Seeing that he was no longer in immediate danger Alexei straightened his rather tall stature and turned to face Jason and Dennis. Collecting his thoughts for a moment, he then answered: "Yes. I was ... kidnapped".

It was obvious that the new arrival was on high alert and so Jason tried to soothe Alexei's nerves. "Doctor Einikov, as was said before our respective governments have asked us to help locate and rescue you from a situation that obviously put you in high risk. We are your friends and we are here to help."

For the next several moments Alexei's eyes moved between Jason, then Dennis, then the girls, and back to Jason. Before saying anything, he stared at Jason for what seemed to be about ten seconds, but then turned around to look at the portal apparatus nearby. He looked at it for about twenty seconds, seemingly inspecting the details of the machinery before he turned back to Jason. With the insightful eyes of an engineer, he then asked: "You transported me here with your transportation portal?"

Of all the things that he could have asked at that moment, Jason and Dennis weren't prepared for this. Jason looked over to Dennis who had the same bewildered look on his face that Jason knew appeared on his own. Looking back to Alexei, Jason then said: "You know about ... about the portal?"

"Yes" was the short and distinct answer from Doctor Einikov.

Dennis rose from his seat at his workstation and came near to where Jason was standing. The two men stared at Doctor Einikov for a moment until Dennis asked "Now, how in all that's holy do you know about the portal?"

"Because, Doctor Greene, I was working on one myself" answered Alexei. He then added with great vigor, "BUT YOU HAVE TO RETURN ME TO MY LAB IMMEDIATELY!"

"Now hold on there ..." said Dennis, trying to use the best of his Texan demeanor to quell the anxiety that was so obviously written across the face of their new visitor, "... you just got here. Why would you want to get back to that hole where they were making you work?"

"Because the work I was doing there in that ... hole ... was keeping my wife alive!" excitedly answered Alexei.

"You're married!" blurted out Mikki, who up to this point had been silent.

"Yes. I am married, Mrs. Marsalis" answered Alexei.

The fact that their new visitor knew her name absolutely floored Mikki, let alone everybody else in the room. Mikki cautiously took a few steps forward and asked, “How do you know my name?”

Alexei all but yelled his response and said “It doesn’t matter! I HAVE TO GET BACK OR ELSE MY WIFE WILL DIE!”

“If you need to go back, then we will take you back” said Jason, “but before you go, you must tell us why she is in such danger, and how you know about the portal!”

Letting out an exaggerated sigh, he took on the look of a frustrated man and said, “because they made it clear to me that if I do not deliver on finding out why their portal isn’t working, then they will kill Brianna!”

All four yelled the same word at the exact same time.

“WHAT!”

Jason followed that with “What portal!? Who has a portal!?”

“I don’t have time to answer! Get me back now, or she’s dead!” replied Alexei.

Jason and Dennis looked at each other again, but then Jason looked to Alexei with a stern look on his face and said, “We can get you back to where and when you need, but you’re going to have to give us some answers first before you go back.”

Eventually seeing that his options were apparently limited and seeing how any more delays in answering the questions of these men might result in the very real possibility that his wife would be killed, Alexei relented and lowered his hands, which had been outstretched up until now, and simply said “Fine. What do you have to know?”

The first question was simple. Jason simply asked, “What portal?”

“The portal is in the possession of my captors” answered Alexei.

“Who are your captors?” asked Dennis.

"For a while they wouldn't tell me, but one time I overheard them refer to themselves as the 'Circle of Seven.'"

"Circle of Seven?" asked Lynne, who had stepped forward herself.

"Yes"

"And you built a portal for them?" asked Jason.

"No" answered Alexei.

"Didn't you just say you built the portal for them?" asked Dennis.

"No, I said that they are having me see why it wasn't working" replied Alexei.

"Then where did it come from?" asked Dennis.

"It was built before I got there by someone who doesn't know the difference between an electron gun and a pea shooter" said Alexei.

"Who built it?" asked Jason.

"I don't know, but it was based on some plans they got from someone else" came the reply from Alexei.

"Who would have plans to the portal?" asked Mikki.

"Again, I don't officially know, but I read a computer file one time that said the plans came from someone named Brinstock."

Reaching out to steady herself on a nearby cabinet, Mikki uttered the same thing that was on the minds of the other three in the room, "Oh my god!"

For the next twenty seconds, the news that Kenji was somehow involved in leaking plans for the portal percolated down in the minds of Jason, Dennis and their respective wives. With each passing second, the news that he had betrayed not only Jason like he did, but also the most secret of all United States secrets ... this made Jason and Dennis more and more angry.

With wide eyes, Jason exclaimed "My god! That guy was even more of a snake that I thought!"

Ultimately, Jason gathered his wits about him and then asked a new question that came to mind. "Were you successful?"

"With what?"

"With making your portal work!" replied Dennis, knowing exactly what it would mean to the world if a criminal organization had access to a portal.

"Yes, and no" came the somewhat evasive answer.

By this time Jason's typical casual demeanor had been replaced with one of anger, and so with a monotone voice that Mikki had never heard before he said only one word.

"Explain."

Taking another breath to gain his bearings, Alexei could see that he needed to reveal to Jason and Dennis what had been happening so that they could see that while he didn't like some of the things he had done, he was in a no-win situation.

"When I came a few nights ago, Brianna and I were taken from our bedroom. All I remember is being attacked and injected with something. Everything went black after that. When I regained consciousness, I was in the room where you took me. As I came to, there were some men there that explained that I had been brought there to complete the machine, the portal, and that if I didn't, they would kill Brianna."

"And so you just took their word that they hadn't already killed her?" asked Lynne. Her 'straight-shooter' personality seemed to have no veneer at this moment. Truth be told, none in the room were all that happy right now.

"Of course I didn't, but if there was at least *some* possibility that she was still alive, I had to try" answered Alexei. "Wouldn't you?"

For the next ten seconds the only sound in the room was the liquid helium cryogenic pumps that were still running. After letting that thought percolate down, Jason once again said only one word while showing no expression on his half-lidded eyes.

"Continue."

"For the next few hours I masqueraded like I was working on the programming for the portal, when in reality I was thinking about what my options were and what I had to do. Meanwhile I had no idea what this device was for initially, however it became clear that the intention was to create a method of transferring matter from one location to another by creating an Einstein-Rosen bridge. You see, and Einstein-Rosen bridge is a bridge or an artificial wormhole that ..."

"... We know what an Einstein-Rosen bridge is" interrupted Dennis who was also speaking with a mono-tonal edge.

Alexei paused, then replied "Yes ... of course you do, Doctor Greene."

"Well I don't!" blurted out Lynne.

Jason was about to tell Lynne that he would explain it to her later, but then decided against it. He thought to himself that the more Alexei was talking, then perhaps the more they would learn information they would need to know otherwise. He looked over to Dennis and did a slight nod of his head. By now, working together as long as they had, Dennis and Jason had a nearly telepathic communication ability and so Dennis remained quiet.

"Well" glancing toward Lynne, "another name for an Einstein-Rosen bridge is a wormhole. You see, it is impossible to travel faster than light, and so if we wanted to go a place that is far away, say ... to the galaxy that is closest to the milky way named the Andromeda galaxy ... it would take us somewhere around ten billion years to get there with the technology we have right now."

Then reaching over and grabbing a sheet of paper on a nearby table, Alexei took the flat sheet of paper and said "Now imagine that this paper represents space-time, and imagine that the Milky

Way is at the left end of the sheet and the Andromeda galaxy is at the other end of this sheet. Remember it would take ten billion years to travel from one side to the other, right? But what if we could bend space ..."

Alexei bent the paper so that the two opposite ends of the page were now laying on top of each other.

"... so that instead of having to travel ten billion years to get to Andromeda, all you have to do is walk to the next block and you're suddenly there. That is what the portal does, and that is what they wanted me to fix."

"So ... did you?" asked Dennis.

"Well, as I said before yes, and no. Yes I fixed it, but when I saw what it could do I buried a limitation in it so that it was only able to transfer about a pound of matter instead of the unlimited abilities that it would normally have" answered Alexei. "I also buried deep down in the computer source code a different limitation that would only allow them to transfer something three times before it would completely destroy itself."

"Why did you do that?" asked Jason, who was now intrigued that he would sabotage the system like this.

Alexei looked over to Jason and replied "Because while I had no idea what they were planning on using the portal for, I did know that they were bad people and they couldn't be allowed to have something this powerful in their hands. I hoped that I would be able to find a way to get Brianna out of danger and get away myself before they would discover what I had done."

"Weren't you worried that they might discover the limitation before you had a chance to escape?" asked Mikki, who up to now had been silent.

Looking to Mikki, Alexei answered "Yes I was, but I had to take that chance. Even if it meant that I would have to die, this technology couldn't be allowed to fall into their hands permanently."

Then resuming a very agitated state, he added "But now, I am running a huge risk being away from their lab! The longer I stay here, you are making me risk Brianna's life! PLEASE take me back there before they discover I am gone!"

Jason had been listening for the last few minutes to the story that Alexei had spun, and in that time he decided that he liked Alexei. While he wasn't happy that he had fixed the other portal, he understood the no-win situation that Alexei was in, and so he understood why he did what he did. He also liked that he was willing to risk his own life to make sure these criminals, these people who called themselves the Circle of Seven, didn't have a portal at their disposal. While he had never heard of this criminal organization before, he was sure the President had, and so he mentally filed that away for later discussion with President Kirken.

There was something else that dawned on Jason. The more he thought about it, and the more he listened to how Alexei was worried about getting back "in time", it dawned on Jason that Alexei must not know all of the abilities of the portal.

"Doctor Einikov" said Jason, "I can guarantee you that Brianna will be safe, and you do not need to worry about her."

"And just how can you possibly guarantee that!" shot back Alexei, who was greatly agitated, to the point of being frantic.

"I can guarantee that because not only do we have sitting behind you the original portal that Admiral Brinstock stole the plans for, but it has an ability that you don't know about yet" said Jason.

Breaking character as his telepathic sidekick, Dennis turned to Jason and said, "Are you sure you want to tell him about this?"

"Why not?" asked Jason to Dennis. "He already knows about the portal, and he was also willing to sacrifice his life to keep it from getting into the wrong hands."

Dennis appeared to be thinking about it for a few seconds, but then with a nod, he turned to Alexei and said "Like my partner here said, the portal sitting behind you is the original portal that Jason and I invented. It's the one that Brinstock stole the plans for."

"I assumed as much shortly after I arrived here" replied Alexei. "But that doesn't help me now! I need to get back so that Brianna won't be hurt any further!"

"Any further!?" shouted Mikki. "What have you done?"

"It isn't what I have done" retorted Alexei. Then stumbling backwards and into a nearby chair, Alexei slumped over and buried his face in his hands. He then said with an obvious tear in his voice "Shortly after I got to the laboratory, I refused to work, but they presented me with a box. I opened it and ..."

"And what?" asked Jason.

Gulping down some air, Alexei worked hard at gaining his bearings. He then said "The box had a finger in it. Sitting on that finger was Brianna's wedding ring!" Alexei broke down in uncontrollable tears. Dennis looked over to Jason, and Jason was already rushing to Mikki. Mikki was suddenly wracked with her own bout of tears over hearing that her close friend from college had been treated so terribly.

With red tear streaked eyes, Alexei looked up again and said "Please ... I beg of you ... let me go back!"

Dennis walked over to Alexei, knelt down on one knee near to him, and said "Listen buddy, I know you might not understand this yet, but I can tell you that we can make sure that absolutely no harm will come to your wife."

"How can you possibly make that sort of claim?" asked Alexei with obvious scorn in his voice.

"Because our portal that you're sitting next to ..." said Dennis.

"Yeah ..." said Alexei.

Dennis continued "It also has the ability to travel in time."

Alexei looked at Dennis for a grand total of ten seconds before he scanned over to Jason, in order to see if this was just a horrible joke being played on him. Jason had a very serious face though, and so apparently there was no joke.

“Time travel” said Alexei.

“Yes” answered Dennis.

Letting a few more seconds go by, he then returned his gaze at Dennis and said, “But that’s impossible!”

“Actually, it’s possible” replied Jason.

“How?” asked Alexei.

“Suffice to say that if we wanted to, we could place you back in that lab about two seconds after we snatched you” answered Dennis. “But ... we have a better idea. Instead, let’s find Brianna and grab her the same way we grabbed you. And we’ll do it from a point in time BEFORE any harm has come to her. OK?”

Seeing that the tell-tale earmarks of a sick joke were nowhere to be found, Alexei decided that he had no choice other than to go along with what Jason and Dennis were saying. This isn’t to say that he believed them, just that he had no choice.

“Ok” was the simple response from Alexei.

“Ok then. Let’s have you move away from the portal while Jason and I look for her” replied Dennis. He then led Alexei to stand at a distance from the portal aperture near Mikki and Lynne. By this time, Jason had resumed his place at his console and started working up the coordinates to find his college friend.

Starting from the point where Alexei and Brianna were abducted and then separated, Jason manipulated his controls to follow the locations where Brianna was kept. In doing so, it quickly became evident to Alexei that they indeed had the ability to see, at least, what had happened in the past. This alone was astounding to him and his attention was quite riveted on the events unfolding in the portal.

As it turns out, after some time Jason and Dennis discovered that Brianna was actually kept in the same building where Alexei had been forced to work, however she was just in a locked room on a different floor. Even better news was that they took her wedding ring from her ... but not her finger. They had apparently used her ring on another finger from an unknown source to coerce Alexei to work.

Simply put, Alexei was floored. He not only saw these other locations, but it was obvious that he was witnessing events that had occurred days ago. It was true! Time travel through these artificial wormholes WAS actually possible!

Eventually, Jason and Dennis arrived at a point where Brianna was alone in her locked room, and so it was the perfect opportunity to grab her. Positioning the portal window in the same way he had when Dennis snatched Alexei, Jason locked his station, and strode over to the portal. Using the same moves as before, Jason touched the portal field and was instantly transported to the same room where Brianna was being held.

From her perspective, an otherwise quiet room was suddenly invaded by a cacophony of light, and then suddenly she wasn't alone. Normally she would have screamed, but when she saw Jason standing there in front of her, she rushed to her friends' side and hugged him tightly. Jason returned the hug, and while his arms were wrapped around Brianna, he reached back and touched the invisible portal window, thus transporting her back with him to the laboratory he shared with Dennis.

It was then when a very appreciative Alexei rushed to her side and grabbed hold of her like he would never let her go again.

"Thank you!" was all Alexei could say amidst the tears of an appreciative man.

"You're welcome" said Jason as he hit the disconnect button on his console. The portal window instantly disappeared and as soon as the cryogenic systems were shut down, the room was silent. Meanwhile Mikki had rushed to the side of her friend and they all hugged and consoled each other until the tears eventually subsided.

Looking again to Jason, Alexei said "I don't know how to thank you for rescuing us!"

"You're welcome" said Jason. "But the only thing I'm worried about now is that they have a working portal on their hands. I just hope they don't use it in a bad way."

Letting out a small sigh, Alexei said "I think they have."

"What do you mean?" asked Dennis.

"A couple of days ago, I was restrained by their guards when they appeared to connect to some closet somewhere. After several minutes they appeared to receive some signal, and when they did, they sent a one-pound package to that closet and shut off the portal. I don't know what happened after that."

"We have to disable that portal somehow" said Jason.

Releasing his hold on Brianna, Alexei thoughtfully walked while stroking his goatee. After thinking for a few seconds, he said "I have an idea."

"What's that?" asked Jason.

"I built into the system those limitations, right?"

"Yeah, that's what you said" answered Dennis.

"Well, part of those limitations was a test system. If I type in a special password into my terminal in my lab, then that will hardwire those limitations and kill any further use of their portal."

Jason looked at Dennis, and Dennis looked back at him. Jason looked over to Alexei and said, "So be it."

Taking the necessary steps, the portal was restarted and then positioned back to the lab at a time right after Alexei had been snatched. Alexei traveled back to the lab, and immediately went to his terminal and typed the special password that would disable any further use of this portal. The password was simply the name of a cat he had when he was a boy.

He typed the password M-R-K-I-T-T-Y and pressed ENTER. Then immediately walking back to the portal, he returned to the safety of Jason and Dennis's lab. The portal was shut down and once again the lab was silent.

Once again, Jason and Dennis had used the portal for the betterment of humanity, and they were more than happy it could be used this way once again. For his part Alexei was keenly impressed with what he had learned from the other two scientists. Jason and Dennis, though, were about to learn something too.

Something that would completely blow them away.

CHAPTER 28

RUSSIA IS, OF COURSE, AN amazingly large country. Though it was only part of the original Union of Soviet Socialist Republics, it was by far the largest of those republics. Since the breakup of the Soviet Union on December 25th, 1991, the direction of the Russian republic has sometimes been unclear, but it is easy to see that they have been inexorably moving forward toward democracy, albeit with similar growing pains that other democracies, such as the United States, had to endure. On one hand economic diversity in Russia has grown well over time, but on the other hand things like religious and social tolerance has seemingly died a noisy and troubled death, retrenching its way back to the morass once found during the dark ages.

In addition to the normal problems of a growing democratic society, the problem of organized crime and the commensurate bribe-laced corruption that tends to come with it has also been a particular thorn in the side of altruistic governmental authorities.

The mob, as some like to call it, has their own agenda of course, but they also let themselves be hired for a price, if in fact the price is attractive enough to merit their attention.

Within the last several months, the Circle of Seven had been working on the plans for a fantastic and somewhat unbelievable technology they had obtained from Admiral Brinstock. They had among their ranks several scientists that had been coerced in one way or another to work for them, and it was these very scientists that had been tasked with the job of translating the plans into a workable portal apparatus, much like the one that Jason and Dennis had perfected in their laboratory at Midway Magnetic.

Back in the late 1980's, the USSR undertook a major project in a town called Protvino. This project was the brainchild of several scientists at the Russian Institute for High Energy Physics, and with its completion it would be the largest particle accelerator in the entire world. As with most particle accelerators, tunnels had to be dug underground in a circular shape, and the specifications for this accelerator outlined enormous circular tunnels that would span a total of 50 kilometers. Those tunnels had been completed and they were ready for the hardware to be installed that would guide protons around the circuit in an enormous buildup of energy, eventually allowing those scientists to deduce the building blocks of the universe through massive collisions in a chamber designed to detect microscopic particles.

It would ... that is ... had the project not been cancelled. Eventually the collapse of the Soviet Union and the commensurate economic difficulties and funding cuts that came with it caused the whole project to be thrown into the trash can.

When representatives of the Circle of Seven approached the Russian government with a proposal to buy the half-completed facility, the politicians were all too eager to sell. Up to that point they had been spending roughly 80 million rubles, or 2.7 million dollars, to just keep the tunnels from flooding. Selling the facility and being able to repurpose that capital over to other popular pet projects was very attractive to them, and so the red tape that typically accompanied such a transaction seemed to vanish. Once it had been purchased, it was at this facility where the Circle of Seven scientists eventually designed … and eventually failed … to create the portal technology. They were able to create the particle accelerator technology of course. The methodologies in creating such technology had been known for years. But the creation of the technology that made it possible to form a portal field itself eluded them. They just couldn't seem to get the field to form.

It was then, when the upper management of the Circle of Seven decided they needed to get some additional help in the form of the planet's brightest minds. At the top of the list was Alexei Einikov who happened to be working at his privately-owned facility in Saint Petersburg, and it just so happened that one of the other names on that short list of scientists, an American scientist named Brianna Plant who was a world-renowned electronic engineer and roboticist, was working with Doctor Einikov. On top of that, it came to their attention that the two engineers had recently become romantically involved with each other. This would make the task of forcing Einikov to "play ball" even easier.

Their "acquisition" (most would call it kidnapping) was accomplished without much effort, and after being apprehended they were immediately separated. They didn't have much call for Brianna's expertise just yet, but it was decided that she might come in handy soon enough. In the meantime, Alexei's love for her coupled with him not knowing how safe she was or wasn't led to him deciding to perform the work that they "requested" of him.

Still though, the massively intelligent Doctor Einikov remained two steps ahead of his captors even though he didn't know how he might be able to get out of his current predicament. It wasn't until Jason and Dennis grabbed both him and the love of his life that his salvation became clear. The tears of both Alexei and Brianna were plentiful, which of course led to some tears being shed by the others in the room during their reunion. It wasn't until a few minutes had passed that Alexei released his body-to-body hold on his wife right there in front of the portal apparatus so as to look her straight in the eyes.

"Thought I lost you my wife!" Said a very emotional Alexei to Brianna.

"I thought you had lost me too, my husband. I thought all we had accomplished was not only going to go up in smoke, but I thought I was going to never see you again!"

"That's all in the past now, my love. All that matters now is that you're safe" consoled Alexei. As he pulled her into yet another hug, she luxuriated in the strong arms of her tall but gentle husband. As she laid her head on his chest, her eyes closed with a look of comfort and safety on her face. His embrace felt so strong, and yet so gentle to her. Hearing a small noise to her right her eyes opened, only now to see her best friend in the world, Mikki. Without thinking much about it, Brianna quickly released her grip on Alexei and immediately rushed to Mikki's arms. The two friends embraced each other for several moments in silence, until eventually Brianna said "Oh Mikki, I'm so happy you're here!"

"I'm here Pepper" consoled Mikki as she slowly rubbed circles on Brianna's back. "I'm here."

The others in the room didn't want to interrupt the reunion between Brianna and Mikki, and so while Mikki made overtures to introduce Brianna to Lynne who was standing nearby, Dennis and Jason stepped closer to Alexei. Dennis was the first to speak.

"Doctor Plant just mentioned something about all you had accomplished. What exactly were you two working on?"

Alexei's eyes were trained on Mikki and Brianna at that particular moment and so the question didn't even really register with him. Jason could see where their new visitor was looking and so allowed him the time that he evidently needed. Eventually though, Alexei's gaze faltered and with a slight smile he glanced at Jason. It was only then that Alexei realized that Dennis had asked a question earlier.

"I'm sorry. Did you say something?"

"I was just asking about what you and Brianna were working on" replied Dennis.

Breathing deeply, Alexei answered "We were working on the ability to completely map the neural network of the human brain, Doctor Greene."

"Mapping the neural network of a brain?" asked Dennis. "Sounds like you've got your work cut out for you" replied Dennis.

"As far as what we have published to the scientific public, that would be correct" replied Alexei, "but we haven't exactly been completely forthcoming about our progress."

Furrowing his eyebrows, Jason responded "You didn't falsify your published research, did you?" Jason's body language showed that he was once again suspicious of Alexei.

"No, Doctor Marsalis, not in the way you are thinking. We didn't exactly publish the truth about our research, but the truth of the matter is that we have achieved more success than what we have published. Brianna and I have actually been able to successfully map the entire neural network."

"Successful ..." said Jason.

"Yes" answered Alexei.

"Mapping the human brain neural network ..." added Dennis.

"Yes" answered Alexei once again.

As Jason and Dennis gazed at a suddenly mute Alexei, the two scientists digested this new revelation.

"You're telling me" said Dennis, "that you are now able to map the human brain?"

"Yes" came the reply.

"With what results?" asked Jason.

"Well" replied Alexei, "we were just about to perform a complete scan and mapping when we were abducted, but according to our research and calculations, we should be able to replicate the memories, and thinking processes of whatever brain we choose to scan."

With slightly open mouths, Jason and Dennis looked at Alexei for another several seconds, before they turned to each other, and with wide eyes conveyed to each other that they both knew the significant impact such a capability would have.

"Well doesn't that just beat all you ever stepped in" came the unfiltered Texan response from Dennis.

Jason, ever the pragmatist, asked "That means that if you are successful, it is possible that you would create a computer that is, for all intents and purposes, sentient."

"Yes" came the repeated response from Alexei.

"But if that happens" prompted Jason, "then what about when the time comes when you have to turn the computer off? Won't that mean you'd be killing that sentient being? That 'copy' of the person you just scanned?"

Alexei slightly nodded his head while the corners of his mouth curled up in a slight smile. "I can see that you and Brianna are cut from the same cloth, Doctor Marsalis" replied Alexei. "As it happens, Brianna and I had just spent the entire evening debating that very subject just before we were kidnapped."

At that moment, Brianna had approached her husband and heard what he had just said. As she once again placed her arms around Alexei, Brianna added "I am of the opinion that before we move forward with this, we need to be prepared to do this on a computer that will never be shut off."

"Actually" responded Alexei, "I had a thought about that. We could always save the entire scan to memory that stays after the power is shut off, like a hard disk. If everything works the way we think, we could just 'save' the new sentient being and retrieve them later."

With a thoughtful look on her face, Brianna showed that she not only understood what Alexei had just said, but that it was an acceptable alternative to her.

Taking in an unhurried breath, Jason shook his head from side to side. He then said "This is … overwhelming, to put a fine point on it. Well, all I can say is that I am so glad you are here where you are safe Pepper."

"I am so glad to be here with you too, but …" Brianna looked around herself at the room where she now stood which was nothing like the veritable dungeon where she had just been standing. She then added "… where is … 'here'?"

"There is a very good answer to that question" answered Jason, "but before I can answer that, I need to have a little conversation with the president." Jason then gestured to a comfortable lounge that had some couches and chairs and said "Until that happens, please take some time with your husband over there while I make some phone calls. OK Pepper? Trust me, there will be answers to your questions."

Brianna looked at Jason in the eyes and smiled at the pet name that only she, Jason and Mikki knew, and said "I trust you." Taking the proffered hand of her husband, she walked with Alexei to the lounge and sat with him. The last thing that Jason saw was Alexei suddenly realizing something, and then inspecting Brianna's hands. Apparently, the severed finger he had seen earlier from the representatives of the Circle of Seven was only a ruse.

Meanwhile, Jason got on his secure phone and made a call to a very important phone number.

"Office of President Kirken. May I help you?"

"Yes, this is Doctor Jason Marsalis. May please speak to President Kirken?"

Seeing that the President's "Do Not Disturb" light wasn't on, President Kirken's personal secretary Susan replied, "One moment please Doctor Marsalis."

Susan placed Jason on hold and dialed the intercom to President Kirken's phone on the resolute table. At that moment, President Kirken had been standing in front of his desk having an impromptu meeting with the Secretary of Defense, but he had purposely not turned on the DND light in case a call came in from Jason.

Reaching over to his phone, President Kirken punched the intercom button and spoke. "Yes?"

"Doctor Marsalis is on line one for you Mister President."

"Thanks Susan" replied President Kirken. Then looking over to the Secretary of Defense, he asked if the secretary could step outside for the moment while he took this call. The secretary left the oval office, and once the door was closed, President Kirken picked up the handset and opened the line.

"Jason, this is President Kirken. I hope you have some good news for me."

"I do, sir. The good news is that both Doctor's Einikov and Plant have been rescued from their captors."

"The good news?" queried the president. "I take it there is some bad news?"

"Yes sir, I'm afraid there is" came the reply from Jason. Jason then explained to President Kirken that the organization responsible for the abduction is a group that calls themselves the Circle of Seven. He also explained that apparently Admiral Brinstock had supplied this criminal organization with plans for the portal while he was still alive.

"You're telling me that they have a portal in their possession?!" questioned an almost yelling president.

"Not exactly" answered Jason. "They needed Doctor Einikov to debug the portal, which he did, but not before he built into it a self-destruction circuit which we have just activated. While they still have the incomplete plans the admiral gave them, the portal has been rendered inoperable and useless, and it is unlikely that it can be resurrected with the scientific minds at their disposal."

"Well at least they didn't have time to use it" responded President Kirken.

"I'm afraid it appears that they may have used it once before we had the ability to disable it. According to Doctor Einikov Agents of the Circle of Seven sent a one-pound package somewhere. We don't know where it was sent, and we don't know the contents of the package."

"A one-pound package?" asked the president.

"Yes sir. At that point, the portal had been limited to that amount of mass by Doctor Einikov" answered Jason.

After taking a moment to think about it, President Kirken put two and two together and arrived at a grim conclusion. "I'm afraid I know where they sent that package."

"Oh" replied Jason. "Where?"

"Last week there was a bombing in New York at a transportation company on the eighty seventh floor of the Miritrans building. The investigators believe it took about a pound of a material called Azidoazide Azide, but they were not only baffled how so much of it was synthesized, but also how it found its way onto the eighty seventh floor of the building. It was only because the Miritrans building had been built after 9/11 that the lessons learned from the collapse of the World Trade Center were used, otherwise the heat from the explosion would have brought down the entire building as well."

There were a few seconds of silence on the phone while Jason and the president processed this information. Sensing that Jason had something additional to say, President Kirken said "OK. Please let me know if there is anything that changes with that. Is there anything else?"

Regaining his bearings after hearing about the Miritrans building, Jason replied "Yes sir, there is. It is apparent that this organization is very familiar with the location where Doctor Einikov and Doctor Plant have been working, and so we feel that returning them to that location would not be wise at this time. Having said that, I will add that his ability to examine, debug, and fix the other portal means that he would be a very useful ally in our efforts with the portal here. I would like to request that he be allowed to remain here at the lab facility."

With a tentative tone to his voice, the president asked, "You do know what that means, don't you Doctor Marsalis?"

"Yes sir, I do. While he and his wife Brianna have so far only seen the portal room, it would mean he would see where it is located" answered Jason.

"Wife?! They're married?" asked the president with notable surprise and a slight laugh in his voice.

"Yes sir. They were apparently married only three weeks ago" replied Jason.

The line was silent for a few moments until President Kirken spoke again.

"Provided you can get their assurance that the location where the portal is kept will remain secret, you have authorization to make your offer. Meanwhile I am going to direct the FBI and CIA to get intelligence on this Circle of Seven you spoke about. I need to know what they're up to."

"I couldn't agree more, Mr. President. If there is anything you need us to do, let me know" answered Jason.

"I will. Kirken out." The line went dead.

Looking up toward the lounge where Alexei and Pepper were seated, Jason hung up the phone and then looked toward his friend. Dennis, for his part, was chatting with his wife Lynne.

Walking toward them, Jason held out his hand to Mikki who was standing nearby. The motion made it clear to Mikki that Jason wanted to have a small chat amongst the four of them.

Approaching Dennis and Lynne, Jason said "Hey you guys. Can I talk to you for a minute?"

"Sure. What's up?" asked Dennis.

"I just got off the phone with President Kirken, and he authorized us to offer this location as a safe house for Alexei and Pepper."

"Here? They would stay here?" asked Lynne.

"Yep"

"Why?" asked Mikki.

Always on the same track as Jason, Dennis answered, "Because they can't go back home. Those black-masked idiots that kidnapped them would probably just kidnap them again if they went back."

"But that means" replied Lynne, "they would know where the portal is ..."

"Yes" answered Jason.

"... and that means they would know what's outside the portal room" continued Lynne.

"Yes" answered Jason.

"Are you sure they can handle that?" asked Mikki.

"Don't really have much of a choice" replied Jason. Then Dennis added "That, and the fact that he was willing to basically sacrifice his life to keep this technology from falling into the wrong hands makes him A-O-K in my book."

The four of them stood there looking at each other for a few seconds until they all simultaneously looked through the doorway to the lounge at the newlywed couple. As it happened Alexei and Brianna had noticed that the others were talking among themselves, and so the newlyweds were already looking at the others. When they saw Jason, Dennis and their wives simultaneously look over, they rose and approached the group.

"I have a feeling that you are talking about us?" asked Alexei.

"Yes, we are. I've just been talking to the president of the United States, and he has authorized me to make an offer to you" answered Jason.

"An offer? From your president?" asked Alexei.

"Yes" responded Dennis, "and let me tell ya, this one's a doozy."

Alexei looked at Brianna, who returned the look. Alexei looked back at the group and said "What is the offer?"

"As you can probably imagine, returning you back to where you were living is probably a bad idea" responded Dennis.

"We were just talking about the same thing" replied Brianna. "We were kidnapped from there, and so we know they already know where we would be if we went back there."

"Exactly" answered Jason. "And that is what had led us to relocate you here where we know this Circle of Seven you spoke about will never find you."

"What makes you so sure they won't find us here?" asked Alexei.

"It's because of where this lab is located" answered Jason.

"Where is it located?" queried Alexei with a quizzical look on his face.

Looking at the rest of the group, Jason could see that they all had smiles on their respective faces. Truth be said, there was a smile on his own as well.

"Before I answer that" said Jason as he looked back to Alexei and Brianna, "What I am about to show you is probably the most highly guarded secret in the whole of the United States, let alone the entire world. There is only a handful of people that know this facility exists. Not even Vice President Monroe knows about this. I need to have your unqualified and unreserved assurance that what I am about to show you is something that you will keep completely secret. This is not just a simple request from me, but it is a requirement from the President of the United States. Are you willing to give me your assurance?"

By the look on their faces, it was obvious that Alexei and Brianna were more than intrigued by the prospect of learning something that was of such utmost secrecy. Alexei looked at Brianna, then back at Jason and said, "We agree." Brianna was nodding her head.

Jason stood and said, "Will you please follow me?"

Taking a tentative look at each other, Brianna and Alexei stood and followed Jason. Jason stopped near an exit door and placed his hand on the handle. Looking back at his two guests Jason paused, and then opened the door.

There before him was an immaculately decorated lounge, and beyond that lounge were immense floor to ceiling windows looking out from the two hundred sixty third floor of a gleaming glass skyscraper.

A skyscraper standing right in the middle of an island named New Galimar.

CHAPTER 29

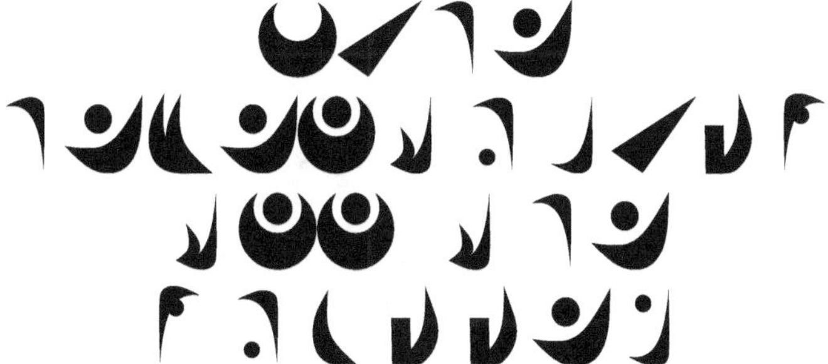

Jason had just opened the door and as Alexei looked through it to the other side, he could see that the world on the other side of the door was completely different than anything he had ever seen. Pausing for a moment, all he could hear was the sound of his own breathing even though the laboratory that he was technically still standing in had its own sounds from the array of electronic devices strewn about. Rather than being on the verge of passing out as many would be in this circumstance, his senses were all on high alert and he was mentally taking care to remember all that he was seeing.

And what he was seeing was none other than amazing.

The room on the other side of the doorway had what appeared to be an open beam ceiling that was taller on one side than the other. The floors were made of inlaid wood paneling and were occasionally accented with area rugs of different designs and colors. On the far wall were windows that extended from the floor to the ceiling and they appeared to be about four to five meters tall. Each window was two meters wide and there were at least ten of them on the one wall. Some of the windows had been slid to the side though allowing for a person to walk out onto a balcony that overlooked the rest of the island. There were light chiffon curtains that extended from the ceiling to the floor in front of the windows, and they were undulating back and forth in the light breeze wafting through the room.

In the center of this long rectangular room were several conversation centers outlined by the arrangement of different couches, chairs and tables. The colors of the upholstery were mostly light-colored pastels and each of the tables were adorned with tasteful statues or similar pieces of art. Light was mostly filtering in from the windows, but there were what appeared to be crystal chandeliers hanging down from the ceiling high overhead. The light, and especially the patterns from the crystals in each chandelier, must have been dazzling at nighttime.

Brianna, for her part, was standing behind her husband and was equally as stunned as her husband with what she could see so far. After looking at the scene through the doorway before her, her eyes darted to Jason and Mikki who were standing together, but to the side of the door. The two of them had smiles and expectant looks on their faces, and it appeared that Mikki had a brightness on her face as if she was about to squeal with delight. She appeared to be really happy to share this with her friend.

After a comparably short period of time, Alexei finally took a step forward, which of course prompted Brianna to do the same. Stepping through the doorway, he reached out to the doorjamb to steady himself and he took in more and more of the staggering beauty of the architecture of this room. Already on sensory overload, he steeled himself for more and eventually he completely entered the room. Step by measured step he ultimately made his way to the wall of windows across the room, and then onto the balcony to look out over the island. Looking to the left and to the right, he could easily see three massive curved pylons that stood in seeming guardianship over the island, and below them he could see what appeared to be vehicles that were scurrying about in mid-air. The island was enormous and seemed to extend from horizon to horizon. There was a grouping of buildings in the center of the island, one of which was the one he was standing in, but then there were what appeared to be arms of land extending outward to the sea. There were countless waterways and harbors on those arms of land that were all beautifully decorated with greenery, and throughout the island there was tasteful architecture that complimented the flora rather than detracting from it.

One of the first things that Alexei noticed was that even though he was standing in direct sunlight there on the balcony, the light didn't seem harmful. Normally he would avoid the sun because of the pain it inflicted on his skin. He was naturally tan-skinned and so he didn't really need to lie out in the sun to get a tan, which was just fine with him because for some reason the sun always made him feel so uncomfortable.

But this place was different somehow. He couldn't quite put his finger on it, but in some way the whole vista before him was both completely new and yet familiar. He felt as if he could stand there in the sun all day and never feel the worse for it. But how could that be?

Brianna stepped up behind him and placed her arm around the waist of her husband. As she looked out toward the vista before them, she heard her husband say, "The contemplation of beauty causes the soul to grow wings."

"Well said" replied Brianna as the rest of the group joined them.

"I agree" said Mikki. "Did you just make that up?"

"Not exactly" replied Alexei rather enigmatically. Then seeing the puzzling look on Mikki's face, Alexei continued "It was Plato that said that originally, and it seems to be used regularly in connection with the story about the Greek god Eros and Psyche."

"I'm not sure I know that particular story" said Brianna.

Looking out toward the ocean Alexei thought for a moment, but then said "Eros and Psyche were Greek gods that fell in love in an unusual way. Eros, who represents love, had wings, but Psyche who represents the human soul didn't have wings but was excruciatingly beautiful. So much so that Venus, the mother of Eros, became horribly jealous and tried to ruin Psyche's life only to be foiled by the fact that her son fell helplessly in love with her."

"One way that Venus then tried to foil the relationship between her son and Psyche was to trick Eros into making Venus agree in a pre-nuptial agreement to never lay eyes on Eros. They could interact with each other in all the ways that married persons would, but it would always have to be in complete darkness. Nevertheless, Psyche completely fell in love with Eros without ever having seen him. The beauty of his personality was enough for her."

"Bummer!" said Lynne.

"Indeed" replied Alexei. "So, she enjoys night after night with her mystery lover/husband in ultimate marital bliss until eventually her meddling sisters convinced her that it must all be a trick, and that Eros must really be a hideous monster since they had to stay in the dark. They convince her that she must find out if this is true and kill him, etc. etc. One night she lights a lamp while he is asleep and takes a peek at him and is blown away by his beauty. She gets a little too close though and her lamp drips oil on him. He awakens and flies away wounded more by her treachery than the oil."

"So, Psyche saw his beauty. Did she grow wings?" asked Mikki.

"Not right away, no" answered Alexei. "Venus, using this betrayal as a reason to punish Psyche, then puts her on a grueling and literally impossible path of redemption. Luckily the gods understood the unfairness of Venus' revenge and help Psyche complete her impossible tasks. After trekking down to Hades and back, Zeus felt she had earned her place in the heavens with her husband Eros."

"So, in the end Psyche, or the human soul, grew the figurative wings necessary to live on Mount Olympus, and this was presumably from contemplating both the physical and spiritual beauty of her husband Eros. And if that's not beautiful and amazing enough, they eventually had a child and they named the child Pleasure."

Looking out toward the incredible vista before them, Brianna then said in an understanding voice "And so that is how 'The contemplation of beauty causes the soul to grow wings.'"

The rest of the group looked out as well and they all shared a small moment of silence.

In time, Alexei turned around to the rest of the group standing next to him and searched out Jason's eyes, saying the first thing that came to his mind.

"What is this place?"

Smiling, Jason answered and said, "This, my dear Doctor Einikov, is the island of New Galimar."

A mouth that was slightly open now went slack and Alexei's eyebrows scrunched together with a look of disbelief or disorientation.

"New Galimar?" asked Brianna. "Is there an old Galimar?"

That honest and innocent question made Dennis, Lynne, Mikki and Jason burst forth with laughter, which in turn made Brianna laugh as well although that wasn't the reason for her sincere question. Alexei wasn't laughing though, and because of that, he ended up hearing laughter coming from more than the small group of people he had arrived with. Following the sound of laughter, his eyes scanned to the far end of the room where there were two people sitting quietly. Their wardrobe both contrasted and matched the colors and feeling of the room, and even from this distance he could see they were both quite attractive.

As he was finishing his laughter, Jason looked over and could see that Alexei was gazing with a look of wonder toward the other end of the room. Following his line of sight, it was only now that Jason discovered they had unexpected guests. Looking over to Dennis, he tilted his head indicating that he wanted Dennis to follow him. Jason and Dennis walked up to Alexei, and Jason touched the back of one of Alexei's shoulders.

"Alexei, I have some friends I would like you to meet." Applying gentle pressure to Alexei's back, the three men and their respective wives migrated over to the group at the other end of the lounge. Seeing the approaching group, the seated individuals stood and in doing so revealed themselves in all their tall splendor.

Upon approaching the group, Jason was the first to speak.

"Alexei, this is Lord Khreelon Tellindor and his wife Lady Terri Tellindor. Khreelon and Terri, this is Doctor Alexei Einikov and his wife Doctor Brianna Plant." Then turning to Brianna, Jason quickly said "Or is it Einikov now?"

Smiling, Brianna nodded and said, "I've chosen to stay with 'Plant' professionally, but privately I am Doctor Brianna Einikov."

Khreelon turned to Alexei and Brianna, and pressing his open palms together above his head, then lowering the still-pressed palms down to his chest resulting in a bow, he said "I am very pleased to meet you."

Without really thinking about it, Alexei turned to face Khreelon and very pregnant Terri and repeated the gesture. The difference though was that Alexei said, "May you have peace."

This simple gesture on the part of Alexei went completely unnoticed by Dennis, Lynne and Mikki, however it definitely didn't miss the attention of Khreelon, Terri and Jason. How was it that Alexei knew the words of the formal greeting of New Galimar? Was it just a lucky guess? And there was something else about Alexei that was strange too. Something like ... maybe it was something familiar? Like maybe he looked like someone familiar?

"I am honored by your greeting Doctor Einikov, although I am a little surprised by your visit" replied Khreelon. Then turning to Jason, Khreelon asked "Has President Kirken decided on a shift in the policy of secrecy about New Galimar?"

"Not exactly" replied Jason. "Alexei is a scientist from a country named Russia, and Brianna is a scientist from The United States. In the interests of creating continuing growth in goodwill and international communication between our two countries, President Kirken asked Doctor Brianna Plant here to work alongside Doctor Einikov on a common area of interest. She did that, and ..." turning to smile at Brianna, "... she ended up falling in love with her new partner."

"But ... not long thereafter, the two of them were kidnapped by a criminal organization that we had never heard of before. They were forcing them to work on a portal of their own, which Doctor Einikov later sabotaged. Using our own portal, we rescued them from their captors. We knew we couldn't return them to their former research laboratory since they would be at risk of being kidnapped all over again. Since they have capabilities that are more than compatible with our research, and since they had already shown themselves to be trustworthy even to the point of personally sacrificing their lives if necessary, President Kirken decided that they could be trusted with knowledge of the portal, and where it is located."

All through this explanation on the part of Jason, Alexei couldn't take his eyes off of Khreelon.

"I see" said Khreelon. Then turning to Alexei and Brianna he said, "I am sorry for your experiences of late, but I hope you will find your stay here to be enjoyable."

"Well, based on what I can see so far, that shouldn't be difficult" said Brianna. Then turning once again to look out the window, she added "I can't believe the view we have here. How many stories is this building?"

"We aren't on the top floor, but this is the two-hundred and sixty-third floor of this building" answered Terri.

Brianna's mouth hung open in astonishment. "Two-hundred and sixty-third floor? As far as I know, the construction materials in use today wouldn't support such a structure!"

"That's because they haven't been invented yet" answered Jason.

Alexei and Brianna turned to look at Jason. "OK. You're going to have to explain that one" replied Brianna.

Letting out an audible breath, Jason answered and said, "What I mean is that it hasn't been invented yet on earth."

A few seconds went by, and then Brianna shook her head and said, "... not helping!"

After being silent for a while, Dennis spoke up and plainly said "What he means is that New Galimar isn't from Earth. New Galimar is from the planet Galimar." Then pointing to Khreelon, Dennis continued "This here is a real, live, and breathing alien from another planet, and this island is actually a ship that was built on another planet."

"Mmmmmmm ... technically it was built in orbit above Galimar" said Khreelon with a smile. Terri nudged him in the ribs with her elbow and with a smile all her own.

Jason, Dennis, Mikki and Lynne were all giggling. Brianna saw the humor and was smiling.

Alexei was almost ready to pass out.

Reaching behind him, he felt for and eventually found the arm of a chair in which he quickly took a seat. His reaction wasn't quickly seen by the group but eventually Brianna looked back to her husband with the intention of sharing the levity of the moment, but that is when she saw a look on his face she had never seen before. It wasn't necessarily a look of pain, but it definitely wasn't one of pleasure either. He was obviously experiencing some sort of distress.

Rushing to his side, she sat down in a chair next to him, and with her hands on his arm she said "What is it, my husband? Are you all right?"

Her questioning of Alexei drew the attention of the rest of the group and so all were now attentive to the two seated doctors.

His eyes were fixed on the carpet in front of him, and without looking up to his wife, he replied "Yes. In fact I think I am more than OK." Then looking up to Khreelon, he asked "Who is the leader of this island?"

"We have no single leader" replied Khreelon. "Our government is centered around a single ruling body made up of the oldest and wisest of our population. It is called the Grand Council of New Galimar."

He hadn't received the answer he was looking for, so he decided to take another tack. "Yes, but when your ship came to earth, was there a single person responsible for the entire ship?"

Khreelon thought this was an odd question. In fact, all in the room actually thought so, Khreelon nevertheless answered the question and said "Yes, in fact there was. His name is Ehobak Aramine. Do you want to meet him?"

"Yes" said Alexei. "I would very much like to meet him."

"As you wish" replied Khreelon. Stepping to a communication panel on the back wall, Khreelon got in touch with Ehobak and requested his presence.

Jason looked over to Dennis and made a questioning look while simultaneously raising his shoulders. Dennis replied with a shake of his own head and with open palms indicating that he was just as in the dark about Alexei's behavior as Jason was. In the meantime, Alexei rose and walked back out to the balcony with Brianna quickly following. Once they got there, it was obvious they were quietly talking amongst themselves and so the rest chose not to intrude on their discussion.

Mikki, Lynne, Terri and Khreelon approached Jason and Dennis, and Mikki was the first one to speak.

"Do you know what's going on here?"

"Not a clue. Do you?" asked Terri.

"Nope" answered Mikki.

The group looked out to the balcony and watched the two quietly talking amongst themselves. They couldn't hear what was being said between Alexei and Brianna, but at one point, Alexei apparently said something that was completely astonishing to Brianna. She took a step backwards and her eyes and mouth were hung wide open. Reading her lips, it was obvious she had said "WHAT?" to Alexei.

"That didn't look good" said Lynne.

"Nope" agreed Dennis. "She just looked at him like he's two sandwiches short of a picnic."

"Doesn't look like she's mad though" added Mikki.

"No. Doesn't look like it" agreed Jason as he witnessed her still rubbing circles on Alexei's back.

While they were all watching the two out on the balcony, Mikki then looked to her left at Terri and decided to touch her on her shoulder. When Terri looked over, Mikki made a motion with her head that she wanted to talk to her privately away from the group. The two slowly made their way off to the side and Mikki was the first to speak.

"So tell me, have you swallowed a basketball?" said Mikki as she motioned her head toward Terri's distended belly.

"Tell me about it!" replied Terri. "This is my first, and so for a while I was just thinking that all is normal, but ... look at me! I'm as big as a house and I'm only ten weeks along!"

"Ten weeks!" exclaimed Mikki as she once again looked down at Terri's belly. Comparing the current size of Terri's belly with her own when she was pregnant with Jace Junior, something didn't add up.

"Are you sure everything's all right?"

"Yeah" replied Terri. "The one doctor I went to on the outside of the island said Coral is perfectly fine in every way, it just appears to be growing at a really quick pace. I've also been visiting the medical facility here on New Galimar although it's still only staffed by medical students. They're a little stumped as to why it's growing so fast too, as they pointed out that while humans are full term at nine months, normal Galimarians are full term at a little over fourteen weeks. The only ideas they have about why I seem ready to pop any day now is because the child is a combination of human and Galimarian DNA."

"But does she appear to be normal in every other way?" asked Mikki with a concerned look on her face.

"Oh yeah" replied Terri in a nonchalant manner and with a smile on her face. "I saw a scan of her, and she looked beautiful! In fact, while I was watching, she reached up and started sucking her thumb. It was so cute! And I have to say, I've never felt better. I thought I'd feel really drug down and tired, but ... nope!"

A visibly relieved Mikki smiled back and once again looked down at Terri's belly, currently draped with the chiffon style fabric of Terri's outfit. Mikki placed her hand on the belly and after a few seconds she felt the baby move. "Oh my gosh, she just moved!"

"Oh yeah. She's been jogging around the track for the last six weeks" said Terri. The two women shared a light-hearted chuckle amongst themselves.

Just then, a door to the room opened and in walked Ehobak. Walking over to Khreelon, the two men greeted each other. Other than Alexei and Brianna who were still on the balcony, they all came together in a circle.

"Khreelon here tells me that we have two new visitors?" asked Ehobak.

"Yes, that's true" answered Jason. He then related to Ehobak the story of how Alexei and Brianna had been kidnapped, but also that they are top scientists that President Kirken had authorized to be here.

"I see" said Ehobak with a newfound look of understanding. "But he asked to see me?"

"Well, not by name exactly" answered Khreelon, "but he asked to see the person that was in charge when the ship was coming to earth."

"So, he knows that we are from Galimar?" asked Ehobak.

"Yep" answered Dennis as he was gesturing to the couple on the balcony, "and it appears to have set him back a piece."

Pausing for a moment while looking toward the balcony where Alexei and Brianna were standing with their backs to the group, Ehobak finally said "Well, I'd like to meet them."

The group migrated to the balcony, and upon hearing them the two scientists turned around.

"Alexei" said Khreelon, "This is Lord Ehobak Aramine. Ehobak was the captain of the ship as it was traveling to this planet."

Alexei considered Khreelon for a moment, then appeared to come to a decision. "Don't you mean he was the captain of the ship as it was traveling to ... Eden?" asked Alexei.

Now it was everyone else's turn to drop their mouths open and exclaim collectively.

"WHAT?!"

"How in all that's holy did you know they called this planet Eden?" exclaimed Dennis.

Looking back and forth between the ones gathered around him, Alexei straightened his back and said, "It is because my father and mother told me."

"Who are your father and mother?" said Ehobak as he now noticed that there was something familiar about Alexei, much the same way Khreelon had noticed earlier.

Alexei responded. "My name is Doctor Alexei Einikov, however this is a name that I only recently took on about thirty years ago." Then reaching up to remove the green contact lenses from his eyes, Alexei looked back toward Ehobak and Khreelon with irises that were completely black and said, "Originally my name was Thane. I am the son of Docius and Sa'Urri ... Docius and Sa'Urri Atlantis, and as such, I am full blood Galimarian."

Under their breaths, Ehobak and Khreelon both said the same thing.

"Docius"

Other than that, there was absolutely nothing said by anyone while the fallout from this particular bomb began to settle in the minds of all assembled. Jason, Mikki, Dennis, Lynne and Terri were all mentally thinking the same thing though, and that was a resounding "OH MY GOD!"

A full thirty seconds passed before Ehobak suddenly realized something. "That's why you wanted to see me and why you looked so familiar." Then, taking several steps to stand closer to Alexei, he looked Alexei in the eyes and said "Docius was a close friend, and in you I see the perfect combination of Docius and Sa'Urri in your face."

"Yes. I remember father telling me about you and how leaving his friends was the hardest part of going to live with ..."

Alexei's voice faltered for a moment while he glanced at the others gathered around him.

"... to live with humans."

Mikki couldn't hold it in any more. "Oh my god."

"It's true" said Brianna.

Jason and Mikki whipped their heads around to Brianna. "YOU KNEW?!"

A small smile played itself across her face, but then Brianna looked at Mikki and simply answered, "Yes." Then looking toward her husband, Brianna added "Alexei had never been romantically involved before me. The idea never interested him, and he had always referred to the idea as nothing more than getting mixed up with such 'entanglements' that would get in the way of his work. But once he met me, and more specifically once he decided he wanted to marry me, he knew that he could never give his heart to someone that didn't know the truth about his past. One night he told me about all of this, and even though it was a little hard to swallow, I knew that I loved him and that I still wanted to marry him."

Khreelon spoke up and used a small expression that he had heard Terri use a few times. "Wait a minute ... How long after they went to live with humans did you arrive?"

"It was about five years after they made landfall in a country called Greece" answered Alexei.

Shifting the slant of his head to the other direction, Khreelon said "That was about two thousand five hundred years ago."

Now Jason was the one blurted out what everyone else was thinking. "WHAT?! You're telling me you are about twenty-five hundred years old?"

Looking at Jason, Alexei answered with a diminutive yet earth shattering "Yes."

Another several seconds passed before any had the presence of mind to say anything. Then with a deep breath, Ehobak smiled and said "How are my old friends Docius and Sa'Urri? They must be pretty proud of what you've been doing!"

Alexei's face turned gloomy as he replied "I'm sorry to say that they are no longer alive. My mother was killed during an earthquake, and father was the innocent victim of a crime in Athens where he and I lived."

With a sorrowful look to his own face, Ehobak responded "I am so very sorry to hear about that Alexei. Please accept my heartfelt sorrow."

Alexei nodded his head but didn't say anything.

"I am sorry as well Alexei, but there is something else that just doesn't connect with me. If you grew up around Athens Greece, how is it you have a Russian name?" asked Terri.

"That's because" answered Brianna, "his name wasn't always Alexei Einikov."

"It wasn't?" responded Terri.

"No" answered Alexei. "As I said my name when I was born was Thane. At my celebration of Hin, I chose a different name that reflected the culture of where I lived. I chose the name Socrates."

The response floated around the room for a while as this new information took a little getting used to.

"I suppose that makes sense" responded Terri. "A lot of people name their kids after someone famous. But that doesn't ..."

"Actually ..." interrupted Alexei, "I wasn't named after Socrates the philosopher." Then looking around to those that were gathered in the room, he then said, "I ... AM ... Socrates. The philosopher."

Once again, another bombshell had just been dropped. Dennis quietly thought to himself that just when he thought he wouldn't ever be surprised by anything else, something new drives up and smokes its tires in his driveway.

"How could you be the philosopher Socrates?" responded a slightly incredulous Terri. "The accounts of the death of Socrates are well known and documented"

"Yes, I know. By Xenophon. He was a friend of mine" answered Alexei.

"If that's true" said Jason, "Then why would you allow him to write something about you that wasn't true?"

"It wasn't a matter of me allowing him to write something about me that wasn't true" answered Alexei. "I asked him to write that apocryphal history about me."

"But why?" asked Lynne.

"Well ... as time went on, and especially after I lost my father, I began to notice that I wasn't aging in the same way everybody else around me was aging. Everybody was getting old, but I was just staying the same. In time it became noticeable by everybody and so I started to wear things that would make me look older. I would shave part of my head to look like I had lost my hair, and I would grow a beard to hide the absence of wrinkles. Eventually that didn't accomplish what I needed and so I had to come up with a solution. I asked my closest friend Xenophon to start writing a history about me and my death."

"So, if you faked your death" asked Terri, "What did you do after that?"

"Oh, this is the best part!" said Brianna with a smile on her face. The group thought the smile was a little out of place, but Dennis mentally braced himself for another cloud of smoke from the tires.

"At the time, I had a student who was very sick. He had no family, and he was a recluse with no friends. Most of those around him found him to be an arrogant ass, and so all his contemporaries chose to avoid him. I however saw enormous potential in him, and I was more than sorry to learn that he was going to die soon."

"When the time for him to die was eminent, I was the only one with him and so I chose that time to tell him about who I really was. I asked his permission to use his name and reputation after he passed so that I could live on as a young man again who had miraculously recovered from a horrible sickness. He couldn't speak, but he nodded his head. Thirty minutes later he died, and I took on his name and his life, leaving my old life behind. His name was Plato."

“You’re telling us that you’re not only Socrates, but you’re also Plato?” asked Terri.

“Oh, it gets even better” responded Brianna with a smile.

“Oh? And how is that?” Asked Mikki.

“In time I had to do it again, and again. Through the ages I had to repeatedly take on new names and lives. Sometimes it was a fictional name and life that I made up, and sometimes it was someone like Plato that was about to leave this world with nothing left behind.”

“So, who else were you? Was it anybody we might have heard of?” asked Mikki, who was starting to be incredibly intrigued by actually knowing the man who lived these lives.

“Are you sure you want to know? I’m sure it will be rather hard for you to believe.” asked Alexei, sensing that this was perhaps too much for the group. He sensed wrong though. The group of intellectuals in the room had all come to the conclusion that this fantastic of a story could not have just been created out of thin air. That, and the irrefutable fact that he was indeed Galimarian led them, one and all, to conclude that the yarn Alexei was spinning was indeed true.

“Of course we do!” answered Terri. “Who else?”

“There were several that you probably have never heard of, but others … you probably have” answered Alexei.

“Such as …” prompted Terri. Her archaeology mind was in full gear now.

“After Plato I became Aristotle. During what you would refer to as the dark ages I stayed out of the way for the most part, but eventually my desire for research got the best of me and when I was living in Italy I took on the name Leonardo DaVinci, and later Galileo Galilei. After my bad experience with the church while living life as Galileo, I moved away from Italy and settled in England. While there I decided to ingratiate myself to the church in the area and I became a theologian, while at the same time I indulged my interests in math, physics and astronomy. I arrived at some conclusions in the field of mathematics that I thereafter published under the name that I used at the time ... Isaac Newton. Right after I faked his death, I moved to North America and lived life as an inventor named Benjamin Franklin. Recently though, I created a new life under the name Alexei Einikov, and I have taken all the things I have learned through the ages and brought them to the fore with my current research."

Dennis decided that this had just gone from tire-smokin to setting the whole truck on fire.

By this time, all in the room had to find a seat since they were only now realizing that they were standing in front of someone who was no less than one of the greatest scientists and researchers in the known world. Collectively, all their breaths were taken away, and the realization of whom they were talking to basically put their minds in neutral.

All of this didn't have the same effect on Ehobak and Khreelon though, mostly since they weren't as familiar with human history as the rest of the group. Since that was the case Ehobak plied him with another question.

"How is it possible that you have been able to live this long without the benefit of our Galimarian technology?"

"For years I wondered about that myself" answered Alexei, "But it wasn't until I was able to use a modern electron microscope that I received the answer."

Pausing for a moment, Alexei continued "On the night of my celebration of Hin, my father did something that I always assumed was a normal part of the ceremony. On that night, we each slit our palms and held hands. Our blood mingled. I always assumed that this was a ritualistic ceremony and nothing more, but when I looked at my blood under an electron microscope, it was then that I discovered something that wasn't in any other blood sample I had ever seen."

Knowing where this was going, Khreelon said one word that explained everything.

"Nanites".

"Yes" affirmed Alexei, "Nanites. Apparently, my father knew that my life expectancy would be comparatively short, and that the only way for me to live as long as he expected to live was if he shared his blood with me, thus putting nanites in my blood stream."

Seeing that this information was a little hard for the majority of the group to process, he and Brianna found their own seat and waited for the thoughts of the group to come back into the room. After a few moments of quiet contemplation, Jason was the first to speak.

"So why didn't you ever attempt to come back to New Galimar?"

"I wanted to" answered Alexei, "but honestly I didn't know where it was. For reasons that I didn't understand at the time, my father and mother hid the actual location of the island from me. I didn't understand why until many centuries later when I realized that if the world knew where New Galimar was, it would probably corrupt it, as man tends to do with many things around him. In time I came to appreciate that even if I actually did know the real location of New Galimar, I would need to keep it a secret."

Alexei hesitated, then continued "But ... that wasn't until after I told some people about it. The story I told when I was Plato changed over time and eventually went from an island with incredible technology that Docius and Sa'Urri Atlantis came from, to the current version where there was an island that fell into the sea named Atlantis."

Once again, time passed as all that Alexei said was processed in the minds of those present. Finally, Mikki asked a very obvious question. The others were a little surprised that they hadn't thought of the question themselves.

"So ... what name should we call you?"

Alexei smiled and said, "Originally I chose the name Socrates since I liked that name. I still do."

Upon hearing that, Mikki stood and presented her outstretched hand to him. "It's very nice to meet you Socrates. I am Mikki Marsalis and this is my husband Doctor Jason Marsalis. I hope you find your new home comfortable."

Socrates stood, and after shaking the hand offered to him, he smiled and embraced Mikki with a hug.

Hugs were shared by one and all, and from that point on, Alexei was once again known as Socrates. As he stood there in the warmth of their affection, he finally knew what it meant to be at home. No longer would he ever have to masquerade as someone else. No longer would he have to bid goodbye to someone he had affection for.

As he closed his eyes a tear found its way, followed by many more.

CHAPTER 30

TIME IS A STRANGE THING when you think about it. When you are looking forward to some impending activity, the hours, minutes, and even seconds leading up to it seem to drag on interminably. But once the activity comes, the march of time suddenly shifts into high gear and before you know it all is done and over and you are reflectively thinking on the great experiences just enjoyed while at the same time somehow wishing it wasn't in the past so quickly.

Before moving to New Galimar, Mikki would normally have to come into Jace Junior's room and repeatedly coerce him to get up and get ready for school, but ever since he and his parents had moved to the island, this was seldom the case ... unless he had stayed up later than he should have the night before of course.

When they first moved to the island, Jace wasn't sure he would like the move. As you would expect, he was overwhelmed with the fact that his dad and mom were now living and working with aliens from another planet, but in his little mind he wasn't so sure where exactly that left him. When he lived in his old house in northern California, he had a lot of friends and he liked his school and his teachers. But what would it be like in this new place? He was pretty sure there wouldn't be anybody he could … you know … hang out with.

Then he met Malick.

Malick lived in the home next door to where Jace settled with his mom and dad. From a human standpoint, it appeared that Jace and Malick looked to be the same age, however since Galimarian and human biology were so different, Jace may have been twelve years old, but Malick was about thirty-five. Still though, they were mentally on a par with each other and so their personality compatibility caused the boys to become friends right away.

Being that this was New Galimar, and as such there was no crime to speak of, Mikki had to become accustomed to her son being away from the house for long periods of time without worrying. Each day the boys would strike out and explore the vast island around them, and that of course led the two of them to meet more like-minded young ones. Before long, there was a group of around ten of them that spent all their free time together.

And while there was free time, that isn't to say that Jace didn't still have to go to school. School on New Galimar though took some getting used to. First of all, everybody in the school knew who Jace was and so he was somewhat of a celebrity since he was the absolute first human that any of them had ever met.

Second, the course of study that was given to the students was designed to match the abilities of each individual. A teacher might have twenty or thirty students under his or her care, but there was no guarantee that any of those students would be studying the same thing that their fellow student sitting next to them was studying. Since the teachers and school staff weren't exactly sure what academic niche Jace would fall into, they decided to keep his individualized course of study confidential between them and his parents. They needn't have worried though. Jace had always exceled in school, and in fact he surprised them all since he was only twelve years old yet appeared to be at the same level as several other Galimarian students who were double or even triple his age.

As time went on, and as his group of friends grew, there were more and more things that piqued his interest. Nothing, though, came close to a conversation he had had with Malick last night. It was just Jace and Malick sitting outside around a fire pit that lent some warmth to the cool night. They were in a garden area that was planted between their respective homes and the aroma of flowers and greenery occasionally wafted by and enchanted their noses. Malick had asked Jace if he liked living here and if it was hard moving away from his old place.

"I didn't think I'd like being here" replied Jace, "but I didn't really know for sure. It was hard when I got here cause I didn't know anybody. Then when I found out that I was going to be one of the only humans living here, I thought I was going to basically be a huge weirdo in everybody's eyes. Everybody would want to look at me, but nobody would want to get any closer."

"What about now?" asked Malick.

"It's different now. When I met you, and when we became friends, it got easier" answered Jace frankly.

This comment made Malick smile as he thought about how being Jace's friend caused him to be somewhat of a celebrity too, since anybody who wanted to meet Jace would invariably come and talk to Malick first, as if he was some sort of go-between.

After a few seconds of staring at the fire, Jace thought of something. "Do you have any games we can play?"

"We do" replied Jace's friend. "What kind of games have you played before?"

"Mmmmm ... depends on what kind of games you mean. I loved playing video games. Old school ones like Super Mario, or

Metroid. But when my parents and I played games, we always played board games like Scattergories, Monopoly, or Life. There were some others, but ... yeah. Games like that"

He may as well have been speaking Greek or Latin as far as Malick was concerned. He gave Jace a strange look, and that is when Jace realized that his friend had likely never heard of any of those games. "Sorry. I guess you've never heard of those games, have you?"

"No" said Malick. "What are they like?"

"Well, if you're talking about the video games" explained Jace, "you have a game console that is hooked up to your TV ... I ... I mean your vid screen ... and then you play the game that is on the screen. You use a game controller that you hold in your hands to control your character in the game. Those other games are what we call board games. They have a playing board that is laid out in front of you, and you have game pieces that you move around. You roll these things called dice that have numbers on them, and when you roll the dice, you move your piece on the board the number of places that are on the dice."

"You'll have to show me how to play them sometime" said Malick.

"Okay."

Malick nodded as he continued to stare at the fire. A few seconds later he said, "I think you'll like the games we play here on New Galimar a lot."

"Oh yeah?" asked Jace. "Like what?"

Malick looked over to Jace and smiled. Remembering what his parents told him about not overwhelming Jace with too much, he thought to himself that Jace would probably go nuts over what he had to show him.

"I can't really describe it" said Malick. "It's something that I'll have to show you tomorrow morning when we are able to round up the rest of our friends. What I can tell you though is that it is something that will totally surprise you and I don't think you'll want to play your other games again after you see this one."

"Really?!"

"Really" replied Malick. "Since there isn't any school tomorrow, I'll come by in the morning and pick you up. I'll call the rest and have them meet us there."

"You're not gonna to tell me what it is?" whined Jace.

Seeing an opportunity to have some sport with his new friend, Malick replied "Nope. You're just going to have to wait. Trust me. Using a phrase you have used before, it will blow your mind!"

"No fair!" came the reply from Jace as he slunk back down into his seat with his arms folded. The smile on his face, though, showed that he wasn't actually mad. The conversation had interested him and so now he was looking forward to the morning.

Sure enough, morning eventually came as it always does, and Jace was up and out the door with hardly any intervention on Mikki's part. He would have rushed out the door without eating if it wasn't for Mikki demanding his attendance at the breakfast table. Shoveling his food down as fast as he could, he asked if he could be excused and then rushed out the door to Malick's house, only to see him emerging at the exact same time.

"Hey Jace. You ready?"

"I've been ready since last night. What is this game?!" asked Jace rather insistently.

"You'll see" replied Malick with what Jace found to be a very irritating smile.

Just about then, a transport car came up and parked in front of them. Up to this point, Jace and Malick had always walked to wherever they had gone. But today was going to be different. Normally, only adults are allowed to order a transport car, however

Malick had asked his father for permission to use one to go to the place where he wanted to take Jace, and since this place was quite some distance from their home his father agreed. Getting on their network terminal, Malick's father ordered one and indicated where the car was to take his son and Jace, as well as when it was to pick him up to bring him home.

Looking over to Malick, Jace was a little hesitant, but quickly got over it when his friend climbed aboard. The gull wing doors to the transport car closed behind them and the car immediately started moving. It traveled rather fast actually, and with no "driver" in the car it felt a little strange to Jace to be sitting there waiting for the car to eventually get to its destination.

Eventually the car pulled over to the side of the road and the door opened allowing the two boys to emerge. There before them was the rest of Jace's new posse, and they all had smiles on their faces. As they were walking up to the group, Jace had an idea.

"So, what is this place?"

First to speak up was a girl named Kathlia. "It's a place where you can ..."

"NOPE!" interceded Malick. "I am keeping this as a surprise for Jace! You can't tell him!"

The rest of the group immediately could see that this was a good plan since they knew what was waiting for Jace. Seeing that his plan had been foiled, Jace huffed with mild annoyance, however he figured he would know soon enough now.

The group walked forward toward a glass-encased building in front of them. This building wasn't as tall as the rest of the buildings that surrounded them, but it did have something that the rest of the buildings didn't have. There were lots of lit up sculptures on the grounds outside the building, and it appeared to be a place where a lot of other young ones were congregating. The side of the building had some lit-up words written in Galimarian, but that didn't help Jace much since he hadn't mastered reading

Galimarian yet. As they approached the building, the doors to the building opened and they all entered.

Just inside the building was what looked like a reception area with a counter running along the right-hand wall, but that wasn't what initially took Jace's attention. This room was wall to wall and floor to ceiling with what looked like black glass panels. It almost looked like the panels were windows and behind the windows were star fields complete with planets, moons and enormous gas clouds. It was as if one was floating in the middle of space in a glass box, and the planets, moons and comets were all passing you by. It was an incredible sight to Jace, and he was immediately mesmerized.

As soon as the group entered, the person behind the desk looked over and said "Khazine! I was wondering when I would see you again!" Jace looked over in the direction of the voice and saw a slightly older Galimarian, who looked like a later-aged teenager.

One of the girls in their group named Khazine looked over and smiled sweetly at the young person at the reception desk. Walking up to him, she said "Hello Alervahn. Yeah. I've been busy with school mostly, but we all came here today to introduce the game park to our new human friend here. His name is Jace."

"Human?! I think I remember hearing that we had some humans come live with us, but I didn't think I'd get the chance to meet one" said Alervahn. Then turning to Jace, he said "Welcome to New Galimar! Did the group tell you what we do here?"

"No" replied Jace. "I've been trying to get them to tell me, but they kept saying it was a surprise."

"Indeed" said Alervahn. "I'm sure it *will* be surprising to you." Then turning to the rest of the group he said, "The standard package?" The group nodded their heads except for Jace who had absolutely no idea what he was in for.

One by one, Alervahn passed out what appeared to be pendants to be worn around the neck. When Alervahn gave one to Jace, Jace went to put it on, but Malick stopped him, saying that it wasn't time yet. After all in the group had received their pendant, Alervahn opened a door to the right of the reception desk and allowed all to enter.

The room where they entered was a very comfortable lounge. It was quite large and there were dozens of people quietly seated around the room in various conversation nooks. Except for a few of them, they all seemed to have their eyes closed which seemed to be pretty strange to Jace. The room had an open architecture and there was multicolored carpet throughout the room. Half-walls were tastefully placed here and there so as to delineate congregating areas, and each area was either a raised-up area that you would step up to, or it was a sunken pit that was lined with couches and pillows. Off to one side there was what appeared to be a concession stand where you could obtain food and/or drinks. The lighting of the room was similar to what Jace had seen before with Neon lights surrounding the ceiling/wall corners, and the colors of the neon would cycle through different colors. As with the reception area, the ceiling of this room was made of glass, and it also had the scene of stars and planets passing by. Even though there were several dozen people in the room, it was unusually quiet, since most of the people here were wearing their pendants, and they were sitting there with their eyes closed. Jace thought it almost looked like they were sleeping.

The group entered the room and found an unused conversation pit. As they stepped into the pit all took their seat and expectantly looked at Jace. It was Malick who spoke first.

"Well, my friend, I'm sure you are wondering what this place is."

Jace nodded expectantly.

"This is a what we call the game room, but the games we play here are different than the ones that you have described to me. To play the game, all you have to do is put on the amulet."

Jace looked down at the pendant in his hand and realized that this must be something similar to that time that he attended the wedding for his fathers' friend Dennis. As soon as he realized that, he was immediately intrigued and put on the amulet.

As soon as he donned the amulet, the scene of the lounge in front of him vanished and after a little bit of a light show he was immediately greeted by a scene where he was standing on what looked like a glass pathway, and just like the ceiling in the lounge where he knew his body was still seated, all around him now was what looked like stars and planets. Out of thin air there were other people appearing next to him, none of whom he recognized. One of them walked up to Jace and said "Well? What do you think?"

Looking around Jace responded "It looks cool." Then turning to this stranger who asked the question, he said "What is your name?"

The person looked at him with a strange look, but then realized something and started to laugh. "I guess you wouldn't know! I am your friend, Malick. What you see right now is my avatar in this virtual reality world, and it is in this world where we will play our games."

"Oh WOW!" exclaimed Jace. He thought to himself how this totally beat any video game that he had at home. "How do you play?"

"Let me show you our favorite game" said Khazine. That is when she and Malick reached onto their forearm and pressed some buttons. Jace hadn't realized it before now, but he also had the same type of control mechanism on his forearm, but he decided not to mess with it until someone showed him how to use it.

After pressing the buttons on their control pads, the group was all transported to a place in space, and it appeared that a game grid was set up in front of them. Magically wrapping itself around, Malick and Khazine were each outfitted in what appeared like a battle suit complete with helmet. Khazine levitated from the platform where the rest of the group was standing and moved to a platform that looked to be around fifty feet away. Situated in front of her was what appeared to be a floating ten-foot wall, and as soon as it appeared, she moved her outstretched arms to the left and right which caused the wall to make the corresponding movement back and forth. As he looked over to Malick, only then did Jace realize that Malick had been positioned on a similar platform fifty feet in the opposite direction, and he had his own movable ten-foot wall in front of him.

As soon as both players were positioned properly, what looked like a round ball appeared in the middle of the game grid between them. As soon as it appeared it started to move toward Malick. Malick moved his arms, which in turn caused the wall to move correspondingly. The ball made contact with the wall, bounced off, and made its way toward Khazine.

As the two worked their barriers back and forth, it gradually occurred to Jace that while the way it was being played was certainly better than anything he had experienced before, the complexity of the game … or the lack of it … was nothing compared to what he had played on his video game consoles at home. For a little while he was trying to figure out why this game seemed a little familiar, but then it suddenly hit him.

"Pong!"

"What was that?" said another in the small group that was watching the game with Jace. Jace didn't answer though since he was still amazed at the overall experience.

It didn't really take that long though before Jace became a little bored with the game, which was in sharp contrast to the level of interest displayed by the others in the group. Each of them were more than engaged with the gameplay, and when Khazine won the match, they whooped and hollered over the victory of their friend.

As the two players shed their virtual battle gear, they walked over to Jace to see what he thought. Jace tried to be diplomatic about it, but his lack of interest in the game was immediately apparent to Malick.

"Didn't you like the game?"

"Oh yeah … but I've played something similar to that before and honestly it doesn't really present much of a challenge to me. Are there any other games we can play?"

"Yes, but none that are as good as this one" replied a somewhat disappointed Malick. "I was hoping that you would like this place."

"Don't get me wrong!" exclaimed Jace. "I think this place is great, but I really wish I could show you some of the games I have played before so you can see what I mean. There's this one that I really like to play called Super Mario Brothers that is really fun!"

Malick seemed to be thinking, but then after a couple of moments he said, hang on. I want to check something in the real world to see if it is possible. I'll be right back."

Just then he waved his hand over the control panel on his forearm and instantly disappeared in a mist.

"What just happened?" asked Jace as he looked over to another member of the group.

"It looks like Malick wanted to ask the managers of the game park a question, and so he needed to exit the game grid. He'll be right back" replied Gerilan. Right about then, another mist appeared, and in about five seconds Malick materialized in front of the group again.

"I was right!" exclaimed Malick.

"About what?" asked Khazine.

"I asked the manager if it was possible to scan your memories Jace to see if we could reproduce this game you mentioned here on the game grid. He said it was, and that if it was ok to scan your memories to extract the game, he could program it into the grid fairly quickly."

"Of course it's ok!" said a rather excited Jace. "What do I need to do?"

Malick showed Jace what to do on his control panel in order to indicate to the manager on the outside that it was ok to scan his memories for this game. It only took about what felt like fifteen minutes for the process to complete, and as soon as it did, Jace found himself at the opening of the Mario brothers game but now he wasn't just looking at a two dimensional version of the game, but rather he was looking at a complete three dimensional version of the game. When there were characters that needed to be jumped over, he actually jumped over them, etc. etc.

The new game was an instant hit on the game grid, and before long not only was Jace's immediate group playing the game for the rest of the day, the entire set of visitors that day, all one hundred and thirty people, were enthralled with this new game. Without even trying, Jace was an instant hit with all the gamers on the island.

It brought an immense amount of happiness for Jason and Mikki to see their son acclimatizing to life on New Galimar as well as he had. After thinking about it for a while, it really wasn't that surprising since the Galimarian people were so peaceful and easy to get along with. Jace's set of young friends weren't any different, and the speed at which he formed friendships with a group of young ones from his school was remarkable.

On this particular day while Jace was out playing games with his friends, Jason and Mikki had been invited to a picnic with the rest of their friends. It was easy to enjoy such a picnic since you didn't actually have to be in close proximity with each other. That, and the fact that they wanted to include their amulet companions in the festivities led to the decision to hold the picnic in the virtual reality world of the amulets.

While sitting in their respective living rooms, Jason and Mikki went in-world and joined the rest at a beautiful countryside spot where there was a large blanket spread out, and everyone was sitting on the blanket. While it was pointless to "eat" anything while in-world, they still decided to enjoy things like playing instruments or a game of catch. It was a really peaceful setting. Upon arrival, Jason immediately sought out Dennis while Mikki walked toward the seated group and was a little surprised to see Terri.

"Hey you! I didn't think I'd see you here!"

"Oh?" asked Terri. "Why not? Didn't want us around to spoil the fun?" said Terri with a glint in her eye and an obvious smile on her face.

"Of course not!" responded Mikki. "I just thought you'd be more or less preoccupied with the new baby. How is Coral doing?"

"She's great" answered Terri. "As the doctors predicted, she has been developing at a highly increased rate. In fact, even though she's only two months, she is already walking and is starting to string together sentences. It's actually staggering how fast she is progressing."

"Sentences! At two months?! Are you sure she isn't going to be like those kids that get old before their time?"

"I don't think so. The doctors on Galimar think she's just racing to catch up to the hybrid DNA in her cells, but at any rate, they also said that when she is ready to accept it, they will give her the nanites to help stabilize her cell function. I'm a little guarded in my personal prognosis, but I have a feeling she'll be ok."

"Wow" was all that Mikki said for a little bit. Eventually, she added "Sentences huh? Did it sound like she knew what she was saying?"

"Oh yeah. This morning for instance, she said that she liked the oatmeal I made for her and that she wanted to play with her dolls after breakfast. When she got down from the breakfast table, she left the room saying, 'I love you mama!'. I totally lost it!"

"Oh my god! That's incredible!"

"What's incredible?" said a curious Jason who was only now joining the group with Dennis, Khreelon, Ehobak and Socrates. Seated already was Ruavu, Lynne, and Brianna who Terri had already been talking to when Mikki arrived.

"Oh, it's just that Coral is already talking and walking around, and it's only been about two months since she was born!"

"Walking and talking! That IS incredible!" exclaimed Dennis.

"Indeed" responded Khreelon. "This is far and away the fastest I've ever seen a child develop in all my years."

"… many though they are" quipped Terri as she was looking at her husband Khreelon with a smile. Khreelon looked at her with instant blue eyes and said "Well, I had to wait for the perfect woman!"

"Boy he knows how to butter his bread, doesn't he?" said Lynne. The rest of the group chuckled at the comment, while Khreelon and Terri paid them no attention.

"Well, if you're here, where is Coral?" asked Brianna.

"We just put her down for a nap before we got here" said Terri. "Put her in her rainbow pajamas and put her teddy bear next to her and you won't hear a peep for at least a couple of hours." The rest of the group showed looks of understanding.

"So, what were you guys talking about earlier before I so rudely interrupted?" asked Mikki.

"Oh, I was just telling Brianna about when we were introducing the Galimarians to the new president" replied Terri. "I swear it was so hard not to laugh when he dropped his drink upon seeing Ehobak, Ruavu, Khreelon and myself!"

"Oh my god, that must have been so funny!" chimed Brianna.

"It was!"

"I almost wish I was a fly on the wall during that meeting" said Lynne. "I think if I was him, I'd want to know everything about the

Galimarians. Like where they live, how long they've been here, why they came here in the first place, what they want with earth, etc."

"Actually, that is something that I've been wondering about lately" said Brianna. "What was the main reason why the Galimarians came to earth in the first place? Was there something wrong with the planet Galimar?"

"Not at all" replied Khreelon. "Galimar was, and I assume still is, a beautiful planet with endless natural wonders. The people of Galimar are just as beautiful as the planet and I have to say I'm really sad that we weren't able to go back home."

"So, if it is such a beautiful place, why did you leave?"

"Paliminium" answered Ehobak.

"Pala-what-ium?" said Dennis.

"Paliminium. Element #126 on your periodic table of elements. It's the element that makes it possible to achieve anti-gravity and is the basis of the propulsion drives on the Arageena and the shuttles."

"OK. There's another word I'm not familiar with yet. What's an Arageena?" responded Dennis.

"The Arageena is the name of the ship that carried us eventually to earth, and is now the basis of the island of New Galimar. You see, while Paliminium is incredibly useful to us, it wasn't found anywhere on Galimar. It was named after a planet where we first discovered it called Palimine and so we called it Paliminium. We would have just gone back there to get some more, but the sun near that planet exploded in a massive super nova and destroyed the planet."

"Isn't that the same thing that happened to the planet you were originally going to visit when you set out on your voyage?" asked Terri.

"Yes" answered Ehobak. "Long range spectroscopy indicated that a planet whose name was Eden had stores of Paliminium on it, but its sun also went super nova just as we were getting there. That explosion threw us out of our own galaxy and into yours."

"So, you say that it has anti-gravity properties" said Jason. "How does that work?"

"So far, none of our scientists had been able to explain how it worked before we left" replied Ehobak. "Perhaps they figured it out after we left, but so far we just don't know."

"I wonder there if any of it on Earth" pondered Jason mostly to himself.

"This is something else we don't know" replied Ehobak. "In its raw state, it gives off a subtle blue-green glow and so it is easy to visually spot if you are looking for it."

"Do you have any scanners that can look for it?" asked Dennis.

Ehobak smiled. "I'm afraid our abilities don't exactly match the kind of technology that I've heard are featured in human science fiction stories that I've been exposed to."

Dennis smiled at Ehobak and Khreelon at the reply, then looked over to Jason. As with many times in the past, the look on Jason's face told Dennis volumes, and in this case told Dennis that something in their conversation had just triggered a line of thinking in Jason that was probably going to lead to something very interesting. Jason was staring at a patch of grass in front of him, and Dennis could see his eyes darting back and forth.

"OK. I've seen that face before. What do you have cookin up there?" asked Dennis.

Jason looked up to Dennis and the rest of the group who had heard the query and were now just as interested in what Jason was thinking. "Well … I was just thinking about the portal."

"As you often do" injected Dennis in a slight bit of comic relief.

"As I often do, yes" smiled Jason. "I was just thinking about how we've already modified the portal to have two portal windows that sit right in front of each other in order to facilitate site to site transfers, right?"

"Right" responded Dennis.

"So, it isn't anything new to utilize the portal field in ways that we had never even imagined when we first designed the device, right?"

"Yup. Right again"

"So, you know how earlier we were talking about using spectroscopy on the starlight that pours through an alien planet's atmosphere? And how by doing that you can learn the composition of the planet based on the wavelengths of light present, and how every element has a certain atomic structure, which leads each to absorb/reflect different wavelengths?"

"Yeah ..." said a now very intrigued Dennis. "You're thinking about using a spectrometer with the portal, aren't you?"

Smiling back at his friend, Jason replied "Exactly, but I'm not just thinking we should limit it to an optical spectrometer. I think we could have a whole array of detection devices such as a mass, time-of-flight or even magnetic spectrometer."

Socrates, who had been mute up to this point piped up and said, "Or how about hooking up any other range of detection devices, like even DNA sequencers? Or Lidar? Or Gas Chromatography?"

For a small while, the physicist brains of Jason, Dennis, Socrates and Brianna were now burning at top speed, thinking through everything that had just been said. The rest of the group including Ehobak and Khreelon were astute enough to realize that something special was happening right before their eyes. Something extraordinary was being invented right in front of them. Mikki's face showed a half smile as she mentally likened it to the spectacle of watching a baby being born.

"I'm sorry guys, but I can't see any reason why this wouldn't work" said Brianna.

"Neither can I" responded Jason. "I'm slightly embarrassed we didn't think of this before."

"So, if you do this, what capability would that give you" asked Terri.

Jason and Dennis looked at each other, but before they could respond, Socrates said "It means that we would be able to have exactly what Ehobak was referring to earlier. We would be able to actually have a science fiction scanner that would allow us to scan for whatever substances we may want to look for."

"Not only that" added Jason, "But since we can dial in any position we want, we can do it for whatever position on the planet, or even the galaxy, that we want. We would really have a real live science fiction scanner."

"Yeah" added Dennis. "One that we could use to look for that ... what was that element #126 you were talking about earlier?"

"Paliminium" answered Ehobak.

"Right. Paliminium. We can use this scanner to look anywhere we want on the earth for it, and if we find it, we can then refine it and use it to make anti-gravity devices."

Standing up, Terri said "Well. It looks like my work here is done. I think I've sufficiently made sure that science has moved forward!" Everybody in the group chuckled. "Meanwhile, I need to check on the baby and make sure she's ok.

"Awww ... do you have to go already?" whined Lynne.

"Sorry babe. Being a mother is a new experience, but I'll tell you there's a lot of instinct built in that I never knew was there."

"That's for sure" agreed Mikki.

Khreelon stood and put his arm around his love. "Talk to you all later!" said Terri. After making the appropriate strokes on their in-world amulets, both Khreelon and Terri vanished.

"The thing is, all this still doesn't explain why Paliminium does what it does. Why does it float?" asked Jason.

"Good question. Something to ponder while we are making our new toy" smiled Dennis.

Jason smiled back at his friend. "Indeed!"

Meanwhile, Khreelon and Terri awoke from their amulet-induced sleep feeling refreshed as always. It was because of their need to live part of the time at Terri's apartment in Brooklyn Heights that the Grand Council of New Galimar agreed to boost the signal for the amulets, thus allowing them to be at their New York apartment while still being able to communicate through the amulets with their friends on the island. Terri's responsibilities as U.S. Ambassador to the island of New Galimar meant that she sometimes needed to be on the island, and sometimes she needed to be in New York and Washington.

As they opened their eyes there in the living room of the apartment, the first thing they noticed was the flashing of blue and red lights outside the windows to her apartment. With a quizzical look on her face, Terri made her way over to the window and pulled aside the curtain while Khreelon made his way over to the front door that seemed to be slightly ajar.

The scene made her blood run cold. There were several emergency vehicles, and several of the personnel were grouped around one spot in the middle of the road. Paramedics were working feverishly.

Their focus was on a little girl laying on the pavement in rainbow pajamas.

CHAPTER 31

Camp David, as it is commonly known, is a peaceful place where many presidents of the recent past have gone to "get away from it all". In reality, while it was often used to achieve a level of relaxation that was seldom afforded to the president when he was in the oval office, many times it was also used as a place where world leaders could meet together and discuss matters of international interest with little or no interruptions from the outside world. Even though the setting of camp David is located in the heavily wooded and serene hills of the Catoctin Mountain Park near Thurmont, Maryland, it is actually considered a military installation called the "Naval Support Facility Thurmont" and is run by a joint contingent of Navy and Marine personnel ... not to mention the secret service whenever the president is visiting.

In comparison to the posh and stylish surroundings of the White House, the accommodations at Camp David are rather rustic. This of course suited President Kirken and his wife Suzette just fine, as it did for many other presidents. Their home ground of Utah was rife with bucolic and heavily wooded surroundings, and so whenever they needed to get back to their roots, a weekend at the camp was just what the doctor ordered. One of their favorite pastimes was snuggling with each other in front of the fire in the fireplace. Winter was the best time for that. Today though it was Saturday morning and the couple was just finishing the dishes from breakfast that morning.

"What are you planning on doing this morning darling?" asked the first lady.

"Oh, I have some work I have to do for a few hours. Why? What did you have in mind?"

As she sipped on her second cup of coffee that morning, she leaned against the kitchen countertop and wistfully gazed out the bay window over the sink. Her hands were both cupped around the mug of steaming brew even though it wasn't necessarily that cold in the house.

"I dunno" came the unengaging reply.

The president looked at his wife and saw the faraway look in her eyes. "What is it?"

Looking back at him, she smiled, took a small sip from her cup, and replied "Oh ... I was just thinking about how I miss the times when we could go to a small town and window shop with nobody paying much attention to us. I was just watching that hitchhikers guide movie where it said something wouldn't be done without", she did air quotes, "orders signed in triplicate, sent in, sent back, queried, lost, found, subjected to public inquiry, lost again, and finally buried in soft peat for three months and recycled as firelighters. I just feel like doing anything with you these days requires that kind of planning."

That prompted her husband, whom she always referred to by his first name 'Ernst', to laugh out loud.

“I can sympathize with you on that one” replied her husband as he removed his glasses and wiped the tears of laughter from his eyes, “but back then there weren’t elements in the world that equated my well-being with all that is going wrong in the world.”

“You need to assign some scientists the task of making a magic wand so you can solve everybody’s problems” replied Suzette.

“It sometimes seems like if I had a magic wand and solved all the problems of the world, my love, the world would just go looking for more problems.”

With a flick of her eyebrow and a nod of her head, Suzette conceded to his conjecture and took a more relaxed and unhurried pull from her coffee mug with no words in reply. Coming over to stand next to her, she took one hand and snaked her arm through his as they both looked outside and watched the snow fall.

“Actually” said Suzette as she broke the silence, “I was thinking I would make a few calls to my mother and sisters. After that, I was going to see what kind of progress I could make on that quilt I’ve been working on.”

“Sounds nice. I should be done in about four hours with my work.”

“OK babe” came the reply from the first lady. “Go save the world for me. I’ll see you soon.”

Leaning over for a quick kiss the president replied, “One ‘save-the-world’, coming up!” With that, he retreated into his personal study down the hall and closed the door.

President Kirken’s personal study at Camp David was about as normal as any home office. There were bookshelves lining the walls, and while many of those shelves indeed carried books, several of them just simply had stacks of papers. His desk of course had a phone, computer screen, keyboard, and various business paraphernalia. The wall across from his desk had another fireplace and mounted above the fireplace was a wooden steering wheel for a ship. His father who had been a merchant marine during World War Two and later the captain of an oceanographic research vessel associated with the Woods Hole Oceanographic Institution gave it to him when he had started running for public office some thirty years ago. When he gave it to him, he said to always remember that no matter what he did in life, the lives of those he was responsible for must always be more important than his own.

As he entered the room, he stood in front of the fireplace and placed his hand on the wheel and, for a moment he felt a connection with his dad once more whom had passed away about ten years ago. Glancing up to the top curve of the wheel, words were carved into the wood in Latin saying, "Ex Nihilo Nihil Fit". His dad explained that the Latin phrase meant "Nothing comes from nothing", meaning that if you do nothing, you'll get nothing, whereas if want something then you need to work hard for it. As he progressively worked his way through various bastions of government in the last thirty years, he never forgot those words. For all of those years this wheel hung on the wall of his office and his dedication to the work of serving the people of America showed he never forgot his fathers' words.

Wrapping his hand around the nearest handle he started to turn the wheel on the wall. As if it was the dial to a combination lock, he turned the wheel back and forth five times. Upon turning the wheel a sixth and final time, the door to his study automatically locked and the one and only window to the room was quickly blacked out by a descending metal cover. The lights to the room turned red, and the paneling on the east wall receded and slid to the side revealing an elevator door that was now opening. Releasing his hold of the ships wheel, President Kirken walked over to the car beyond the opened door and stood in a frame that was uniquely shaped and formed according to his body.

Once the doors closed, a protective padded frame closed itself around his body such that he was completely snug in the frame. It was a necessary step because just then, the car quickly descended vertically, but then tilted until eventually the car traveled along its path horizontally at a speed of about sixty miles an hour, all while the president laid in the car on his back. This evacuation tube system was a holdover from the cold war days, and it was designed to quickly whisk the president away in the event of a nuclear attack. Being that the car was only designed for the president, it always perplexed President Kirken on how he was supposed to leave his family at Camp David to fry in a nuclear strike while he was safe in some bunker. It never made sense to him, but then again, nothing nuclear *ever* made sense to him.

The journey eventually ended deep in the middle of a nearby granite mountain. Once his car came to a vertical and complete stop, the doors opened, and he was able to step out into a facility that was brightly lit and well appointed with the latest in electronic gadgetry and necessary furniture. Overall, the bunker was segregated into various functional areas. The tube that transported President Kirken to the facility deposited him in an office that was dedicated to the president. The door to that office let out into a large main room that served as a central area with high ceilings where people could congregate, converse and plan their next moves. Conversation areas were set up and strewn throughout this main room made up of couches, chairs, and tables. Jutting off from this great room, several other smaller rooms and facilities that supported the personnel that found themselves at this facility could be found. There was what amounted to a dormitory with beds and lavatory facilities. Another wing to the facility was where a kitchen and eating areas could be found. There were several smaller offices that could be commandeered by any who needed them, and there was a large utility room where the necessary machinery to support this facility could be found.

Water to the facility was supplied by a well that had been dug, and electricity was supplied by outside electrical suppliers. In the event of a nuclear strike, it was doubtful that that electrical services could be counted on, and so the facility had available to it fuel in the form of a direct tap into a nearby Strategic Petroleum Reserve storage. While most of the oil stored in the SPR was made up of crude oil, and while most of those storage fields were located along the coastline of the Gulf of Mexico, there were other storage facilities peppered around the country in the northern states, and some of those facilities stored refined oil and other petroleum products. The one near this facility stored refined gasoline and so the supply of fuel to the generators in this facility was virtually endless.

As President Kirken stepped out of the transport car and into his office, he emerged into the great room and waited in a chair. He didn't have to wait long, for not long after he took a seat the room filled with the characteristic light from an arrival using Jason and Dennis' portal, and shortly thereafter Jason, Dennis and a new person that President Kirken had never seen before arrived.

"Jason! How are my star physicists?" asked the president.

"Mr. President. It's good to see you again" responded Jason. With a smile, Dennis reached out his hand and the president responded with a handshake. "Hello Mr. President. Quite a place you have here" said Dennis.

"Yeah. It's a relic from the cold war days, and so that's why there isn't anybody here at the moment. I thought it would be a great place to meet together since extremely few people know it exists."

"I can see that. Are those beds I see through that door?" asked Dennis.

"Yep. Sure is. And There's a fully stocked kitchen out through that door over there. I'm afraid most of the food is freeze dried, but once it's reconstituted, I'm told it isn't half bad."

"Freeze dried" bristled Socrates. "I've never found anything freeze dried that ever merited the title of 'food'"

"I'm with you on that one pal. It may not be half bad, but I'll bet it probably isn't half good either" added Dennis with a slight smile.

"I suppose you might be right" responded President Kirken to the newcomer, "but I would counter that it is much better than the alternative of starving."

“Then would I suppose you’re the one in the right, Mr. President” acceded Socrates.

Taking the opportunity, not to mention the lull in conversation, the president stepped over to the new arrival and extended his hand. “I am President Kirken. Doctor Einikov I presume?”

“Yes Mr. President. It is an honor to meet you.”

“The honor is all mine” responded the president. “Doctors Marsalis and Greene have told me some good things about you Doctor Einikov.”

“You don’t know the half of it” interjected Dennis with a roll of his eyes.

The president looked over to Dennis and with scrunched eyebrows and a smile he said, “This isn’t going to be another time when I should be sitting and not holding a drink is it?”

“Probably not a bad idea, Mr. President” replied Jason.

“Well, before we get started gentlemen, I want to inform you that I have decided to get my vice president involved. She doesn’t know it yet, but the material that I will be sharing with you will be the beginning point of a special task force that she will be heading up. As you know, the existence of your portal and all that goes with it including the island of New Galimar I have classified as ‘Most Secret’ and is on a need-to-know basis. I have familiarized her already with some of this material, but I have to say that it was obvious she didn’t really believe all of it. Even so, I have instructed her to clear her schedule for this afternoon, and I would like you to use the portal to retrieve her to this facility. Can you do that for me?”

Jason and Dennis always relished the few and far between occasions when they could share the portal technology and the existence of New Galimar with anybody, and so they were more than ready to do as the president requested.

“Of course!” said Jason. “How do you want to do this?”

President Kirken answered by pulling out his secure cell phone and dialed a phone number. As the call was ringing, he looked over to Jason, Dennis and Socrates, and showed a sly smile.

"Hello, Brynn?"

"Yes, Mr. President. This is Brynn. What can I do for you?"

"Brynn, are you at the White House as I asked?"

"Yes sir. I'm just sitting here in my office catching up on a little paperwork, and I have cleared my calendar as you requested."

"Good. Good." Then the president made an up-motion with his face toward Jason and Dennis, and winked. He then said "While I am on the phone with you, I'd like you to go to the Oval Office."

Jason and Dennis smiled at President Kirken and knew exactly what he intended and immediately walked over to where the portal window was still positioned, although it was currently invisible there in the underground facility. Stepping through it, they returned to their lab on New Galimar, and made the necessary preparations.

"Sure, Mr. President" said Brynn. "But I thought you and the first lady were staying at Camp David this weekend?"

"That's correct, Brynn. But I need you to help me with something that is of great national security."

"Of course, Mr. President. What do you need me to do?"

"Well Brynn, remember how we had that chat earlier in the week about the new task force that I was going to be setting up?"

"Yes."

"And remember how I also told you about some technologies that you were going to have to be familiar with as you head up this task force?"

"Unh ... yes. I remember Mr. President."

As he sat there alone with the president, Socrates could see the president smile a bit. He could see President Kirken was enjoying this, probably as much as Jason and Dennis were.

"Now Brynn, I know that the information I shared with you was a little hard to believe, but trust me when I tell you that the superficial information you already know won't even hold a candle to the entire reality of it all."

"Well, Mr. President, while I have to admit that I do have a hard time believing all that you told me, I will also say that I trust you to be a good and honest man."

Just then, President Kirken received a text message from Jason telling him that all was ready and that the portal had been established.

"I'm glad you feel that way Vice President Monroe. I've always known that picking you as my running mate was a good choice, and as I said to you the night we were elected, I intended to make sure you were not just a figurehead, but rather you were going to be an integral part of this presidency. Do you remember me saying that?"

"Of course I do, Mr. President. I am very glad to be of service to the country, but especially to you as well. Oh ... and by the way, I am here now in the oval office as you requested."

"Good. Now I have to warn you that what I am about to do will be very disorienting for you, but I need you to trust me when I tell you that you are in no danger and that any and all questions you have will be completely answered. OK?"

"Yes sir."

"Good. Now ... I need you hang up the phone to step over to the fireplace."

"OK sir. Good bye."

"Bye"

President Kirken snapped shut his folding cell phone and looked over to Socrates with a grin. Having been an eager observer of the human race for a very long time, he knew exactly what was happening here, and sure enough, about 45 seconds later, the room lit up with the typical portal light show and Jason, Dennis ... and Brynn ... appeared. With eyes that showed the same bewilderment as her voice, Brynn was the first to speak.

"What ... THE HELL ... just happened?"

The four men just looked at each other and laughed. Brynn wasn't laughing though, and as soon as he could compose himself, President Kirken answered.

"I'm sorry Brynn, I have to say I was just as confused when I learned about this technology the first time too. Here ..." the president pulled out a chair for the Vice President and continued "Take a seat and I'll explain everything. I'll answer any questions you have, and these men here will fill in any gaps."

Vice President Brynn Monroe slowly took the seat, followed by the rest of the men who were all standing. It took the better part of the next hour to cover all the information about Jason, Dennis, Admiral Brinstock, the impending disaster with the Yellowstone super volcano, the discovery of the island of New Galimar, the alien race living on New Galimar, the Tectonic Stabilization machine, and finally the portal and its abilities including time travel.

Simply put, Vice President Monroe was thunderstruck. When it was evident that there were no more earth-shattering revelations to tell her about, she stood and wandered a short distance from the group to chew on this information for a few minutes. The men all knew what she was going through, and truth be told having reiterated all the information again from beginning to end like they just did, it was a bit surprising even to them how much had happened in such a relatively short period of time. They all decided to remain quiet as she mentally chewed on it all.

“I’m sorry guys” responded Brynn, finally breaking the silence. “I just … this is a lot to take in.”

“Oh, trust me Brynn” responded President Kirken, “I know exactly what you are going through.”

There was just a nod from the vice president, but after another ten seconds or so, she asked “This is how those supplies miraculously showed up on the ISS, isn’t it?”

President Kirken smiled at the fact that his very intelligent vice president put two and two together so quickly. “Yes” was his short response.

With a slight nod and with squinted eyes, she responded “I was wondering that day in the oval office what you were thinking about, and later how you somehow pulled those astronauts butts out of the fire.”

The president didn’t verbally respond, but simply nodded with a smile.

Brynn looked back over to Jason and Dennis, and said “And you must have been the ones to snatch those supplies from the VAB and transported them to the ISS, aren’t you?”

Dennis smiled, put up his open palms and said “Guilty”.

Brynn walked over to the two men and extended her hand. “Gentlemen, I may be the vice president of the United States, but before that I was an astronaut that lived on the space station for several months. From the bottom of my heart … *thank you* … for saving the lives of my friends!”

Slightly emotional, Jason and Dennis both stood and shook the hand of the vice president. Then turning to President Kirken, she then added “And thank you for making the arrangements.”

“Of course, Brynn. Like you, they are some of our best national assets, which makes them like family to me. I take care of my family.”

Brynn nodded, and at that point realized that all these revelations were taking their toll on her. She plopped down in her stuffed chair and let out a rush of air and simply said "Wow."

"I'm sorry about forcing your feet back down to the earth now Brynn" said President Kirken, "but I have to move this meeting along because there are some very important issues that you need to hear regarding the new job I'm giving you with this task force, and there are some things that Jason and Dennis have said they need to share with me too."

Straightening her back, she resumed her professional demeanor and simply responded "Of course, sir. No problem."

Taking the cue, all in the room resumed a seated position.

Turning to Jason and Dennis, the president said "All right guys. Lay it on me."

Jason and Dennis proceeded to recount the conversations that had recently taken place on New Galimar between Jason, Dennis, Alexi (also known as Socrates), Khreelon, Ehobak, and all their respective wives. Saving the best for last, they culminated the story with Alexi telling the president how his real name was Socrates, and how he was the actual personage of history. He explained how he was the beneficiary of the blood-borne nanites that had been given to him by his father, thus leading him to be very long lived. He then explained how he had also been other well-known people of history.

"Are you telling me you are Socrates? The actual Socrates of history? And even Ben Franklin?"

"Yes sir" came the short but powerful reply."

The president secretly thought for a moment that his previous comment about being glad that he wasn't holding a drink had ended up being prophetic. Like Jason and Dennis on the previous day, President Kirken was completely floored at the knowledge that he was standing before one of the greatest and most influential men of the ages. As was the case quite frequently when it came to Jason and Dennis, he once again found himself without words. He simply sat back in his seat and stared at Socrates with wide-eyed wonder.

"Well" said the president once he gathered his wits together, "It is a pleasure to have met you … uh … Socrates."

"Thank you, Mr. President. It is an honor to meet you as well"

"Well gentlemen and lady, I appreciate you all coming here to meet with me" said President Kirken as he looked back at Jason and Dennis as well. "I have some information to share with you on this new threat you told me about, but admittedly, I don't have very much."

"Are you talking about the group called the Circle of Seven that abducted Socrates?" asked Dennis.

"Yes" replied the president. "According to the people I have sniffing around, they are a group of people that seem to think they can run things better than anybody else, and it also seems like it might be some sort of secret society made up of super-rich individuals. We're still looking into it, but they seem to do a really good job of covering their tracks." Then turning to Brynn, he then said "I am assigning you the job of running a task force to not only learn all needed intelligence about this group, but once you do I want you to do whatever is necessary to eliminate them as a threat. You will have the complete weight of the presidency behind whatever decisions you make. All I ask is that you keep me informed of your progress during our daily conferences."

"Yes sir" responded the vice president.

"They must be doing a great job of covering their tracks." said Jason. "If this is the first you've heard about them, then either they just came onto the scene, or they have the best program of secrecy I've ever heard of."

Taking a deep breath and opening his eyes wide while still staring at the ground, Socrates answered "Oh … they haven't just come onto the scene."

"Oh?" asked President Kirken.

Looking up at the other men in the room, and more specifically President Kirken, Socrates replied "I am actually very glad to have the opportunity to speak with you Mr. President since their existence and their activities will probably directly affect not only your presidency, but the course of human history in the years to come."

Had this type of conjecture come from anybody other than the men in this room, the president would have probably taken it with a grain of salt. "A rather large grain" thought the president as the statement from Socrates floated around the room.

"Tell me why you feel this way" requested the president.

Socrates, who had been sitting up to this point in a chair at one end of the conversation pit where they were all seated, stood up and thoughtfully paced as he spoke. The president, along with Jason, Dennis and Brynn remained silent as they observed what looked like Socrates choosing his words carefully. Ten seconds passed, but then he said "I have always said that those who fail to prepare are also those who are preparing to fail. In the time that I have carried the burdens of my personal mortal coil, I have learned that those who see the calamity coming, and thereafter prepare for it, are also those that live another day." Then turning to look at his friends directly, he continued "The challenge is to have the eyes that can not only look, but also to have eyes that can see; eyes that can not only see what is happening in front of them, but to have perceptive powers that are trained to distinguish the difference between normal pedestrian and meaningless details of daily life versus the elements and features of life's experiences that all point back to a common thread. It's the ability to see how the minutia of the human experience can sometimes point back to those few who might be puppeteers pulling the strings of society."

It was obvious to the others in the room that Socrates hadn't lost his touch for waxing philosophic, nor had the number of years that he had spent on the earth dulled his clear-thinking abilities. Knowing that it was best to allow Socrates the time he needed to fully express himself, they all unanimously and independently decided to remain silent.

"For centuries I had pondered on the events of history" continued Socrates. "The more I did, the more it appeared to me that there was a common thread ... an overall course toward which the ship of humanity inexorably sailed. At times, it appeared this course would lead mankind to an eventuality of destruction. At other times, it appeared mankind would bounce back in a refreshing renaissance of discovery and exploration. The ebb and flow of man's growth versus destruction seemed to be unstoppable, and yet while I had no ability to prove my conjecture, I always felt there was someone ... or something ... pulling the puppeteer strings, causing events of history to play out according to a pattern of thinking that never originated from the puppets. I was never able to prove my theories in this direction."

Then taking his seat once more, Socrates looked into the eyes that were already staring at him and added "Until now."

"Until now?" asked Dennis.

"Yes" answered Socrates, "Until now."

"What do you mean?" inquired the president.

Interlacing his fingers in his lap while his elbows rested on the armrests, Socrates leaned forward in his seat and continued.

"When I was abducted, I had the ability to overhear conversations between my abductors in a room about four doors down from the room where I was forced to work for them."

"Four doors down from the room where we took you?" asked Dennis. "How could that be possible? Were they blowhards?"

"No" answered Socrates with a slight smile. "I'm not really sure why this is the case, but I have always had hearing that was much better than those around me. At any rate, their conversations over the course of the three days I was there proved to be quite informative. Apparently one of their number was new to the fold and so there were several in the room who were enlightening him on the history of the group."

"The first thing I learned was that they call themselves the Circle of Seven and that the group has been around for about as long as I have. They originated in Greece, but soon thereafter spread out to three different points on the compass. One group centered itself on the Italian peninsula, another in the area of England, and finally another in the area of Egypt. This latter group called itself the Circle of Seven, and it was they who were responsible for the scientific breakthroughs recorded in the Library of Alexandria. As a side note, I had planned to visit those centers for learning there in Alexandria, and in fact I was only a week away from traveling there when I received word that the Romans had destroyed the libraries in their raids. I was very disappointed."

"You had planned to visit there, huh?" asked the president in an uncharacteristically casual yet obviously intrigued manner.

"Yes. I have always been a student of the sciences, and I had heard that there was a lot of research being done there. I was anxious to visit Alexandria since its centers for learning were originally proposed by a student of mine named Demetrius of Phalerum. But, as I pointed out, the Romans came and destroyed things there to such an extent that I changed my plans and traveled with some of my other students to assist with pursuing their areas of study. Eventually I settled on the island of Lesbos and taught a young prince." Socrates paused for a moment, then said "But ... I digress."

Jason leaned over to Dennis and barely whispered "I think that young prince he's talking about is Alexander the Great"

Socrates looked toward Jason and said "Don't believe it. He wasn't that great."

Caught in the whisper, Jason leaned back in his seat and belatedly realized Socrates had just said his hearing was better than most. With a slight guffaw, Jason put both hands up and said "Ahhh ... you caught me!"

"What was that?" Asked President Kirken.

"Jason accurately speculated that the prince was the man known as Alexander the Great" replied Socrates.

The president soaked in the fact that he was sitting with a man who not only knew these people of history, but in this case, was one himself. As what seemed to be a regular event for him lately, he once again slowly shook his head and simply said "Astonishing."

"It was during one of those conversations with the new recruit" continued Socrates, "when I learned the manner in which they recruited the most elite and senior of their governing body. Apparently, as a group they decide to invite a personage of society that would probably help them to meet their goals of world domination, control and exploitation. If that invitee agrees, then all is well and good from their perspective. If he or she refuses, then that one is ruthlessly eliminated in order to cover their tracks. I found out that they had just invited someone in New York recently, and when he refused, they bombed his entire business."

Suddenly sitting forward, the president shouted a single word.

"Miritrans!"

"It has to be!" exclaimed the vice president.

The other three men looked at the president and vice president, but it was Socrates who asked the question that all three were thinking. "What's a Miritrans?"

"It's the bombing in Manhattan that happened a couple of weeks ago" answered the president. "Blake Chambertree was the head of that company, and it must have been him that they invited to be a part of their group."

Then sitting back in his seat, he then added “He must have refused to be a part of the Circle.”

“More than likely” agreed Socrates. “That is the way they have always done business. Invite well known, powerful and influential people of history to be a part of their ruling body. If they refuse, then eliminate them.”

“I wonder who else met their demise that way.” pondered Jason.

“Actually, they happened to mention a few” answered Socrates, “and it’s a who’s who of society.”

“Like?” Asked President Kirken.

“Like ... Julius Caesar, Peter the Third of Russia, Archduke Ferdinand, Emiliano Zapata, Abraham Lincoln, and more recently John F. Kennedy and Robert Kennedy.”

At that point, a nuclear bomb could have been detonated near the bunker and none of the others in the room would have noticed. Having just had the real reason for the assassination of such historical figures finally explained to them left them all dumbfounded and completely speechless. As if forgetting to breathe, after about twenty seconds they one and all took a deep breath and looked at each other.

“You’re kidding!” As soon as he said it, Jason silently berated himself for saying something so stupid.

“Not kidding” answered Socrates. “I was just as surprised as you when I heard it, but that isn’t the half of it.”

“Not the half of it! What else could there be that would top that?” exclaimed the president.

“I also learned that they collectively steered the social and political engines back in the late thirties and early forties. That steering not only led to the outbreak of world war for their own profiteering, but they also spurred the creation of the Manhattan project since they wanted the other two cousin organizations to be destroyed.”

“How would the Manhattan project do that?” asked Brynn, echoing the same question that hung in the minds of the others.

“It would accomplish it because the other two organizations were meeting with each other at two key cities in 1945. Those two cities were Hiroshima and Nagasaki.”

Once again, all were speechless.

Knowing that there was a criminal organization that needed to be stopped was one thing, but now learning that this organization had not only been right under their noses all along, but that they are powerful enough to engineer the destruction of millions of lives ... solely for the purpose of increasing their own wealth? They all struggled to wrap their minds around this revelation, and for several minutes, none of them were doing a good job of it.

Jason stood and contemplatively paced around the room, as did the president. All in the room were lost in their respective thoughts. Dennis and President Kirken were aghast that there could be people that were so diabolical, so callous, and so without mercy that they could ever do such a terrible thing.

While Jason was just as floored at the thought, he was also simultaneously not only thinking about how this organization could be destroyed, but he was also thinking about something else.

Startling the others out of their reveries, Jason asked “You say they engineered societal unrest, eventually resulting in world war?”

“Correct” answered Socrates.

“And so that must mean they were the ones behind Hitler rising to power?”

“Correct again. In fact, he was a member of the governing body of the Circle of Seven.”

“Oh my god” muttered President Kirken.

Seeing that his best friend was on to something, Dennis spoke up and asked, “What are you thinking?”

Jason, who had been standing a few paces away from the rest, walked back to the conversation pit and sat down and said "Don't get me wrong, I am just as blown away with all this information as you are. But I also have to say that, depending on how you look at it, there is actually some good news in all this."

"How in all that is holy can you POSSIBLY find anything in this that is good news?" asked Dennis.

"Well, think about it. We are now possessors of knowledge that has been hidden from all of mankind for centuries. Sir Francis Bacon once said that knowledge is power, and in this case that is certainly the truth. For instance, imagine what would happen once we find and neutralize this organization? The reason for assassinations? Gone! The reason for world war? Gone! The murderous calamities that have caused the growth and prosperity of mankind to repeatedly stall?"

Then using his index finger to hammer itself into the armrest of his chair to enunciate each word, "ALL ... GONE!"

After letting that soak in for a few seconds, a smile found its way to his face when he then continued and said, "Now imagine what the world would be *then* like?"

Needless to say, all those in the room, two of which could be the architect of such national change, had a lot to think about. Minute by minute the issues became clearer and clearer. The balance of billions of lives could not only be saved, but the health, prosperity and cultural prosperity of all humankind could attain a level that none had ever even thought possible.

Jason could see that his point had been made. All in the room were looking back and forth between each other with wide eyes. Just when he was about to say something more, Jason's phone rang.

"Hello, this is Jason."

"What?"

"WHEN!" shouted Jason. The look of horror on his face was unmistakable.

"Is she still breathing?!"

This of course REALLY got everybody's attention.

"Good."

All in the room breathed a tacit sigh of relief.

"Walter Reed?"

"OK. I'll meet you there! Bye."

Jason looked to the president.

"Mr. President, I need to go. Coral Tellindor, Terri and Khreelon's daughter has been hit by a car while crossing the street. She is apparently in a coma and is currently being transported to Walter Reed Medical Center."

"Coral?" asked Brynn.

"I'll fill you in on Coral in just a minute" said the president to his vice president. Then looking back to Jason, he said "Jason, if there is anything that you need for her care, just call my cell phone. Day or night."

"Thank you, Mr. President," replied Jason as he rose from his seated position. "I'll pass that along to Terri and Khreelon. I'll also check with the medical doctors on New Galimar for their input."

Then turning back to Brynn, he added "Madame Vice President, unless you want a very long walk, I suggest you allow us to return you to the oval office."

And with that, and little commotion, the underground facility was once again completely quiet. After watching the others disappear through the portal window, President Kirken looked around and considered the main room of this underground bunker and conversations that had just taken place. He thought how the very idea that war would possibly be completely eradicated … all during his presidency …

He shook his head back and forth, and with a smile on his face, he returned back to his escape chute transport back to Camp David.

CHAPTER 32

It's often been said that Miami Florida is somewhat of a melting pot of society. As with a lot of expensive real estate, it is common to have thirty-two million dollar mansions located on the water with their own dock, and yet only ten minutes away you have people living two and sometimes three families to a single home just trying to survive. Some would say that the rich must coexist with the poor, because who else would clean the pools or change the bedding. Others would point to the remarkable gulf between the rich and the poor and talk about how that gulf widens more and more each decade.

These ones who honestly care about that gulf, and more specifically the poor living conditions that some have to live with around the world are usually the same ones that set up foundations that try to effectively distribute food and clean drinking water to third world countries. Many times, these are the same ones who philanthropically donate millions or even billions of their own money to get things done. They are true hearts in a seeming world of darkness.

Bart and Rennie, however, are not among them.

Both Bart and Rennie are somewhat of an enigma to any that try to figure them out. They have both reputedly been around for decades even though neither of them appear more than 30 years of age. Bart could easily be on the cover of Abercrombie & Fitch, and in fact he once was, and Rennie could equally be on the cover of Sports Illustrated or Victoria's Secret catalogs although she wasn't as keen to be in the spotlight.

Bart and Rennie have done well for themselves. Living in a Miami mansion that according to public records cost one hundred two million, they live the privileged lives of the super-rich in Miami. Their home is right on the water, yet even so, the pool that can be seen from the water is massive. The living structure itself is more cubic in its design, and yet there seems to be hundreds of windows all around. Some of the walls are nothing BUT glass, and so the home lends itself to an open and airy feel. Their favorite spot is next to the pool and they can be found there much of the time.

The enigma exists because of a few different things. First, it appears that they never need to work. Some think this is because of good investing, some think this might be because of some illegal activities, but most just don't really care. Those that find themselves in their presence quickly figure out that it is much healthier to not ask questions. If you are lucky enough to enjoy their epicurean parties, it is much better to just enjoy the hedonism of the moment and don't speculate.

The second part of the enigma stems from the fact that even though they are certainly a couple, they seem to be very free with their affections to the opposite sex. As a case in point, on this particular day they are both relaxing next to their infinity pool, but Bart has two bikini clad beauties lounging right next to him in his covered cabana, while Rennie has basically the same thing lounging next to her, with the genders reversed.

The final dimension to the mystery of Bart and Rennie is that they both appear to be from Ireland, although there is never any discussion about that particular heritage. The people that all appear to work for them all have a similar accent to them, and in fact there is one particular individual that has come calling on Bart for some business that seems to be cut from the same Irish cloth. As Bart reclined on a large cushion in the cabana soaking in the attention of the beautiful brunette and red-head next to him, a very muscular man wearing, black pants, black t-shirt, black sunglasses, and a black disposition approached.

"Sir, your two-o'clock appointment has arrived" said the body-guard in a voice that seemed to be two octaves lower than every other human male alive.

Bart glanced over to his mate Rennie and saw that she had heard the announcement as well. Somewhat under his breath, yet loud enough for Rennie to hear, Bart replied "It figures. Just when things are getting interesting with me lasses."

"G-wan with ya" replied Rennie with an equally thick Irish brogue. "You'll be done with it in a few shakes. Sure, an I'll see to it your entertainment won't run off, now will you ladies?"

Seeing that Bart was standing up and leaving them for the moment, Bart's lady friends each made their own whimpering sounds while sticking out their bottom lips. "Sorry ladies, but business calls. I'll be back in two shakes of a lamb's tail."

As he walked back into the house, he was joined by another equally muscle-bound body guard and with his guards flanking him on each side, he emerged from the front door and entered the garage.

The garage was large enough to hold seven cars, and the doors to each bay was a single pane of tempered glass. Each of the parking bays held an impressive specimen of mechanical might. There was a McLaren 600LT, Bugatti Veyron, Ferrari F60, Lamborghini Veneno, Koenigsegg Agera RS1, Aston Martin One, and finally a

Porsche Panamera. Each of the cars had their use, in Bart's opinion. For instance, if he just needed to take a short ride into town, he might take the Porsche, but a more interesting night on the town would require a more interesting ride such as the Koenigsegg.

Be that as it may, though, he wasn't here to drive. No, but it seemed like someone had taken him for a ride and needed to be attended to. Standing with yet another imposing black suited guard, was an older and somewhat disheveled man. Bart was the first to speak as he entered the garage with his own goon squad.

"Hello Aidan."

Hi ya, boss. How she cuttin?" The accent was obviously from the northern part of Dublin.

"Oh, I'm fine Aidan, but it seems to me you made a holy show of it at the bar last night."

With a slight jitter to his voice, Aidan knew exactly what Bart was referring to, although he was praying that he was wrong.

"I ... I don't know what you mean. Me and a few of my mates were tossing a few of the black, and we was just effin' and blindin' all night with a few of the slags, boss. I got a bit knackered so I kipped in me car. That's all."

For a few moments, Bart looked Aidan in the eyes while saying nothing. With each passing second, Aidan's blood pressure rose until finally Bart broke the stare-down. Taking a few steps toward Aidan but then passing him Bart walked over to a tool chest against the wall of the garage. Like everything else in the garage, everything was pristine and perfectly clean. Dirt and grime had no place in this garage, and as he opened one of the drawers to the toolbox, Bart saw that even the tools in the chest were all wiped clean.

With his back to Aidan, Bart spoke up and asked, "How long have we known each other, Aidan?"

"Jeeeze, it's been donkey's years, boss!"

“It has” agreed Bart while nodding his head. “And all during that time my friend, how long have you believed I’m so thick that I wouldn’t know exactly what you were doing last night?”

Aidan took in a silent but very labored breath as he was quickly coming to the conclusion that his activities the previous night were exactly why he was here now. Hoping beyond hope that he was reading Bart wrong, he tried one last attempt to feign ignorance.

“I … I don’t know what you’re talkin about boss.”

Still without turning toward Aidan, Bart raised his voice “OI! Bring in the whelp!”

Just then Aidan heard a sound to his left and slightly behind him. Turning that direction, a door opened and two of the guards carried in a very battered and bruised man by the shoulders and essentially dropped him to the ground in a heap next to Aidan. Instantly recognizing his drinking buddy from the night before, Aidan realized there was no getting by the fact that, as usual, Bart knew exactly what was happening last night, and that there was going to be no escaping his wrath.

“Jonsey here had a very interesting tale of the events last night, and it sounded a little different from your story, Aidan.”

“Sorry boss” came the foreshortened reply from Aidan. “I was a bit fluthered and I … I don’t really remember …”

Cutting Aidan off in mid-sentence and suddenly spinning around from his position in front of the tool chest, Bart came face to face with Aidan while holding a Heckler & Koch USP Match 9mm handgun about one inch from Aidan’s forehead. Though completely at odds with his maneuver though, Bart’s voice was characteristically calm and even as he spoke again.

“Are there any changes to your story you’d like to make, Aidan?”

Feeling every nerve ending in his body suddenly fire while simultaneously feeling the blood draining from his face, Aidan instantly started to sweat while his eyes flitted back and forth between Bart, the gun pointed between his eyes, and Jonesy who had just partially thrown up from the beating he had obviously just suffered.

"I ... uh ..." stuttered Aidan, "... I may-y-y-y ... have told a few of the guys at the table about what you and I did in the keys last week ..."

Aidan looks again at the crumpled mess next to him, and only now does he see the blood mixed in with whatever else was just vomited onto the perfectly painted concrete floor.

An emotionless "Uh huh" came from Bart. Contrary to what Aidan was expecting though, the gun pointed at his head slowly lowered until Bart's arm rested at his side. Bart then turned back to the tool chest behind him.

"And what part of 'secret' didn't you understand about that secret trip, Aidan?"

Bart continued to turn away from Aidan, and in doing so placed the gun on the chest ... much to the relief of Aidan.

"Boss, I didn't mean anything by it. I swear I just was blowing off a little steam with the boys!"

Nodding his head, Bart appears to be thinking for a moment, but then says "See I have a problem now Aidan. Your makin' a moran of yourself last night and telling those boys about our shipment made Jonesy here get a little greedy. Now that he knew where it was hidden, he was in the middle of skimming a bit off the top of that shipment last night when we found him."

Now that his eminent demise seemed to be averted, Aidan looked down again at Jonesy with disgust.

"You thick chiseler!"

"Aye, he's thick, but I'm afraid he wasn't the only one actin the maggot last night Aidan" agreed Bart.

"Boss. I'm sorry. It'll never happen again. I promise!"

"Aye. It won't"

Just then, two shots from a silenced gun rang out in the garage. The already quivering lump of humanity on the ground descended into a final slump, only to serve as a landing pad for the equally lifeless body of Aidan. As he turned to see a pool of blood form underneath the body of his one-time friend, Bart looked over to the white McLaren and glided his finger underneath a drop of blood that had splattered.

Turning to one of the guards he spoke in disgust as he walked out and said, "Clean up this mess before it messes up the paint." His two bodyguards followed him and upon returning to the pool he was once again a charming host to his guests. Now standing at a distance, the guards blended into the architecture and once again were barely noticeable.

Bart decided to grab a pint from the fridge since these activities always seem to make him thirsty, and as he did so he looked over to Rennie who was already looking at him. With a quick nod of his head, he wordlessly asked her to meet him in the private den. Perfectly understanding his request, Rennie turned to her boy-toys and excused herself.

The den was decorated more like an office than a place of comfort and relaxing. On the wall there were what appeared to be star charts, and on another wall, there were several tables that had blueprints sprawled out. Bart had his back to Rennie as she entered the room, and with a pint of Guinness in his hand he was leaning over those blueprints of what appeared to be a ship of some kind. The ship wasn't one designed for the sea, but rather it was something quite aerodynamic. It appeared like something that NASA was more apt to develop.

As Rennie entered the den and closed the door behind her, she began speaking to her husband. The Irish accent had now completely vanished.

"Is it what you thought?"

Bart finishes taking a long pull from his Guinness and with a hissing swallow answers his wife.

"Yep."

Rennie slowly shakes her head and looks to the floor. "Stupid imbecile. People of this world aren't even worth a lead bullet."

With a breathy chortle, Bart nods and says, "Well said."

"But, my love, I have just learned something that I'm sure will brighten your day."

"Oh?"

(Later that week, in a secret location deep underground in the middle of the inner city)

"...and will serve as a brave and obedient soldier and risk my life for this oath at any time. I give my will, my heart, and my soul to the enlightened ones. They are my guide for all that I do. If the enlightened say I live, then I live. If the enlightened say I die, then I die. We are the enlightened ones. We are the illuminated."

Having just led the invocations which were always recited at the beginning of each meeting of the Circle of Seven, BarDringol looked out and surveyed those in attendance. The nine attendees made up the most influential men and women of the world. It occurred to him that even U.S. Presidents would feel privileged if they gained an audience with this group.

"Welcome, my brothers and sisters, to this emergency meeting of this most sacred bastion of civilization" continued BarDringol. "May we all guide the world around us for the betterment of mankind, and may we all have the bravery to make hard choices for the good of our organization."

All spoke up and replied in unison, "Amen."

"As you all know, my mate has called a rare emergency meeting of the circle, and so I call upon her to speak to us."

“Good!” spoke one of the others out of turn. “I hope Rennie can give us a good reason why I had to cancel my trip to the Balkans.”

With an icy stare, she turned to that one and said “I realize Mr. Smith that you are new to our fold and so I will grant you a one-time exception, but when we are in this meeting we do not go by our manufactured monikers, but we are called by our real names. I am not Rennie, but rather I am MenGala RenIval, and my mate is MenGala BarDringol. You may address us as BarDringol and RenIval. Do you understand?”

The powerful yet recalcitrant member of the circle responded and said “A thousand apologies. I mean no disrespect RenIval. I am simply pointing out that we all have billion-dollar companies that need our attention.”

“Oh, I am well aware of how busy we all are, however as I said we have a level one emergency that needs our attention.”

Hearing that this was a level one emergency situation got everybody’s attention now. A level one situation hadn’t happened for about eighty years, and so this must be something that is of extreme importance.

“All right, you have our attention” said Mr. Armand.

“Thank you” answered RenIval. “As you all know, BarDringol and I are the only remaining members of the original seven that formed the Circle some two thousand five hundred years ago.”

“Yes, we are aware of this, and we are also aware of how you continue to refuse to share how you have enjoyed such long life” responded another member of the group who himself was head of a several major pharmaceutical companies.

Feigning a small smile, RenIval responded “Well perhaps once this news is dealt with, we will finally share that information with you Mr. VanRaton.”

“I would hope so.”

"Nevertheless, as you all know the primary purpose of this group has always been to seek out and destroy 'Coral of Eden'. Everything else we have done must remain secondary no matter how profitable it might be."

"Of course, RenIval" responded Mr. Armand, "however up to this point Coral of Eden has remained little more than a riddle, the answer to which has remained as elusive as the tooth fairy or the location of Atlantis."

That particular response garnered a short reaction of laughter from both BarDringol and RenIval.

"Nevertheless" continued RenIval, "it appears that Coral of Eden has now appeared, and if we strike now, the primary mission of this group will finally have been fulfilled. There is even a minor detail that may work to our advantage."

"Oh? And what detail is that?" asked another of the group. BarDringol was the one to answer.

"Apparently the demon child has been injured and is currently in a coma. She is being held at the Walter Reed Medical Center in Bethesda Maryland."

"How do you know this is the very one we have been looking for all this time?" asked Mr. Armand.

"Because" responded BarDringol, "the collateral evidence that came with the primary information removes all doubt."

"Exactly" added RenIval. "Along with the information about Coral came information about her parents. Her mother is a human, but her father is a different story."

"Her mother is a human, but her father is a different story?" asked Mr. Armand in an even and emotionless tone. "RenIval ... I am a busy man and I do not respond well to jokes."

"Oh, this is no Joke Mr. Armand" answered BarDringol. "Mr. VanRaton?"

"Yes."

"You wanted to know why RenIval and I are so long lived? Well now you have your answer."

The group remained silent and considered what had just been said. While all who sat at the table were brilliant, truth be said … it actually took a while for it to completely dawn on each and every one of them exactly what was being revealed. Long held assumptions sometimes die a slow and painful death, and this was no exception. The realization that the human race is not as unique as they had once thought was not only hard to accept for these masters of their own universe, it had an uncomfortable and unfamiliar effect.

It was humbling.

For them though, being humbled didn't spawn further modesty and unpretentiousness like it would on the part of most. To these sociopathic megalomaniacs it caused nothing less than anger. To think that they may not be the most powerful was unacceptable, and one by one, each of them came to the conclusion that whatever existed in their way had to be eliminated. The one question that remained was exactly where these two that were standing before them … actually stood.

"So, you're not from earth" said Mr. Smith flatly.

"No" answered BarDringol and RenIval simultaneously.

A few more seconds passed. Then Mr. Armand asked, "What are your intentions?" He was just as emotionless as Mr. Smith.

Seeing that their associates needed to be assuaged, RenIval decided to soften her response and said, "Our intentions, my friend, haven't changed one iota. The primary mission is to eliminate Coral of Eden. The only other mission on our agenda is to continue guiding humanity in the way we always have. No change. You will always be the beneficiaries of our efforts."

Which of course was a lie, but she wasn't going to share all of her and her mate's long-range plans.

"How exactly did you come by this information?" asked Mr. Snow.

"As you know, we have several benign viruses that look for a specific combination of phrases and words in the target computers" answered RenIval. "If they sense what we are looking for, then they report back to us. One of the infected computers at the pentagon pinged us, and after validating the info, we have now brought it to you."

"What other information came with this?" Asked Mr. Corcus.

Continuing her pretense of softness and comradery, RenIval answered "It also included a rather tantalizing mention of a certain island where the original transportation portal has been removed to. It also included information that representatives from that island are being sent to the medical center with a pod that has suspended animation abilities. It is their intention to use this pod to prolong the life of Coral of Eden until they can systematically arrive at a treatment plan. It is this treatment that must be stopped."

"What island?" asked Mr. Snow.

"That's the problem" responded BarDringol. "It didn't reveal where the island is. We need to find a way of locating it."

A few seconds elapsed, but then Mr. Armand responded with a rather chilling idea.

"I would assume the President of the United States knows."

The rest in the room turned to look at Mr. Armand, but then they all had looks of quiet contemplation. Several stroked their respective beards and Mr. Snow reached up to caress his prematurely balding head. The ambient temperature in the room seemed to drop a few degrees at the mention of the president. Invitation of the president hadn't happened since the early 1960's, and that hadn't ended successfully. In the past two-hundred plus years, it only ended successfully once.

"I'm not so sure that is an option, Mr. Armand. Doing that in the past has rarely ever resulted in a successful adoption into this organization" said Mr. Corcus.

"Perhaps" acquiesced Mr. Armand, "However we could use our powers of persuasion to get the information we need, and then deal with his possible resistance later."

A few more seconds strolled by, but then there was an almost imperceptible consensus on the part of all. Minor head-nods seemed to make their way around the table.

Renlval decided to push the idea. "All in favor of recruiting the President of the United States in the typical manner, say aye."

All did.

"Any opposed?"

None were.

"The motion to recruit the current President has passed. Mr. Armand, I assume you will head the recruitment effort as usual?"

He nodded.

"Then the only remaining question is how we are to eliminate Coral of Eden."

Mr. Corcus leaned forward in his seat and asked, "What is the current status of our portal?"

Mrs. Edgemont, who had been silent up to this point spoke up and replied "As you all know, the primary scientist we had working on the portal has disappeared. We believe he and his wife were retrieved by the designers and operators of the original portal, although we have no idea how they were able to discover our secret location. Due to this, we have relocated our lab and our portal to a different location, and it is now operational in that new location."

"Then in that case" answered Mr. Corcus, "I propose we send an explosive to the room where the child is located using the portal."

"I have anticipated such a need" replied Mrs. Edgemont, "and so all I need is the go-ahead from the group and the operation can be completed as we wait."

RenIval then said, "All in favor of sending an explosive device to dispose of Coral of Eden once and for all, say aye."

Once again, all did.

"Any opposed?"

As before, none were.

"The motion is carried. Mrs. Edgemont, please proceed" commanded RenIval.

Taking out her cell phone, she dialed the necessary number. All in the room heard her side of the call, telling them to proceed with sending a device and where to send it.

As she waited, the technicians dialed the coordinates into the portal where the explosive device would be delivered ... the same portal that Socrates had hacked. They brought in the explosive device, set it in front of the portal window that had been dialed to the room where Coral lay in a coma, and set the timer on the device to five seconds. Pressing the green button on the device, they pushed it through the portal to the other side ...

Only ... because of the hack that Socrates, had placed deep in the circuitry, the explosive device disappeared, but then reappeared right back in the lab from where it had been sent. Socrates had changed the navigational system on this portal such that anything that was sent through it would wind up right back at its starting point.

Four seconds later, the lab and the apocryphal portal ceased to exist.

CHAPTER 33

Casey Emerson was a new graduate from California Polytechnic College, San Luis Obispo. While his counselors at the college all felt that Casey would go a long way in life based on his grades and aptitude with all things electronic, even they would probably raise an eyebrow at what he was doing right at this moment.

About three months ago, Casey knew he was about to graduate from college and so he naturally knew he needed to start getting applications out there. In this regard he was somewhat of a late bloomer as most of his classmates had already been sending out employment applications by the handful for a few months already. Casey, on the other hand, was so focused on this thesis project though, it actually slipped his mind. His thesis project was a device that he hoped would better detect gravity waves. It was based on some existing technology at the Laser Interferometer Gravitational-Wave Observatory, also known as LIGO located in both Livingston, Louisiana and Hanford, Washington. Back in 2016, the first of several gravitational waves were detected, and those were mostly the result of binary black hole mergers or the collision of two neutron stars.

Casey felt that there must be many more cases of gravitational waves being generated than what had been detected, and so he set out to create a detector that could detect waves that were fainter than the ones already detected. This was a herculean task since the current detectors were so sensitive, they could detect wave spacing of less than a ten-thousandth of the charge diameter of a single proton. According to Wikipedia, that would be the equivalent to measuring the distance from Earth to the Proxima Centauri sun which is 4.2 light years away with an accuracy smaller than the width of a human hair. An ambitious goal indeed, one that many of his professors tried to dissuade him from even trying to pursue.

That is ... until he actually did it.

Being a new graduate with a published paper outlining this new technology for detecting such gravity waves was something that got the attention of the company whose reception area was where Casey found himself. Being here meant that he had to fly from his home town in California to the main headquarters of Gravionics, Incorporated in Miami, but that was certainly something that he was willing to do if he had even a remote chance to work with this company.

According to what he had looked up about Gravionics, the company was a combination think-tank and scientific research and development lab working on a few different projects for DARPA, or the Defense Advanced Research Projects Agency. It sounded like just the kind of job he was hoping he would find, but to get a pure research position so fresh out of college was probably a pipe dream. Nevertheless, he was contacted by the hiring manager at Gravionics last week in response to the application he had originally sent in. The manager said they would like to speak with him, and they even ponied up for the roundtrip airfare for Casey to come out and talk. That must mean something. Right?

As he sat in the plush chair there in the reception area, he looked out the glass windows. Even though he couldn't see any rain hitting the ground from this high up in the skyscraper, he could certainly see the angry clouds as well as the rain that was pelting the window. Glancing over to the reception desk and the wall behind it, he thought about how he was supposed to be here at 1 PM, and it was now 1:05. More from being nervous than from anything else, he checked his watch and saw that it told the same time as the clock on the wall. Just to make sure, he unzipped his case with the intention to compare his iPad to his watch, but right about then he realized he was just being ridiculous. With his leg vibrating up and down, something he always did when he was tense, he was the picture of nervousness. Willing himself to calm down, he stopped the leg movement and tried to breathe deeply.

Meanwhile the receptionist who had been watching him from a distance could easily see that this guy was really keyed up. She took pity on him since she knew that he was the fifteenth one to come in for an interview. He probably wasn't going to be the last one.

About that time her phone rang, and she reached over to answer it.

"Reception. This is Katrina."

"Yes Sir. Right Away."

Looking up she addressed the nervous kid in the reception chair.

"Mr. Emerson?"

Casey looked up almost as if he was startled and said "Yes?". He silently thanked God his voice didn't crack.

"Ms. White will see you now."

Casey stood and gathered his satchel, only to realize too late that he hadn't re-zipped it. About two dozen papers spilled out from the satchel where the cover had flung open, and they proceeded to individually take wings ... at least it seemed like that to the now blushing cadet.

Taking pity on the kid, Katrina came out from behind her desk and helped Casey gather his things together in one place again.

"Thank you, Miss. I really appreciate that!" As he stood and regarded the older but still very beautiful receptionist, his toothy grin belied the fact that he was still monumentally embarrassed by the accident.

"Don't worry about it, Mr. Emerson. It could happen to anyone."

"Oh, you don't have to call me Mr. Emerson. My name is Casey."

"It's very nice to meet you Casey. My named is Katrina, but if you don't walk through that door to meet Ms. White, then my new name will be mud." Her smile seemed to light up the room.

"Ah. Gotcha. Wouldn't want that to happen" said the new recruit as he moved toward the door. "Thanks again!"

The receptionist waved to the kid as he stepped through the door. She thought to herself that someone really needed to take him to the store and buy him a healthy dose of confidence. Oh well. Things come with time.

Not far after the door, a woman stood in the hallway looking his way.

"Ms. Emerson, I presume?"

"Yes sir. Ms. White?"

"The one and only. Come on in" said Ms. White as she motioned toward his office. She had a manner about her that was quite casual which immediately put Casey at ease.

"Thank you, Ma'am."

Casey entered the room and immediately was struck at how large and opulent the office was. The carpet was a plush grey carpet, and it had a large window. The company offices were located on the 18th floor of a high rise building and so this office had a really good view. There in front of him was a nice park eighteen stories below, but not far beyond that, was the ocean. Not only was there a desk in this office, there were several bookshelves, and there was a separate conversation area complete with couch, love seat coffee table and chairs. Casey took a seat in front of the desk and set his case down to his side on the floor.

"Can I interest you in anything to drink? Coke? Water?" said Ms. White

"Some water would be nice. Thank you!"

Ms. White took her place behind the desk and punched a button on the phone.

"Yes ma'am?" Came the cheery voice on the phone.

"Erica, would you please bring in some cold water for Mr. Emerson and bring my usual as well, please."

"Right away ma'am."

"So ... Casey, is it?"

"Yes ma'am. Casey is my first name."

"Good. I like to be on a first name basis as much as possible. My name is Brooke."

"It's nice to meet you Brooke."

"The pleasure is all mine, Casey.

Just then Erica entered carrying the drinks and glasses with ice on a platter. She laid the platter on the edge of the desk, which Casey was only now noticing had hardly anything on it. She handed a glass and the bottled water to Casey with a very pleasant smile and eyes that seemed to sparkle as she looked Casey directly in the eyes. He had to fight against the urge to inspect the rest of this beautiful and very curvaceous secretary, and thankfully he was successful. He secretly hoped that he wouldn't have to fight that particular battle too much more since she was very attractive.

Erica handed Brooke her drink, and after she thanked her for it, she excused herself and closed the door behind her.

Noticing the battle Casey had with keeping his eyes trained in the right place, Brooke smiled and made a slight shake of her head. "You know, we recently had a companywide meeting where we discussed exactly what 'sexual harassment' was" said Brooke with a slight chuckle in her voice. She then added "I know it isn't easy sometimes."

Knowing he had been caught, Casey blushed several shades of red, though he could see that Ms. White was smiling herself. He hadn't blown the interview already.

"Yes ma'am. She is very attractive" agreed Casey. Then perhaps deflecting the subject, he said "Thank you very much for the water."

"Eh, don't worry about it. The least I could do."

After taking another drink from her glass, she reached over to a folder and said, "So Casey, it looks like you just graduated from Cal Poly San Luis?"

"Yes ma'am."

"Tell me a little about your field of study."

"Well ..."

And with that Casey spent the next several minutes going over the subject of his thesis project, and what advances he had made with it. It was actually a well-traveled mental road for Casey and so answering questions about the project as well as what had led him to his discoveries came very easy. The conversation between the two of them ebbed and flowed easily, and while Casey had no idea about Brooke's training and qualifications, it was apparent that she had more than a working knowledge of physics and electrical engineering.

"Very interesting project you have there, Casey."

"Thank you, ma'am."

"Tell me something, how much do you know about what we do here?"

"I have to admit I don't know too much. I know that you run some projects for DARPA, but beyond that there aren't many details."

"Yep, I suppose that would be true since many of those projects are for the department of defense, and so security has to be pretty tight. On that note, do you have any sort of government security clearance?"

"No ma'am."

"OK. There isn't any kind of criminal history with you, is there?"

"No ma'am! Not at all!"

"OK. Good. That will make getting a security clearance easier."

That comment was a little perplexing to Casey. It almost sounded like he was already going to be working here. But … how could that be? He hadn't been offered anything yet …

"I like you Casey" said Brooke interrupting Casey's thoughts. "You have the kind of stuff we need around here. Knowing what you know about Gravionics, do you think this is the kind of place you'd like to work?"

"Definitely, ma'am. I've always wanted to work as much as possible in research and development."

"Well, if you're going to work here, you're going to have to drop that whole 'ma'am' thing. Can you do that?"

"Oh. Um, sure, B – Brooke."

"Good. Good. Well, I have to admit something to you Casey. I've already been doing some checking up on you and based on what I have found, I've been able to get a security variance for you in anticipation of you passing the full background check." Then reaching over to a drawer, Brooke pulled out a stack of pages and pushed them across to Casey. "This is a pretty standard non-disclosure agreement that I'd like you to sign. Once it's signed, I'd like to give you a little tour around our facility."

"Ok" said Casey as he took the pages from Ms. White and started to read them.

"Take your time reading the agreement. I'll be right back." And with that, Brooke rose and exited the room for a few minutes.

Casey was thinking that this interview was going much better than he expected. Getting a tour of the research facility? Are you kidding!? This felt like he was a kid getting a tour through a candy factory!

It only took about five minutes to read through the document, and not long after Casey had signed it Brooke returned with a visitor security badge, and she exchanged the badge for the NDA that Casey had just signed.

"Let's take a tour!" said Brooke with a smile on her face. "You're welcome to leave your case here since we'll be returning here when we're done."

The two of them emerged from the office and made their way to the elevator. Swiping her own security card and punching in a security code on the panel inside the elevator, the car descended from the eighteenth floor above ground, to a facility that was located on the fifth floor below ground. When the doors opened, the two were met by a security guard that closely inspected the cards and then checked them against information in his computer. After clearing them to enter, Brooke pushed open the set of doors next to the guard and was immediately greeted by a laboratory that was no less than a complete dream for a guy like Casey.

“Wow” was the unfiltered reaction from Casey which caused Brooke to smile.

“Yeah, I’ll bet something like this makes your mouth water doesn’t it?”

“Oh yeah” was all Casey could think of saying. Truth be said, he was in complete awe over the technology he was seeing in this laboratory. Millions of dollars’ worth of detection equipment was in this room alone, and it looked like this room was just the beginning!

“Yeah. The owners of this company are a husband and wife living here in Miami. When they see something they want, they aren’t afraid to spend the money to get it. But, if you think this is something special, then you better hold on to your seat cause what I’m about to show you will really knock your socks off.”

Casey couldn’t think of anything that would be more amazing than what he was now witnessing, but as he was soaking in the sights before him, he suddenly realized that Brooke had already moved off in search of more. Casey leapfrogged toward his tour guide and immediately caught up with her.

“This next thing is something that the world doesn’t know about yet, but it is some technology that we are perfecting for release to the public sometime later this year.”

Just then, Brooke pushed through a set of doors that had two large “No Admittance” signs on them and entered a room that seemed straight out of a science fiction movie.

“Take a look at this here Casey”

Brooke motioned Casey to come closer to a black colored laboratory bench that had had a device laying on it. The device was roughly rectangular in shape and measured roughly twelve inches long by five inches wide by about four inches high. It had various LED displays on it, not to mention several switches. Reaching over to the device, Brooke flipped a switch and it started making a noise. It took about five to ten seconds for anything to happen, but then something amazing took place.

With no tethers, and no support structure, the device spontaneously raised up and floated about four inches above the bench.

Initially Casey was intrigued, but not necessarily surprised. There had been a lot of research and development recently on superconducting materials and their effect on magnetics. Part of the effects that had been achieved by many other scientists was a sort of levitation effect, but only while the superconducting material was kept at a super-cold temperature, and only while the material was in the proximity of a magnetic field.

"Did you guys come up with a superconducting material that maintains its conductivity at room temperature?" asked Casey who by now had lost all traces of his previous nervousness.

"MMMM ... not exactly" said Brooke with a smile. "We have something here that is much more interesting than that."

"Oh? What would that be?"

"What you are looking at here, my boy, is the world's first anti-gravity device" said a rather proud Brooke.

Casey looked from Brooke, back at the floating device, and back to Brooke.

"Anti-gravity" said Casey. It wasn't a question. Just a statement that belied an undercurrent of disbelief.

"Yep" replied Brooke. "Here ... see that dial right there on top?"

"Yeah"

"Go ahead and dial it up, but only just a little bit."

Casey reached over to the floating device and turned the dial just one click to the right. As soon as he did that, the device raised up to floating about six inches above the table.

A few seconds passed, then Casey looked back at Brooke and said, "You're telling me that this has nothing to do with magnetic repulsion against the metal in this table?"

"That is exactly what I'm telling you. In fact, this table is purposely not metal. It's made of a non-ferrous carbon fiber material" replied Brooke.

Seeing that Casey might need a little more convincing, Brooke then said, "Try pushing down on the top of it to see if you can make it go down."

Tentatively, Casey reached over to the device and with his open palm pushed down on the top of it to try and make it dip back down to the table. Not only did the device resist his pressure, but to Casey it felt like it was itself sitting on a solid table.

A table that just wasn't there.

"Oh my god" came the once-again-unfiltered response from Casey.

"Yeah, that's pretty much the response we get from anybody who has the privilege of coming down here" said Brooke.

Casey looked back to Brooke at this point, and asked "Then … I have to ask. Why am I here?"

Brooke smiled to Casey and said, "For that, let's go back upstairs so we can talk."

With that, the two of them switched off the device. Gradually the black box floated back down to the bench, and only now did Casey see that one of the digital read-outs had stopped counting up, but not before showing that it had been operating for fifty-seven seconds. Eventually they re-boarded the elevator back up the eighteenth floor. As they were walking back into the office where they had started their meeting, Casey didn't even begin to notice the secretary that had earlier brought the water. He was far too blown away by what he had just seen.

Resuming their respective seats, Brooke was the first to speak.

"I can see Casey that you are pretty surprised at what you just saw."

"Surprised isn't quite the word I would use, Brooke. That device is no less than revolutionary! Do you realize what that technology would mean?"

"I'm sure YOU realize it. Don't you?" said Brooke enigmatically.

"I certainly do! If you can make an antigravity device like that, then you can make ... Oh my god ... So many things! How about creating a vehicle that doesn't use tires! Or how about a different vehicle that just floats up and up until it gets to the space station! With this technology, combustion-based rocketry and space travel will be a complete thing of the past!"

"Exactly" was the simple yet mysterious response from Brooke.

Then something occurred to Casey that he had to ask. "How is that technology possible? How have you been able to achieve anti-gravity?"

"Good question" replied Brooke. "For now, let's just say that a material was discovered on a south pacific island that makes this technology possible. Unfortunately, the doctor that discovered this material came to an untimely death recently, but that wasn't before he allowed us to take over all research and development of that particular material."

"The stuff was just floating around on this island?"

Letting out a small chuckle, Brooke responded "Not exactly. In its raw form, it actually glows with a very pleasant pale blue glow, but it doesn't float until you process and treat it with different processes."

"I see" answered Casey. "But ... I have to ask again ... why are you showing ME all this?" asked Casey.

"I'm showing you all this, Casey, because we were very impressed with your breakthroughs with gravity wave detection, and your understanding of the field. That, coupled with your understanding of electronic engineering, means that we want to offer you a job here at Gravionics. We want you to not only work with the technology you just saw, but to enhance it and develop it into the very types of devices you just mentioned."

"Wait" said Casey, "You're offering me a job here to work in the lab that we were just in?"

"Mostly, although you'll have a more conventional office as well."

"An office too? Have I seen it?"

Brooke smiled. "You're sitting in it."

Casey immediately scanned around the room he was seated in. Coming close to losing consciousness, he got a grip on himself, and all he could come up with was a simple "Oh my god!"

Meanwhile, at the Johns Hopkins University Applied Physics Laboratory, the Project Manager of the Parker Solar Probe satellite was hunched over a monitor analyzing data coming in from the probe along with one of the senior physicists on the project. Apparently, there was something that one of their analysts referred to as a "burp" in the Sun's corona, and he wanted the Project Manager to see it.

"There! See that? Starting right then the corona started destabilizing" said the physicist while pointing at the screen.

"When did that happen?" asked the project manager.

Checking the readout again, the technician replied, "It started at 13:32:34 Eastern Time."

The project manager straightened his back and stroked his beard while he was thinking.

"Any ideas on what happened?"

"No sir. All I know is that everything was happening along a predictable pattern, but then for exactly fifty-seven seconds the corona started destabilizing. Then, as quick as it started, it suddenly stopped."

"So according to the data you have so far, are there any long-term effects that we need to be concerned about?"

"Not right now sir, but I can tell you that had it not stopped, then there would have been hell to pay with communications satellites. As it is, it's lucky the probe was currently so far away from the sun."

"So, all we're talking about is knocking out some satellites?"

"For now, yeah. But if this happens again, and if it happens for a sustained period of time, then who knows what long-term effect it will have on the stability of the sun itself."

"You're telling me that the Sun is at risk?!"

"For now, ... no. But like I said ... if it happens again ..."

CHAPTER 34

"ARE YOU GOING TO TALK to him?" asked Kriss.

"No!" Said Jillintor with wide eyes, as if even asking the question was extremely embarrassing.

"Why not?" said another in the small group of girls quietly sitting in the library named Lissa.

"I don't know! Just ... because!"

"Just ... because ... isn't a reason. Don't you like him?" asked Kriss.

Jillintor knew, based on something her brother Nafan said, that Bristal liked her, but was it mutual? Did she think he was interesting? Maybe. He was studying medicine just like she and her brother were, and so they shared a lot of the same classes. Granted, most of those classes were executed through the online portal in the family home where she lived with her parents and brother, but ...

"Jill!" said Lissa a little too loud for the library. The administrator of the library looked up from her desk and glared across the room at the gaggle of girls that were all congregated in the corner. Jill had been lost in her own thoughts.

"What?!" replied Jill in a hushed voice.

"Well?! Don't you like him?" asked Kriss.

Looking over to the young man sitting two tables over, she spied his marvelous physique and manly good looks. If she had been honest with herself, she would admit that she was indeed interested, but isn't the girl supposed to be a little hard to get?

With a wistful look to her eyes and a breathy exhale, she finally replied "He *is* gorgeous."

The rest of the girls looked over and they all had to agree, although several of them weren't looking at him, but rather the guy sitting next to him.

Without thinking much about what she was saying or who she was saying it to, Brinna said "I think the guy next to him is pretty gorgeous too.

"Ugh … I could have gone all afternoon without hearing that!" said Jill with mock horror. The guy sitting next to Bristal was her brother Nafan and so, of course, she didn't look at him that way. Truth be said though, while she had no romantic feelings, she had to admit that her brother was a good-looking guy.

"Ohhhh … get over it. He's attractive, and so you're going to have to just weather through hearing about it!" said yet a different girl in the group, Jill's best friend named Lorah. She was quite a bit older than the rest of the girls, and so she seemed to have a more seasoned view of things.

While they were talking though, Nafan stood and started walking toward the group, which of course caused several of the group to get slightly tongue tied. As he approached the group, he interpreted the sudden hush to mean that they didn't think he was anything to take seriously ... which of course was far from the truth.

"Hey Jill" said Nafan, "You ready to go?"

"Go?" asked Lorah with a pleading look, "But you just got here!"

"Sorry girl" replied Jill, "We have to leave to meet with Socrates and Brianna."

"Ohhh ... now?" said Lorah with a continued pleading tone to her voice.

"Yep. They're waiting for us."

"I think it is so cool you two get to hang out with them!" said Kriss. Like Jill and Nafan, Kriss was equally interested in the medical arts they were all learning, but she was also very curious about the experiences of the two newest arrivals from the outside world.

"It is" said Nafan, "but they are so far ahead of us. I'm usually completely lost when I'm listening to them."

"Aren't they accommodating?" asked Lorah.

"Very" said Jill as she was slinging her satchel of learning materials over her shoulder. "But that doesn't change the fact that we have a long way to go before we'll ever be as smart as they are."

"Intelligence isn't a measure of what you know my sister" said Nafan, "It's simply a measure of your ability to learn and remember. You'll get there soon enough, and we all know it."

The act of giving a reassuring compliment to his own sister in front of them sealed his measure in the eyes of the rest of the girls. Having lived with it for years though, Jill was quite used to it. Even though she was so much older than him, it always seemed to her that he was the wisest. She knew she wasn't a dummy, of course, but he always seemed to know the right thing to say to help her.

"Are you ready?" asked Nafan as he looked to Jill.

"Ready as I'll ever be" replied Jill with a smile. "Lead the way little brother."

Turning to the rest of the group, Jill waved as she walked away. The group was silent as they watched the two walk away and, of course, Jill and Nafan were the subject matter for the next ten minutes. All, unfortunately, to the suffering of their coursework.

The siblings stepped onto the lift and descended several dozen stories, until finally they arrived at street level. Emerging from the gleaming glass and polished metal building, they stepped toward the street where a transport vehicle was already waiting for them. While they were descending to the street, Nafan had already ordered a car to come for them using his personal communicator, whereas Jill's mind was still thinking about Nafan's friend in the library.

To look at Jillintor and Nafan, they basically appear like your typical late teen, early twenty something college student brother and sister. As such, they still live with their parents and are extremely dedicated to their studies.

Typical ... except for the fact that they aren't typical, nor are they in their early twenties.

Jillintor, or Jill as she likes to be called, as well as her brother Nafan live on the island of New Galimar. Being the only two children of Ehobak and Ruavu Aramine, they could have had an easy ride of course. Their father was not only the designer of the ship known as the Arageena that came to earth from Galimar, but Ehobak was also the captain of that same ship. He hadn't really had any official duties since he and the bridge crew had officially handed over administrative powers to the newly formed Grand Council of New Galimar many years ago, but still, Ehobak and his family were very well known.

Jill was still young though, young enough to get into trouble and old enough to know better. Nafan, on the other hand, was younger by two hundred years. To look at them, they looked roughly the same age and so most wouldn't have realized Nafan's youth since he carried himself so maturely. Indeed, Jill had always wondered why he always seemed to be the one who was older and wiser.

The car pulled up to another, yet equally impressive structure where Socrates and Brianna now worked. This structure was located on one of the "arms" of land that made up the snowflake shaped island of New Galimar. To call New Galimar an "island" is somewhat of a misnomer since New Galimar was actually the exposed top of a very large interstellar ship that was mostly submerged under the sea; the same ship named Arageena that brought the Galimarians to earth so many years ago. These same land arms are now covered with a great deal of vegetation and so even though the understructure of the island is nothing but technology, the visible portion of the island appears to be nothing but a lush forest of tropical vegetation, lightly peppered with tastefully built architecture such as the medical sciences building where Socrates and Brianna now work.

The car stopped and the door automatically opened allowing Nafan and Jill to emerge onto the walkway that led to the front of the building. The walkway meandered between various landscaped features such as ponds containing some of the aquatic life Galimarians had found in the local oceans, or small knolls with trees and flowering shrubs. Everything was perfectly groomed by the automatic caretaker robots that occasionally scurried around the pathway in front of the two walking siblings.

Upon approaching the building that seemed to have no door, a small portion of the glass on the side of the building seemed to melt away revealing a doorway to the inside. A short ride up to the thirty-fourth floor led them to the laboratory where Socrates and his wife Brianna not only worked but also lived ... albeit in an adjacent apartment.

"You made it!" said Brianna.

"Was there any doubt?" asked Nafan sincerely.

Jill turned to her brother and said with a smile "Oh stop being so ridiculous!" She then added "It's just an expression of greeting among humans silly!"

Nafan didn't say anything in response, but he appeared to be deep in thought. It was times like this when his youth and lack of experience showed through. He didn't like it though. He wanted to be more grown up like his sister. What's funny is that she sometimes wanted to be more like him.

Then turning back to Brianna, Jill said "But to answer your question, yes we did! As promised!"

"That's awesome" responded Brianna. "Come with me. Socrates and I have just finished replicating our experimental environments and so we can start moving forward again with our work."

"Being that this is a medical science building" replied Jill, "I realize that you must be doing something with medicine, but it wasn't really clear to me what exactly you are doing."

"That was on purpose" said Socrates as he entered the room where the other three were setting their things down and preparing to don their lab coats. "In the outside world, we always had to be secretive about our work for a lot of reasons. It's taking some time to get used to not having to do that here."

"Why would you have to be secretive out there?" asked Jill.

"A few reasons" answered Brianna. "First, there are some who have no morals and so if they can steal someone else's work and say it was theirs, they would then reap any monetary rewards from such work, and we would get nothing."

"Second" added Socrates, "there are others who are equally devoid of morals and who always seem to be looking for a way of taking peaceful technologies, such as what we are working on, and weaponizing it for use in warfare."

"That's sick!" responded Jill.

"Indeed" said Socrates.

"What exactly are you working on that could be made into a weapon?" asked Nafan.

"Brianna and I have been working on a device that can map the entire neural network of a brain" answered Socrates. "We are at the point now where we are ready to start testing."

"What would the scan reveal?" asked Jill who was now extremely interested.

"Well" answered Brianna, "according to our research and calculations, we should be able to replicate the memories, and thinking processes of whatever brain we choose to scan into a computerized neural network."

There was a few moments of silence on the part of the Jill and Nafan, but then Nafan said with a look of wonder in his eyes "That means that if you are successful, then it would be possible for you to create a synthesis of a person that is, in every way, sentient."

"Correct" answered Socrates.

Jill and Nafan looked at each other, and each noticed that the other's mouth was slightly agape.

Looking back at Socrates and Brianna, Nafan asked "Have you done it yet?"

"No" answered Brianna. "We had to replicate our working environment here in our new laboratory first. Fortunately, Jason and Dennis have allowed us to secretly use the portal to retrieve our materials from our old lab in Russia."

"Russia?" asked Nafan.

"It's the name of an organizational grouping of land and governmental structure where we lived. Russia is just one of many nations on earth" explained Socrates. "While I was living there, I hid the fact that I was Galimarian, and as such was much longer lived than the rest of earth's population."

The mention of how long-lived Socrates is, and how the rest of humans aren't as enduring touched a very secret, yet equally raw nerve deep down in Brianna. She didn't want to lose her love, or even for him to feel the loss when she wasn't around anymore.

Just then, the personal communicator units for all four went off. These units, also known as PCU's, aren't really anything that spectacular when compared to technologies that the outside world has. They simply allow person to person communications if desired, but it struck each in the room as odd that the PCU's for all four went off at the same time. Checking the message, it was an emergency message, and they were all asked to meet in the portal room on New Galimar.

Simultaneously, each in the room looked up from their respective PCU's. Knowing that each had received the same message, they all dropped what they were doing, grabbed their things, and left for the portal room.

The ride to the portal room only took about ten minutes, and they all shared the same transport car to get there. Upon arriving, their own happy faces were met with the much more solemn ones of Jason and Dennis.

"What's going on?" asked Brianna who was instantly afraid of the probable response.

"I'm afraid there's some bad news" said Jason. "We just received notification that Terri and Khreelon's daughter Coral has been in a pedestrian-on-vehicle accident on the mainland."

"Oh my god!" responded Brianna.

"What's her status?" asked Jill.

"She is in a coma and is currently in the hospital."

"But she's still alive?" asked Socrates.

"Yeah. But the doctors don't have a whole lotta good things to say about her prognosis" answered Dennis with a rather glum look.

Putting on his medical hat, Nafan asked "What are they doing for her?"

"Aside from a broken leg and a couple of ribs" responded Jason, "the bigger problem is that she is suffering from swelling on the brain resulting from blunt force trauma. Apparently, she hit her head on the hood of the car, and the doctors say her brain bounced back and forth in her skull causing the coma. That cranial swelling is the reason why they are planning on opening her up as soon as possible to relieve the pressure."

"Yeah" added Dennis, "and so we called you guys here to see if there is something New Galimar can do for her that is a little better than sawing off the top of her head."

"Definitely!" responded Nafan.

"There is?" asked Jill as she looked over to her brother. "We haven't even started to study neurology and neurosurgery in med school yet! What can we possibly do for her?"

"We need to get a suspended animation pod over there to arrest her condition degrading any further" answered Nafan. "If we do that, then we and our colleagues can take our time studying and getting really good at what we need to do to help her.

"Why didn't I think of that!" asked Socrates to himself.

"Don't feel bad!" responded Jill. "We just studied this stuff in school and even I didn't think about it."

"What do we need to do to make it happen?" asked Jason.

"We'll need to get a pod to the hospital as soon as possible" answered Nafan. "How long do you think it'll take to get one to the hospital?"

Smiling, Dennis answered "About three seconds with this baby." He was patting the portal frame with his right hand.

"OK. Good. The portals are all housed in the undersea habitat where we slept waiting for you to revive us, Jason. Do you remember where that is?"

"Sure do" answered Jason.

With no further delay, Jason sat down at his portal control console, and Dennis sat at his. Between the two of them, the artful dance of control manipulation was choreographed so well that within the span of 90 seconds, the portal was not only online, but was connected to the undersea habitat.

"Ok. Do what you need to do" said Jason to Nafan and Jill.

The two stepped through the portal aperture and within the span of three seconds, the noise level meeting the ears of the two siblings went from the noisy hum of the portal room, to the very peaceful and calm sounds of the ocean surrounding them. The habitat was thousands of meters under the surface of the ocean, and so Jill decided that when all this was over, she wanted to come back and maybe spend time studying down here.

Jill rushed over to a control console and dialed up a pod to be delivered to one of the embarkation alcoves along the far wall. As she was walking over to the alcove, she saw her brother searching through some of the side rooms for something.

"What are you doing?"

"Well, unless you plan on carrying that suspended animation chamber on your back sis, I am looking for an anti-grav platform that it can ride on."

"Ah" said Jill. "Good idea!"

Jill arrived at the delivery alcove and waited. Behind the back panel of the alcove, massive machinery was set in motion allowing for the selection and delivery of the requested suspended animation pod. These pods were all kept in a huge storage area that was not only four-thousand meters wide and four-thousand meters long but was also two-thousand meters tall. Hundreds of rows stretched endlessly in all directions within this storage facility, and it was on these rows where the Galimarians waited for hundreds of years recently, each in their own suspended animation pod, awaiting the time when Jason would fix the problem with the tectonic stabilization machine in the modern era, and thereafter come here to revive them all.

It only took about a minute for the back panel of the alcove to open, and an empty suspended animation pod was delivered. The gleaming ovoid pill-shaped pod was white all over its entire surface except for the smoked glass panel on its front. This window allows outside personnel to look into the chamber where the person is kept in suspended animation in order to make sure that all is well. The pill-shaped pod is tilted back at a forty-five-degree angle and is fixed onto a pedestal that can sit on the floor. Right when the pod appeared, Nafan arrived at Jill's side with the anti-grav platform. Transferring the pod onto platform was an easy chore since the pod delivery systems were built to do it. Returning to the location where the invisible portal window was still waiting for them, they were instantly returned to the portal control room where Jason and Dennis immediately shut down the portal and made preparations for connecting to the hospital room where Coral was kept.

As they waited for Jason and Dennis to redirect the portal to Coral's hospital room, Jill and Nafan waited patiently near Socrates and Brianna. Jill looked over to Brianna and looked like she wanted to say something to her but didn't end up saying anything. Brianna saw the look on Jill's face, and said with a small smile on her face "Is there something on your mind?"

Realizing that her face had betrayed her thoughts, Jill looked down at her feet and thought about how to voice her thoughts. She nodded her head, and eventually looked up to see that both Socrates and Brianna were looking at her, which made her feel even a little more unsure how to ask the question she was thinking.

"I'm not sure if this is rude to ask this kind of question or not, and so I don't know how to ask it."

"I'm sure it isn't, but even if it is, I know that you wouldn't knowingly try to be rude. What do you want to know?" said Brianna with a reassuring tone to her voice.

"Well" stammered Jill, "I was just wondering if, well, I notice that you look very different than Jason, Dennis, or any Galimarian

I've ever seen. I was wondering if you are from earth as well, or if you are from somewhere else too like we are."

Brianna immediately smiled which had a very reassuring effect on Jill. Brianna thought about how Jill and Nafan were from a world where walking among beings from other planets wasn't unusual, and so her asking if Brianna was from another planet was an innocent question and nothing more.

"I can see why you would ask that kind of question, and I don't think it's rude at all to wonder about that."

"Oh good!" responded Jill. "I wasn't sure if I should even ask."

"No. You're fine" answered Brianna. "The answer to your question is that I am from earth too, just like Jason and Dennis here. Remember how earlier we were talking about how earth has different nations?"

"Yes"

"Well, while I grew up in an area called the United States just like Jason and Dennis, my ancestors came from a place on the other side of the globe called China. Because these two areas are so far apart, there are genetic differences among the different nations that result in us looking a little different than each other. People on earth all have two arms, two legs, two eyes, one nose and so forth, but these genetic differences cause subtle differences like those that you see in me. Understand?"

"Yes. Completely. Genetics is something that I really look forward to studying, and in fact I was ..."

"OK. We're there!" interrupted Jason from the other side of the room. Looking at the portal window, the image was just now coming into focus. There on the other side of the portal window was a typical private hospital room complete with a hospital bed and a wide array of medical machines all hooked up to Coral.

There were also two men dressed in black with black ski masks over their faces. Each of them had a gun with an unusually long barrel. The holes drilled in the end of the barrel appeared to be the visible part of a silencer.

"What the hell are they doing!" asked Dennis who was no stranger to guns having grown up in west Texas.

Being pre-occupied with his control station, Jason hadn't been watching the portal itself. Upon the outburst from his friend, Jason immediately swiveled his chair around and saw the danger the little girl was obviously in. With no comment Jason jumped from his control station, and with a seeming single leap jumped through the portal window with Dennis right on his tail. Appearing with several flashes of light, Jason and Dennis materialized in front of the two assailants which of course caused them to take a step back since they were definitely not expecting anybody else to be there.

"Back off if you know what's good for you!" said Dennis with as much bravado as possible. As soon as he said it, he thought how his chivalry might have been a little ill-thought since the other guys had guns with silencers, whereas all he brought with him were his fists.

The black-clad invaders took about five seconds to regain their composure, and upon noticing that both Dennis and Jason had nothing close to the weapons they carried, they said "Out of our way!"

Jason took a step forward, but just as he did, the room started to glow with bright lights again, only this time from the area near the windows. The two assailants looked over to the bed, however both Jason and Dennis were laser focused on the guns pointed towards them. As soon as Jason saw the opening, he lunged for each of the attacker's guns which were held directly in front of them but near their bellies. With each of his hands Jason grabbed the barrels of the guns and directed them upward and away from he and Dennis. This motion caused three things to instantly happen.

First, the trigger finger of each attacker had been resting on the trigger of each respective gun, and so swiveling the guns upward caused both triggers on each gun to be simultaneously pulled.

Second, since the guns had been swiveled upward, the silenced bullets from each gun didn't travel into Jason or Dennis, but instead traveled upwards and entered the skull of each aggressor from underneath the chin.

Finally, since Jason's hands had been wrapped around the exhaust holes of the silencers, his hands were immediately burned from the intense muzzle flash.

Upon hearing the gunshot, Dennis' attention was immediately directed toward Jason who cried out in pain. Dennis thought Jason had been shot and so he lunged to his friend to catch him and help stay the inevitable bleeding that would come from the gunshot wound, however much to his relief, Jason stood up while the two attackers slumped to the ground. That whole side of the hospital room was now a terrible and macabre mess, especially the ceiling above the attackers.

"What happened!?" shouted Dennis.

"I lunged for the guns and shoved them up. I guess they ended up pulling their own triggers" said a very wide-eyed Jason.

Due to the noise of all the commotion, Khreelon and Terri, who had been down the hall from Coral's room, slammed the door to the room open and were horrified to see the mess where the two masked men had been standing. It was an enormous amount to take in all at once.

That is ... until Terri yelled "CORAL!"

Spinning around to look, there on the other side of the room was a bed, several life-support machines ...

... and no Coral.

CHAPTER 35

THE SPEED OF LIGHT IS a speed that seems quite ominous when you first look at it. While the speed of sound is only around one thousand two hundred thirty-eight kilometers per hour, the speed of light is vastly quicker. Imagine you are in the United States in a city on the west coast called Los Angeles. Then imagine traveling at the speed of light to another city called New York around forty-five hundred kilometers away on the east coast. How long would it take? About six *hundredths* of second.

And yet when it comes to measuring distances in space, there is no better way to do so than to measure them by calculating how long it would take light to travel between those distances. Take, for instance the sun that earth revolves around. When light leaves the sun and travels toward earth, the earth is so far away from the sun that it takes a full eight minutes for that light to finally get to earth. That distance though, which is one hundred and forty-nine million kilometers, is still close enough to the sun to cause your skin to burn if you are exposed for too long.

Even though the sun of our local solar system is often referred to as a yellow dwarf, and even though there are suns in our galaxy that completely put our sun to shame in terms of size and power, our sun still commands immense respect. To illustrate, if you took a pinhead sized piece of the sun and somehow placed it on the surface of the earth, you wouldn't be able to safely stand within one hundred and forty-four kilometers of it.

Being that the sun is so powerful that you can't even look at it with the naked eye, it has taken some time to come up with a way that would allow scientists to not only look at it, but to scientifically take it apart and, piece-by-piece, learn about all that is going on under the surface. For instance, why is the atmosphere of the sun over three hundred times hotter than its surface? This mystery, and many others, are the reason why the revolutionary Parker Solar Probe was built. The probe, launched on August 12th, 2018 was built to pass only three million miles above the surface of the sun. The ingenious design allows for it to use four instrument suites built into the spacecraft that are designed to study magnetic fields, plasma and energetic particles, and to image the solar wind.

Meanwhile, in a non-descript business park near Miami, Florida, Casey Emerson is working on an experiment for a company called Gravionics that is tied to not only his own destiny but is tied to the fate of our sun and every living plant, animal, and being in the entire solar system.

Gravionics, a company wholly owned by a Miami husband and wife team named Bart and Rennie MenGala, is the sole owner of the rights to research and develop industrial and military uses of a new mineral that was discovered off the coast of Australia on an island called New Caledonia by a biologist named Nixon McConnell. This discovery made him quite famous among his contemporaries, however a series of events led to Gravionics being the only company allowed to develop technologies for the mineral that was dubbed “Connellium”.

First, he was convinced to sign over the rights to Connellium to the Gravionics corporation under the terms of an agreement that has remained sealed to this day.

Second, Doctor McConnell met with an untimely death when the fuel sensors in the fuel tanks of the Lear jet he was using developed a short and caused a spark leading to an explosion that destroyed the plane and all its inhabitants.

These details were never discussed with Casey though, and truth be told, he wasn’t really interested in them. He wasn’t a callous person in any way, but rather he was exceedingly thrilled to be working on a technology that would, in his mind, not only make the world a better place, but would also open up space travel to the commoner.

The laboratory experiments already established that Connellium not only had the ability to generate an anti-gravity field, but they also indicated that the more power you apply to the mineral then the stronger anti-gravity it generates. The problem now was generating a significant amount of power in a relatively small amount of space. One idea was to use an RTG, or Radioisotope Thermoelectric Generator, such as was used on the Voyager spacecraft. A compact power source for sure, but aside from a large amount of heat that is generated, the units only generated about 470 watts of power which was significantly less than what Casey was looking for.

Other ideas were proposed ranging from generators using internal combustion engines, to the latest of battery cell technologies. Ultimately, it was another DARPA project that came through with the kind of power output Casey needed. It was essentially a complete nuclear power plant that was about the size of a small car. This small plant could generate upwards of three hundred kilowatts and was developed to help developing countries have the power they need.

For Casey though, this relatively small generator just might make it possible to lift a payload the size of a space capsule off the ground. With the current power availability, it won't make it to space yet, but this will be a significant step in the right direction. Casey was standing in the middle of a large warehouse, and near him was a crane carrying the experiment. It was moving way too fast.

"Hold it! Easy with that thing! It's worth a hundred times your yearly salary!" shouted Casey into his walkie talkie.

The forklift driver was somewhat of a lunk, and it sounded like he had some sort of Irish accent. The walkie talkie crackled back with the words "Sorry boss!" It sounded like the guy was actually chuckling. "Didn't mean to startle ya!"

"You didn't startle me, and I'm not your boss, but I don't want you to be in trouble with the owners of Gravionics who have invested a LOT of money in this device" responded Casey.

Unbeknownst to Casey who could not see the crane operators face, the mention of the owners of the company seemed to have a definite effect on the driver. He even seemed to sit straighter.

"OK. I'll be more careful sir! Where do you want it?

'*that's a little more like it*' thought Casey.

"Right where you have it is fine. Just set it down. Gently!" answered Casey.

"Yes sir."

The driver gingerly fingered the controls to the crane, and the heavy load settled down right on target. The device was essentially a larger version of the small tabletop device that Casey saw when he was interviewed for the job. According to the calculations that Casey had made based on the tabletop device and based on the notes written by the previous scientists working on the project, Casey felt that when the switch was flipped this device should not only float but should rise to a height of about five meters. The roof to this warehouse was about twice that and so there shouldn't be any clearance issues. Even so Galileo Mark II, the name Casey gave to the device, had an outer case made from hardened steel. Along with some ballast weights that were integrated inside the device, its overall weight was increased to meet the requirements for this test of ten thousand pounds. There were plans however to increase the lifting ability incrementally.

As he neared Galileo to render a final inspection before the test in ten minutes, Casey was stopped in his tracks by a huge thunderbolt outside. Judging from the loudness, it must have hit nearby. He remembered hearing a thunderbolt one time when he was visiting Disney World in Orlando Florida. He was standing under the "golf ball" in Epcot Center when it happened, and he swore the bolt must have hit the ball itself. It was easily the loudest thing he had ever heard up to that time, and it made him feel really small next to the hand of mother nature. Having moved to Florida from California now, he wasn't as used to Florida as were many of his co-workers. California, at least the part he lived in, didn't have nearly as much rain as Miami seemed to get. It rained nearly every day in the summertime, but at the same time it seemed to clear up just as quickly.

He approached Galileo and opened the forward access panel where the controls to the generator could be found and saw that all systems with the generator and the anti-grav device were nominal. Within the device was of course a master computer, and this master computer had a countdown timer running that was in charge of monitoring all systems on the device, and if all systems were green, then it would allow the forward motion of the test. Casey could see that the countdown timer was proceeding, and in fact it was now thirty seconds away from starting the generator. Before the computer could sense the access panel being open, and hence holding the countdown because of it, Casey closed the panel and stepped away. Looking up, he could see that the now-cooperative crane operator had moved the crane away, and so now the only thing above the device was thirty feet of empty space under the roof the facility.

As he backed away from Galileo, he and the other researchers took their positions behind a three-inch-thick panel of a ceramic compound called aluminum oxynitride, also known as transparent aluminum. Even though this panel is primarily made of aluminum, it is optically transparent, and even though it is only three inches thick, it had the same strength as a glass panel a foot thick. As he stood there quietly watching the countdown on the control panel in front of him, Casey mentally stepped through the steps that the on-board computer would follow during the test.

According to the test parameters, the computer would first start the generator and wait until the power output would rise to the energy requirements of the Connellium reactor. Once that had been achieved, power would be incrementally applied to the Connellium while at the same time an altimeter would be monitored to gauge the effect of the power on the reactor. The goal was to rise fifteen feet off the ground, and it should be able to achieve that within a relatively short amount of time, say ... fifteen seconds or so.

Once it achieved the necessary height, ancillary Connellium thrusters built into the side of Galileo would be energized for the purpose of gauging the maneuvering ability using the mineral. This part of the experiment was a secondary goal, and not one that Casey put much faith in. It was basically an afterthought, and if it didn't work it wouldn't surprise him that much.

After a hypothetical rotation of three-hundred and sixty degrees, Galileo would hover in place for about ten minutes allowing for a team to take measurements in the warehouse and outside. Part of the team wanted to know if there was any stray radioactivity, and others were looking for any detectible magnetic fields. Several experiments were set up around the test area and those experiments were all set to run when the countdown computer reported that power was being applied to the reactor. Once ten minutes had elapsed, the countdown computer would then slowly decrease power to the Connellium reactor until Galileo ended up resting in its original position on the floor. All systems on the device would thereafter be incrementally shut down in reverse order.

That's if all went as planned.

Glancing back down to the control panel in front of him that was an exact duplicate of the same panel he had viewed on Galileo itself, he could see that the computer had just turned on the generator. Slowly the power output rose, and within twenty seconds, the output reached Max-A, or the amount of current that was required to operate the Connellium reactor. In five percent increments, the computer then applied that power to the reactor.

Casey watched the device like a hawk using his binoculars. At five, ten, fifteen, twenty, and twenty five percent, nothing really seemed to happen. But then, at thirty percent, Casey could see a small box that was about ten feet away from the device shift slightly. Something was happening!

Thirty-five percent.

Underneath Galileo there were dozens of thermoplastic supports that suspended the device off the floor. These supports were yellow colored cubes that were roughly eight inches tall. As he was watching the device, it didn't really look like there had been any movement, other than that box of course. But just then, one of those cubes under Galileo shifted about three inches to the right. What had formerly been supporting a ten-thousand-pound structure was no longer touching the payload.

Galileo was floating!

Casey's eyes snapped back down to the control panel.

Forty percent.

With a somewhat jerky motion, the device suddenly rose two and a half feet from the ground. The suddenness of motion greatly surprised the team watching the test with Casey, and many of them were startled back. It was instantly obvious that the transition between voltages needed to be much more gradual in the future, and Casey made a mental note to change that in the programming of the test computer for future tests.

Forty-five percent.

With each additional application of energy to the Connellium reactor, Galileo rose more and more, albeit with jerky motions, but nonetheless the device rose. By the time the desired altitude of fifteen feet had been achieved, the needed power to achieve this height was eighty percent. According to mission parameters, the countdown computer stayed its progression of power to the reactor and so the unit remained at fifteen feet off of the floor.

The next part of the test involved the rotational movement of the device and with keen interest, Casey watched. As time progressed, he could see on the readout in front of him that the countdown computer was doing what it was programmed to do in applying power to the maneuvering Connellium thrusters, however nothing seemed to happen. Looking again through his binoculars, he could now see that, while the device wasn't rotating at all, there was an unexpected wobble to the device. It didn't appear to be anything unstable, but it was readily apparent that the thrusters were not working. Sure enough, as soon as the hypothetical rotation thrusts ended, the wobble ceased, and so it was obvious the thrusters were to blame for the current instability. Galileo was now rock solid ... floating fifteen feet in the air.

Now it was time to wait for ten minutes.

Outside the warehouse, the weather was getting bad. The tropical depression bearing down on Miami was typical this time of year. Sometimes these storms mutated into full blown hurricanes, but fortunately this storm wouldn't get that bad. There was a lot of rain for sure, but nothing that Miami hadn't seen thousands of times before.

But not everything was quite so fortunate.

As Galileo was hovering fifteen feet above the ground, and while the team was just about ready to great out the champagne, at eight minutes and thirty-seven seconds into the flight a lightning bolt hit the warehouse. Like that day when Casey was standing underneath the geodesic sphere in Epcot Center, the crash of the thunderbolt made the hearts of all the team stop for a moment, and several of them fell to the floor thinking there had been an explosion on Galileo. There hadn't been though. The lightning had hit the lightning rods on the outside of the building, and most of the energy bled off to the ground. There was one lightning rod that hadn't been grounded correctly though.

When this lightning rod had been installed about ten years prior, it was the end of the day and the technician who installed it had his mind on other matters. That night he was due to propose to his girlfriend, and so he was thinking more about that, than the fact that he had selected the incorrect insulator when installing the grounding cable to this rod. As a result, when the lightning hit, a portion of the bolt arced over to the rod with the faulty wiring. The surge of electricity didn't bleed to the ground as it should have, but rather the power fed into every metal part built into the walls of the warehouse where the experiment was being conducted. This upwelling of electricity caused an induction field throughout the entire warehouse, and that field induced a flood of unanticipated power directly into the Connellium reactor.

After recovering from the shock of hearing the loud bang from the lightning bolt, Casey checked the console in front of him and saw a completely blank readout. The electrical surge had apparently wiped out the computer.

Putting his binoculars to his eyes, Casey immediately saw two things. First, Galileo was nowhere to be found.

Second ... there was a hole the size of Galileo in the roof.

At the exact same time when the lightning bolt hit the warehouse in Miami causing the Galileo experiment to go awry, ninety million miles away the Parker Solar Probe happened to be passing the point where it would be the nearest to the sun during its whole mission. At that very moment, a portion of the sun massively destabilized which resulted in a fiery protuberance called a Coronal Mass Ejection. CME's happen all the time, however this one was one of the largest ones that had ever been recorded by solar observatories on earth.

Unfortunately, the CME was aimed in the exact direction of the probe, and within a hailstorm of multi-million-degree heat, the probe was reduced to atoms.

CHAPTER 36

"An accident? What kind of accident?" asked Bart.

"It happened while the team was testing phase two of the Galileo project" replied Brooke White, general manager of Gravionics Corporation.

"Say a little and say it well, Ms. White. That didn't answer my question" said Bart with an even stare to his eyes. The dichotomy of the thick Irish accent combined with a stony demeanor seemed to Brooke as if Bart could look all the way into her brain and find the answer himself.

"Sorry, sir" said Brooke. "What I meant to say is that the test was going perfectly. The Mark II Galileo device floated fifteen feet above the ground, and it held steady there for about eight minutes. At eight minutes and thirty-seven seconds though, a lightning bolt hit the building, and apparently it hit a lightning rod that wasn't properly grounded when it was installed. The bolt energized the building in its entirety. The good news is that nobody was hurt, and the even better news is that device survived the lightning bolt."

"And the bad news?" asked a heretofore silent Rennie.

Brooke's eyes flitted over to Rennie, even though her head didn't move in her direction. Taking in a deep breath to stay her nerves, Brooke stuttered "Th-th-the bad news is that the when the massive amount of current hit the device, the Connellium reactor caused the Mark II to shoot out through the roof. Its velocity was so massive that it apparently left the earth's gravitational influence, and the last time we checked, it is still speeding away with no chance of ever returning."

As Brooke waited for a reaction from the two owners of Gravionics, she tried to calm herself. She had heard back-room whispers about what happens to people who ... displease ... the owners of the company, and she really didn't want be one. She didn't know if those stories were entirely truthful, and she thought that they were probably wildly exaggerated, but ... you never know.

Both Rennie and Bart sat motionless while they stared at Ms. White. Brooke couldn't tell if the two of them were simply assimilating the news, contemplating exactly how they would fire her, or deciding the right size of box to stuff her remains in after ...

"I assume you have fixed the problem with the lightning rods?" asked Rennie with her characteristic Irish Brogue, which in turn broke Brooke out of her downward spiral.

"Yes ma'am! We found the rod that was the cause of the whole problem, and we found two others that were also installed improperly."

"And you have made plans for taking what you've learned with this experiment and taking the next step with the project?" asked Bart. His eyes were still cold and emotionless.

"Absolutely. Our lead researcher, a brilliant guy I hired recently named Casey is already starting on it. He forecasts having a new test unit in three weeks."

After an almost interminable period of silence, Rennie finally blinked and looked over to Bart. “Then I think we’re done here, unless there is anything else you want to say?”

“Naw” said Bart. To Brooke, Bart’s accent almost seemed thicker.

The two owners of the company stood, which of course prompted Brooke to stand.

Sticking his hand out to Brooke, Bart actually smiled and said “Let us know when the next test is scheduled, Ms. White. Rennie and I will want to be there.”

A much-relieved Ms. White replied “Yes Sir. I’ll be sure to do that!”

Bart and Rennie walked Brooke to the door to their office and shut the door behind her.

“Did you see how nervous she was?” said Rennie with a slight trace of mirth. “I think she was about ready to defecate.”

Bart laughed and reached out to his wife and slid his hand around her waist, which caused her to reflexively put both her hands on his shoulders. The two were nose-to-nose in an often-practiced pose.

“Do you blame him?” said Bart with a smile on his face. Once again, his Irish accent had completely vanished. “You *are* rather intimidating.”

That comment, it turn, made RenIval laugh out loud. She then added “She’s just lucky I’m in such a good mood now that the demon child is no more.”

“Not so fast there my love. First, all the blood and guts in that room were from those fools we sent. Second, I still don’t see a body.”

“Perhaps, but we do know for sure she never left the room” replied RenIval. Then looking to the side while still in her husbands’ arms, she added “Unless ...”

"... unless they swiped her with a portal" said Bart as he finished his wife's sentence.

Now deep in thought, the two of them released each other's hold, and stepped contemplatively apart. After thinking about it for a few moments, RenIval finally said "Yes, but if that's true, then why would her parents and the others have reacted that way? First, we know from the video feeds in the room that those two men suddenly appeared there which means they came there using the original portal, wherever that is. Second, we know that they are friends with the parents of the demon child based on the way they interacted with each other. Finally, we know that all in the room were surprised that the child had vanished, and so we know they didn't take her. The only conclusion is that she was somehow vaporized from everything that happened with the gunshots and the portal sending those men."

"I don't know" responded BarDringol. "Seems like some shaky ground to rest our hopes for revenge on."

"Well unless I hear differently" said RenIval, "I'm going to concentrate on our escape plan, and this little project at Gravionics is the key in that particular lock."

Just then an intercom on the nearby desk where they were standing made a sound, and BarDringol reached over and pressed a button. Assuming his Irish demeanor again, he said "Yeeah?"

"There's a Uriah Shylock here to see you Mr. MenGala."

BarDringol glanced over to his wife, who sported the same quizzical look as her husband.

"Send 'em in"

Clicking off the intercom and verifying the light was out, BarDringol looked once again to RenIval and said "Strange. He never shows up in daylight."

With no words but with a nodding assent, RenIval showed she was thinking the same thing. After only five seconds, the door to the office opened on its own and in walked a man that seemed to be the embodiment of all that was unholy on the street. BarDringol and RenIval walked and talked a good game in the underworld of thugs, but even they seemed to stand slightly taller when Mr. Shylock came into their presence. Still though ... he got things done.

"Uriah" said BarDringol with a timbre to his voice that was slightly higher than he would have liked.

"Bart" graveled the visitor. His voice sounded more like grinding of bones than that of human speech.

"Unusual to see you here ..." said Rennie.

"... During the day?" interrupted Uriah. "Yes, but I have come into possession of some information that you would want to know immediately. It's about the portal."

Even the mention of the portal caused Bart's blood to boil. The back-stabbing betrayer scientist they had working on it not only disappeared along with his wife, but the quisling had even sabotaged the only portal the Circle of Seven had so that it exploded when they tried to use it. To say Bart wanted to see Doctor Einikov's blood run through his fingers was an understatement.

"I already know about the portal, Uriah" said Bart with a tone that belied his contempt. "The entire city block where it was housed was leveled."

"Not that one" answered Uriah.

With a slightly irritated tone, Bart replied "What are you talking about, Uriah?"

"I'm talking about the portal that the admiral had." Uriah let a couple seconds elapse, then added "I'm talking about the original one that was made in California."

"What about it?" asked Rennie. She was more in command of her emotions regarding Doctor Einikov, however she was no less ready to see the life slip away from the good doctor's eyes.

"I found it."

"WHERE?" asked Bart.

"Ohhhhh .... That's the best part" answered Uriah. "It's on an island ..."

"We know that already, Uriah" said Bart who was still irritated. "We came from that island ourselves, but when we left, we didn't think it was important to keep track of where it was since we could never go back, and so we have no idea where the place is!"

Uriah continued, "... and I can take you right to it."

It took a few seconds for the news to sink all the way into the minds of the two titans of industry he was talking to, but when he saw the sinister eyes that formed on BarDringol and RenIval just then, even Uriah was surprised.

The first sensation that Terri felt was the sound of rushing water. She was far too out of contact with reality at that very moment, however soon enough the darkness that permeated her field of vision started to clear and she could then hear that the rushing water sound was subsiding, but the bright lights of the lamps just above where she was lying were starting to come into focus. She then realized that she was lying on something very comfortable, and there were several out-of-focus people standing around her.

'This doesn't make sense' thought Terri. As she laid there, she blinked her eyes a few times and that seemed to start helping make the faces around her come into focus. What was happening? Why was she lying in bed and why were her friends, whom she how recognized, standing around her? 'Let's see ... the last thing I remember was standing in the hallway of the hospital and talking to the doctor about ...'

"CORAL!" yelled Terri as she shot up and sat forward in her hospital gurney. Without regard to the IV stuck in her arm, her only thought was to run to the room where the little girl had lain.

Almost involuntarily, Khreelon and Lynne reached out to Terri to steady her and to halt her forward, which of course Terri was going to have none of it.

“Let me go!” said the frantic mother who was dealing with the knot stuck in her own throat. Seeing the arms and hands that were restraining her, she was ready to use her nails and even teeth to free herself. She had to get to her baby!

“She’s gone Terri!”

That comment stopped her in her tracks, and she looked to the source of her comment, which only now she realized was her own husband, Khreelon.

“She … She’s …” Terri couldn’t say the word. She took in a very labored and very stuttered breath while her own enormously open eyes began to fill with tears.

Lynn could instantly see what her friend was thinking, and so she jumped in and said, “We’re not saying she’s dead, Terri.”

Instantly setting her sights on Lynne, Terri said “Then what the hell ARE you saying? WHERE’S MY BABY!”

“We don’t know” replied Khreelon. Terri looked back to her husband, whose own eyes were as bloodshot as Lynne’s, and no doubt her own.

“What do you mean, you don’t know?!” asked Terri in a very irritated tone. She wasn’t at all interested in passing her words through any ‘nice’ filter. “I know what I saw, and I saw a hell of a lot of blood!”

That’s when Lynne and Khreelon explained what had happened in the room with the two masked gunmen, and how Jason had grabbed the guns they were holding and ended up turning the guns on the gunmen themselves. They told her about how they had no idea where they were from and they had no ID on them at all. Nothing was known, except that they both had a tattoo of an eagle on their right wrists. They also explained that somehow, in some way, Coral had completely disappeared, and nobody knows where she is or what her condition is.

As they finished their story, Terri sat on the edge of her bed and just started crying. From the depths of her soul the tears welled up and spilled out, which of course caused the hearts of those around her to break as well. Jason with his bandaged hands as well as Dennis came into the room by this time and witnessed the terrible sight of a woman who had lost her daughter and had no idea where she was or if she was ever going to come back. Tears were flowing freely in the room, and Lynne looked over to her husband Dennis. With a pleading look in her eyes, she asked "Isn't there anything you can do? Can you look at the security tapes for the hospital to see if someone took her?"

Dennis, who was having his own hard time keeping his emotions in check over the situation, replied "Already did. Nothing."

Jason then answered, "There is something else we can do."

Dennis looked over to Jason and instantly knew what Jason was thinking. "The portal."

"The two men looked over to Terri who was already looking at them, and simultaneously said "We'll be right back!" They then seemingly ran out of the room leaving Terri, Khreelon and Lynne to listen to the innocuous yet oppressive sounds of the hospital. Khreelon sat down next to Terri and put his hands around her to comfort her, but Terri could only think of one thing she wanted. She wanted the comforting shoulder of her amulet companion right now.

Without thinking about the effect it would have on him, she simply said "No!" with no malice in her voice. She stood and said "I need Quorlynn" as she walked over to a chair. She got comfortable, put on her amulet, and was instantly transported to a parklike setting where she always found her friend.

As was usual when Quorlynn materialized near Terri, she was about to casually greet her friend when she instantly saw that something was wrong. Terri was sitting on a park bench in the world of the amulet where Quorlynn lived and she had her face in her hands. It was obvious she was crying.

Quorlynn sat down next to Terri and put her hand on Terri's shoulder and said, "What's wrong my dear?"

Terri looked up, and with a tear strewn face and stuffed up nose, Terri said "Oh Quorlynn! It's so horrible!" Terri broke out in a brand-new gale of tears. Quorlynn reached out and hugged Terri close to her chest, so far having no knowledge of what had her best friend so upset.

"I'm here sweetie. I'm here" said Quorlynn as she gently stroked her back. "Tell me what has you so upset?"

Terri told Quorlynn about what she had at first heard, then seen in Coral's room. She then related what Lynne and Khreelon had just explained.

"You're telling me that Coral is now missing?" asked Quorlynn.

"Yes!"

Quorlynn looked off to the side and seemed to be in a deep contemplation of her own.

"I just had to come talk to you" said Terri.

"Didn't you say Khreelon is with you right now?"

"Yes" answered Terri. But ..." Terri didn't finish the sentence.

"Isn't he upset by this too?"

"Well ... yeah. I mean I saw him crying too."

"I can imagine he was" replied Quorlynn. "Didn't he try to comfort you?"

"Yeah. I guess so" answered Terri.

"But you came here to talk to me instead?" asked Quorlynn.

"Yeah" said Terri. "You're my best friend, Quorlynn. I knew you would know what to do!"

"Honey, I do know what you should do actually. There are two things I need to tell you" said Quorlynn.

"Yeah?"

Quorlynn stood and walked away contemplatively, as if she was thinking deeply about something.

"Terri" began Quorlynn, "I can't tell you how I know this. What I mean is ... I don't exactly know how I know what I'm about to tell you, but the fact remains that I do indeed know what I am about to tell you is the truth."

"OK. What is it?" asked Terri.

Turning toward Terri and looking Terri straight in the eyes, Quorlynn said "Terri, I can tell you for a fact that your daughter Coral is OK. Again, I don't know why I know this, but I can tell you for a certainty, she's safe."

"What's telling you this?" asked Terri.

"Well, again ... I don't know how I know this, but every fiber in my soul is screaming at me right now, and those fibers are telling me that she's safe and sound. What's more, I know she'll be back in your life. I don't know when, but she will."

Terri took a deep breath and looked down to the ground in order to soak in the words Quorlynn just said. She thought about how not only is Quorlynn a sentient being living in a world of technology that they simply don't understand, but Quorlynn is literally thousands of years old. If there was anybody that would have the wisdom of the ancients, Quorlynn would be it.

Slightly shaking her head back and forth, Terri simply said "OK. I'll have to trust you on that."

Truth be said, Terri was rather relieved at Quorlynn's words. Quorlynn had never been wrong, and Terri really needed her to be right, right now.

"What is the second thing?" asked Terri.

Quorlynn walked back over to Terri and resumed her seat on the bench. Taking Terri's hands in her own, she said "Terri, my friend. You have a man out there that is hurting just as much as you are."

"I know, but I just had to run to you my friend for the comfort I needed" said Terri.

"I know, honey. But sweetie ... Khreelon is really your other half. He waited thousands of years to find you, and you waited as well for the right one too. I know that for a long time, you were on your own, and you got into the habit of relying on yourself when adversity came along in life. The thing is ... while I love the fact that you hold me in such high regard, he really should be the first one you run to when things go bad. He's your soulmate, sweetie. And I'm betting that he is hurting just as much as you are."

Quorlynn let a few seconds pass until she spoke again.

"Remember what I said though. I know for a certainty that your baby is OK, and I'm sure that soon her whereabouts will become evident."

A tiny "OK" was the only response Terri could think of saying while she stared at the grass in front of her.

Picking up Terri's chin with her finger, Quorlynn said "Go to your man, honey. Be there for him and let him be there for you. OK?"

"OK" said Terri. Then reaching out to Quorlynn for a hug, Terri said "Thank you."

"You're welcome" replied Quorlynn.

And with that, and a few swipes on her virtual amulet, Terri returned to the hospital room where Lynne and Khreelon were still gathered. Looking up at Khreelon, Terri rose and walked over to her husband who was sitting on the bed. Sitting next to him, she put her arm through his and laid her head on his shoulder.

"We'll get through this together, my love" said Terri. Khreelon, who had been weeping, simply nodded his head.

EPILOGUE

BEGINNING IN 1951, THEN-PRESIDENT HARRY S. Truman established an organization that he named the Science Advisory Committee. It had gone through several name changes through the years, and during Nixon's era was even done away with since the members of the panel at that time didn't agree with some of the policies that he had on his agenda.

It was eventually restored to its place in the Whitehouse though, and it is now referred to as the President's Council of Advisors on Science and Technology, or PCAST.

The current chairman of PCAST called an emergency meeting and asked that the president be at the meeting. To get the president's attention the chairman, a Doctor Cavanaugh, characterized the subject matter of the meeting as a matter of national importance. Indeed. It certainly was.

Per the request of the president, the twenty-one-member council assembled in the cabinet meeting room and waited for the president to arrive. Normally the tone of conversation in the room as they waited would be light. They would discuss the status of each other's families and perhaps make arrangements for golf later in the week. Today though was different. VERY different. Oh, they were thinking of their respective families. But not in the way you might expect.

Soon enough President Kirken arrived, flanked by his ever-present secret service guard. "Good afternoon everyone."

As the council members stood in respect, they all replied their greetings to the president, and in doing so President Kirken could immediately see that something was wrong.

Taking his seat and seeing that the door to the chambers was now closed, President Kirken said "I know that Doctor Cavanaugh characterized the subject matter of this meeting as a matter of national security, and I see by the somber tone in the room that something is indeed on your minds."

Being the current chairman of PCAST, Doctor Cavanaugh was the first one to speak.

"Mr. President, after reviewing some information that has recently arisen, and running measurements we have taken through various computer models that we have, as a group we all came to the unanimous conclusion that we needed to bring something to your attention that you should know about. As I said in the memo to you, the information we are about to discuss will have very far-reaching effects. To give you some background, I've asked Doctor Winton to be the first to speak."

"Yes, thank you Doctor Cavanaugh" said Doctor Winton. "Mr. President, to begin with I'd like to lay some groundwork for a few moments about the Parker Solar Probe satellite project. The probe was launched from Kennedy Space Center on August 12th, 2018 and it was built with several scientific detection and measurement devices that would give us a better understanding of our sun. This information would lead to our being able to better predict changes in its surface and perhaps take away information that might eventually lead to our being able to replicate its energy generating abilities, but on a much smaller scale in the laboratory. As part of the mission parameters, it would pass close to the sun several times in an elliptical orbit, and it would use the gravitational well of Venus to slingshot it closer and closer each time. The last pass near the sun would end up being only about three million miles away from the surface of the sun, which is vastly closer than we are on earth at about ninety-three million miles away. As you may remember I am the Project Manager of the Parker Solar Probe satellite project." He then paused while looking around at some of the others in the room. "At least I used to be."

"You're not the manager anymore?" asked President Kirken.

"No sir."

"Who is the manager now?"

"Nobody sir."

The president displayed a very quizzical look to his face.

"I realize that it doesn't yet make sense, sir, but it will in just a moment" explained Doctor Winton.

The president relaxed his face, breathed, and said "OK. Continue."

"Yesterday afternoon, our solar observatories that had been visually monitoring the progress and trajectory of the probe witnessed what is called a coronal mass ejection from the sun that coincidentally happened at the exact moment when the probe was at its nearest point. While that ejection was the largest ejection we have ever had on record, unfortunately it hasn't been the first one we've seen lately. This one though was so large that it had a catastrophic effect on our probe. From what we can tell, it was completely destroyed."

The president displayed a surprised look on his face, but then said, "I'm very sorry to hear that, Doctor Winton, but how does that equate to something that threatens national security?"

"The answer to that question" replied Doctor Cavanaugh, "has to do with the fact that our sun is a two octillion pound gorilla in the room. Quite literally, we live near a continuous nuclear explosion happening twenty-four seven. This gorilla has a love hate relationship between two forces. On the one hand the continuous nuclear explosions happening deep in the core of the sun causes all of its matter to want to eject out into the solar system. If that happened, of course, not only would the sun cease to exist but all life on earth, indeed even the earth itself, would completely cease to exist as well."

"OK" said the president as he nodded his head.

"On the other hand," continued Doctor Cavanaugh, "you have the force of gravity. The sun is so big that it generates its own gravity well that is sufficient to keep all its matter in the same spherical field. While the nuclear fire in the core wants to tear apart the very fabric of the sun, its own gravity causes the sun to stay together and continue its life-giving operations. Does that make sense so far?"

"Yes" replied President Kirken.

"Good. So now this leads us to the problem. The problem is that the sun appears to be losing its material, or its mass, at an alarming rate and we have no idea why."

"Hasn't this type of thing happened before?"

"Yes sir, it has" replied Doctor Valorio, another of the scientists gathered at the table. "Back in 1989, there was a massive CME that happened which caused massive power outages in Quebec, Canada, however the most significant solar storm on record happened way back in 1859. If that one had happened today mister president, satellite electronics would be completely wiped out and we would be essentially returned to the dark ages both figuratively and literally. It's almost like we're sitting at the wrong end of a shooting gallery. In 2012 for instance a huge solar storm that was probably equal to the 1859 event happened, but fortunately it was pointed in another direction and not at the earth."

"Exactly" continued Doctor Cavanaugh, "however what we are talking about is something much more dire than those events Doctor Valorio mentioned."

"How much more dire?" asked a now very concerned president.

"What we have been witnessing has been an apparent pattern of coronal mass ejections that lead us to unanimously believe that our sun is losing its overall mass, the cause of which is unclear. If this pattern continues, then our sun will destabilize and explode in a supernova. As I said earlier, it will probably mean the end of our entire solar system."

This set the president back in his seat, and in a very uncharacteristic moment his mouth was hanging open. Finally, he uttered one word.

"When?"

"We have run the statistics that we have gathered together through several computer models to see exactly when that would happen" replied Doctor Cavanaugh. "According to every one of them we have run, we calculate that we only have two years until our sun will explode and all life on earth will cease to exist."

The End ... or is it?

www.ingramcontent.com/pod-product-compliance
Lightning Source LLC
Chambersburg PA
CBHW071337020726
47502CB00001B/136

* 9 7 8 1 9 4 5 9 2 5 1 3 9 *